DRAGONFLY WINGS
Dragonfly Trilogy, Book Two

Elizabeth Ann Boyles

Copyright © 2020 by Elizabeth Ann Boyles
All rights reserved.

No part of this book may be reproduced in any form or by any electronic or mechanical means, including information storage and retrieval systems, without written permission from the author, except for the use of brief quotations in a book review.

This is a work of fiction. All of the story's names, characters, incidents, places, and dialogues are products of the author's imagination or are used fictitiously. Any resemblance to actual events or persons, living or dead, is coincidental.

Scripture quotations are from the King James Version of the Bible.

Cover design by The Killion Group, Inc.

For supplementary insights, visit the author at
www.elizabethannboyles.com/my-books

*Dedicated to Sherry and Scott—
You bring great joy to our family!*

Dear Reader,

Decades ago in Tokyo, I became acquainted with descendants of my great-great-uncle, the first United States consul in Nagasaki, Japan. My cousins commented on how congenial their grandfather had been. I wish I'd probed to discover more details about this ancestor. If only I'd realized that someday I would imagine stories around a fictional consul's life.

In the story, the Japanese family names are given first, following the country's custom, but I took liberties with the complicated use of Japanese titles and phrases reflecting status. For example, the straight-forward title of Shōgun is used for the exalted ruler.

You can find lists of the characters and selected terms in the back material.

So now, the daughter of a samurai and a New York adventurer are waiting to entertain you as their quests continue.

first day. But with these classes, she would meet Americans twice a week, maybe even the amazing United States consul himself. She had to comport herself with the dignity required for a samurai's daughter. But inside her, fireworks exploded.

"That paper does *not* concern you."

She started and then bowed. "Ah, good morning, Grandfather. The strange paper attracted my curiosity." She crumpled the precious notice, fitting it within her fist, bracing for his next words.

"It announces barbarian trickery. Throw it into the fire."

Her hands obeyed, but her heart didn't let go. The paper disappeared in a fiery puff.

She darted a look at her grandfather. Despite the thinning white hair, his firm jaw hadn't softened a bit. His dark eyes glittered with determination. She'd occasionally wheedled a concession from him in her childhood, but not recently.

"What is it now?" He picked up a metal stick and poked the brazier's charcoal chunks.

Her chest tightened. "I regret the trouble I've caused."

"Trouble especially in my arranging your marriage." He gave the coals a final hard poke.

"Instead of being a burden, I . . . I think there might be a way for me to contribute to our family."

"And how is that?" He motioned to the teapot, then lowered himself onto a cushion with a groan.

"Might not Father find translation work . . . tedious? Perhaps I could aid him—do the most routine parts—if I spent only a little time studying languages."

She glanced at the Eldest again and sighed. Of course, he knew she didn't think her father's work was tedious. Of all words to choose, why had she said *tedious*? As Dutch Scholar

CHAPTER 1

July 1859 (Year of the Sheep), Nagasaki, Japan

Taguchi Sumi took a closer look at the charcoal bucket for the brazier in her home's main room. A wadded paper lay half buried as though intentionally concealed. She plucked it out and uncurled the tight ball, careful to keep the black dust from dirtying the *tatami* floor's spotless straw mats.

Her breath caught. Words written in the squiggly English alphabet as well as in Japanese leapt off the page. Tingling with excitement, she tore through the Japanese translation.

English lessons. Taught by Americans. One class for young men. Another for young ladies. Unbelievable! Nothing on earth could be more wonderful. Nothing.

Two afternoons each week. Even once a week would have thrilled her.

Third house from the Oura River Bridge in the new international sector. She could walk there in an hour.

Three weeks had passed since the Westerners' arrival, cracking open her country's two-hundred-fifty years of isolation, and she hadn't glimpsed a single foreigner after that of the Second Rank, her father had access to the writings of the world, like having a banquet at his fingertips. And he didn't just read about the Westerners. While interpreting for the American consul, he met them every day.

Her grandfather grunted and pointed to the cushion across from him.

She filled his *chawan* bowl with the golden tea, her shaking fingers spilling only a drop, and set the bowl on his nearby stand. At his stern look, she quickly took her place, kneeled back on her heels, smoothed her kimono, and straightened her spine.

He slurped the steaming tea, then dabbed the moisture from his cheeks. "The barbarians are perilous in ways you refuse to accept. Their *ideas* can destroy the naïve. Moreover, Kato-*dono* has agreed to continue as matchmaker. He will search out another worthy family—one who would deride the study of barbaric languages, no matter the reason. Or pretense."

Sumi forced down the acid rising in her throat.

"When Kato-*dono* hesitated because of the botched negotiations with Kurohashi Keiji-*san*, I convinced him that your unseemly interest in the foreigners had been an ignorant phase. You should thank the gods he is still willing to represent us, especially since the age of eighteen far exceeds the time for betrothals."

She swallowed, afraid to speak. The matchmaker would no doubt seek another man as repugnant as Keiji-*sama,* who had belittled her, ranted against foreigners, and worst of all, applauded—actually relished—the banishment of a pitiable man to the coal mines for possessing one ancient *Kirishitan* charm.

"Do you remember the old tale of Urashima Tarō?" Her grandfather's voice sounded less gruff.

"Yes." She kept her eyes lowered. "It appealed to me as a child."

"When the young Tarō left the sea princess's underwater palace, a calamity lay in store. Describe it."

"Returning home, Tarō found years had passed and his family had died. Yet—"

"Dallying in an alien place destroyed the boy's natural life." He leaned forward. "Moreover, the ocean covering the palace enabled sharks to prowl. Invisible. Dangerous. Waiting for people foolish or stupid enough to go where they did not belong."

Sumi blinked. Sharks weren't in any version she'd heard.

"Childhood stories have a kernel of truth worth noting."

Sumi respectfully bowed her face to the mat, then gathered her courage. "May I ask if the story might be looked at in an additional way? How Tarō might have avoided the curse?"

"Eh? There is no other way." He squinted at her as she looked up. "The tragedy of the story was *not* the curse of aging. It was the boy's neglect of service to his family." Her grandfather plunked down his tea bowl. "Without *loyalty* you are nothing!" He rose and pointed his finger at her. "No matter how you wish to construe the story, I forbid you to attend that class." He headed for the door.

Sumi stood and bowed to his back, then stared at the paper's ashes. Loyal? She *was* loyal to her family. Couldn't she be loyal yet explore a little? Dip her toe into new waters without being swept away? Or attacked by sharks? Her grandfather had toured the largest domains, climbed Fuji-*san*, visited the Shōgun's magnificent Edo castle. He hadn't been in a magical underwater palace, naturally, but close to it.

Glancing toward the doorway, she caught her grandfather

looking back. Likely as not, he had no idea how much pain he had just inflicted. And he couldn't know how much she yearned to please him, yet how impossible it was.

He continued toward his room, and she turned in the opposite direction, holding back a forbidden tear.

At their home's entrance, the summer heat already seeped through the paper panels. She slid back the *shōji*, seeking a breeze, but found none. Pulling out her fan, she sat on the veranda's step, imagining years of empty days ahead.

A dragonfly flew past, its wings a flash of silver.

She straightened and watched it dart from one bush to another, heading all the while toward the front gate as though daring her to follow. A poem she loved came to mind. Revising another poet's *haiku*, Bashō had written:

> *Simple pepper pods*
> *Add gossamer wings to them*
> *Behold: Dragonflies*

Pepper pods and dragonflies. One essence to the poem's authors, but not to her. A pepper pod drooped in a garden until picked. But the dragonfly, admired by all samurai, could visit new, distant places on a whim, and then, after overcoming any defying insect, return unscathed.

The stalwart creature's sudden appearance could be a sign, couldn't it? Life had to offer more than an utterly disagreeable husband combined with endless flower arrangement, tea ceremony, embroidery, and plucking the *koto*'s strings. Her days already progressed as slowly as the poet Issa's snail crawling up Fuji-*san*, stone by stone by stone.

Oceans no longer separated her from the foreigners. They were here, in her city. She closed her eyes, picturing the tall, confident consul during the welcoming procession. He couldn't be an uncivilized barbarian. Her father wouldn't have said he had a calm, thoughtful disposition if he were. She'd sensed his fine life's energy, his *ki,* herself.

Regardless of danger, whether real or make-believe, she had to find an opening into the world beyond, into the tantalizing world the consul inhabited.

CHAPTER 2

The following morning, cooler air blew in from the ocean, inviting an outing. Seeing her father gazing at the book shelf over his low desk, Sumi bowed. "Father, please excuse my interruption." She drew in a shaky breath. Had her grandfather foreseen her request and already blocked it?

He turned toward her. "Yes? What is it?"

"Might I accompany you on one of your visits to the international sector? I would like to observe the strange sites you mentioned." She drew out her fan and tried to maintain an unruffled countenance while slowly fanning her face.

"I suppose you'll need to see the area sooner or later." A smile flickered at the corner of his mouth. "If you have no lesson today, you may come with me. Perhaps we can satisfy a little of that boundless curiosity of yours."

Her spirits rose as she bowed her thanks. Somehow, against all odds, he had gained her grandfather's permission to become a linguist. Of course, that was before anyone knew the Shōgun would open the country to the Americans, and then to other countries as well. But her father's victory showed the impossible could become possible.

An hour later, she wiped damp palms on her cherry-colored kimono and met her father downstairs. She nearly tiptoed out the house even though her grandfather was in the back garden, where he didn't like to be disturbed. Her father and she each rode in a *kago*, the hammocks swaying from the broad poles carried by jogging, bare-legged porters. At the Oura River Bridge, they left the *kago*.

Her father waved her forward. "Walk next to me. Foreigners, both men and women, walk side by side. In fact, when entering buildings, the men insist that the women enter first."

Sumi immediately complied despite unease at not following three steps behind. Did foreign women get used to such regal treatment?

After they passed through the guard gate, the road filled with swaggering sailors, workmen, horseback riders, men and women in bizarre outfits, and aggressive peddlers hawking fans, umbrellas, ink stones, and other paraphernalia. Two seagulls swooped overhead, their squawks mixing with the caterwauling of fishmongers selling eels and squid. The strong smell of seawater announced the bay's proximity.

Sumi drank in as many sights as she could, her body tingling with excitement. Her country's door had opened wide, and hers had creaked open a tiny bit in spite of her grandfather.

The dark river next to her teemed with sampans and large barges. Six men unloading barrels of whale oil shouted to each other in a language she'd never heard her father practice—not sounds of English or Dutch. She turned toward him.

"Russians," he said, anticipating her question. He pointed to several Chinese with long pigtails earnestly bartering for *daikon,* foot-long white radishes, from a green grocer.

"Foreigners' cooks. The world has come to us. To our own city."

They walked by the third house from the bridge. Its occupants had turned the Japanese house into a semi-foreign one. White wooden planks and glass windows took the place of the original sliding panels. Sumi forced her eyes away from the building. Behind its strange exterior lay the English treasure trove. She sealed her mouth against the pleadings longing to burst forth. *Forbidden!*

Up ahead, a group of foreigners chatted, two men and two women. The ladies wore the amazing mushroom-style skirts that nearly swept the ground. A hat covered with feathers perched on one lady's head. The other lady wore a smaller, less startling hat with one feather poking up. The foreigners talked and laughed in a familiar fashion. Then the lady with multiple feathers signaled to another couple across the road and marched over to them. The foreign women enjoyed astonishing freedom, the extent almost dizzying.

As they drew closer, she noticed a cane poking out from under the elderly man's arm. The cane's top curved into the shape of a . . . a parrot's head. Could that possibly be his clan's insignia? The characteristics of such a bird would hardly make an enemy tremble. She snickered at the thought of a parrot swooping down on a helmeted warrior.

The man gave the lady's words his full attention. Gray streaked his once dark hair and beard. Why foreign men wanted hairy faces was beyond her.

At that moment, the man recognized her father. He held out his hand—the *handshake* she'd heard about. The white-haired lady turned toward them and smiled. Then the second man, whose back had been toward Sumi, turned around.

She took a step backwards before she stopped herself. The tall American consul faced her. Only thirty years old, according to the documents her father had seen, yet he was a powerful country's envoy. Although he didn't shave his pate or wear his hair in a topknot, he had to be an extraordinary samurai.

The consul and her father shook hands too. No one bowed. When the elderly lady spoke, white teeth showed. They weren't coated with black enamel. Wasn't she married at such an advanced age? Didn't all married women dye their teeth and pluck their eyebrows?

English words swirled all around.

Her father said something that caused the three foreigners to look at her. She raised her fan, but dared a peek at the consul's face. He didn't at all have the sinister look attributed to barbarians by so many of her countrymen. His gray eyes appeared just as kind as when she'd seen him on the day he'd landed. In spite of his brown beard and the swath of hair over his lips, his jaw exuded strength, as expected of a samurai. She'd heard a rumor through her friend Taki that he was a good swimmer, accounting for his muscular, lean look.

She fanned her warm face. She would give everything she owned to be able to understand the conversation.

What luck, Taguchi Kenshin thought. Maybe encountering a friendly American couple as well as the consul would satisfy Sumi, and she wouldn't pester him with as many questions.

"It's a nice day for a stroll, isn't it?" Margaret Pendleton asked. "I'm sure having your beautiful daughter as your companion makes it all the more delightful."

"Yes, thank you for kind words." Kenshin carefully followed the foreign style of accepting rather than denying compliments. He glanced at his wide-eyed daughter, noting that her kimono did bring out her rosy complexion and contrasted well with her glossy, piled up hair. "Sumi asked to see this new area. Maybe her hope was to meet people from other side of the world."

"I imagine you've influenced her quite a bit, Mr. Taguchi," Consul Cardiff remarked, making no effort to mask an admiring glance at Sumi.

"I may have." *Might as well brag as they do.* "She study pictures in my foreign books, and I teach her a few vocabularies. Her mind remember well."

Mrs. Pendleton's face lit up. "My, that's splendid. You probably recall the notices you translated for us about holding English classes."

"Yes. Very generous." Bragging had been a mistake.

"We count it a privilege to spend time with young people." Mr. Pendleton pushed his square, wire glasses closer to the bridge of his nose. "Keeps our old minds agile. When I retired from teaching back in Connecticut, I didn't know how much I'd miss the younger set."

"If you wouldn't object," his wife continued, "I would be pleased for your daughter to join my class of young ladies. I'm certain she'd learn quickly."

"Thank you for fine invite," Kenshin hedged.

"We will devote our time to the most basic vocabulary and phrases, but if your daughter has already learned some of the words, she can practice using them in real conversation." Mrs. Pendleton wrinkled her brow as if deciding what to say. "Eventually, I'd like to introduce a few of our stories and excerpts from great literature, but I doubt our beginning students can handle that anytime soon."

"Vocabularies take much time to learn." And vocabulary, Kenshin realized, would be a thousand times safer than stories, some of which might be from the *Holy Bible*. The *Kirishitan* beliefs might not be truly evil, but the authorities thought so. And although the government no longer banned the suspect book from entering the country, the religion was still illegal for Kenshin's countrymen, punished by life-long banishment.

"If your daughter chooses to attend, the first lesson will be next Tuesday, as you probably remember." Mrs. Pendleton's brown eyes were gentle, her voice warm and inviting.

"What a good opportunity for the young lady," Consul Cardiff chimed in. "I heartily recommend she take advantage of it." He glanced at Mrs. Pendleton. "And it appears her attendance would also aid the other class members."

Mrs. Pendleton nodded. "Having a student who already knows a little English would be a great help."

"Now that our two countries have friendly relations," the consul added, "it behooves us to master each other's language, doesn't it?" He swept his hand toward Kenshin. "As you have so admirably done yourself."

"I am poor speaker, but I work to improve. I value wise words." *Words that could hide sharp teeth.* "We take no more your time."

Cardiff dipped his head to Kenshin. "I'll see you tomorrow." Then he smiled at Sumi. "I hope you have an enjoyable outing . . . and choose to join the class."

She blushed and bowed.

Setting out again after the exchange of farewells, Kenshin rubbed his forehead, his thoughts in a muddle. He hadn't planned to tell Sumi about the class. However, Consul John Cardiff was not only his superior, but also a powerful country's diplomat. If Cardiff hinted disapproval of anything involving Kenshin or his family, the authorities could demote him from Interpreter of the Second Rank to Third Rank. Or Fourth. Or even eject him from the guild altogether. It didn't take much to upset the two Nagasaki governors, and he'd been on shaky ground since the morning of the consul's arrival when he'd advised the vice governor to proffer his hand in greeting, only for the official to be met by Cardiff's deep bow.

He swatted away a buzzing bluebottle fly, wishing he could do likewise with Cardiff's recommendation.

He glanced at Sumi, whose eyes were bright with interest. She would be thrilled to attend lessons taught by a native English speaker. And English fluency, handled discreetly, would be a valuable asset to her generation. John Cardiff was right about that.

His clan's anti-foreign sentiment was the biggest problem by far. But he didn't have to blindly submit to the reactionaries' views or to self-imposed ignorance like that of the Kurohashi family. He would never purposefully challenge his father's actions—he knew his place—but he'd have no regrets if the next person proposed for Sumi's betrothal was the exact opposite of the obnoxious scholar, Keiji.

So, what should he do about the class?

Sumi twirled her yellow parasol. Her father, seemingly lost in thought, hadn't said a word since they'd left the foreigners. What had they discussed? The newest inventions? The young consul's heroic escapades? She wouldn't be left out if she could attend the English lessons. Fresh disappointment gripped her.

"Father," she said, daring to speak first, "why does Grandfather oppose the foreigner so? Perhaps they have medicine to cure cholera and other terrible diseases. More of their inventions like the *telegurafu* might benefit our country."

Her father stood still and frowned. "The foreigners may bring desirable things but also disputes and untested customs with unknown consequences." Then he shrugged and started walking again. "But whatever the disadvantages, more and more foreigners *will* come on shore. Whalers to be restocked. Steamship captains for coal. Traders for customers. And the *Kirishitan* no doubt craves converts, as his predecessors did hundreds of years ago."

He waved his hand toward the white warehouses sprouting up next to the bay. "The Western giants have vast resources. There's no stopping the incoming flood—for good or bad. And for the present, I choose to think for good."

"Couldn't Grandfather also choose to think for good?"

"He may eventually."

Not soon enough.

"Now, wouldn't you like to know what I discussed with the foreign couple?" He puffed out a breath. "I have good news for you."

While Sumi listened about the class, a battle raged. If the matchmaker introduced a traditionalist like her grandfather wanted, only a little time remained to explore the world outside her gate. She should take every opportunity. And the foreign lady specifically invited her.

But no, the gateway to the English classes had clanged shut, barricaded by her grandfather's final words. Disobeying—

unthinkable. Disloyal. Wrong.

Her father stopped speaking and looked at her.

"I fear Grandfather would object." She couldn't bring herself to say he already had.

"Only if he believed the classes were harmful. As he has more opportunity to evaluate the Westerners, he'll see the benefits of knowing their languages."

Sumi kept silent despite an inner nudge to admit the full truth.

"The foreigners' ways are odd, but you needn't fear for your safety. Mr. and Mrs. Pendleton live near the gate, so it would be safe enough even at those times I couldn't walk with you. Of course, you shouldn't venture farther into the international settlement alone."

"I understand, but—"

"It's unlikely anyone opposed to foreigners would care about these small classes, or even be aware of them." He stopped and looked at her. "Nothing has happened since the rude warrior bellowed against the foreigners that first day. He's probably moved on to a city more traditional than ours, where he has a better chance to stir up trouble."

She'd assumed the masterless warrior had been apprehended, but at least he was no longer a concern. "I am happy our city is rid of the scoundrel." She struggled to smile.

Her father's brow furrowed. "Do you not want to be in the class?"

"Yes, more than . . . I want to be of help, as much as possible, but—"

"Then I will arrange for you to attend. You can assist with the translation work after you gain enough fluency. As for your honorable grandfather, I believe he will agree to your aiding me in the future. However, there is no sense in troubling him now with this matter."

"But he has . . . he's—" Her father's last sentence registered. Not tell the Eldest? Was that possible? Blinking in astonishment, she bowed. "Thank you. As incompetent as I am, I *will* do my best in the class."

Like a storm cloud blotting out the sun, fear overshadowed the first rush of bliss. If only her secret could be buried deep in the waters below the Buddha's lotus blossoms! A shiver ran up her spine. Deceiving her grandfather could never attract any god's help.

CHAPTER 3

Taguchi Yoshikatsu stepped onto the back veranda to breathe the evening's fresh air and to think. More and more trouble was brewing. His granddaughter had not dared to argue about the English classes after he forbade her attendance, but her countenance had argued for her. Despite his efforts to shield Sumi, the despicable barbarians enticed her. They always had. He'd even had to rebuke her as a child for climbing their tallest pine tree, trying in vain to glimpse the tall sails of the annual Dutch ship.

He peered at the moon, its light dipping in and out of the branches. Its bright orb shone not only on his garden, but on the foreigners making themselves at home, desecrating Nagasaki. A travesty like none he could remember. The early shōguns had rid the country of the colonizing foreigners and the subversive *Kirishitan*. But now the barbarians would again spread their insidious poison.

He recalled the terrified voices of the messengers who told of the Americans' black warships steaming into Edo Bay *against* the wind six years earlier. And then his own shock at the Shōgun's capitulation to the foreigners' demands for trade despite his title of Barbarian-Expelling Generalissimo.

His shoulders sagged. His family had sworn undying loyalty to the Shōgun. He could not lift his sword, or even a stick, against the foreigners. Worst of all, his son had to obey the order to be the American consul's interpreter—almost as degrading as handling a dead animal.

Wispy clouds passed in front of the moon. A slight breeze sprang up, carrying an unidentified sound. He stiffened, straining to separate the faint rustle from the usual night noises.

A prowler!

He grasped the dagger hidden behind the back step. Leaving his clogs by the veranda, he crept barefoot toward the darker shadows and the scarcely audible footsteps.

A twig snapped under him despite his years of samurai training.

The footsteps paused and then became pronounced, moving along the side garden's wall.

Yoshikatsu rushed to the side gate and opened it a crack, ready to jump the intruder.

A gaunt samurai, the only person in sight, strode by, carrying a half-closed lantern. It cast enough glow to illuminate the crest on his faded, yet elegant tunic—an emblem belonging to Yoshikatsu's own Chōshū clan. The frayed tunic suggested the high-ranking nobleman might have left the clan to live like a masterless, wandering samurai, a *rōnin*.

Yoshikatsu gripped his dagger more tightly, but held back. He dared not accost a Chōshū samurai outranking him, whether or not he was a *rōnin*. But if the warrior had skulked in their garden, why?

Probably not to rob the house.

He slipped out of the gate. Hugging the wall, he trailed the bobbing lantern.

Just as the samurai reached the front of the nearby bronzeware shop, the lantern's light vanished.

Yoshikatsu halted. Had the stranger *entered* Merchant Omura's place at this late hour? Or had he suspected a tracker and snuffed out the flame? Neither possibility reassured him.

He made his way back to the garden, listening for any sound of being stalked himself.

The moonlight now cast a more ominous spell over the rocks and bushes. He surveyed the shifting shadows, then studied the back side of the house facing him. The open partition of Sumi's room gaped in the pale light as if intimating her vulnerability.

After this, he would always carry his dagger. Too many of his Chōshū clan strayed toward fanaticism in their hatred of the foreigners. He had to find Sumi a refuge without any more delay. In the future negotiations for her betrothal, he'd make sure her enthrallment with barbarians didn't disrupt the proceedings again. Eventually she would appreciate his fidelity to the right path for her and their family line.

CHAPTER 4

August (Month of the Rooster)

On her way to the Pendletons' home, Sumi stopped to purchase more embroidery thread. At the tailor shop's entrance, her gaze was drawn by a towering black hat among the people in front of the neighboring store. Her breath quickened, and she moved a little closer. A tall foreigner, wearing dark blue trousers and a white coat, stood among the shoppers. His profile resembled the consul's. Could it be?

She strolled in his direction, apprehensive yet yearning to meet him.

Then she halted. What was she doing? If he were the consul, they couldn't converse. The most she could do was greet him in English, ask if he was well, and sing the song she'd learned in the first week of the English classes about rowing a boat. She chuckled despite her disappointment.

John Cardiff browsed through the rolls of silk displayed in front of one of the box-like, two-story buildings crowding the busy thoroughfare outside the international sector. The shopkeeper had enthusiastically beckoned him to take a look, a big contrast to the two previous shopkeepers who'd treated him like a pale-faced demon. He'd taken a real interest in one shop's huge yellow and blue shrimp, octopuses, slithering eels, and all sorts of live fish until the owner had practically shoved him out, alternating scowls and gestures with bows.

This shop's silk was the best he'd seen, better than the excellent quality of rolls he'd ordered previously from a local Chinaman. He would need to come back with Interpreter Taguchi and make an offer on behalf of his trading company, with the goal of eventually buying directly from the source.

Managing his company while fulfilling his role as honorary consul demanded every ounce of energy he possessed. Before he'd been recruited to be a part-time diplomat, he had put all his effort into Cardiff & Associates, owned by him and his older brother Edward, operating in Shanghai. Now John labored to represent his countrymen *and* make a profit in a place both fascinating and unsettling.

He fingered a roll of shimmering turquoise silk, imagining how his fiancée would admire its color and texture. Although Catherine might need time to fully embrace Japan's dissimilarity with New York, she would enjoy perusing these shops from the first day. If Japan turned out to be hospitable enough—a big if—he would do his best to persuade her to take part in the adventure, properly chaperoned, of course, until their marriage.

"*Shita ni iyo! Shita ni iyo!*" rent the air.

He twisted toward the street. Six men marched down the road, obviously shouting commands. In the distance, a military formation swept forward, completely filling the road. All the nearby people, toddlers and silver-haired elders alike, instantly knelt with their heads bowed to the ground. Behind him, the shopkeeper dragged in the upright banner announcing the store's contents in giant, Chinese-style characters and shuttered the entrance.

Was the governor approaching? A warlord? The Shōgun himself?

John's new manservant, Goda, bowed and urgently motioned for him to kneel.

Out of the question. A representative of the United States of America could not take such a subservient position, groveling in the dust. He crossed his arms and shook his head.

Four columns of men carrying tall poles with banners drew near. Several kneeling men near John clamored with gestures for him to copy them.

He motioned for Goda to follow and moved back into the shade of a cherry tree's branches stretching over a wall. The more inconspicuous, the better, but he couldn't do anything about his six-foot height. He could refuse, however, to give in to the needles of fear pricking his spine.

"*Sumimasen,* Cardiff-*sama.*"

He turned toward the voice. His interpreter's daughter, Miss Taguchi, stood before him and bowed. Where on earth had she come from?

"Hizen *Daimyō* come." She knelt gracefully next to his servant and gestured for him to do likewise. "Please."

"No, I cannot." He shook his head.

She stared at him for a moment, then looked down the road at the advancing formation. She pointed to the oncoming warriors and then to the ground. "Please. Hizen *Daimyō*. No good."

He shook his head again, trying to think.

Hizen was a nearby province. *Daimyō* probably meant *warlord*. How insulting would a refusal to kneel be? A dispatch from the consul general at the capital's legation flashed through his mind: *Avoid processions. High threat of unprovoked attack.* But in heaven's name, how could you avoid one if you didn't see it coming until too late?

Miss Taguchi glanced back at him again and ran her fingers across her throat.

He nodded and shot up an urgent prayer.

The first row of ten warriors strode by. Not moving a muscle, John tracked them with his eyes.

Nothing happened.

The second row came, sporting muskets as well as their swords. These samurai also seemed oblivious of him.

Then a warrior in the third row pointed at him and yelled. Other warriors joined in.

Miss Taguchi, eyes wide with panic, again motioned for him to kneel.

A shiver sliced through him. Hadn't this warlord and his underlings been informed of the Treaty of Friendship's terms? He had to show his status—and fast.

He searched his pockets. A watch. Japanese script. A letter from home. *Dear God, is there nothing of use?* The consul general's dispatch? Yes, there, in his waistcoat's inner pocket.

He pulled the paper out and ran his fingers over the gold seal.

The entire procession halted. Two samurai swaggered toward him. One of them whipped out his sword, its edge glinting in the blaze of sunlight.

John's pulse raced. Only one swipe of the razor-sharp weapon would finish him.

The other samurai shouted guttural commands at those kneeling in front of John. These bystanders, including the interpreter's daughter, threw themselves down fully prostrate. His manservant stayed kneeling upright—now a target.

Heart pumping, John held up the dispatch. "Look here!" He strode forward between the bodies that inched farther aside.

The hate-filled eyes of the closest samurai, three feet away, drilled into him.

John heard a rustling and looked back. Miss Taguchi had risen onto her knees. Goda had stood up and was stepping forward.

"No!" John yelled. He motioned for them to get back down.

Miss Taguchi obeyed, but Goda stepped closer to him. Words poured from the old man as though he were the messenger for a king. He pointed at the sky, once, twice, three times—punctuating his shrill pronouncements.

Regret engulfed John. He should have fled. He never should have put his manservant in this situation. *Lord, have mercy! I didn't mean to gamble with his life.*

Goda bowed, then prostrated himself.

John spread his legs to better block the servant and Miss Taguchi from view. He puffed out his chest and pointed to the seal as though it alone could overpower the sword. In the past he'd stared down more than one adversary, but none intent on killing for a master's honor. Sweat poured down his back.

The closest samurai seized the paper and rubbed his thumb over the shiny seal, muttering.

More yells came from the procession. Two more warriors drew their swords and veered out. Was the whole phalanx next?

John fixed his eyes on the first samurai. The warrior's glare held John's.

The surroundings faded. Only the warrior's flint-hard face remained.

John gave a slight bow, having no desire to force the man's hand, and flicked his eyes to the paper.

The samurai followed his glance, then shoved the paper back to John. After a livid look that traveled the length of John's body, the warrior barked orders at the other three and led them to rejoin the procession.

Chest heaving, John stepped back into the shade of the tree. When Goda looked at him, John nodded his approval. What a gem he had in this man. And what a horror he'd just witnessed, far worse than the first-day incident with the samurai bellowing for the barbarians' expulsion.

He breathed a shaky prayer of thanks.

A clanking sound drew his attention. A small group of policemen, holding metal poles, had gathered nearby. Did the samurai withdraw because of these lightly armed police? Or had it been because of his manservant's speech? Or the shiny seal? Or his own bravado? He huffed a breath. Perhaps he'd never know.

Miss Taguchi, Goda, and the other bystanders continued to kneel while seventy or so samurai passed by. Then the Hizen warlord himself came along in a palanquin, its black lacquered compartment hanging from a thick beam. The six porters halted the palanquin on the road in front of John. He stiffened, sensing the warlord's examination.

Removing his hat, John bowed while still standing, then raised his head slowly.

Would an order come to slay him after all?

Three fingertips from under the compartment's veiled opening gave the slightest of signals, and the porters moved forward.

He could breathe again.

At least two hundred attendants and their servants followed the noble, bearing umbrellas, armor, and row after row of black lacquered boxes.

John grunted. With his one servant, he must have looked not only weak but ridiculous.

After the last of the procession paraded past, Miss Taguchi rose along with the others lining the street. She blotted her face and mustered a weak smile "You are that." She pointed to a dragonfly flitting past, then looked into his eyes for a brief moment, apparently expecting a knowledgeable response.

He hadn't been called an insect before. Was it a compliment or an insult? A dragonfly seemed better than a moth or—heaven help him—a worm. Since she wasn't frowning, he said, "Thank you."

She turned as red as a firecracker. "Come well, ah, come," she sputtered.

"You are welcome," he corrected.

"You are welcome," she repeated. "Good teacher. Thank you." Her eyes shone.

"Good student," he responded. And a very brave and pretty one, he thought, noting her oval face and sparkling eyes. But he would not become the slightest bit interested in any native. He was engaged to the prettiest and best lady in both hemispheres. And commitments were meant to be kept.

"Meet again. Goodbye." Miss Taguchi gave a sedate bow. If still flustered, she didn't show it.

John returned an equally low bow, determined to show respect to ladies whenever he could. He wished he could tell her how much he appreciated her efforts to help him, that he admired her remarkable bravery. As she walked away and entered one of the reopened shops, he rebuked himself for his ridiculous desire to follow her.

Behind John, a hawker of soybean cried "*Nattō, nattōō.*" A leg man trudged past, lugging a load of charcoal on his back. John glanced around. Housewives and workers bustled in both directions. The whole street had resumed its interrupted activities. No one appeared bothered in the least that the samurai had threatened to slaughter him.

He beckoned to Goda and began retracing his steps to where he'd left his horse and newly acquired groom, Nobu. The groom, recommended by the Taguchis' neighbor, Merchant Omura, never seemed to relax, but at least the superbly competent man could be counted on to have John's horse ready in a future emergency. From this time on, he'd always have the horse close by. He would carry a concealed weapon too when visiting threatening areas. And that meant he'd carry his revolver most of the time since a threat could obviously arise anywhere. Anytime.

The next day, in response to John's urgent request, Governor Nakamura sent a palanquin and six officials to escort John to his residence. Since the palanquin was required for official visits, John gritted his teeth and squeezed into the nearly square box, four feet long and three-and-a-half feet high. Within minutes, the palanquin metamorphosed into a sweltering oven. Sweat drenched his sticky clothes. Unable to straighten, he stayed bent forward over his crossed legs. He'd ridden in an uncomfortable sedan chair in Shanghai, but this was worse.

Arriving at last, he hobbled forward with as much dignity

as he could marshal. Three samurai ushered him into the governor's domicile through the wide gate reserved for warlords. At least this show of respect was a far cry from the treatment the Dutch received during the previous two centuries. When permitted off their prison-like island, they'd had to *crawl* before the authorities and even perform impromptu dance steps and songs to satisfy the officials' whims.

After two of the city's vice governors and more samurai conducted John to the cavernous audience room, John took his place on a dais facing Governor Nakamura's dais of equal height. The Shōgun's black crest of hollyhock leaves emblazoned screens that lined three walls, trumpeting the governor's authority as the military dictator's direct representative. As usual, dozens of samurai squatted on mats, forming a large rectangle in front of the daises. A special guard next to Nakamura held his sword. John imagined the uproar if President Buchanan received a diplomat at the White House with crouching soldiers and a loaded pistol. But the less-than-warm welcome accommodated his mood.

After a half hour of cordialities and the usual refreshments of yellowish-green tea, sweet bean confections, and tobacco pipes, Nakamura fixed John with a hard stare and leaned forward, his white, flat hat casting a shadow on his forehead.

The two interpreters tensed like hunters, ready to pounce on each word. A red-haired American sailor, loaned from the United States frigate, had the task of translating John's English into Dutch, and Mr. Taguchi, not yet able to handle technicalities in English, had to translate the Dutch into Japanese. And then vice versa.

"I presume a situation troubles you," came from the governor via the translators.

John nodded. "Indeed. Yesterday, without provocation, four Hizen samurai threatened my life during their warlord's procession."

"I assure you the clansmen meant no harm." Nakamura fingered a tassel on his large fan during the translations. "They were merely clearing the way for their master."

John gave a slight shake of his head. "I had already moved back from the road. Without question, my adversaries wished to draw blood simply because I maintained the honor of the United States."

The governor tilted his head and smiled as though managing a small child. "You appear whole and healthy. Clearly our subjects respect the laws."

John waited to reply until sure of the governor's full attention. "If a foreigner is attacked here—God forbid—the Western nations will hold the assailants' clan fully responsible. *Military* consequences would be a strong possibility even though I would urge restraint. I am sure we both want to avoid such a dilemma."

As the translations droned on, John watched Governor Nakamura's round face. No eyelid quivered. The attending vice governor nodded his head occasionally. The *metsuke,* the Shōgun's agent-spy, continued taking sips of sherry while recording every word in the daybook to be sent to the shogunate officials in the capital city, Edo. No one appeared to take his dire warning to heart.

Suddenly one of the younger officials jerked his head back toward the governor, but not before loathing contorted his face.

John checked his notes. During the opening formalities, the man had been introduced as Governor Nakamura's second son, Kohei. Studying him, John judged him in his twenties.

Kohei looked straight at John again. Except for the ice in the man's eyes, his stony expression now concealed his contempt.

Did others of these breathing statues feel the same hostility, but hide it better? Could the basket-hooded warrior who shouted the first day be among the samurai watching him from behind? A chill invaded the warm room.

Nakamura ran his eyes over John and wrinkled his brow. "You need not fear. Many precautions are assuring your safety. I have told Chief Inspector Sato to put the city's forces on higher alert."

John forced himself to appear composed at the mention of Sato.

"You are in good hands." Nakamura gestured at a screen.

The chief inspector stepped out and gave a deep bow to the governor and a stiff, shallow bow to John.

John returned a similar bow, remembering Sato's fury during an incident the day before the official welcoming ceremony. An American, who had taken passage on the same naval ship as John, had accused John of supplying the opium the man himself tried to smuggle. John had proven his innocence, and Chief Inspector Sato—with grim reluctance—had submitted to John's and the frigate captain's disposition of the case.

John wasn't at all eager to deal with the inspector again, and he imagined the feeling was mutual.

Sato's strong features exacted attention: a jaw more square than most of his countrymen's, a broad forehead, deep, penetrating eyes. A powerful countenance, even when not irate. Someone who could do a great deal of good . . . or harm.

Chief Inspector Sato bowed low to the governor a second

time and backed from the room.

"Now that the issue of safety is settled"—Nakamura's proud smile resembled the look of a chess champion—"do you have other concerns?"

John's skin crawled at the cavalier treatment. Yet what use would there be in repeating the same threats?

"Yes, I most certainly do. The three American ships I reported previously still face disastrous ruin. It has been *four* weeks since the port authority barred them from unloading cargo." The ships' captains had ranted and pled for John to *do something*.

"Very bad for ships' owners." Nakamura waved a hand toward the *metsuke*. "We already referred the problem to the shogunate's High Council in Edo, however."

John bit back an angry retort. He wouldn't gain respect by losing his temper. But would the governor pay attention to anything he said? Bankruptcy for traders could come far too easily, as the owners of the three ships would experience anytime now. And the government's stonewalling could damage his own trading house once his company's ship returned from the American West Coast.

If his venture failed, his post as honorary consul would be yanked away too. He'd be forced to work in his future father-in-law's carpet company in order to repay the investment the man had made in John's journey to the Far East. And Catherine? She might end their engagement.

He squared his shoulders. He'd come too far and endured too much, to suffer defeat now. Like opponents wielding off-balance thrusts in a slow-motion swordfight, the duel with the governor continued. Coinage problems. Hindrances at the Custom House. The Russian bazaar's unfair advantage.

In the end, he achieved nothing—nothing to show for all that effort.

By the concluding formalities, the second son Kohei had already left. John worked to imprint the man's features in his memory: average height, a sharp, dour face with the usual shaved pate and samurai topknot. Another agitated person to guard against—one which John's words no doubt further enflamed.

And Governor Nakamura? He projected politeness, but he could simply be more adept at hiding hostility. How could an outsider ever read these people's true intentions?

He climbed back into the palanquin, forgetting to remain bent over. He rubbed his sore head. How nice it would be to trot along on his horse instead of roasting in a box. In fact, how nice to sit in a chair instead of negotiating pretzel-shaped on the dais. He stopped himself. Life overseas always brought struggle, separating the fittest from the pack. Nevertheless, one thing above all had to change. The authorities had to take the foreigners' safety much more seriously. What would it require—a murder? A massacre?

CHAPTER 5

Sumi strolled toward home from the foreign sector, humming the second American song she'd learned in the English class. She wouldn't use most of this song's vocabulary about Yankee Doodle or the first one about rowing a boat anytime soon, but singing with the other seven class members was a new and fun experience. And today's interesting class had helped settle her mind after the horrific confrontation with the Hizen *daimyō*'s procession two days earlier.

The consul's bravery still gave her chills. He truly had been like the dragonfly. A dragonfly didn't slink down in the dust. It drew from towering strength, like the poet Issa had written:

> *Distant mountain peaks*
> *Reflecting in the small eyes*
> *Of the dragonfly*

She'd seen a woodprint of distant Fuji-*san* soaring above the countryside. She raised her chin. She would remember the extraordinary consul's example of standing strong.

Two young boys rolled a hoop past her. She chuckled at its twisting course over the cobblestones, sideswiping a startled sweet-potato vendor's stall and wobbling past a cluster of housewives haggling with a knife grinder. A goose flapped, barely escaping the hoop's threat.

A whiff of wood smoke reminded her of the refreshing bath waiting at home. She put her hands in her sleeves and squeezed her arms. The weather was *mushi atsui*, like a hot, wet blanket, but she didn't care. It was a grand day to be alive.

A dead leaf caught in her sandal, and she bent to remove it. At that moment, something odd swished over her, catching several hairs.

It thudded against the wall.

She stared in disbelief. A samurai's dagger! If she hadn't bent down, it would have struck her! She crouched, darting her eyes in every direction.

The bamboo at the end of a noodle shop's wall swayed. A samurai's blue tunic flashed as the warrior leapt behind an adjoining wall.

She stifled a scream. He had meant to hit her. Kill her! A samurai would never disappear, leaving his weapon, otherwise. But why? Why target *her*? Trembling, she struggled to breathe. He would try again. No warrior accepted failure.

A husky laborer plodded by. She fell in next to him even though his large frame didn't offer much protection. Seconds later, she cringed, realizing the man's size might give no protection whatsoever. The assailant could lurk on either side of the road.

A loose cobblestone caught her foot. She pitched forward and barely caught herself. Choking back a sob, she let the laborer go on ahead.

Two porters toting a *kago* entered from a side street and stopped in front of a seaweed stall, letting their passenger out.

Pushing forward with all her strength, she cut before another woman.

"Take me . . ." No, she couldn't guide the warrior to where she lived. The lead porter raised his eyebrows and shot a look at his partner. "Take me down this road to Merchant Omura Kowa's bronzeware shop. I'll pay for your top speed."

Her hands wouldn't stop shaking. When she tugged at the packet tucked in her sash, four of its coins fell onto the cobblestones.

Frowning, the porter took the rest of the coins from her and squatted to gather the scattered ones.

She slid into the *kago*'s hammock. The two porters took off at a fast jog, causing the *kago* to swing and jerk. She clutched its sides. Could they possibly outpace a samurai? She squeezed down on the cushion as much as possible, her mind spewing questions.

Surely her attacker wasn't the *rōnin* from weeks ago. Hadn't her father said the scoundrel had moved on? Was she a target because she'd risen to her knees during the warlord's procession? But that had been for only a second before she'd prostrated herself. How about her father's work? Could a crazed clansman be so enraged that he'd strike anyone in the family? Or was it because of the forbidden classes? She groaned at the unfairness, at her helplessness . . . at her weakness.

The *kago* passed the last gate between the city's wards on her route and stopped. The lead porter called for her to climb down.

Her stomach dropped. She poked her head out. "Go on! You must go on!"

"This is all you paid for."

"I, I don't have any more coins . . ." Her voice choked.

"Then climb down, miss. I have a family to feed."

She stumbled out. Her gaze swept the street. Shoppers, vendors, two pilgrims, a musician, a storyteller—ordinary people. Was the samurai behind her? Ahead of her? She was only fifteen minutes from her home, but it might as well have been hours and hours.

The toy store next to her had banners and displays right up to the road. She ducked into the shop, dodging a painted puppet dangling from the ceiling. Long whistles in the shapes of segmented dragons filled the shelf to her right. Beyond them, the painted eyes of wooden warriors glared at her.

Harmless toys, a place for children, she told herself. But her galloping heart didn't slow down. She crept farther into the room and stood still in the dim light, listening while she scrutinized the dark corners for a place to hide.

The creak of a stair step alerted her to an elderly woman, slowly descending from the residence above. Most likely the owner's mother. The little old woman didn't look like she could mount any defense if the attacker guessed Sumi's whereabouts. Even a hard push would probably incapacitate her. But how about the gray shawl around her shoulders? Could it work as a disguise?

Sumi interrupted the elderly woman's welcoming sales speech. "Excuse me. I'm . . . I'm very cold." Her teeth chattered as though to prove her words. "I'll exchange my silk sash for your shawl."

"Begging your pardon. Please keep your beautiful sash." The woman wrapped the shawl around Sumi and patted her shoulder with a tsk. "I suggest you go to your home and rest. No mistaking that fever. Perhaps you can return the shawl when you're up and around. And"—the woman pointed to a shelf full of tops—"our toys delight every child. No mistaking that neither. Maybe you could honor our store—endorse it, eh."

"Yes, yes. I'll highly recommend this place." *If I survive.*

Sumi pulled the shawl over her head. It covered only the front half of her kimono when she stood straight, but more when she leaned forward. Bent over like an old grandmother, she shuffled out the door.

One step. Another step. Breathe. She yearned to race home, but that would be fatal. She must go slowly, even more slowly.

A shadow flapped and reached for her. Breathing out little gasps, she glimpsed a fluttering store banner from the corner of her eye. *Stop quaking. Normal people don't jump at shadows. And certainly not brave ones, ones like dragonflies . . . or the consul.*

Another step. And another. Until finally—Omura's shop.

At the shop's vestibule, she bent farther to remove her sandals. She placed one hand on the small of her back, mimicking an arthritic ache. Deliberately swaying, she took the single step up into the store.

The merchant dozed at his low stand, an abacus in his hand next to his strings of cash. She crept through the room toward the display on the far shelf.

Someone entered the shop behind her.

She froze. Surely the assailant wouldn't kill her right there! One more minute and she could be safely home!

The man spoke to wake Omura.

She glanced back.

A real customer rapped on Omura's stand.

She slipped into the rear garden and scurried through it to the back hedge, panting. Removing her *obi*, she squeezed through the vine-covered gap between the two connecting plaster walls, scraping an arm.

Home! She was home! She rewrapped her *obi* around her waist and lurched into the house.

The maid Kin stood before the stairs with a worried frown.

"There is no need for my bath or supper tonight." Sumi tried to steady her wavering voice. "Tell my family I am tired and beg to be excused." She turned back toward her grandfather's room, wondering how she could struggle through the usual greeting obliged by her return.

"Excuse me," Kin said, taking a step after her. "The eldest master is already in the bath house."

Hiding her relief, Sumi nodded, then veered around the maid to trudge up the stairs.

She pulled a futon from her room's cupboard and fell on it, covering herself with a blanket in spite of the late afternoon's warmth. Her body still quaked. Her mind reeled. Could she tell her father or her grandfather about the dagger? No, especially not the Eldest, who had warned about sharks. If anyone in her family knew about the attack, she would be guarded like a cricket in a cage.

All at once, Sumi threw back the blanket and sprang up. She'd seen an odd flicker of a shadow in their garden the night after she'd learned about the English lessons. Could the shadow have been her attacker? She rushed to the wall's partition and closed and barred the rain shutters. Her cousin Kiyo, who shared her room, was staying at a friend's home overnight and wasn't there to object.

Lying down again, she lay with her eyes wide open. Her enemy would not make her cry. She was a samurai's daughter.

Sumi puttered around her room the next day. She took up her neglected needlework, but put it down after tangling the threads. She fingered a writing brush resting in its ornate box next to her low dresser and picked up the ink stone to dampen it. Somehow she had to pass the time, to ease the fear.

After writing "English" across the top of a piece of foreign paper, she hesitated. Was even that dangerous? Were the gods themselves punishing her for the English lessons? Were they incensed by Pendleton-*sensei*'s two small references to the *Holy Bible*? She brushed a swath of ink through the word and crumpled the paper.

Moving to the open window panel past her dozing yellow cat, she gazed down at the garden, a sight she'd always loved until that moment. The shifting shadows in the area beyond the pear tree looked innocent enough. The summer day appeared to be an ordinary one. However, *ordinary* had vanished. A chill ran through her, remembering the horror of the previous day.

The Buddha was right. Everyone's existence consisted of illusions. Safety was an illusion. The garden—no. Despite what a monk might say, the garden was not an illusion. Its beauty might be, but the rocks, bushes, trees, and their shadows were there. Real and menacing.

CHAPTER 6

Sumi waited by the front entrance, watching for her father's return. Why was he so late? She hazarded going to their gate and peering out. Did her father lie somewhere wounded? Dying?

She should have told her family about the attack right after it happened, not letting a day go by, let alone three. If her father were still alive, she would tell her elders even if it meant she'd never leave the house. Never again see the tall consul with the amazing gray eyes. Never learn the foreigners' modern ways, their ideas about life's riddles, or the mysterious contents of their holy book.

She sighed. How could she have been so thoughtless? So disloyal, to use her grandfather's word?

At that moment, her father rounded the corner and turned into their gate, nodding to the bowing gatekeeper.

"Oh, Father, you are all right! I was frightened for you." She bowed low, hiding the threatening tears of relief.

"Certainly I am all right. Why wouldn't I be?"

"You are home later than usual. I thought—"

"You worry too much. A samurai's daughter must be

brave." He stepped out of his straw sandals at the vestibule and into his slippers in front of her kneeling mother. "Our daughter trembles at everything these days, like a rabbit seeing a fox ready to spring."

Her mother murmured something in reply and cast worried eyes on her. Sumi opened her mouth to reassure them, to prove that she wasn't like a cowardly rabbit, but no words came. She hurried inside behind her parents.

After nibbling at her supper, she lingered downstairs. As she hoped, her grandfather retired to his room early. Then her father drew out his pipe and began to answer her mother's question about his late return. Sumi knelt on a cushion next to her. Kiyo knelt opposite them.

"An excited crowd milled around, not too far from our sector's gate. Blood splattered the ground. Chief Inspector Sato questioned every bystander."

Sumi's breath came faster.

Her mother set down her needlework. "Had someone very important been injured?"

"A masterless samurai, deranged by all accounts, was caught stealing from a store. He was young, not more than seventeen. He fought the shopkeeper and the guard trying to apprehend him. Even tried to stab the guard with his dagger just as the chief inspector decapitated him."

Sumi gasped. Was that her attacker? Now dead?

Her mother wrung her hands. "Terrible, but how fortunate Chief Inspector Sato was close by."

"Close this time, but what about next time? He has the foreigners' safety now on top of his regular duties." Her father shook his head in disgust. "He and his men cannot be everywhere at once, and these *rōnin* infesting our countryside need to be reined in."

"Pardon me." Sumi cleared her throat and strove for a more disinterested tone. "May I ask whether this was the *rōnin* who threatened the Americans the day they arrived?"

"Highly unlikely. The one today acted like a common thief. And as I already told you"—his tone sharpened—"we can assume the hooded one moved on."

Her mother replenished their tea.

Sumi waited impatiently while everyone slurped the hot tea for several minutes. Finally she could hold off no longer. "May I ask what the thief tried to steal? Toys?" She grimaced. The word *toys* had slipped out.

Her father tilted back against the wall, a slight smile twitching his lips. "Certainly not toys." He paused and the smile disappeared. "It *did* take place by a toy store. Why do you ask about toys?"

"Oh . . . you said he was deranged. I . . . I just guessed he wouldn't steal any usual thing. I don't know why toys came to mind." She forced a little chuckle as if amused by her own absurdity, then bit her lip, trying to restrain her excitement. Surely the deranged samurai had been her assailant. He must have tracked her until she disappeared in front of the toy store, so he blamed the store owner, who fortunately escaped harm.

Her cousin rolled her eyes. "Aren't you a little old to be preoccupied with toys?" Kiyo, a year older, never missed an opportunity to seize on Sumi's supposed immaturity.

Her parents stared at Sumi as if they shared Kiyo's line of thought.

"A few days ago, I saw a dagger on the road and wondered if a samurai had been in a fight—one who was bad-tempered or not quite right in his head." She folded her hands to hide their tremble, hoping she sounded more reasonable.

Kiyo muffled a snort.

A puzzled frown creased her mother's forehead. "You left the dagger alone, surely."

"I wouldn't have touched it for anything."

Her father squinted at her quizzically. "Don't let your imagination run wild. A warrior probably dropped it while peeling a piece of fruit. That's all. You needn't be concerned about such a small incident as a lost dagger or about my safety either."

She bowed in acknowledgment, while relishing her relief. She pushed her palms down on the floor, as though to anchor her exuberance.

Her parents were studying her.

"I haven't felt well for several days. I feel much better now." Despite her parents' solemn faces and Kiyo's leer, she gave them all a careful smile.

Her silence had not been disastrous. Her father was safe. She could venture out. She wouldn't have to give up the English lessons after all. Of course, she'd also have to go to her *ikebana* lesson first and practice yet another interminable way to arrange cut flowers, but that was all right. Her attacker was dead. Dead!

Chief Inspector Sato, clothed in his spotless, gray tunic and *hakama* wide trousers, drew his dappled horse to a halt. He had checked the neighborhood for signs of anything suspicious and was satisfied all was well. The interpreter's daughter, the makings of a flower arrangement in one hand and a parasol in the other, strolled by the side of the road a little in front of him.

He had thought of her as a child for a long time. Once when he'd been visiting her grandfather, she'd even been scolded for climbing a tree during a coming typhoon to rescue a kitten. But in the last year or two, she'd grown into an attractive lady.

While he watched the young woman's progress along the road, he mulled over the previous day's incident at the toy store. Normally, he liked the challenge of unraveling plots. But this crime didn't fit the usual patterns. For one thing, the samurai's ravings had included words about the *traitorous interpreter*. That had to be Taguchi Kenshin, the young lady's father. Moreover, the criminal hadn't actually been a deranged thief as the crowd assumed, but a Chōshū samurai concealing a suspiciously large pouch of silver coins.

Dead men couldn't provide answers, but the samurai's raw youth indicated older associates lurked in the city. Agitators who could cause a lot more difficulty. Possibly the *rōnin* who had disrupted the welcoming procession the first day. That shrewd scoundrel had still evaded capture.

The young lady drew in her parasol and bowed to a passerby. What a graceful sight she presented in her dark green kimono. His family's status and hers matched well. Her father couldn't help his repugnant assignment as the barbarian's interpreter. Eventually, Interpreter Taguchi could return to his more reputable work of translating foreign treaties.

Sato rubbed his chin. Maybe he should find out why this member of a good family was not yet married. But no, even after three years, his dead wife's face still dazzled his mind. And pained him.

His horse snorted, causing the young lady to glance around. She picked up her pace, not as carefree as he'd guessed. Good. She'd better keep an eye on her surroundings. If the youth who raved against her father had conspired with like-minded Chōshū clansmen, those seasoned samurai would not overlook his death—the death of a martyr.

He clucked at his horse. He'd spent enough time in the area.

However, he rode past the *ojōsama* at a slower gait than he intended.

CHAPTER 7

John kneaded the back of his stiff neck, having persevered through another meeting with the governor. During their discussion of carrier pigeons, a conversation more relaxed than usual, Governor Nakamura had abruptly held up his hand and issued the long-overdue permission for the three waiting American ships to unload cargo. Despite John's relief, unspoken questions needled him—riddles, wrapped in the enigma of a complex language, rife with cultural innuendos.

A few more minutes and he'd be out of the palanquin's torture chamber. Today he genuinely appreciated the ancient temple the city's current governor provided for his residence until the consulate could be finished. The musty temple, guarded at its entrance by two giant statues of fearsome gods, always stood empty except for the monks, the lead priest, a few young acolytes, and an occasional female worshipper bowing before the gilded Buddha. He needed the peace and quiet in which to settle his thoughts and write Catherine his weekly letter.

A growing sound of voices caught his attention as his palanquin entered the *Terramachi* main street. Poking his head out the palanquin's reed curtain, he stared, dismayed to see men, women, and children packing the dusty road ahead. Surely they weren't headed for his refuge. But in the distance, the steps leading up the temple's low hill were black with masses of people. A puff of smoke issued from one of the stalls that had mushroomed at the base of the hill, no doubt satisfying a mob of hungry customers.

Once he made it inside the temple, John gaped at the gigantic, orange paper lanterns newly suspended from the main room's forty-foot-high ceiling. A jostling throng occupied all the floor space beneath. The pungent smell of incense invaded his nose and throat. Mr. Taguchi had mentioned that the *Obon* observance honoring the dead would begin that night. But his interpreter hadn't even hinted at what that meant for the Buddhist temple . . . and him.

He squeezed through a crush of persons intent on peering into his two rooms in the temple's auxiliary section. Feeling like a circus's main act, he made a quick bow. While his bow was returned, he slipped through his door and whipped it shut.

Four tiny holes appeared in his door's paper panel. Eyeballs met his when he looked through two of the openings. He rummaged in his desk for a jar of glue and quickly pasted paper over the holes.

No sooner had he pulled his chair up to his desk than more holes appeared. No doubt the sight of his four-poster bed, which had required the removal of the panels dividing the two rooms, his large wardrobe, oak desk, and three straight-backed chairs provided an irresistible temptation when added to himself.

John sat with his back to the door, and reread his family's newest letters, forwarded via Shanghai. Two from his mother and even one from each brother. But none from Catherine. He ran his hand over the first one he'd received from her two weeks earlier, safely tucked next to the consul general's missive in his inside pocket. If she had any idea how her letter buoyed him, she'd write every day. At least, he hoped she would.

He turned to the twelve-week-old New York newspaper. Its main headline described the high hopes of prospectors heading to Virginia City, due to a remarkable silver lode. Farther down the page, an article described the growing rancor in congressional debates over slavery and states' rights. He shook his head. Resolving the travesty of slavery without a split in the Union looked impossible.

At suppertime, the Chinese servant charged with delivering John's food was nowhere to be seen. John kept his back to the door and chomped on an apple-type pear, two small sausages, and four rice balls left over from noon. Leaving his oil lamp unlit, he prepared for bed.

Although dog-tired, he couldn't sleep, grumbling to himself about the eyeballs. Normally the people's stares didn't bother him, and these shouldn't. The curious eyes were nothing like the hate-filled glare of the Hizen samurai. What's more, if looks could kill, the governor's second son Kohei would have rid the earth of John—in front of Chief Inspector Sato's *good hands*.

The owner of those hands might not care a whit about foreigners' lives. What caused these warriors' obsessive dedication to their master? Not a one of them valued individuals' lives, other than their highly exalted master's.

Even Mr. Taguchi had mentioned how his daughter's future betrothal—if her grandfather managed to accomplish his aim—would be good for their status, but probably displeasing to her. Apparently her grandfather hadn't considered the young lady's wishes in the least. Seeing an arranged marriage played out in a

Japanese maiden's real life made the well-known practice much more troublesome.

The first time he'd seen Miss Taguchi, she had been a picture of sedate loveliness. But she'd shown a completely different side of herself before the warlord's samurai—a daring, heroic one. Hopefully her use of a few English words meant she was attending Margaret Pendleton's class.

What was her given name? Sushi? Hardly. Sumi, it was Sumi Taguchi, or Taguchi Sumi in Japanese style. He snickered at how she'd compared him to a dragonfly. Someday maybe he'd be able to ask her why she'd called him an insect.

He knocked his head with his fist. *Stop it! Stand for what's right and worthy of a Christian, earn a profit, and return home. Home to Catherine.* He covered his head with his pillow to block the revelers' noise and tried to find a more comfortable position.

The next thing he knew, the peal of the temple gong reverberated in his ears. The chants of the monks, accompanied by tom toms and cymbals, started within minutes. Thinking it couldn't possibly be morning, he cracked open an eyelid. The dim light of dawn crept through a gap in one of the wooden shutters.

He rose, stubbed his toe, and cursed. A bottom drawer in the wardrobe stuck, and he yanked it out of its slots. He barely restrained himself from pulling on his boots and tromping through the temple hallway instead of using the required indoor slippers.

He puffed out a breath. *What's the matter with me?*

He knew instantly.

Tucking his Bible under his arm, he strolled outside and found a good spot under a willow tree by the temple's pond. A swallow overhead twitted a cheerful song as the sun's rays lit up the sky. White lotus buds floated at the edge of the pond, a few already displaying their pink-tipped petals against dark green leaves—a big contrast with the cattails in the pond where he'd fished growing up. Homesickness threatened, but for only a moment, restrained by the exquisite lotus blossoms.

Balancing his Bible on his crossed legs, he turned to his two favorite psalms. *The Lord is my shepherd; I shall not want . . . If I take the wings of the morning, and dwell in the uttermost parts of the sea; Even there shall thy hand lead me.*

John paused and reread the last verse. That *hand* was the hand that mattered. The Almighty was just as powerful in Nagasaki as he was in New York. Just as trustworthy as he'd been during the typhoon on the East China Sea or when John faced the hostile warlord's inspector on a LooChoo island. He looked at the blossoms again. And just as awe-inspiring.

A zigzagging rabbit bounded past with a ferret in pursuit. The two creatures rounded the other side of the pond and tore right into the monks' dining area. Three men, yellow robes flying, rushed out, shooing the frantic ferret. John couldn't help laughing.

The ferret had lost his breakfast, but not his life. He admired the Buddhist regard for all such animals. Yet his relationship with the Creator God was what he'd needed to calm his spirit.

The next evening, John took advantage of an invitation to view the *Obon* observances with a small party of expatriates on the merchantman *Adaline's* gig. The light boat, anchored in gentle waters ninety yards from shore, offered a panoramic view of Nagasaki.

The *Adaline*'s captain, the host for the evening, netted a small straw packet bouncing on the waves and pulled it onto the deck. Myriads of similar ones clumped at the mouths of streams. Everyone in the party gathered around the packet.

Richard Pendleton tapped the object with his cane. "I've been told these straw vessels start out carrying *sake* and other delectable items to pacify the fabled ocean demons." The Pendletons had become John's friends during the short voyage from Shanghai to Nagasaki. Richard had retired after thirty-eight years of teaching history in a Connecticut preparatory school. Being evangelical-minded Presbyterians, the couple took a special interest in the Japanese religious beliefs.

Richard pushed the straw vessel onto its side and looked over his wire spectacles. "As we can see, the cargo is missing, possibly taken before ever reaching the bay."

"At least it may have cheered up the fishermen's quarter," the British consul remarked with a laugh. "Guess I wouldn't mind a little cheering up myself." Sir Edman straightened his black cravat and took a furtive glance at the wine glasses on the refreshment table behind him.

"That's why it's there. Please. Don't insult the cook." The captain stepped over to the table. "In fact, we should use this opportunity to toast Consul Cardiff's successful negotiation for offloading our cargo."

John grinned at the praise. "What can I say? The governor up and changed his unfathomable mind." His chortling cohorts probably thought him humble, little realizing the truth.

Happy for the dishes laden with Western food, John took a heaping plate of hors d'oeuvres. He settled in one of the chairs near the ship's railing that offered a good view. The others followed his lead.

Margaret Pendleton, her brown eyes sparkling, gestured toward the high purple hills behind the city. "Look how the paper lanterns resemble a carpet of light, shimmering clear to those hilltops. Have you learned their significance, Richard?" She scooted her chair closer to her husband's.

"They're meant to light the way for ancestral spirits, I believe."

"Oh!" Sir Edman's wife, Anne, set down her fork. "What a strange idea."

Richard's brow knitted. "Although we know the Japanese people's beliefs are sadly mistaken, the hope that dead loved ones visit their homes brings them comfort."

John looked again at the thousands of flickering lanterns. It appeared all the people in Nagasaki, estimated at 60,000, were engaged in the rituals. The small group of Christians separated from the scene by the dark waves seemed isolated. Insignificant. Were they the ones who were right in worshiping Almighty God and these multitudes wrong?

He had examined the New Testament's evidence while a Hamilton College student. Confidence in Jesus' claims had led to placing his faith in Christ. Answers to desperate prayers while risking every cent he owned in the last few years had strengthened his beliefs. So, the answer had to be *yes*.

But what about all these people? The peace from his time under the willow vanished.

John's secretary at the consulate, Henry Mann, waved his hand toward the city. "So many sounds, lights, and odd beliefs!"

"It's overwhelming," Henry's wife, Beth, said. She turned

toward John. "I don't know how you remain so collected, Consul."

"I'm not feeling collected right now, madam. The people's beliefs *are* troubling, and I haven't gotten over my run-in with the Hizen samurai or the hooded warrior our first day."

At Mrs. Mann's grimace, John added, "On the other hand, the ordinary Japanese people attract me. The laborers' broad grins. The ladies' shy smiles. The attention to artistry everywhere. In fact, my original goal in venturing overseas no longer seems adequate."

"Which was, if I may ask?" Margaret Pendleton eyed him expectantly.

"A profitable trading company, an honest enterprise. One that didn't smuggle, especially not opium." John felt his color heighten when the shady company he'd once innocently invested in came to mind. "Of course, that's still my goal for my company."

Richard nodded and pushed his spectacles higher on his nose. "The path of integrity is the only path our God honors. It's good too, John, that you don't seek to liberate the *backward peoples* under Manifest Destiny. I doubt many here want that kind of liberation. But I believe we can make a significant difference in the lives we contact, one by one."

"And have you found that possible?"

"Not yet. It's far too soon."

"I'll be interested in hearing your progress. Like I said, making a profit's not enough. I'd like to make a contribution here too. That may involve just being true to my faith, not hiding it under a bushel, so to speak. But looking at the scene before us, my light is a pinpoint."

Henry cleared his throat. "Perhaps you've guessed we're

considering leaving after the agreed-to year is finished. I couldn't ask for a better chief than you, sir, but Beth's nerves are frayed."

"I hope you'll reconsider." John sighed inwardly at the prospect of finding a replacement. "You're a genuine asset to the consulate."

"Beth's making a valiant effort, but long-term may be asking too much of her—of both of us. We keep thinking about the tale we heard on the ship about the forty-seven *rōnin*. Beth, especially, can't get it off her mind."

"Remember, the event occurred in the last century." John chewed his final bite of shrimp, trying to savor the flavor despite the disagreeable topic. "I wouldn't pay attention to that old tale."

"Let's hear the story, John." Sir Edman glanced at his wife, who wrinkled her brow. "Apparently it's famous."

John gestured toward Richard Pendleton. "Richard's the one who told the tale on the ship. He's a better storyteller."

"Then go ahead, my good man." Sir Edman held his fork of crabmeat halfway to his mouth. "If we don't hear the tale now, we'll be in suspense until we wring it out of someone else."

Richard sighed. "The damage's done, I guess." He raised an eyebrow at Beth Mann. "I'll just give the tale's bare bones." He placed his plate on one of the stands in front of the chairs and tented his hands. "So, the story goes that at the turn of the last century, a rural warlord visited the Shōgun's castle. When the castle's Master of Protocol, named Kira, didn't receive the customary gift for his guidance, he gave the naïve warlord the wrong information.

"Having lost face, the warlord attempted to assassinate Kira, but only wounded him. The Supreme Council condemned the warlord to death by suicide. The man sliced into his intestines with his own hands."

Lady Edman sniffed into her handkerchief.

"Then, the Shōgun confiscated the dead warlord's castle and booted out forty-seven of his warriors. The now masterless warriors, called *rōnin,* formed a secret pact to assassinate Kira. What people find disconcerting is that the chief *rōnin* disguised himself for over a year as a drunkard."

"You see what I mean," Henry broke in. "These warriors don't forget an affront, and they go to any length to avenge a real or imagined wrong." He surveyed the group. "But don't let me interrupt."

"Well, they sure enough sought vengeance," John said, "but we really don't know how the people, even warriors, would behave now in a similar situation."

"Right," Pendleton said with a nod, "But, to conclude the tale, the forty-seven *rōnin* did eventually slaughter Kira and his warriors. The government returned swift judgment, condemning the *rōnin* to ritual suicide too."

Sir Edman leaned forward. "So, why are these forty-seven still talked about?"

"It's hard to understand," Pendleton said and turned toward John.

"The ultimate examples of loyalty, it seems." John selected one of Japan's small sweet oranges from a nearby bowl and scraped off part of the peeling, wishing he could as easily peel away Japan's enigmas.

"Are there still *rōnin* roving today?" The captain swept his hand down. "Undercover?"

"Right now we just know of one," John said, wiping his fingers on a napkin. "The warrior who bellowed insults when the Manns and I first set foot here doesn't appear to have been apprehended. The Nagasaki governor assured me there's no reason for fear, that we're in good hands."

"Exactly what troubles us." Henry's voice rose. "That belligerent *rōnin* could be lying in wait, biding his bloody time. We're always looking over our shoulders."

John turned his chair to face Henry better. "We have to stay observant. I learned the hard way to avoid *daimyō* processions. But no place is entirely safe, not even the small town I'm from in New York. And life in our country may become much less secure with bloodshed looming over our feuding states."

"Well, you have a point," Sir Edman said, choosing a smoked-salmon canape from the tray a sailor held out. "Life everywhere, including Her Majesty's England, brings risks. To tell the truth, *rōnin* and even the mob interrupting my botanical research a few weeks ago haven't bothered me as much as the blasted isolation and inconveniences. Every time that general store of Jake's gets in something decent, it's snapped up before the news travels half a block."

When the couples began exchanging suggestions on managing their households, John stretched and moved toward the boat's aft railing on the excuse of taking a look around the harbor. The stronger sea breeze whipped foam against the boat and ruffled his hair. He could swear the wind whispered Catherine's name.

He hated being alone at gatherings. *How are you, Mr. and Mrs. Smith? What's that? Yes, I've kept busy all right—running the company, meeting with officials, settling disputes . . . missing my fiancée.* Of course, he never spoke the last phrase out loud, never talked about the loneliness that gnawed at him late at night when he wasn't engaged in his work or busy investigating his unusual surroundings.

What might Catherine be doing at the moment? Painting? Reading his letter? Writing a letter, explaining her *good* reason for neglecting their correspondence?

He peered past the flickering lights of other ships, toward the harbor's distant entrance, cloaked in darkness. Miles and miles and miles of ocean lay beyond. He compressed his lips. He didn't want to go back to New York anytime soon even if he earned a large enough profit. He wanted Catherine to come to Japan. He wanted her to share this fascinating experience. Together, they could reach out to these extraordinary people and possibly show them a little of the Almighty.

He looked back at the couples, absorbed in their own conversation, enjoying each other. This country and its people enchanted him. He could face the risks, knowing God was with him. But at times like this, he wished he could whisper endearments in a loved one's ear.

CHAPTER 8

November (Month of the Rat)

The damp, cool day mirrored Sumi's downcast spirits as she headed to the Pendletons' home. Her grand opportunity had ended. All her hard work for the last three months—useless. Today she would just thank Mrs. Pendleton for her patient teaching and express regret for no longer participating in the English classes. She had no choice. She couldn't bear to see her mother suffer, especially knowing the English classes were to blame.

Everything had gone smoothly until three days ago. Each Tuesday and Thursday afternoon, she'd walked for an hour to attend the lessons. Since her friend Taki was in the class, Sumi had been able to repeat conversations they'd had, leaving the impression she'd been at Taki's house all afternoon.

Then a high fever attacked her mother. The wretched gods must have finally noticed not only her deception but also the more frequent references to the foreigners' religion.

A small Shinto shrine sat next to a huge chestnut tree near the road. Sumi hesitated under the gateway's red lintel. Should she enter? At a Buddhist *tera* the previous evening, her family had offered incense to Kannon, the thousand-armed goddess of mercy. Chanting *Hail, Great and Merciful One,* they had pled for her mother's recovery. But other powers might need to be appealed to as well.

Straightening her back, she walked up to the stone font in front of the small, slate-colored building. She carefully washed her mouth and hands. Maybe her thoroughness would cleanse some of her guilt and please the spirit. Staying in the shrine's antechamber, she clapped her hands four times to get the spirit's attention as her grandfather had often done and then whispered the sacramental call.

She waited a respectful minute before voicing her plea. "Spirit of this tree, I beg you to persuade any angry spirit to leave my mother alone. I am the evil one." Tears welled. She took a deep breath. "I will stop attending the Westerner's classes. I was wrong to forsake my country's ways, and I was wicked to disobey my grandfather." A sob escaped from deep in her throat.

She struck the shrine's bell three times, bowed, and dropped two copper coins into an altar box, where they clinked against the coins already there. Silence surrounded her. Maybe the spirit hadn't cared about her heartbreak or even listened. But then maybe it had.

When she arrived at the Pendletons' home, Mr. Pendleton hurriedly explained that his wife had gone out with a newly arrived American acquaintance, but a qualified person had volunteered to take her place. When Sumi opened her mouth to make her apology for not staying, Mr. Pendleton put his finger to his lips and hustled her into the drawing room to join the class.

She glanced at the teacher. No, it couldn't be! The spirits might forgive her for having been trapped by Mr. Pendleton if she didn't speak in class. But how could she keep quiet when facing the consul?

Not looking at any of the other students, she slipped into a chair in the second row. Risking another glance, she saw puzzlement on the consul's face before she looked down. Blood rushed to her cheeks. She moved her head so the girl in front partially hid her. If only she could be invisible.

"I'm happy you could join us, Miss Taguchi. We are learning the names of useful objects." The consul held up a pen. "Could you name this, please?"

The words struck like a physical blow. Cardiff-*sama*'s gray eyes stared at her.

She mumbled, "*Sumimasen,*" not daring to even say "excuse me."

His brow furrowed. "All right. I understand this object is not well-known here. I introduced it before you arrived." He called on another.

A few minutes later, his eyes moved in her direction again. "Let's practice our greetings." He smiled at the person sitting on Sumi's left side. "How are you, Miss Akimoto?"

Miss Akimoto readily answered, "I am fine, sank you."

Sumi held her breath. *No, call on another, not me. Please not me.*

"Now, Miss Taguchi, how are you?"

"*Sumimasen.*"

Her friend Taki leaned over and whispered, "I am very well, thank you."

The consul still locked her in his gaze. "Please answer, Miss Taguchi. You can do it. I'm sure of that."

"*Sumimasen.*" Sumi closed her eyes. She was dying inside. He didn't call on her again.

On her way out after the class finished, the consul spoke in a low voice to Mr. Pendleton as she passed. "It's too bad Miss Taguchi is slow in grasping English. I expected her to be more advanced by now, especially since she had a small head start."

Sumi bit her lower lip.

Mr. Pendleton reached for her arm, preventing escape. Perplexity wrinkled his brow. "Why, John, Miss Taguchi is Margaret's best pupil. She's far ahead of the rest of the class. She understands us right now, don't you, dear?"

Sumi nodded and bowed, ashamed she'd represented her teacher so poorly.

Chagrin flickered on the consul's face. "I'm afraid I misjudged you, Miss Taguchi. I apologize." He gave a slight bow. "Please, may I walk you to the sector's gate?"

"I . . ." She licked her lips. "Uh . . ." Her mind wouldn't form any words.

"I won't delay you long. Perhaps something is troubling you. I'd like to help if I can, just as you wanted to help me at the procession last summer."

"Thank you," she managed to murmur. She'd have to explain her poor behavior despite the risk. Maybe talking *after* the class differed from talking *during* the class.

As they walked side by side, she told him about her mother. "It is fault of me," she blurted out. "I did not follow my grandfather's order. He forbidden this class, and I hide . . . er . . . hid the truth."

"What would that have to do with your mother's illness?"

"The gods know sickness of mother worse for me."

"I still don't understand."

"I cannot say well." She fanned her face. Why couldn't she think? For one thing, the consul seemed even taller than she remembered and more imposing in his black, fitted coat. And his eyes! He seemed to see into her soul.

"I mean the God I believe in"—he pointed up to the sky—"is just and loving. He wouldn't make your mother sick in order to punish you. Moreover, in our society, a good grandfather acts as an advisor, not a dictator. And a wise one wants his grandchild to receive the best education possible."

Sumi's hand tightened on her fan. Some of the words were too difficult, but she understood the gist. Cardiff-*sama* had just voiced her private, rebellious thoughts. This kind foreigner with the wonderful, caring eyes and gentle tone could rile the gods too. Suppose they heard his words and attacked both of them. She'd already seen the terrible consequences of the gods' anger.

"Thank you for help." She bowed. "I leave you now." She bowed again.

She walked through the international sector's gate, fighting back stinging tears. For nearly three months, she had longed to meet Cardiff-*sama* again—the amazing warrior who could stand up to a samurai's sword while emptyhanded—and she had just pushed him away.

John glanced back at Miss Taguchi, hurrying toward the Oura River Bridge. Her lemon-colored kimono contrasted with her silky hair, swept up into dark spools and crisscrossed with ornaments. Her quick little steps added to her enticing refinement.

But a huge gap lay between her outlook and his. Yes, she

had to be intelligent to be so advanced in English after all, but from the indications, this pretty native would stay locked into her hermit country's ways. No one could argue she shouldn't be deeply concerned for her mother, but she hadn't grasped his views at all. In fact, he guessed they frightened her. Admittedly, he hadn't understood her reasoning either. And for all he knew, he could have just inserted his nose where it didn't belong.

But at any rate, he should be concerned about the health of his interpreter's wife. He'd find out her symptoms and advise Mr. Taguchi to stay home until she improved. God willing, she would. The American doctor on board one of the docked ships could supply medicine once he knew the malady.

John's groom, Nobu, approached, leading his horse. When the young man noticed John gazing at him, his confident stride disintegrated into a kind of shuffle—a strange idiosyncrasy often afflicting the groom. John shook his head at Nobu, choosing to walk to the consulate. He had ordered his groom to stick close to him, but Nobu's dogged conscientiousness bordered at times on being irksome.

Sumi's mother's fever peaked and then dropped later in the week. Sumi's great relief mixed with numbness. The gods had rewarded her repentance, but once more she faced a bleak future. A future without the Pendletons, without the concerned consul with the amazing eyes, without any foreigner—ever.

She headed to the *Butsudan* to give the god its due. While lighting an incense stick from the candle's flame, she overheard her parents in the next room praise Consul Cardiff's consideration. Her pulse quickened. *What consideration?* Then her father said, "Nothing but the Western medicine could account for your quick improvement." And her mother agreed.

Had all her prayers been irrelevant? She could never believe the gods and the family's ancestral spirits would graciously overlook the use of Western medicine if her contact with foreigners offended them. She extinguished the partially burnt stick.

What would Cardiff-*sama* say about her mother's recovery? He had clearly helped, but he'd talked as though *his* god were involved. Months ago, she'd read the phrase, *God is love,* on one of the three pages she'd managed to obtain from the *Kirishitan* book. But other than what the *Holy Bible* claimed, how did he know his god loved people? And even if that were true, what proof did he have that his foreign god cared about *her* countrymen's affairs? Apparently, even her gods didn't—thankfully.

Since the spirits had more important things to do than afflict her family, she could attend the English classes again. In her whole life, nothing had given her such satisfaction. Such joy.

But what about her grandfather? Shivering a little, she turned toward the front garden. She'd pick a chrysanthemum blossom and two branches of dark green camphor leaves to put in the *tokonoma*, the decorative alcove. At least her flower arrangements had finally become graceful enough to earn her grandfather's occasional approval. She could only imagine his condemnation if he knew about the classes.

CHAPTER 9

Ōta Nobumitsu waited for Governor Nakamura's second son, Kohei, in the park's ceremonial teahouse. The small, square room should have helped calm his mind. It provided an ideal place to form private alliances, for no one dared interrupt its visitors' meditation. However, the close quarters could also become a trap. He would either succeed with an alliance or find himself running for his life.

The room reminded him of his meeting there with Kurohashi Keiji. The naïve man still hadn't fully discarded his strange attraction to Taguchi Sumi despite his reprieve from the betrothal. The Confucian scholar didn't grasp that once the barbarian's poison infected a person, it couldn't be cut out. Although Keiji hadn't agreed yet to collaborate in ridding the country of the barbarians, he expressed less and less patience with the traitorous Shōgun's actions.

Kurohashi Keiji, however, was no warrior. Any contribution he made would be like the sting of a jellyfish. The question now was whether Nobumitsu could safely snag a powerful lionfish.

An hour after the agreed upon time, the second son could

be heard ordering the resident monk to stay outside until called. When Kohei entered through the room's low opening, Nobumitsu made a cursory bow from where he rested back on his heels, not at all as a commoner should behave.

Kohei's face flushed with anger. As required in all teahouses, his swords had been left outside the room.

"*Chōshū no Ōta Nobumitsu to mousu,*" Nobumitsu said, identifying himself before Kohei could order his chief samurai, Retainer Yamamoto, to drag him out.

The son's gaze raked him. "You are the Chōshū nobleman, the *rōnin* that minstrels honor? Now a groom?" He shook his head. "Unbelievable! Prove it."

Nobumitsu pulled out his old traveling paper identifying him as *Daimyō* Ōta's cousin. He rose and handed it to Kohei, who after scanning it, offered a genuine bow.

Nobumitsu gave an equally polite bow, impressed that even the governor's family had heard the new ballad about his exploits. They were myths, but one day ballads would honor his role as *Nobu the Groom*, humbler than even the clansmen who formerly spied out enemy castles in the guise of monkey trainers.

Once the initial cordialities finished, Nobumitsu prepared to broach his perilous plan, as though approaching the lionfish's deadly spines. The second son's strong dislike of the foreigners was well-known, but not clear was whether he would break with his father's submission to the Shōgun.

"I've met a few warriors who wish to prove their loyalty to our country by working to expel the foreigners."

"So? A few?" Kohei looked interested rather than suspicious.

"Although not many in number, we would have the

blessings of the gods if we are careful in our methods. Four of these men are Hizen samurai, who already witnessed the arrogance of the American consul, my so-called *master*."

Kohei narrowed his eyes. "Ah yes, I remember the vile man. And you now pose as his groom? A remarkable sacrifice." He wagged a finger. "That barbarian lectured my father. Dared to threaten him with military action." His hand fisted as he dropped his arm. "Aided by Interpreter Taguchi, another despicable man."

"As you say, despicable. A traitor from my own Chōshū clan. The eldest Taguchi is the only one in the family with a semblance of loyalty." Nobumitsu congratulated himself on his hook. Much could be built upon a common foe. "In fact," he added, strengthening the lure, "the disloyalty of the Eldest's granddaughter led to the early death of a loyalist."

"How so?" Kohei's eyes glittered.

"The granddaughter apes her father in learning the barbarians' language. After one of her classes, she escaped my dagger's retribution by breaking her stride at the last moment. I tracked her, intending to strike again, but she received help from a toy store owner. A young samurai of my clan became incensed over the aid and confronted the owner. Chief Inspector Sato slew the loyalist, but ultimately the granddaughter caused the youth's death."

"Too bad your dagger missed the girl."

"That failure is the only one since my boyhood training." Nobumitsu willed his face not to reveal his shame. "I assume her powerful Chōshū ancestors interfered, not ready for her death. But as she piles up her offenses, they will be."

Kohei glanced back at his retainer, who had remained kneeling next to the entrance. "One miss is not a bad record, eh,

Yamamoto-*san*." He turned back to Nobumitsu. "I suppose you have not finished with the Taguchi family."

"A neighbor acts as a pair of eyes for me. Although just a bronzeware merchant, Omura has sworn loyalty to the Divine Emperor—at the point of my sword. During my last meeting with the merchant, he conjectured that the eldest Taguchi was ignorant of the granddaughter's classes, so I ordered him to report them to the Eldest. Admittedly a small rebuke. Nothing compared to my ultimate plan."

"I have thought about dealing with the interpreter and the American consul myself."

Nobumitsu raised an eyebrow. It would be only right for Kohei to confide whatever move he entertained.

"But better not to share unripe fruit."

Swallowing his objection, Nobumitsu gave a shallow bow. After all, he'd initiated the meeting. He was acting as the recruiter.

"How about this barbarian expulsion you talk about?" Kohei folded his arms. "What's your plan for that? It needs to be thorough or not at all."

Nobumitsu could detect nothing adverse in Kohei's expression. But if the governor's son were leading him into a charge of treason, Nobumitsu would know the second after his next revelation. His shoulders tensed.

"A sudden overwhelming blow by a small group of warriors."

Kohei's face masked all emotion. "What kind of blow?"

"Arson after the foreigners have piled up enough of their illegitimate treasure—all stolen from our countrymen. Assassinations at the same time. No clan taking credit. The foreign nations won't know where to retaliate."

Nobumitsu cocked his head as though expecting approval, while readying himself to break through the room's back panel and disappear into the nearby grove if either man made a threatening move.

"With the right strategy, a few men can wreak more havoc than a large army." Kohei's face still betrayed no emotion. "Where would the strike be?"

"A location at the center of the foreign settlement where a fire could easily spread."

Kohei stroked his chin, his eyes took on a distant look.

Nobumitsu realized he'd been holding his breath and forced himself to breathe.

"It delights my mind."

The abruptness made Nobumitsu blink.

Kohei rubbed his hands together. "Those foreigners' hideous warehouses and businesses would turn to rubble in a night. Houses too. And the river would protect the rest of the city if the wind favored you. When the right time comes, Retainer Yamamoto and three of our *reliable* warriors, who know how to keep a confidence, will work with you."

"Yes, when the stars are aligned and the gods smile." Nobumitsu coughed to disguise the powerful pulse racing through him. Help from within the city's highest echelons would guarantee success. Ridding Nagasaki of barbarians would embolden more and more men loyal to the Divine Emperor. The Shōgun and his followers would end up on a trash heap.

Kohei's lips formed a sardonic smile. "When we succeed, we may rival the forty-seven *rōnin* for notoriety, even surpass that current ballad honoring you."

"May the gods grant such success." He could afford to be

generous with fame, especially before the deed was done.

Kohei ordered Retainer Yamamoto to fetch the monk so the tea ceremony could be performed, sealing their cooperation.

The yellow-robed, wizened monk arranged his utensils in meticulous order. After heating the water, he whisked the powdered tealeaves and water into frothy green liquid.

Receiving the tea, Nobumitsu examined the clay cup, then turned its subtle design away from himself, satisfying the required show of humility. He bowed to the monk and to Kohei, who did the same. As he swallowed the bitter drink, he savored its flavor. Then motionless, he allowed the silence to penetrate his bones, transporting him into a different state—one that connected him to the most elemental core of life: restrained discipline and austere beauty.

Yet no one except Buddhist monks could live that way. He had to exit the teahouse and continue the struggle. But his small force and that of Nakamura Kohei were now united.

The groundswell had begun.

CHAPTER 10

Kenshin waited in the vestibule's shadows while his father bid farewell to Merchant Omura, who apologized over and over for bringing unwelcome information. Their neighbor had insisted on talking with the Eldest One alone. A tempest brewed, and it most likely involved Sumi. Again.

"Call my granddaughter," his father ordered, fire in his eyes.

Kenshin hurried upstairs to find her.

"Your grandfather is calling you. Come quickly. I believe Merchant Omura has brought upsetting news."

"Oh no!" Sumi's face blanched. She pushed her cat off her lap and straightened her kimono.

"Hurry. Your grandfather is in no mood to be kept waiting."

His daughter's hands shook. Whatever the reason, it meant trouble. He led her into the main room—into the storm's vortex.

"You deceived me!" His father marched within an arm's length of her and glowered. "I forbade those English classes, and you spit in my face."

Kenshin steadied himself against the wall. He had never

seen his father so livid. Why hadn't Sumi told him about the prohibition? Or had she tried, and he'd brushed over it?

Sumi's face turned scarlet. "The English classes? I didn't mean to disobey you. Please believe me."

"You attended classes every week for months, but did not intend to disobey my clear order? You greeted me each time upon your return without breathing a word of your deception." His eyes squinted in anger. "I am not a doddering fool."

"Forgive me. You are most wise." Sumi took a step back, bowed, and turned toward Kenshin. "Father, you remember . . . I didn't agree to the class at first." Her eyes pleaded with him.

"Ah, I can tell you what happened," Kenshin said. "I did not know—" His father's hand shot out, warning him to cease talking.

"You undermined your betrothal to the Kurohashi grandson." Her grandfather whipped his fan from his sash. "Now you have defied my authority."

He struck her cheek with the edge of the closed fan.

Sumi's hand flew to the red mark. Forbidden tears shimmered in her eyes.

"To me, you are *dead*." He hurled the fan to the floor, wheeled, and stalked toward his room.

She bowed to his back. "I am sorry, very sorry. I have no excuse."

Her body shook so much that Kenshin feared she would collapse. He nodded a dismissal, and she fled up the stairs. After muffled, angry words between her and Kiyo, the house became silent, as though wrapped in a shroud.

His wife sat still, face ashen, brows furrowed. He picked up the fan and sat beside her.

"I unintentionally encouraged her deception. This is partly, maybe mostly, my fault." *And the fault of the interfering, over-solicitous consul as well.* He sank his head into his hands.

Haru slid closer to him and put her hand on his knee.

He sighed and looked up. "It's like Warlord Mori's lesson for his three sons: three arrows bound together cannot be broken, but one arrow can be. Our family is divided. Our strength gone."

"You and I are together. May I suggest, two bound arrows are not as good as three or four, but better than one?"

"If only our daughter took more after you, less after me."

"There is no reason for such a wish."

He stroked her hand. How thoughtful she was. She probably did wish their daughter were more like herself, but would never even hint at such an idea.

In his room, Yoshikatsu took out his long sword and, sitting cross-legged, rubbed his hand over the gilded scabbard. The sword alone faithfully served him. No one in his household followed the way of honor. He should banish his granddaughter from the home. Her mother's brother would take her in. She would not be homeless.

A crow cawed in the garden. He pictured Sumi years earlier by their pear tree, fighting a snake that threatened a sparrow's nest. He had understood her then. Her adventuresome nature had chafed at the family's necessary restraints, but she always obeyed. Now the unthinkable had happened, not just one time, but week after week, month after month.

The murmur of Haru's and his son's voices floated from the main room. Sending their only child away would break their hearts . . . and yes, his too. He blew out a breath. He could not do it. As he had grown older, he had let down his guard and become soft. Too soft. Far too soft. So attached to his son and granddaughter that he could not enforce right actions in his own household.

He had been vaguely relieved when Kenshin asked at a young age to become a Dutch Scholar, the rivalries between the neighboring clans having taken his older son's life. But he had not foreseen that anyone in his family would adopt the barbarians' ways. For foreigners, the individual counted more than family or master. That idea had crept into his house and festered into an unstoppable disease.

He smothered a groan. A family unwilling to honor him during his lifetime would certainly not honor him after his body perished. Once his son and daughter-in-law died, even if Sumi were married into a fine family, she could not be counted on to offer prayers at the god shelf. Without the prayers, the evil spirits would snare his soul and the souls of his wife and sons.

An owl hooted in the distance. The gray evening would turn into a dark night, like the darkness facing him.

CHAPTER 11

December (Month of the Ox)

Sumi joined the maid at the entrance to her home. Her friend Taki, eyebrows raised in anticipation, held up a small paper packet. Sumi dismissed Kin, then invited her friend to come with her to the back garden. They settled down in her favorite spot by the pond.

"You have half-moons under your eyes," Taki remarked, scooting around on the boulder to see Sumi better. "Aren't you sleeping well?"

"Everything's difficult, Taki-*chan*." Sumi frowned. She couldn't reveal her grandfather's denunciation because Taki might not keep the shameful secret to herself. Her friend, just a year younger, acted a little immature for her age.

"I missed you at the classes the last two weeks. It's your honorable grandfather, isn't it? Has he objected to them?"

Sumi nodded and weighed her words. "He abhors foreigners."

"Why? Your honorable father works for one."

"He remembers the problems from hundreds of years ago

and thinks the foreigners' ideas are dangerous."

Taki's forehead wrinkled. "Oh, then I understand, somewhat. Agreeing with the foreigners' barbaric notions would be dangerous. But do you think anyone might?"

"Foolish people could, I suppose." Like herself—but just *some* of their ideas.

"Their Evil Religion is the most nonsensical, isn't it? Take that idea their god's son rose from the dead." Taki shook her head. "Certainly, the emperors, who we *know* are descendants of the gods, lived on this earth and died, but none came alive again in an actual body. Right? I have to struggle not to laugh when Mrs. Pendleton-*sama* tries to convince us of the Evil Religion's truth. Her cheeks get pink and puffy."

Sumi managed a weak smile, remembering Taki's struggle to keep a straight face. "I'm glad we were in the class together. You do like it, don't you, in spite of the foreigners' strange behaviors?"

"That's the very reason I like it. The peculiarities. Cups with handles, wearing dirty shoes inside the house, sitting in chairs high off the floor to protect us from rodents, I guess. And the strange smells." She wrinkled her nose. "But here." She handed Sumi the paper packet. "Here's a chance to experience even more strange things. Look inside. I've already opened mine."

Sure that disappointment loomed, Sumi carefully drew out a card with a bright border of red berries nestled in pointed green leaves. Inside the border, a message in English had been written in beautiful cursive letters.

"See what it says. Hurry," Taki begged.

She read, "You are cordially invited to a party"—just as she feared—"to help celebrate the Christmas season and our last

English class until the new year. Please join us on Thursday, December 15, from 2:00 to 4:00, in the afternoon."

She swallowed the lump threatening to choke her. Nothing could be more enticing, or more out of reach, as unattainable as a kite tangled on a temple's rooftop.

"It's no use my asking. My family won't permit me to go because of Grandfather." Her fingers covered her cheek although the fan's red mark had disappeared within a few hours.

Taki's face fell. "It will be dull unless you come. The classes without you haven't been as interesting. None of us knows enough to converse with Mrs. Pendleton-*sama*."

Sumi inspected the invitation again. A *Christmas* Party! Christmas seemed a festive celebration, full of good cheer for the foreigners, the opposite of the gloomy atmosphere pervading her home. "I've never wanted to do anything more, but it's impossible."

Taki raised a finger and brightened. "Why don't you spend two days next week at my house? My family won't mind our going. They know we'd *never* succumb to barbaric ideas, even someone as curious about foreigners as you."

Sumi hesitated. Taki's parents and even the gods might not care, but what about her family? Her pulse rose at just the thought. Of course, any objection from her father would simply be out of respect for her grandfather. His not knowing about the party would solve that problem. And she need not consider her mother since she never had an independent opinion.

Her grandfather had shunned her, proving she was *dead* to him. Missing the party would neither restore her to his good graces nor relieve the deep ache from their alienation.

Then too, leaving from Taki's home lessened any danger from an assailant—merely living in her imagination, at any rate.

She would not be a turtle with its head always inside its shell.

A chilly wind blew the afternoon of the party. Wrapping her cloak more closely around her shoulders, Sumi struggled against the impulse to cover her head, to disappear among the cloak's folds. For the last five days, she'd argued with herself that she was justified in attending the party. Hadn't she profusely apologized, then begged her grandfather for reconciliation by her sorrowful looks? And yet he had still acted like she wasn't there. His stony expression day after day stung far more than the whack of his fan. So why should she feel any scruple?

She tried to concentrate on her friend's words. Taki had been chattering nonstop since they set out for the party.

"We decorated the round little cakes with red and green goo called *frosting* at the end of class on Tuesday." Taki wrinkled her nose "That made the too sweet cakes even sweeter, but they look pretty. I hope you'll try one."

"Of course I will. Maybe you can show me which ones you decorated."

"Everything is more beautiful than you can imagine. Wait until you see the *Kurisumasu* tree. It's covered with candles."

Sumi smiled. "I'm sure it's wonderful." If only she could be as unencumbered as her friend.

Before long, they passed the noodle shop that had hidden her attacker. A shiver rippled through her although nothing had happened since that awful day—with one exception. The merchant had told her grandfather about her English lessons.

She rubbed her forehead, questioning for the hundredth

time how the merchant had gotten such information. She couldn't believe participants in English classes were gossiped about in the *sake* house the merchant was known to frequent. So who could have informed Merchant Omura recently, and perhaps also informed her attacker months earlier? Her *dead* attacker?

She sighed with relief when they arrived at their destination a few minutes later.

Entering the Pendletons' familiar parlor, she gazed in wonder. A tall fir tree—the Christmas tree—stood in one corner of the room. The beautiful white candles and red and gold silk balls transformed it into something magical. Taki had been right. She never could have imagined it. In another corner, a table gleamed with lace, crystal, and silver. Her gaze followed the mantel's greenery over toward the third corner, then drew in her breath.

Cardiff-*sama*, wearing a dark blue coat and mushroom-colored trousers, stood talking with Mr. Pendleton and another foreign man. Perhaps because she had become a little accustomed to Cardiff's prominent nose, moustache, and short-clipped beard, his lanky form seemed all the more handsome.

At that moment he looked in her direction.

She dropped her eyes. Had he caught her gawking? Unfortunately, while she had been observing the room, the other class members had taken all the chairs close together, so she stood by them stoically, wanting to blend in with the furnishings.

Mrs. Pendleton, dressed in a gray gown draped with strings of shiny beads, walked toward her. "My dear, we are delighted to see you again." She held out welcoming hands.

Before Sumi could think of a reason explaining her

absence, Mrs. Pendleton continued. "Taki told us you were most likely indisposed. I'm thankful you've recovered your good health." She clasped Sumi's hands for a second and smiled into her eyes. "Now, I wonder if I could ask your assistance in pouring the wassail punch? You are the perfect one for the task." She pointed to the serving table.

At first Sumi's hands were none too steady as she ladled up the warm, spicy-smelling liquid and poured it into the transparent cups, but she soon mastered the technique. She didn't spill a drop even though her heart skipped several beats when Cardiff accepted his cup.

Warmth lit his eyes. "Miss Taguchi, it's a pleasure to see you again. You look lovely this afternoon."

She gulped. "I . . . I don't resemble those words." Nobody had ever complimented her like that. Her cheeks burned.

"Oh, but you certainly do look like those words." He cleared his throat. "I heard your mother recovered. I hope she is still well."

"Yes. Thank you for medicine." She glanced down at her kimono, a favorite green one with embroidered pink flowers. Maybe he admired *its* loveliness.

"I was glad to assist. When you finish serving, perhaps you could join me. I can help you practice your English if you wish."

When all were served, there was still no chair by the other class members. An empty chair stood next to Cardiff's, inviting her, challenging her. She straightened her shoulders and crossed toward him, barely able to tolerate her clogs' loud clacking against the wooden floor.

She sat on the edge of the chair, feeling like an unschooled peasant girl, afraid to look at either the consul or Taki, sure her friend would either be scowling or snickering.

"What do you think of the Christmas party?" Cardiff asked as though nothing were extraordinary.

"It is nice." Remembering the animated conversations she'd observed between foreigners even of the opposite sex, she fastened her eyes on the white scarf tied at his neck and added, "It is like some Japan festivals."

"Why is that?"

"Um, one thing is candles. We use lights during *Obon* too. Do you know?" She fanned herself. Did her words make sense? Was she demure enough? Brave enough?

"Ah yes. I heard the lanterns are used to welcome the ancestors' spirits."

"Also, we use evergreen at New Year's festival." She motioned toward the fir tree. "Evergreen, tortoise, and stork mean long life. Is evergreen same in America?"

"The Christmas tree and hanging of the green are just customs for us now. I think most people would agree the evergreen has lost its original meaning. But please go on. I'd like to know more." He adjusted his chair so he faced her more directly. His gray eyes shone with interest.

Tilting her face away, she looked at him from the corner of her eye. "Another thing is same. You say Jesus, born at Christmas, came from a god, don't you?"

He gave a hesitant nod.

"Our first Emperor, Jimmu Tennō, came from sun goddess through her grandson Ninigi. Yes? You know that, don't you?" She congratulated herself for expressing these similarities although the foreign god—if it existed—had to be a subordinate one. But why did Cardiff seem at a loss for words? Could foreigners be ignorant of the world's history?

"You know about the sun goddess, Amaterasu-Ōmikami, don't you?"

"Only what you just said. It seems this goddess is important in your religion. Correct?"

"Yes, Cardiff-*sama*, and . . . and important for everyone in the world."

"Well, ah, I think there's quite a difference between our idea of Jesus and yours of the Emperor. It will be hard for me to explain this in simple terms." He crossed his long legs and rubbed his chin. "You see, Christians don't believe Jesus was just born from a god, but that He already existed as Deity from eternity past. Furthermore, we base this belief on historical evidence—proof—that Jesus rose from the dead."

Evidence, eternity past—so many difficult words. Could she ever learn this language? And here again was that odd notion of rising from the dead. Her English study hadn't prepared her at all for a discussion of the Americans' religion. But more bewildering was the fact Cardiff, an educated, high official, never heard of the sun goddess. Was the account in the *Kojiki*, the most ancient of texts, familiar only to her people?

"Never mind," Cardiff said. "Your English is improving rapidly. You'll be able to read about Jesus in the English Bible soon, very soon, according to the Pendletons." His eyes twinkled. "I'm glad you are enjoying the party. I think Mrs. Pendleton has planned a game or two."

The hosts were dividing everyone to play something called *charades*. Taki, lips pursed, stared at her, so Sumi carefully avoided being on her side of the room. Since the names to be acted out were those of Westerners, the four foreigners did almost all the guessing. Sumi did correctly guess the American president, *Bukanan,* when Mr. Pendleton pantomimed writing something and then stood at attention and saluted.

"Well done, Miss Taguchi," Cardiff remarked. "I'm glad we're on the same team."

Warmth flooded Sumi. She hadn't made a fool of herself this time.

After the game, Mr. Pendleton brought out his *violin.* The sleek wooden instrument looked a little like a *biwa,* in that it had strings. Mr. Pendleton turned the violin's knobs and made its strings twang—like the strangled meow of her cat when it had been stuck in a tree. Was this music?

Sumi glanced at Cardiff's profile. Why did he fascinate her? She had hung onto his every word even though she hadn't fully understood. Like her, he probed, eager to learn. Yet while she tested her steps to the unknown, like someone tapping for weakness even on a stone bridge, he confidently trod forward. Although obviously exceptional in *his* country, he was supposed to be inferior in *her* country. But he wasn't.

Mr. Pendleton began to play another piece. Now the sounds became delightful. The foreigners sang to the music—words about "joy to the world." Sumi closed her eyes momentarily. She never, ever wanted to forget the quick bright notes and the music's sheer beauty sweeping through her.

At the end of the song, Mr. Pendleton repeated the story that Sumi had already heard in class from Mrs. Pendleton about Jesus' unusual birth, then went on to play a song that began with "silent night" and several other pieces the foreigners requested. The idea that Jesus was born in a stable yet came to be the world's king didn't make any sense, but the *joy* expressed in the songs was definitely appealing. She leaned back in her chair for the first time that afternoon, cherishing every minute.

All too soon, the party ended. Mrs. Pendleton pressed a large wrapped present into each of the class members' hands. Sumi regretted she hadn't brought a gift herself, but Mrs. Pendleton had always insisted they not bring gifts in the past.

"Go ahead. Unwrap it and see what it is," Mrs. Pendleton instructed.

Sumi glanced at the other girls, who looked puzzled too. How strange to open a gift in front of the giver. No matter what the item was, they had better look grateful.

Slipping off the red ribbon and shiny silver paper, she pulled out a thick brown book. The *Holy Bible*! Her heart hammered. From the English lessons, she'd decided the book wasn't evil. She liked Jesus' kindness, and his stories interested her even though they hinted at meanings hard to grasp. But was it wise to take the book? It didn't matter that it was no longer illegal and was written in English, she'd still have to conceal it from her family, and especially from Kiyo, who wouldn't hesitate to report the foreign book to her grandfather. Was it worth the risk?

She wanted the book. Really wanted it. The foreigners, including the consul, valued its contents. After her English improved, she might understand its teachings better, like Cardiff-*sama* had implied. Its wisdom might give her answers to earlier questions she'd almost forgotten about since the foreigners' momentous arrival.

All eyes were on her. "We must be polite," she told her classmates in Japanese. "You can decide whether to keep the book later." She'd keep it herself, she decided, and hide it far back in her cupboard, where no one would find it.

She forced a smile for Mrs. Pendleton. "Thank you. I treasure it."

Taki and the other class members followed her lead.

Mrs. Pendleton's eyes sparkled.

Sumi carefully wrapped the Bible in a scarf she pulled from under her sash. Perhaps it would act like the clay-monkey charm she'd had as a child and keep her safe. The idea of an assailant, still alive, edged back into her mind, but she didn't let it stay for even a second.

It had been a wonderful time, like a fantasy. In fact, she'd experienced something like the enchantment Urashima Tarō felt in the fairytale's underwater palace. Her joy dimmed at the memory of her grandfather's emphasis on loyalty. He would certainly look at her presence at the party as disloyalty.

But in his eyes, she no longer belonged in the family. She was dead.

CHAPTER 12

John adjusted the scruffy pine wreath he'd hung over his desk and lit the fat, red candle purchased from Jake's General Store. Only the calendar proclaimed it was Christmas Day. For the Japanese people, it was business as usual. Later, he would help host a Christmas dinner for the Nagasaki Club at the Commercial Hotel. However, their all-male company wouldn't begin to compare to a celebration with his loved ones. He could almost smell his mother's apple pies. His younger brother Matthew would have organized a sleigh ride pulled by their brown mares, bells jangling amid the merry shouts of the neighborhood children.

Forcing his mind away from the memories, John reached for his Bible. He read the familiar story of Jesus' birth, then scolded himself for his self-pity. After all, his Lord God had come from the glories of heaven to an alien land, and John's situation in Japan hardly compared with that. Enemies weren't challenging him daily like they had Jesus. In fact, there hadn't been a single threat on John's life since the Hizen warlord's procession. These days he concealed his revolver in his saddlebag and sometimes failed to carry it altogether.

Furthermore, a few of the gatherings in the last two weeks had been more enjoyable than expected. His own get-together for his trading company's employees and the consulate's small staff had turned out well. Under the guise of explaining the custom of Christmas, he'd shared Isaiah's prophecy of a coming Savior and how Jesus' miraculous birth fulfilled it. None of his Japanese guests had appeared ruffled during Mr. Taguchi's translation, so it appeared there wouldn't be an angry official remonstrating with him about the Evil Religion in the near future.

But the Pendletons' party had been the best. The English students had probably grasped most of Richard's simple explanation about Jesus' birth. And Miss Taguchi had managed to come out of her shell. He smiled at how his compliment had caused her to blush while maintaining her poise. She'd boldly participated in the game of charades, and although she couldn't sing the carols, her shining eyes made her enjoyment clear. A fine young lady.

He abruptly gazed at Catherine's likeness, copied from a daguerreotype plate. He replaced the Bible and drew out his stationery. Dipping his quill pen in ink, he visualized his fiancée's beauty his last Christmas in New York when they had sat in the glow of her parlor's fireplace. No other lady deserved to occupy his mind.

Close by in the stable, Nobumitsu nursed his anger. He checked his long and short swords and the daggers hidden under deep piles of hay. When the time was right, nothing would prevent him from fully avenging the young samurai and the Taguchi family's treachery.

While minding the consul's horse, he had almost revealed his identity when the interpreter's daughter exited the foreigners' home, having participated in the disgusting festivities honoring the Evil Religion's founder. Luckily for her, he didn't carry his dagger these days. Then he watched her father leave the consul's party with the new Western-style, black umbrella he'd been given. Taguchi had twisted it in the air while he'd pranced to the waiting *kago*. What arrogance.

The continued traitorous actions of the haughty translator and his family had to be dealt with before the final blow. He sent a message ordering Merchant Omura to meet him in the Commercial Hotel's stables, where he would be that noon, tending to the consul's horse.

After more consideration, Nobumitsu sent another message—this one to his cousin, the Chōshū warlord in the castle city of Hagi—breaking the silence of eight years.

Sumi waited until her cousin had finished laying out her kimonos before she took her own out to air in the garden, one of her duties in preparing for the upcoming New Year festival. Kiyo and she seldom argued now, simply because they avoided each other. At least, anticipating the two-week celebration for the start of the Year of the Monkey partly diminished the bad feelings afflicting their home.

The whole household grew increasingly busy. On soot-sweeping day, Sumi helped clean the upstairs *shōji*, liking the *pata-pata-pata* of the paper duster against the panels. Then the groundskeeper and gatekeeper pulled up all the *tatami* mats and lugged them outside, where the two men, the maid Kin, and the cook's assistant beat them with bamboo dusters.

During the final week before the celebration, the cook sang an old rice-pounding song as she made *omochi*, the gooey rice treat. Her voice warbled about the "messengers of the Good – luck god," who for an unknown reason had never heard a cat's fearful mew. The song's familiar words reminded Sumi of creeping into the kitchen as a child and being rewarded by this same servant with a dollop of food along with "Happy Congratulations" as though having survived another year was a big accomplishment. She hadn't understood at the time, but now knew survival *was* a big feat.

Because obligations had to be discharged before the New Year, Sumi purchased red bean confections to repay the Pendletons' Christmas gift of the *Holy Bible*. Not daring to visit the Pendletons' home again, she gave a coin to a messenger boy to deliver the package.

Sumi's mother, appreciative of the Omura family's special attentiveness, presented the merchant's wife with a small pillow bearing her finely stitched needlework. But in Sumi's estimation, her father outdid them all. Because Cardiff-*sama* had held the Christmas party for the consulate's staff, her father invited him to visit their home during the New Year's celebration.

And the consul accepted.

CHAPTER 13

Mid-January 1860 (Year of the Monkey), Lunar New Year's Day

Sumi smoothed her new silk kimono and ran her fingers down its sleeve, admiring the design of purple wisteria against the pale pink background. Would the consul compliment her again? She fought against the heat rising to her cheeks and concentrated on completing the New Year's decoration attached to their entrance gate.

After adding oranges to the pine branches, sprigs of bamboo, and twisted rope, she paused to watch the neighborhood boys flying their kites. The boys shouted taunts at each other while making their dragon, hawk, frowning samurai, and tiger swirl high in the sky. The kites hummed as wind blew through the slices of bamboo attached to the strings, sounding together like a beehive.

All at once, an unfamiliar youth ran up, thrust a scroll into her hand, and dashed away. A strange way to deliver a New Year's greeting, she thought as she hurried to her father.

"No seal," her father remarked.

He unrolled the scroll and immediately rolled it up before

Sumi could get more than a glimpse. She caught the words, *You welcome the foreigner, but jeopardize—*

"The messenger gave no explanation for his abruptness." Sumi lingered for a minute in case she could learn more.

"A prank possibly," her father huffed. "I don't know. Today is not a day for riddles. Have you finished your preparations?"

"Almost. I'll be ready before any visitors arrive."

Her father's earlier light-heartedness had disappeared. Was the note a prank, or was it a threat? Or a warning? Whatever it was, she wouldn't let an unknown message get her down, not on the day of Cardiff-*sama*'s visit.

A steady flow of New Year's guests visited their home the rest of the morning. Taki spent an hour with Sumi, playing *uta-garuta*, a game of poem cards, before leaving to make visits to other girls in the class, accompanied by her maid. Normally, Sumi would have accompanied Taki for a short time, but she couldn't risk missing the consul.

Mid-morning, her mother and Kiyo left to worship at the Suwa Shrine, but Sumi begged off, promising to make the trek to gain the gods' blessings later in the week with the maid Kin. Whenever she bid a visitor farewell at the gate, she looked down the road until the gatekeeper bowed, waiting for her to reenter.

Her mother and Kiyo returned, the noon meal was eaten, and still Cardiff-*sama* hadn't appeared. Had an emergency arisen that prevented his coming? Maybe he'd simply changed his mind, fearing a dull time. Maybe he'd forgotten.

The green sprouts at her feet and the sun's rays peeking through the gray skies didn't dispel the wintry chill or her worrisome thoughts. After the latest visitor left, she turned to enter the house.

Then she stopped. Hoof beats on the cobblestones drew closer and slowed. She held her breath, listening. It could be Chief Inspector Sato, leaving his usual card, or another samurai acquaintance. Or it could be the consul.

A voice commanded his horse to halt—in English.

She retreated to the veranda to call her father, nearly stumbling in her haste.

Cardiff dismounted at the gate and took a large box from his groom. Sumi's father rushed past her and met him on their path. Cardiff looked over her father's head in her direction.

She bowed and sucked in a breath.

"I have two gifts I wish to present to the fine house of Taguchi," he announced. "They arrived on my company's ship, which just last week returned all the way from the United States of America." He looked toward her again and raised his voice slightly. "For the Honorable Eldest One."

"That's kind of you." Her father bowed. "I will . . . uh . . . give them to my father at a later time."

"I'd like to show him how one of them works. It won't take but a minute."

"Umm . . . I will see if he can join us."

After pulling off his boots at the vestibule despite being told it wasn't necessary, Cardiff bowed to Sumi's mother and to her. For a minute, Sumi thought he was going to bow to Kin also, but he gave a slight smile instead. Her father led him to the guest's seat of honor in front of the main room's *tokonoma*, then hurried to get her grandfather, who had abruptly retired.

Sumi pulled her gaze off the consul and glanced around. Her heart beat faster. She was the only one left who could entertain their guest. Kneeling on a cushion near him, she looked up at him. "We are happy you visit us." She yearned to say more—to explain the festival's customs, ask about his country's New Year's celebration, inquire about his work and the ship's voyage. But what if she said the wrong things? How had she managed to talk with him the other times?

"I'm happy to be included in your special celebration." He gave her a warm smile. "The chance to see how you and your countrymen live means a lot to me."

She had to speak. "I wish I may see how you live too."

The consul looked surprised, almost startled. She must have said the wrong thing. Of course, she couldn't invite herself to his place. She hadn't meant to. Warmth crept up from her neck.

Just then her grandfather strode into the room, scowling.

Cardiff rose, bowed, and handed him a beautifully bound book. "This is a set of Currier prints—popular paintings in the United States. I want you to have it because I hear you are a fine artist."

Sumi's father translated and bowed.

Without a word, her grandfather plunked the book down on a nearby stand.

Seemingly unaware of the rudeness, Cardiff opened the large box and took out a machine that had two bells attached to it. "I hope you find this apparatus interesting." He also handed it to her grandfather, who set it down more gently next to the book and shrugged.

Cardiff bent over the machine. "This is a miniature electric generator. Allow me to crank this turbine." He turned the machine's handle in fast circles while Sumi's father translated his explanation.

The generator's bells, connected by wires, chimed. Everyone stepped back except her grandfather. Her mother threw her hands up in amazement.

"Look at that!" Her father reached down and turned the handle himself. "An instrument that harnesses our action and carries it through wires. It works exactly like the books describe." His eyes shone.

"Like magic," her mother said.

"Your gifts are . . . are very nice, Cardiff-*sama*," Sumi said in English. "Splendid." He had known exactly what her father and grandfather would like. The American was strange—looking everyone in the eye, thanking his groom, practically smiling at their maid. But how could anyone not like him?

Her grandfather apparently could manage the feat very well. He continued scowling and said nothing. She had never witnessed his being impolite to a guest before. Why did he have to consider *every* foreigner his enemy?

A moment later, he picked up the book of paintings, turned his back to Sumi, and gave a nearly imperceptible bow to the consul, who fortunately returned a deeper bow. "You will see to our guest's needs," he growled to her father before striding out of the room.

With her grandfather no longer in the room, Sumi breathed easier.

John, relieved the family's obvious killjoy had exited, sat down again on the blue and gold cushion in front of the winter *kotatsu*. He liked this low, quilt-covered frame over a built-in pit. The charcoal heater in its depths warmed his legs, and the quilt allowed the warmth to rise to his waist. In fact, he'd order one for each of the three Japanese-style rooms being built into the consulate.

Mr. Taguchi's wife, Haru, placed refreshments on the tray in front of him. "There's nothing, but please eat much," was translated. Only John seemed aware of any contradiction. He ate just enough of the shredded cuttlefish and salted radishes to be polite, but relished the red rice and the sweet bean drink, topped with small, floating rice balls.

Miss Taguchi's parents directed her to play a selection on the *koto*, the Japanese zither, while he ate. He had no idea what music from the instrument's thirteen strings should sound like, but thought she played well enough. She, however, apologized for her "poor playing." Why, he wondered, did everyone in this country continually apologize?

When John laid his chopsticks down horizontally with a sigh of contentment, Miss Taguchi rose and poured him another drink in a small cup. "This is *toso,* to make you young. You cannot know our New Year's custom without it." Her cheeks turned rosy, and she bowed.

"I wouldn't want to miss a chance to renew my youth." John grinned, but put the cup up to his lips with foreboding. However, the taste was surprisingly good, a sweet *sake.* "Delicious. Thank you." He bowed without rising and noticed her pleased look.

At Mr. Taguchi's invitation, John moved to where he could lean back against the wall. He stretched out his legs, the *kotatsu* having successfully counteracted the outside chill. He took in the beauty of the rich, dark beams overhead, the skillfully carved peonies in the transoms, the spotless, cream-colored *tatami* the women padded on in their mitten-like socks. Everything was mellow and quiet, simple yet elegant—a big contrast to his boyhood's animated and sometimes boisterous family gatherings. Not better necessarily, but captivating.

And then there was Miss Taguchi, working so hard to reach out to him. Funny that she'd almost invited herself to his bachelor rooms. He'd barely held back a chuckle. The family was taking great pleasure in entertaining him. Truly, the Japanese could be a cordial and generous people.

"Would you like for us to demonstrate a game of *go?*" Mr. Taguchi suggested during a pause in the conversation. "My daughter can be my opponent. She knows the game well. She quickly learned strategies, even a few complex ones, by watching others play the game when a young girl."

"That's a fine idea. And I can well imagine how quickly your daughter mastered the skill. I've already noticed her talent in acquiring English. We were able to converse easily the last time we met."

Miss Taguchi visibly tensed and busied herself with laying out the game pieces.

Mr. Taguchi tilted his head and turned toward his daughter with a perplexed look.

John bit back his next words. He'd better not elaborate on the Christmas party. After all, the girl's grandfather had objected initially to her English studies. He motioned toward the quiet young woman with brooding eyes. "Might your wife's niece be persuaded to participate also?"

"Kiyo-*san* does not know this game or any English. *Go* takes much concentration, even more than for *shogi,* or chess as you call it. Household activities suit her."

After hearing the Japanese translation, the niece excused herself, her displeasure revealed by the merest flicker of a frown. Although sorry for the girl, John refrained from commenting. The family's relationships were truly none of his business.

The board game's few simple rules proved easy enough. Players captured either the stones made of white shell or the black slate stones as well as conquering unoccupied territory. However, concentrating on the various moves' ramifications posed a bigger challenge. His attention strayed to the sparkle in Miss Taguchi's eyes each time she, or her father, made a strategic move. When John's gaze returned to her face for the fourth or fifth time, he determined to exert every ounce of will power to keep his eyes on the board and his mind on analyzing the plays.

The game developed into a close one. An equal number of black and white stones had been captured, and a group of stones were in danger of being surrounded, one move away from being in *atari*, John guessed.

"This might be a good move." Miss Taguchi's hand hovered next to a white stone.

Her father's face drooped momentarily before he masked his feelings.

She moved her hand to a different intersection of the board's lines. "No, I believe this is better."

John looked at her before he caught himself. Although she was the picture of innocence, he suspected the move she hadn't taken would have threatened a more significant number of her father's white stones. Must be the custom of *saving face*. If he ever played this game with her, he would insist she give him no slack whatsoever—which being a novice, meant he'd lose. He could just imagine the young lady's consternation at such an outcome.

Lengthening shadows on the tatami mats caused him to glance at his fob watch. How had three hours passed so quickly? The game had been delayed from time to time as visitors were greeted, but most of the time had been spent gathered around the *go* board. He shouldn't wear out his welcome. Nevertheless, he'd stay a little longer to see the final moves Miss Taguchi made . . . and her father also, of course.

The next minute, the niece barged into the room, speaking in excited, rapid Japanese.

Mr. Taguchi asked several rapid-fire questions.

"If there is a problem,"—John looked from one to the other,—"please don't let me keep you from attending to it."

"Kiyo saw a stranger in our back garden. Probably a neighbor's servant who got drunk on his master's liquor. He exited our side gate."

Mr. Taguchi's wife came close and spoke softly in her husband's ear. He frowned.

"Actually," John said, "I'd better heed the warning Governor Nakamura gave a few weeks ago, the one about needing an armed escort when out in the evening. Not that I feel any danger from a neighbor's drunk servant." He smiled, but sobered at the thought that the revolver tucked in his saddlebag wouldn't do much good in the dark if a *rōnin* accosted him.

His interpreter's face remained solemn. "Very wise to follow the governor's instructions."

John rose. "I am sorry to leave your gracious hospitality." *Genuinely sorry.* He hadn't had this feeling of belonging since leaving New York. In fact, he might be happy to stay in Japan indefinitely if only Catherine would join him. If she did, she'd find this family delightful too. How could she not?

CHAPTER 14

The Taguchi family, except for the grandfather, warmly bid John farewell at the gate. His interpreter presented him with a pot of blooming jonquils and a packet of wrapped dried persimmons. "A wish for Happy Longevity in the New Year," he explained.

After John had returned the requisite bows, he extended the gifts to the groom to carry. But Nobu didn't notice.

"Nobu! Here, take these now," John said, raising his voice.

Only then did Nobu wrench his eyes off the Taguchis' house.

The smell of burning wood gave John a moment of homesickness. He pictured smoke curling from his New England home's large central chimney. But what smoke was this? Not from wood kindled for the Japanese evening baths.

Another plume of darker smoke rose from the rear of the home. A fire!

"*Almighty God, help this family!* John raced back through the front gate. A gong sounded an alarm from the sector's guard station. Farther away, a temple bell pealed. Shouts came from inside the house.

John, along with several passersby, headed around the house toward the smoke. He gritted his teeth at the sight of flames eating into the back veranda. None of them had any equipment. They couldn't combat this fire with their coats or bare hands. He dashed back to the front.

Two neighbors came running with buckets and headed for a storage tub of water. Too little, too late!

John ran into the house and grabbed up whatever he could to help rescue the family's possessions. When he deposited his load, Nobu was standing by the front gate with his arms crossed. "Help them!" he ordered in Japanese. The groom moved toward the house at a snail's pace.

John shouted at him again and ran back into the house. The neighbors and family dashed in and out, carrying all they could. Miss Taguchi brought out three towering armloads of belongings from the upstairs.

Gray smoke filled the rooms. The fire was spreading too fast. John opened his mouth to warn the family when Mr. Taguchi yelled an order in Japanese, and then shouted in English. "Out! Out! We must get out!"

The fire brigade arrived, and the lead man ordered the family and everyone else off the premises. The firemen began unwinding hoses to pump the tub's water.

Miss Taguchi staggered when a yellow housecat scooted out between her feet. John took part of her heavy load as they exited the gate. A scarf's knot slipped, and he glimpsed oiled paper wrapped around the shape of a book. No doubt the bundle concealed the *Holy Bible*. Pleased the dear girl had cared enough to rescue it, he set down his load and tied a stronger knot for the scarf.

"Thank you for kindness." She bit her bottom lip and shook

her head. "I can't . . . can't understand how . . . why the fire."

Suddenly she jerked around, frantically looking in all directions. She gasped and called out. "*Ojii-sama*! Grandfather! I don't see him!"

Nobu pointed toward the house.

Mr. Taguchi turned back through the gate. Three firemen, armed with sharp pikes, stopped him. He hollered and struggled.

Miss Taguchi and her mother wailed.

No one was watching John. He half-leapt, half-climbed over the wall. Disregarding the firemen's muffled protests, he ran stooped over through the main room.

Where was the old man? "*Anatawa doko desuka?*" John shouted.

No answer. The grandfather had headed toward the back of the house earlier in the day. The worst place. John called out again.

Still no answer.

He ran through the next room, shouting. He heard only the hissing and snapping of the fire and distant outcries. His eyes, nose, and throat burned. Sweat drenched his clothes.

One more room. He couldn't give up yet. *Almighty God, lead me to him.*

Eyes streaming, he crawled through the door. A spasm of coughing left him gasping with his head on the floor. A wave of dizziness hit him. Still reeling, he held his coat over his nose, and ran his eyes over the room. Flames crackled along the beams above. Sparks showered toward the straw mats below. *No more time.*

Just then the hazy outline of the old man's shaved head caught his eye. He was lying off to John's right. He lunged and grasped the grandfather's shoulders. *Tatami* next to the back wall flamed up with a whoosh.

Throwing his coat aside, John hoisted the grandfather into his arms. Moving backwards on his knees, he dragged him from the room and through the next one. In the main chamber, he picked him up, and hunched over, stumbled out of the house.

Sumi knelt a little ways back on the cobblestones and watched Cardiff breathing into her grandfather's mouth and nose. Could that possibly help? The monstrous fire shot out of the roof, but what was that compared to her grandfather's still form?

He couldn't die, not now. He wouldn't know she honestly cared about him, that she was thankful for the hours he'd spent painting the seashells for her dowry. Or the time he'd brought her a special toy when she'd been sick. She wanted to scream, or cry, or pray to the heartless gods, but paralysis held her tight.

Cardiff stopped his efforts and looked up, despair written on his face. "I can't get a response. It's no use. He's—"

Sumi's heart fell to her feet. *No! No! No!* Why had she deceived him? Created the chasm between them?

"Look!" someone cried.

Her father, who had been on the opposite side of her grandfather's body, sprang to his feet.

Sumi edged forward, hardly daring to hope.

Her grandfather's eyes were open! His body jerked with rasping coughs.

Cardiff slipped one arm under his neck. Her grandfather looked directly up at him and collapsed.

Was he alive? Breathing? Sumi moved in still closer and

peered down at the same time as her parents.

Yes! His mouth moved. He mumbled something about a painting of his mother.

Tears coursed down Sumi's cheeks. She was *dead* to him, but he was *alive. Alive!*

Her parents and the spectators pressing around began to exclaim about the American's abilities. She gazed at Cardiff-*sama* through her tears. He'd demonstrated again that he was extraordinary—brave and most of all, kind, even to the very person who had been rude to him.

She watched her grandfather's breathing become more regular. How would *he* feel about his rescue? Saved once in the house and once more with the foreigner's breath. Thankful? Or repulsed?

John squatted next to the grandfather and waited for the doctor to arrive. He periodically checked the grandfather's pulse. The old man's breathing was less labored, but his eyes remained closed. At least, he wasn't seeing the raging inferno. John could barely stand the sight himself.

The house's roof crashed through the second floor. The fire swallowed it up with a roar. One section of the front wall collapsed inward. The remaining section was the only part of the building still standing. Then the flames decimated it too.

The once splendid home became debris, with mounds of ashes swirling among charcoaled chunks of tile. Smoldering red embers shone like malevolent eyes in the dusk. An acrid smell of smoke hung in the air.

Miss Taguchi walked over to John. Her kimono, hands, and

face were smudged, and strands of hair hung limply around her face. "Cardiff-*sama*, thank you! In spite of great danger, you saved my grandfather." Her wan smile disappeared into a grimace.

"I only did what anyone would do in the same circumstances. But your beautiful home—I can't express how sorry I am. An unimaginable loss."

She gave a small bow and managed a weak smile again.

The whole scene seemed an unreal tragedy, a horrible backdrop to the young lady trying to be brave. Still, she was poised, graceful with a natural beauty and . . . determination. Or was it stoicism? How much feeling was the daughter of a samurai allowed in a loss like this?

The firemen had begun prodding the home's remains, apparently looking for clues to the cause. Another was speaking with Miss Taguchi's bedraggled cousin, who gestured toward what remained of the side gate. John wanted answers too. Had the stranger in the back garden set the fire? Was there a connection to John's visit?

Only minutes earlier he'd been enjoying the family's companionship. And now nothing remained but desolation. John's chest ached. What would happen to the family?

Mr. Taguchi and his wife joined him and spoke gently to the grandfather, who opened his eyes and mumbled a word in response. The interpreter swiped his arm across his sooty face. "Only the back garden and the servants' separate quarters have survived," he said to John. "Even the ninety-year-old plum *bonsai* we brought from Hagi years ago is gone."

He repeated his words to his wife, then nodded and translated her response for John. "She says we got many things out, and because of you, no one died." Taguchi adjusted the blanket covering his father. Straightening, he said, "We can never forget your kindness."

As John started to answer, the next-door merchant, Omura, rushed up, saying something about the very bad fire. The neighbor stiffened as four policemen approached.

One of the policemen addressed Mr. Taguchi. John joined the group and caught enough of the Japanese to understand that a man called Matsukichi had been caught trying to exit a neighboring sector's gate when the fire brigade passed through. He would be taken in for questioning.

"*Shinjinai*," Merchant Omura burst out. A passionate exchange ensued.

John stepped back in amazement. If he had understood correctly, the suspect was the *brother* of Omura's servant, a recently hired one. What was going on?

A fireman holding charred materials strode up and spoke in rapid Japanese.

Mr. Taguchi turned toward John. "Those greasy rags were found where the fire started. Arson, Mr. Cardiff. No doubt about it."

Anger like a tiger tore into John. "Terrible! The villain!"

Merchant Omura patted his chest several times, as though having heart palpitations. Bowing apologetically, he excused himself.

John watched the neighbor stumble away, then looked around. Other than Omura, no one who acted like relatives or close family friends had joined the Taguchis.

"May I inquire about your temporary lodging, Mr. Taguchi?" John kept his voice low. "I could ask the temple priest to lend your family the use of two empty rooms near mine. I wish the consulate were finished or my company's ship were still in the harbor. Unfortunately, the ship left yesterday for Fuchow and Shanghai."

"Thank you, but my wife's brother will accommodate us. We've already sent a messenger to his home. He'll be here soon."

"Well then, I'll stay and help you move your goods there."

"No, but thank you. When the firemen finish, I will hire porters. Others will help too. As you said, the Honorable Governor advised foreigners not to stay out late without armed guards."

A breeze whipped up ashes, and Haru coughed, ending with a sob. Her husband turned and handed her a cloth from under his robe.

John bowed and moved away. Mr. Taguchi had once remarked how highly his wife cherished their home. Because the house had been so beautifully constructed of wood, she believed it contained spirit, even as a living tree had spirit. Now it was a dead pile of rubble— because of an idiot.

Nobumitsu had kept his head bowed much of the time so that no one could detect his real feelings. He had struck a blow for the Divine Emperor. The two Hizen brothers and he had easily accomplished the task, and no amount of torture would force Matsukichi to divulge his two accomplices.

Looking up, he saw that the crest of the Chōshū clan, a horizontal bar over three circles, still emblazoned the property's front gate. The New Year's soiled decoration hung there too, not bringing the family the intended luck. Too bad the gate and gatehouse had not been consumed, but the main offending structure strutted no longer. The family had received the first part of what they deserved.

One question bothered him. Why had this barbarian risked his life? When the eldest Taguchi had reentered the house, Nobumitsu expected the fire demons to destroy him. After all, the Eldest allowed his family to go astray. But this foreigner, an ordinary mortal despite the misleading gray spirit eyes, reclaimed the man from their power.

Had the barbarian really cared enough about his interpreter's father to face death? An unfathomable idea. But what else could account for such a foolish act?

Cardiff turned toward him and motioned they were leaving. Nobumitsu laughed to himself. His *master* would never manage the spooked horse.

Nobumitsu untethered the wild-eyed, pawing animal, keeping a tight rein. The consul walked up and patted the horse's muzzle, speaking soft words to it. Just what Nobumitsu anticipated.

Murmuring more words, Cardiff took the reins, mounted the still snorting horse, and set off.

Nobumitsu peered into the gathering darkness, waiting for the horse to buck.

The traitorous beast didn't.

CHAPTER 15

February (Month of the Hare)

Chief Inspector Sato guarded Matsukichi's progress through the jeering crowd. The arsonist faced backwards on the gray horse being paraded toward the execution grounds. Two men beating tom toms drew attention to the rider, and a placard around his neck announced his crime.

"You monster! You heinous devil!" a white-haired, grizzled man shouted, following the horse in a frenzied dance. "All our city could lie in ashes!"

"May you be reborn a roach again and again," another shouted, "so I can crush you into dust a hundred times a hundred!"

Matsukichi remained stone-faced, like any samurai condemned to die. Signs of weakness would so disgrace his family that they and their descendants would become like Untouchables, the handlers of dead and repulsive things.

As Sato expected, the painful inquisition had wrung a confession from the criminal within a week. Admission of his brother as a coconspirator would have been even better, but at least Merchant Omura's phony servant had been forced into oblivion as a *rōnin*. The Council had returned the death penalty with unusual speed, perhaps because of the foreigner's involvement.

Sato bowed to the Taguchi family and Consul Cardiff as they took their places at the front of the grandstand facing the pyre. Since the consul witnessed the fire, even entering the blazing house, the governor insisted he view the justice meted out to such criminals. Sato kept his face dispassionate when he faced Cardiff, hiding his ire. Foreigners greatly complicated the job of securing the city, this arson being a prime example.

A police detachment dragged the bound arsonist off the horse.

"Bind him to the pole," Sato ordered. "He loves fire. Let it embrace him."

Kenshin glared at Matsukichi. Even a fiery death was too good for the criminal.

Cardiff, sitting on Kenshin's right, reared back. "No, it couldn't be!" Eyes reflecting horror, he leaned toward Kenshin. "Do you remember when four samurai threatened me during the Hizen warlord's procession?"

"Yes." He'd never forget Cardiff's brazen threat of foreign reprisal. "You brought it to Governor Nakamura's attention."

"Right." Cardiff pointed at the arsonist. "That man was the leader of those four."

Kenshin blinked as the news sank in. Had Matsukichi known of the consul's visit ahead of time? If so, how? His knees twitched, and he stiffened them. "Then I suspect the other three clansmen are in this crowd."

"No doubt watching their martyr die. Vowing revenge." Cardiff's brow furrowed. "Appalling as that is, I must warn you of one more threat. Yesterday I received a consular report about an interpreter in Edo named Denkichi."

"I know of him. The chief interpreter for the British legation." Kenshin readied himself for more troublesome news.

"*Rōnin* slew the poor man! And the dispatch reported a rumor that five hundred *rōnin* have gathered, intending to burn down the Yokohama international settlement. I suppose we can be thankful Yokohama is eight hundred miles away, but it goes without saying, we *all* must stay alert for more trouble."

"The distance helps not, Mr. Cardiff. Many anti-foreign *rōnin* come from southern clans nearest us, my own clan among them." He laid his hand on his sword's scabbard. *By the gods, these evil men had better not try to harm my family.*

The policemen moved back from the pyre. The crowd behind them quieted.

Kenshin turned toward Haru, who had buried her head in her hands. "It will be over shortly. Be strong."

Flames crackled beneath Matsukichi and sped along the straw piled high around his body. Plumes of thick smoke partly obscured his face. "Expel the barbarians!" he roared, straining at the ropes binding him. "I'd die a thousand deaths to crush them and their cursed accomplices!"

Kenshin gritted his teeth. If only the man could die a thousand deaths. And who knew—his foul karma could exact such a fate in the coming eons.

The fire leapt higher. Matsukichi didn't utter another sound.

Deathly pale, Sumi pushed her face into the crook of her elbow.

Kenshin put his hand under her other elbow. "Are you all right? Our family has a long history of overcoming foes."

"The smell—that criminal's smell! I want to vomit it out! I—" She bent over, a series of dry heaves strangling her voice.

He gripped her more firmly, and she straightened.

"I am all right." She cleared her throat. "He is an evil man! Wicked! Such men cannot frighten us into submission, can they? We are stronger, aren't we?" She searched his face.

"Yes. We are loyal samurai, born from samurai!"

"My Calamity Year has only begun. Do the seers always predict a second calamity for nineteen-year-old females? And then a third one, a *sandome-no shojiki?* The worst one of all?" Her body quivered.

"Stop worrying." He gave her arm a shake. "Like you said, we are strong. Our benevolent ancestral spirits are powerful."

Fortunately, his daughter couldn't see the anxiety gnawing at his mind day and night, his dread of undetected enemies. Possible enemies like Merchant Omura.

What legitimate reason could have caused his long-time neighbor to employ such a shady character as the arsonist's brother? On the other hand, had Omura been the one who sent the cryptic warning before the fire, sensing the danger too late? Was his neighbor a fly caught in a web, too weak to escape? Or was he the spider?

The pole holding the arsonist fell with a thud. Sparks flew, and the man became indistinguishable from the last of the burning logs.

Gone, like my house, Kenshin thought. *But my house will rise from the ashes.*

The police directed the crowd to disperse.

The chief inspector bowed to Kenshin. "The guilty one's

punishment has been carried out as the High Council ordered."

He returned the bow. "Your efficiency is appreciated. My father, still recuperating, asked me to convey his gratitude as well."

Sato nodded, then looked at the ladies. "I deeply regret your loss." His eyes softened and lingered on Sumi before he walked away.

To Kenshin's surprise, their daughter gave no hint of interest. In fact, she had stiffened as if resisting the attention. As far as he could tell, Sato exactly matched the kind of person she'd begged to marry, a man more of the world. And as for safety, no one could protect her better than Nagasaki's chief inspector. Whether or not she initially recognized the suitability, he might be an excellent match if their go-between continued having problems finding an interested traditional family acceptable to the Eldest.

A passing glance at Kiyo stopped him for a second. His wife's niece would have a better chance to secure the betrothal the *nakōdo* was negotiating for her if she didn't always look either morose or angry. At the moment, anger seemed to have won out. He couldn't imagine why she should be irritated at seeing the arsonist receive his just punishment, so perhaps it was Cardiff's presence. If so, she'd better overcome her petulance. The foreigners were in Japan to stay.

Kenshin led his family and Cardiff around the noisy crowd streaming away from the grounds, past two criminals' severed heads displayed on pikes, and toward the thoroughfare, where Cardiff's horse and groom waited. None of the family spoke, and Cardiff appeared lost in thought.

Then right before mounting, Cardiff shook his head and groaned. "An awful sight. The man deserved his punishment,

Nevertheless, I hate to see any human tortured."

Kenshin stared in disbelief. "You felt sympathy for your would-be assassin?" *And the arsonist of my home?* He shook his head. "That is hard to understand, Mr. Cardiff."

The consul squinted up at the sky. "The Creator God tells us to forgive our enemy, even to bless him. Regrettably, I fall far short of that high standard."

What a nonsensical belief. Remembering his subordinate position, Kenshin swallowed his retort. He glanced at Sumi, whose face openly expressed incredulity.

Cardiff checked a stirrup, then turned back to ask, "When you rebuild, will you build on the same spot? Perhaps replant the part of the beautiful grounds that didn't survive?"

"We are still thinking about what to do." Relieved their disapproval had not been obvious, Kenshin offered a thin smile. "The property belongs to my clan's warlord. He could claim the land and anything on it whenever he wanted. Because he disapproves of my present work, the danger threatens."

"Your present work? As my interpreter?"

"Yes, not only those Hizen warriors but many in my Chōshū clan oppose the treaties. Luckily, they are not strong enough to overthrow the shogunate. So, I'll continue my duties, and we will rebuild. Somehow." Kenshin motioned to several *kago* porters that he wished to hire them.

Cardiff raised his eyebrows. "I hadn't fully realized your situation. Can you locate suitable property elsewhere?"

"Not much is available. I must obtain my warlord's or the governor's approval for a new location."

"I'd like to help anyway I can."

"Our family will find a solution. We always have." *How could you—or any foreigner— possibly hope to help?* "I thank you for your kind concern." He bowed low.

The consul nodded in return, as proper to a subordinate. Then he bowed to Haru, Kiyo, and Sumi—a foreign custom Cardiff called *chivalry* and doggedly refused to abandon despite Kenshin's hints. The ladies returned his bows, expressionless except Sumi, who smiled behind her fan.

Cardiff's eyes also lingered on Sumi.

She blushed.

Kenshin held back a grimace. Perhaps his daughter was a little too pretty.

"I'll pray your family fully recovers." Cardiff signaled to his groom, mounted, and rode slowly away.

Kenshin stared after him, stunned that the consul thought his god had power in Japan. Another example of the foreigners' ignorant, brash beliefs.

Or was it? A long time ago, when he'd been a young boy traveling on the main island, an unknown god had claimed *all* creation as his own—not out loud, but in the deepest part of Kenshin's soul.

He shuddered. That unknown god and Cardiff's god couldn't possibly be the same. At least, he fervently hoped not.

CHAPTER 16

John put aside his pipe, eager to get down to business. The preliminary exchanges with Governor Nakamura had taken twice as long as usual. Not wanting the Taguchi family to know of this meeting, John had borrowed the British consulate's interpreter, a man with rudimentary English fluency. Clearly the thorny negotiations ahead would require not only finesse but a good deal of patience.

Henry Mann squatted nearby, and John signaled his secretary to start taking notes, then turned back toward Nakamura. "It is regrettable Interpreter Taguchi suffered due to his outstanding service to the Shōgun's government."

"The fire?" Nakamura sniffed his tobacco. "This happens. The city escaped disaster."

"The international settlement escaped disaster as well. To help with the costly aftermath for the not-so-fortunate Taguchi family, we have collected funds toward the purchase of land for their new home."

The governor let loose of his tobacco pouch and stared at him.

"Of course, we expect the city to subsidize the remaining

portion." John had taken up contributions from the small group of fellow Christians who attended Sunday worship at the Pendletons' home. He'd donated almost half the amount himself.

Nakamura snorted. "Consul Cardiff, they can rebuild where they are. The government does not aid *any* purchase of land."

"Most unfortunate." John tamped down his desire to speak candidly, gambling instead on the oft-mentioned custom of saving face. If his strategy didn't work, he'd lose a lot of money with nothing to show for it. But the Taguchi family's situation cost him hours of sleep. He couldn't help but contrast the sparkle in Miss Taguchi's eyes during the game of *go* with the pain inhabiting them after the fire.

Taking a deep breath, he drew out the papers for a supposedly separate business deal. "I'd like to address another matter." He adopted his most conciliatory tone. "My own company is doing well enough to support a mutually beneficial proposal. I believe the city is interested in importing gas street lamps for the new area developing near the foreign sector. I'd like to give my company's offer."

Taking the quill pen and ink from Henry, he dramatically slashed through the price, reducing it to half the original. The genuine shock on Henry's face underscored his action.

The governor, a suspicious glint in his eye, skimmed the papers. He pursed his lips. "Are charges for shipment a future addition? Or charges for unloading at the dock?"

"No additional charges."

"All foreigners I know seek profit, the highest they can get."

"Then I am pleased to be the first not to do so. The lamps will benefit everyone. You see, I have the interests of the general populace at heart . . . as well as the urgent needs of the Taguchi family, whose reactionary clan may *not* value their outstanding service to the shogunate and our city." He caught the governor's eye and arched an eyebrow. *Now, who's the most generous and discerning—you or this barbarian?*

The governor took three puffs on his pipe and ordered the interpreter to reread the contract.

John kept an air of studied benevolence despite his unease. Gambling never appealed to him. He glanced at the samurai in attendance—no sign of the hostile second son.

The governor looked up with an enigmatic smile. "Consul Cardiff, your bargaining grows better. I fear you outdo us eventually. We accept the contract."

"I am glad to hear it." John picked up his pen to add his signature, but paused and caught the governor's eye again.

The governor coughed. "Also, I recall now a small plot of land—a suitable reward for Interpreter Taguchi's unflagging work."

John maintained his poker face despite the flood of relief. "A fine gesture."

During the return ride in the palanquin, his exuberance from the victory made the discomfort hardly noticeable. His spirits lifted further as the porters lowered him in front of the newly completed house he'd moved into the previous week. The first floor supplied consulate rooms and the second provided a suite for his residence. Finally, a real home in place of the drafty ancient temple.

He stopped inside his gate and admired the tall Palladian windows, visible behind the wraparound porch. The house resembled stately New York homes in general, and the windows and porch were fashioned like his fiancée's distinguished house.

Because of the constant fire danger, he'd had tall brick chimneys built for the three fireplaces. One fireplace stood at the end of the large downstairs audience room that doubled as a parlor. Another, having a built-in, coal-burning stove, serviced the kitchen at the far end of the building. A central chimney rose from the upstairs living area. Pipes helped convey warmed air, but braziers to ward off the chill were installed in the three Japanese-style rooms on the main floor. The mix of Western and Eastern design struck John as ideal.

And now the Taguchi family would have a new home too, one they could be proud of. He smiled, amazed at how much pleasure that thought brought him—in fact, more satisfaction than what he felt about having his own place.

Kenshin's mind whirled. Had his eyes deceived him? He held the scroll out for his wife to see. "From the governor. His kindness is incomprehensible."

Haru looked up at him, her eyes bright. "He values your dedicated service."

Kenshin reread the document. The brush strokes clearly proclaimed the *gift* of land. What's more, the location, suitable for a samurai of his status, bordered a park not far from their original home site.

Mostly for his wife's benefit, Kenshin consulted a diviner that afternoon about the house's layout so it would match the flow of the planet's natural energy. The *onmyōji* also advised him on the luckiest day to break ground.

Three days after the construction began, a contingent of skilled laborers showed up to help the builders Kenshin had hired.

"There's no cost to you," the lead man assured him. "Repairs scheduled for one of the buildings on the governor's grounds didn't take long, so the overseer sent us here."

Kenshin squatted to regain his equilibrium. Nothing he knew could explain his good fortune.

Eight weeks later, only the installation of the *tatami* downstairs remained before the family could move in. Responding to Cardiff's request, Kenshin led him on a tour, ending on the front veranda.

"I've always liked the smell of sawdust." Cardiff took a big breath, then began pulling on his boots. "The crew worked fast, but well, it seems."

"Yes, very well. No structure could fully replace the home we lost, but this is adequate—due to Governor Nakamura's generosity."

"You deserved his help, every bit of it."

"I am a poor attendant." Secretly he agreed with Cardiff. The foreigner had undeniable insight at times.

Cardiff stood and drew out a money pouch from his shoulder bag. "In America, neighbors join in a custom called 'housewarming.' Before . . . uh . . . we knew of Governor Nakamura's assistance, some of us collected funds, following this custom." He held out the pouch. "We'd like you to use this gift to further beautify your home."

Bowing, Kenshin opened it, then gaped at the contents. For a minute he couldn't speak. The pile of silver *ryo* had to equal a year's wages or more. "Forgive me, Mr. Cardiff. Our funds are complete. Please use the money for a worthier cause."

Cardiff shook his head. "My friend, your association with foreigners—with me—brought you danger and destruction. We want to help."

"The sum is too large." *How can he demonstrate insight one minute and sheer ignorance the next?* "I could never pay back such a favor."

The consul stroked his beard. Then his face brightened. "Well, I certainly am not seeking a return favor, but there is a *great* service you could provide. Only a handful of Japanese people speak English as well as you and your daughter. If I could be tutored in the Japanese language—not every day, just once or twice a week—it would help me tremendously. And in turn, I would better serve the others who contributed to the gift."

"Of course, we are glad to tutor. It can help our English too. But—"

"Then we have an agreement?"

Kenshin swallowed hard, searching for words.

"There *is* one more favor I'd appreciate if at all possible," Cardiff added as though an afterthought. "You know I have promised to marry a lady in New York?"

He hadn't known, but nodded.

"I've been careful not to ask the company of any of the Western ladies here. Yet there are social events where it would be nice to have a lady at my side—properly chaperoned, where both of us could increase our language abilities." He shifted the hat he held to his other hand. "Might I ask a personal question about your daughter?"

"You wish to ask about our daughter's availability?" Kenshin sighed. How could he object to any question the consul wished to ask?

"If I may."

"She is not betrothed at the present time, due to unfortunate circumstances."

"I hope the misfortune is short lived and works out for her happiness." He cleared his throat. "At any rate, in the meantime, might I have your permission to invite Miss Taguchi occasionally to such social events as I mentioned? Properly chaperoned . . . to be an interpreter?"

Kenshin caught himself blinking. The consul was dead-set on giving the funds. If he didn't respond quickly, no telling what else the consul might request in order to seal the agreement. He exhaled and bowed. "Again, the honor is ours. Although my service to you is too small, I accept these funds."

Kenshin couldn't ask his father's permission for Sumi to help tutor Cardiff, for the Eldest still refused to hear anything about his granddaughter. At least, he wouldn't voice an objection to the arrangement since one didn't give orders concerning a corpse.

Later that evening, Kenshin studied Sumi's countenance. It used to be easier to read her thoughts.

She fanned herself. "Yes, Father. If you wish, I will help tutor Cardiff-*sama.*"

Only the pink in his daughter's cheeks hinted at her joy. She had abruptly cast her eyes downward. At least a few of her responses fit a samurai's daughter. He silently congratulated her.

Then he watched her walk—dance was a better description—out the door.

What would come of this tutoring? Sumi and he would vastly improve their English skills, but at what price? He closed his eyes in thought.

The consul exhibited good morals and self-control. He wasn't a viper like those barbarians who visited the pleasure houses. His daughter was smart even though eaten up with curiosity about the outside world. If she became better acquainted with the foreigners, she would grasp the impassable divide between these strange people and herself. Thus, there didn't seem to be any drawbacks to the arrangement. Not any he could see.

Should he tell Sumi she might be asked to accompany the consul to *social events*? No, *if* the situation arose, he'd be careful to clarify her position as an assistant interpreter, nothing more. And the consul's marital status? Definitely of no consequence.

CHAPTER 17

April (Month of the Snake)

Approaching her grandfather's room, Sumi patted her hair and checked her kimono, trying to settle the flutter in her chest. Why this summons? Did she face a rebuke, another shameful slap, or might the Eldest resurrect their relationship?

The flutter increased outside his room. She should hope for reconciliation, for how terrible if he were to die while they were estranged, as almost happened. Yet reconciliation could mean tightening constrictions. A demand to stop tutoring Cardiff-*sama*. Another betrothal to a person as equally undesirable as Keiji-*sama*.

Smoothing her hair one last time, she entered the lions' den at his word to enter.

He stopped cleaning his paintbrushes and motioned for her to sit on the faded cushion across from him. His dark eyes under his bushy white eyebrows watered while he seemed to search for the right words.

He waited until she drew herself up stiff and still, then said, "I suppose you were told of Regent Ii's assassination by the reactionaries?"

"Yes, Grandfather." She made an effort to speak above a whisper. Would he blame *that* on the foreigners' presence?

"An old man has many experiences from which to draw."

"I will attend to your wise words."

"During my early samurai training, while parrying a thrust, my new sword chipped. The instructor accused me of not testing my weapon and demanded my sword. I thought he intended to take my head, but he threw the sword onto a corner trash heap. 'Everything depends on your sword,' he railed. 'With it, you defend your life. Your honor. Your family name.' From that time, I have relied on only the highest quality of steel."

Her mind skittered through his words again, striving to grasp his point, hoping she'd have an acceptable answer if he asked her a question.

"Why do I tell you this?" He didn't wait for her response. "The regent's assassination this month shows our country's schism. Those opposed to the Shōgun spit on this land when they slew Regent Ii. Now they urge our clan's domain to fire *unlawfully* on foreign ships and start its own private war. So I ask, which faction is loyal to our country?"

Sumi swallowed. She had no idea how to answer, or if he expected one.

He narrowed his eyes, irritation flaring in them. "I curse our home's arsonist. I despise the regent's assassins. Opposition to barbarians has become an excuse for mayhem. The reactionaries rely on untested steel. Henceforth, I refuse to share their stance."

She managed not to shrink back from his controlled fury. Her mind whirled at his words' implications. Did he no longer oppose their country's opening? Could she possibly be on good terms with him and still interact with the rest of the world?

Suddenly tears pricked her eyes. "I know my deceit was wrong, that I greatly disappointed you. I never want to do so again." More than ever before, her apology was genuine.

The eyes under the bushy eyebrows cleared. "I hear you have frequent contact with the American consul."

"I have begun to help Father teach him our language." She could barely breathe, waiting for a sign of his approval or disapproval.

"Is he an apt student?"

"Cardiff-*sama* learns quickly, but is too bold sometimes in using new words."

"I see." He wiped one of the paintbrushes with a cloth, then set it back with the others. He cleared his throat. "I owe him . . . a great obligation, one I can never repay."

"Oh!" *Careful. Stay calm.* "If my efforts in teaching have your approval—"

"How could I object? I owe the man my life."

Sumi bowed. Was she dreaming? His words were too wonderful to be real.

"But my approval—if you want to call it that—extends to Consul Cardiff, not to all foreigners. If good qualities appear through our examination of the Westerners' ways, like in a few of these paintings,"—he pointed to the book of Currier prints that Cardiff had sent to replace the burned-up one—"we can accept those. Only those."

"I will accept only the good." She felt an inexcusable desire to grin.

"From time to time, you may tell me about their customs, both civilized and barbaric. Some of our clansmen wisely call for *Western science; Eastern ethics.* New knowledge must never diminish our virtues: Loyalty. Duty. Honor."

She bowed her acknowledgment.

He sat in silence to undergird his words. Sumi stayed perfectly still with her eyes lowered. Three or four minutes passed before her grandfather broke the spell.

"Now perhaps you will find a use for this." He handed her a traditional watercolor he'd painted of a honeybee hovering above a pale blue hydrangea blossom.

"Thank you. I will treasure it." She bowed to leave and remembered to use mincing steps despite the liberating sense of relief.

Reaching her room, she paused to let Kiyo, more curious than usual, glance over the painting.

"It's lovely, isn't it?" Sumi moved the painting to catch the light better. "But he should try something new. Maybe like those Currier prints. He approves of the book Cardiff-*sama* presented him, you know."

Kiyo didn't answer.

Sumi slipped the painting into a pile of papers stored under her quilts. She wanted to tell her cousin about the remarkable transformation that had just occurred, but Kiyo was scowling as she'd been doing almost nonstop since the fire.

Sumi turned her back, concentrating on the happy things in life. The renewed relationship with her grandfather. His approval of the consul. Her family's new home—entirely satisfactory even though a few people remarked on its smaller size. Even the blooming of the spring flowers in their recently planted garden. Above all, the pleasure of tutoring Cardiff-*sama* once, twice, sometimes three times a week.

She never could have guessed how much she would enjoy those lessons. When Cardiff-*sama* understood the more complex explanations, his contented look warmed her from head to toe. And at the end of the lessons, he never failed to express appreciation. Each time she met with him, his thoughtfulness grew more appealing.

Terrible things had happened in the last year. But now the future appeared promising. It seemed there wouldn't be additional disasters in her Calamity Year. No mention had been made recently of the matchmaker's investigations. And her grandfather would surely find her betrothal to a traditionalist less attractive now that he'd opened himself to new ideas.

Picking up her modern glass mirror, she smiled at her reflection. She wouldn't be a red pepper pod drooping on a bush. Someday soon she'd soar like the dragonfly.

CHAPTER 18

John slowed his pace to match that of Miss Taguchi and his middle-aged housekeeper Kuma. Eager to explore and wanting a break, he had proposed a change of scene for the tutoring session during the series of beautiful spring days. Now he had second thoughts about reaching a temple he'd spied higher on the wooded hill overlooking Nagasaki.

The warm sun and sloping pathway, broken by flights of giant stone steps in the steepest places, made the climb more demanding than he'd imagined. Additionally, the ladies' kimonos, parasols, and slippery straw sandals hindered their progress. His plump housekeeper, beads of perspiration dotting her forehead, already talked about returning home despite the generous bonus he'd given her to accompany them.

They threaded their way through a grove of tall bamboo and came across a traveler's rest house on the far side. John let out a breath of relief. They would have the lesson there after well-deserved refreshments.

At the entrance of the establishment, a young female attendant, eyes widening in surprise, ushered them inside. John immediately liked the place. One wall's panels opened to breezes and a view of the valley underneath the clear sky. The aroma of garlic and ginger wafted in from the semi-attached kitchen. Blue satin cushions with gold tassels on the raised *tatami* invited relaxation. Best of all, no other customers were there to gawk.

Carefully imitating Miss Taguchi's Japanese, he gave the order for a light lunch to the middle-aged owners. The husband poured out a torrent of words about having their first foreign guest, and his wife vigorously bobbed her head in support.

Despite Miss Taguchi's protests, black trays loaded with red lacquered bowls soon covered the matted platform. John identified prawns, steamed fish, murky soup, rice, and pickled vegetables as well as a few threatening-looking dishes that were no doubt appreciated by the others.

"Are you sure you know your own language, Miss Taguchi?" he teased. "No one could call this a light lunch."

"I'm sorry," she began, but stopped. "Oh, you are joking." She raised an eyebrow. "Maybe our light lunches are better than American light lunches." She blushed and quickly added, "I cannot joke like you. My jokes are rude."

"Don't worry about being rude. You and your countrymen are the politest people I've ever met. I know we Americans are too frank—partly to be sure we're understood, I guess."

"Sometimes my countrymen communicate by what we not say. We dig beneath the words."

"Wouldn't it be easier most of the time just to say it straight out?"

"Then we are not polite people. If a friend invites to her home and I refuse with my words, that friend feels bad. The friend and I lose face, both of us."

"Then do you never refuse a friend's invitation?"

She gazed at him with open astonishment. "A friend can tell our meaning."

"This may be a cultural difference I can't fully embrace, but thank you. You're doing very well as a tutor, and your progress in mastering English has been phenomenal."

"I am very poor tutor and student." She cocked her head. Only the raised color in her cheeks showed she accepted his compliment.

"Of course, I won't take those words at face value." He grinned at her look of approval, while noticing her long eyelashes and smooth skin.

He turned his attention to the food. Using his chopsticks to pick up a pickle slice, he stopped it from slipping out of his grip and, more importantly, managed to keep his mind off his tutor's fair looks. He hesitated only for a split second when Miss Taguchi held a bowl of sea slugs before him. He took just one, placed his chopsticks down on his square little plate, and looked at her. Could she understand what *he* wasn't saying?

She motioned for him to take another. "Plenty here. Please take more."

So, my silent communication expresses nothing. He took an additional one and shoved the bowl toward his housekeeper, who accepted it with evident relish. He put both slimy slugs in his mouth and, holding his breath, chewed and swallowed, managing not to gag. He ran his tongue over his teeth and drank some tea.

After the meal, Kuma chose to rest on the soft mat with her small Japanese pipe, but Miss Taguchi didn't hesitate to join him in exploring the grounds. Following a path of moss-covered stones down a terraced garden, they came to a shaded grotto. A thin stream of water splashed down the rocks. "Just the place to study," he pronounced.

She nodded. "A good place to instruct our mind."

He caught himself staring at her. The bamboo, cypress, and bright pines combined to create a magnificent background, accentuating her beauty. He must be careful to think about Catherine, notice other parts of the scene, and definitely instruct his mind.

In the moment of silence between them, a musical note sounded nearby. He followed Miss Taguchi's gaze to where a narrow rivulet glistened over a bed of polished white stones. At the bottom of the gentle slope, the water formed into a shallow green pool, surrounded by ferns. Leaning across the pool, he discovered that a miniature waterfall dropped from the far side. Beneath it, a section of bamboo had been sliced to form a trough and then balanced on a little ledge. When enough water trickled into the bamboo, it tipped forward so that it struck a rock waiting under it.

Straightening, he sensed Miss Taguchi beside him. Their stillness seemed to make them one with the tranquil place. The bamboo tipped again, creating a resonant sound only the attentive would appreciate. Three golden butterflies flitted between the sunshine and shade. Although he was wasting valuable study time, he couldn't move, captive to the scene's loveliness.

Suddenly aware of the pleasure from Miss Taguchi's nearness, he forced himself to speak. "Have a seat please." After waiting for her to perch on a limestone boulder next to the pool, he settled on a neighboring one. "I guess we're usually too busy in America to stop and notice beauty like this. It's a shame."

"Americans have little time for beauty?" She dipped her

hand into the water. "Lovely things—butterflies and green plants and cool water—stay with us a short time." She let a little water drip from her fingers, the sleeve of her royal blue kimono inches above the pool. "Shouldn't people hold them while they can?"

"I'm afraid most of the time we Americans fill our thoughts with fingers . . . er, with what we're doing, or have to do next." *Good heavens! What kind of enchantment is this?*

She abruptly folded her hands in her lap. "Then I should be happy for some of my dull life."

"Yes." He refocused on her words. "You really should be thankful—not for dullness, but for time. And awareness." His gaze swept the scene. "Maybe I can learn to slow down, to take to heart what the British poet Wordsworth wrote. 'The world is too much with us, late and soon . . . Little we see in nature that is ours . . .' And so forth."

"Do you and the Americans often write poetry about beautiful things?"

"Uh, no, *I* don't. Some American *poets* do—such as Emerson and Whitman."

"You have never written any?"

"No, it's never crossed my mind. Have you?" He could just imagine what his family and friends would have said had he done so. His mother had threatened severe consequences if he failed to memorize the poems for his upper grades' English class, whereas he'd gladly studied the other subjects.

"Yes, almost everyone here makes poetry. It helps us remember special times. Do you want to learn to make a *renga* poem? Sometimes we make *renga* at parties."

"Sure. Let's give it a try." More insight into the country's culture could be as beneficial as vocabulary study.

"The words do not rhyme like English poems. Our poets make . . . umm . . . an outline. Listeners imagine meaning."

"I don't seem to have a talent for communication by omission, but please continue."

"I give you example. I know many poems. Bashō wrote my favorite, in its final form. He lived about two hundred years ago, and his poems are called *haiku*." She cleared her throat.

> *Simple pepper pods*
> *Add gossamer wings to them*
> *Behold: dragonflies*

"What meaning do you put for this poem, Cardiff-*sama*?" She looked at him expectantly.

He folded his arms and leaned over to ponder. Was everything in Japan a riddle? Straightening up, he flung out his idea: "Perhaps children like to make toys out of the pods and pretend they're alive. Then the pods could seem like dragonflies." He thought it a fairly good interpretation, an appreciation of child's play. "What meaning will you give it, Miss Taguchi?"

"Uh . . . perhaps the poem says all is one. Pepper pods and dragonflies are not different at their inside . . . I don't know the word."

"At their core, their essence?"

"Yes, their central part—because everything is one."

She apparently noticed his perplexity and quickly added, "Kaga no Chiyo, a woman poet, said, 'Everything we see arises from dreamer's dream.' We think things are separate, but they are not."

"Hmm, so we're fooled by illusion, and life is a dream. A somewhat unsettling idea, at least to me. And like everything else in this country, something that appeared to be simple, isn't.

Yours is the real meaning of —let's see, his name was Bashō—Bashō's poem, isn't it?"

"Anyone can put his idea in the poem. Maybe I have added another new one too, but yours is a very new one." Her eyes twinkled.

"May I ask what idea you have added to the poem?"

She hesitated. "I . . . think a pepper pod might *become* a dragonfly, and then have wings to explore." Her cheeks turned rosy. "Now I will explain how to make a *renga*."

He put off trying to deduce how pepper pods might become dragonflies. *Unusual ideas, but how refreshing to have a conversation with a lady not detailing the latest scandal, fashion, or domestic problems . . . although she's certainly no more informed than Catherine.*

He realized she was talking. "I'm sorry. Could you repeat that, please?"

"Yes, it is complicated. Short poems connect together to make longer *renga*." She intertwined her fingers.

He pulled his eyes away from her slender fingers and beguiling wrists.

"The short poems are called *tanka* and have five lines. We must use the right number of sounds in each line. The first line has 5, the second has 7, then 5 again, then 7 and 7. Excuse my poor explanation."

"Not poor. I think I've got it. By sounds, you mean syllables. But how about your leading off? You start the poem."

She took a moment, then spoke softly.

"Japanese tutor
Making many big mistakes
Writes poor poetry
You need to finish my poem with the two lines of seven, uh, syllables."

He offered,
"Large brush strokes of sable ink
Curl around her student's mind."

She clapped her hands. "Oh, that is wonderful. Now you start the next *tanka* with an idea, a connected idea."

"A related one? All right." He crossed his arms and tried not to look smug.

"Swirling its curled tail
The black cat meows for food
An impatient stare"

He laughed at her look as she strove to finish his thought. His association had been slight at best. A black cat curled up next to the rest house had been his inspiration.

After a long pause, she said,
"Its hungry eyes complaining
No one comes while life passes
Now I'll continue the idea in the next tanka," she added, clearly more caught up in the activity.

"Time must be endured
While wishing for the great Void
To bring nothingness"

He jerked back. "Miss Taguchi, you're not actually yearning for nothingness, are you?"

"Not right now, but maybe in future. Our shrine's priest says it removes our struggles. Do you agree?" She cocked her head.

"No, I'm not wishing for a void that brings nothingness." He cleared his throat. "Not at all. I hope to live forever."

"Here? In the same body?"

"I mean, I expect to be in heaven after this body dies."

"Cardiff-*sama,* if your soul lives forever, how can you escape suffering?"

"Heaven is a joyous, glorious place. There won't be *any* suffering."

Her brows pulled into a frown, and she glanced toward the pond.

"You spoke of the great void," he said, wanting to probe further. "Will you still be you? Will you have some enjoyment of this void?"

She shook her head. "After enlightenment, I will be one with an ocean of energy. No joy, or suffering either, but the priest promises peace." She took a big breath. "Excuse me, Cardiff-*sama*. May I ask how you know 'heaven' will be *joyous*? That is hard to understand."

"See this beauty." He swept his hand in an arc. "It's a hint of heaven, given by the Creator."

She began to fan herself. "Beauty lasts for a very short time. You said heaven is forever."

He racked his mind for an explanation. She was grappling with entirely new ideas, as was he.

"Beauty on this old earth is a fleeting gift. God is the Giver. In heaven, we can experience the Almighty's presence and permanent beauty."

"Please excuse me. These ideas are puzzling. I feel more comfortable with ancestors' spirits, pitiless as they sometimes are. I want to know more, but my mind is lost in—how do you say?—a maze."

"You're in good company. Some of the greatest minds in history have echoed those thoughts." He stood and stretched. "Well, it seems we've not only been swamped by complexities, but our *renga* has also come to an end."

"Yes." Rising, she smoothed her kimono. "We may not become famous poets like Bashō."

"By the way, his poem reminds me of something. You once called me a dragonfly. Why was that?"

"Oh, because of your bravery when you faced the Hizen samurai." Her eyes shone.

"And dragonflies have that kind of reputation?"

"Why yes. They are daring and never retreat. Don't some warriors in America put its image on their helmets?" She patted the top of her head.

"I've never seen a helmet with the image. But now that I grasp the symbolism, I appreciate the compliment although, to be honest, I was quaking inside."

"You are human, but very brave."

He savored her smile. No doubt her charm had made learning about poetry enjoyable. Then he let out a breath, promising himself there would be no more inappropriate feelings.

After jotting down notes about *renga,* Bashō, and dragonflies, he chose a small platform next to the rest house for the ensuing language lesson. They would be in plain view of any approaching customer.

At the session's end, he asked Miss Taguchi to write a note of appreciation that he could give the rest house owners. The kind couple had refused payment.

Handing the wife the note, he tried to tell her in Japanese to read it.

Instead of a polite bow, the lady drew back and threw up her hands.

Miss Taguchi laughed out loud, and then swallowed her chuckles. She spoke to the woman, who then chortled too.

John walked off and heard another giggle from Miss Taguchi behind her raised fan.

"I am sorry," she said as she and Kuma, who was also snuffling and snickering, caught up with him.

"What was so hilarious?" He couldn't believe this polite young lady could make him a laughingstock.

She sighed and lowered her eyes. "You did not say, 'Please read.' You said, 'Please be bride.' The words are much alike."

Remembering the lady's bewildered expression, he broke into laughter himself.

During their descent, he envisioned showing the rest house to Catherine. He would put his arm around her by the grotto and show her the little waterfall and bamboo container. A quiet contentment would fill her eyes as it had his tutor's.

But the question was would, or even should, she come.

When they reached the bottom of the hill, a wild monkey, accustomed to scavenging people's picnic scraps, swung down from a tree. John playfully held out his key ring. The monkey grasped it out of his hand with unexpected strength and swung back up the tree.

Forgetting himself, he climbed after it.

While inching toward the monkey, he heard someone ride up. Peering down through the branches, he saw Chief Inspector Sato, the one on whose *good hands* the international community relied. He also glimpsed Miss Taguchi's upturned face, gaping at him in the tree. Was she pleased with his athleticism or shocked at his informality?

The inspector stood in his wooden stirrups and held up two shiny coins. The monkey, making a pass for the coins, dropped the keys. Sato flipped the coins into his bag too fast for the monkey, which chattered furiously.

After dropping down from the tree with as much composure as possible, John retrieved the keys and thanked the suave officer, who tipped his head without dismounting. Sato rode closer to Miss Taguchi and greeted her. She bowed, and the two carried out the Japanese cordialities.

A twinge of irritation sliced through John. He jerked back at the implication. Jealousy? Impossible. He was engaged. He had also just gained more insight into the vast chasm between her culture and his—belief in ancestor spirits and a Void versus the Creator God. A void didn't equal peaceful nothingness for him. It conjured up black hopelessness.

Despite his momentary feelings at the grotto, there was no danger of any serious relationship developing with a young Japanese maiden, even though this one was undeniably smart and pretty—thoughtful too.

Apparently Inspector Good Hands agreed with that assessment.

CHAPTER 19

On the high hills northeast of Nagasaki, two couriers hurried along the narrow road that climbed between groves of fir and bamboo. Although dressed as common peasants, they were young Chōshū samurai. Twin bundles supposedly filled with onions swung from poles laid across each man's left shoulder.

The couriers came to a massive rock formation overhanging the road. Neither spoke in its shadows, listening intently, until they came out the far side.

The younger of the two breathed a sigh of relief. "If there are robbers on this hill, they missed—"

Three figures swooped down, knives flashing. The less experienced courier collapsed, his throat and chest slit open. One of the robbers jabbed his knife deep into the other courier's arm, knocking a dagger from his grasp. A stab intended for the courier's stomach missed and grazed his side instead. Outnumbered and weaponless, the injured man slumped to the ground, pretending death.

"Didn't put up much fight, did they?" the first robber said. "Easy pickings. Look here!" He emptied silver coins out of one of the bundles. "I knew it!"

The second man grunted. "Stupid men. Making haste like a ghost chased 'em. Huh! No ghost got 'em. They became ghosts." He opened one of the other bundles. "That red-haired devil can get himself plenty of copper with these *onions*."

"He won't be the only one rich," the first one gloated. "Think what the Chinese heavenly smokes'll bring us.'"

"Enough talk. Get the bundles and come on," the third robber ordered.

The wounded man waited until the robbers were out of sight and then wrapped his headband around his arm's still-bleeding gash. His side was not hurt as much. One look at his companion's lifeless eyes and pool of drying blood confirmed the man's death.

The courier found his way down to a farm in the valley below. After the farmer's wizened mother treated him with her collection of medicinal herbs, he continued his journey. Upon reaching Nagasaki, he went directly to the American consul's groom.

"You buffoon!" Nobumitsu hurled his pitchfork into a pile of hay, coming within a finger's width of the courier's head. "Is it so difficult to imitate a peasant? No peasant treats his bundles like treasure. You are a disgusting maggot!"

Nobumitsu shoved the bowing man to the ground and squatted in front of him. "Now listen well. If you fail a second time, *my* dagger will draw your blood, and wild animals will pick your bones." He took a stick and sketched a rough map in the dust of *Tojin Yoshiki*, Nagasaki's Chinese sector.

"Since the robbers deal with a barbarian trading in copper

and opium, you will visit these two teahouses, nearest to the Chinese." He drew X's on the map. "Drop hints your master will sell copper, payable only in silver. Understood?"

"Yes, Sire. Payable in silver."

"When you have the right buyer—the red-haired devil—set up the transaction for the following week. Then report the murder and theft to Chief Inspector Sato."

The courier jerked. "Tell the official? *That* official?"

"You will *not* tell the coins' real purpose." Couldn't the gods have brought him someone with a grain of intelligence? "Say the stolen coins were to purchase silks and spices for *Daimyō* Ōta's celebratory feast."

At Governor Nakamura's directive, Sato provided the necessary copper to catch the American smuggler red-handed. This time the scoundrel wouldn't escape justice like he had when Sato had to yield to the gunboat captain's authority, counseled by Consul Cardiff to give the man a second chance—a ludicrous idea based on faintness of heart.

The police, under Sato's supervision, brought George Jennings in chains before a city examiner.

Hearing the charge through interpreters, Jennings growled, "There's a ban against exporting copper? How's anyone suppose to know that asinine law? You can't arrest me on a trumped-up charge. This man here"—he pointed at Sato—"holds a grudge against me."

Sato almost laughed aloud. He signaled the police to drag the cursing man out.

The treaty with the United States of America specified that

accused Americans be tried under their laws in a consular court. Although Sato despised the demeaning provision, he relished turning this red-haired devil over to Consul Cardiff. The American would regret his former leniency. He'd have to conduct one of the strange foreign trials. A verdict suiting *both* foreigners and Sato's countrymen would be impossible to reach, so let Cardiff try.

But the burning question in Sato's mind—in Governor Nakamura's too—concerned the true reason for the Chōshū clan's clandestine shipment of coins.

CHAPTER 20

John knelt to help Richard and Margaret Pendleton unpack the mouth-watering picnic provisions in a grove close to the foreign sector. He glanced around at the large number of Japanese individuals and families already settled on raised mats under other trees, participating in the national pastime of cherry-blossom viewing. The country's passion for nature was proving contagious for him too. He looked forward to an enjoyable, relaxing outing.

Raising his head after Richard gave thanks for their food, John covered his surprise. An English businessman and his family, known for their aloofness, had stopped to visit. The Pendletons and John scooted to the edges of the spread-out quilts to make room for Robert Morrow, his wife Emeille, and their daughter Josephine. Then the three men aided the two ladies ease themselves onto the quilts, their skirts' yards of chintz requiring most of the space.

"I do believe the natural beauty of this country is unsurpassed," Mr. Morrow proffered, squatting next to his wife. He glanced at the lacy, pink blossoms that met in a canopy over them. He had a long face and jutting chin, partly concealed by a bristling, dark beard. If he felt any enthusiasm for the beauty, it didn't show in his pinched expression.

"Why yes! All these blooms,"—Margaret swept her hand in an overhead arc—"fluttering like countless fairy wings. The Creator has uniquely blessed these islands. And what a glorious day he's provided to refresh our spirits."

"I wish I could describe this land with such rhapsodies of praise." Emeille adjusted her blue bonnet. "The beauty is quite overwhelmed by all the creeping creatures in this damp morass. Last week a three-foot-long snake entered our parlor. My maid tried to kill it with a metal poker, but it slithered away. We haven't seen it since."

"A snake in the house would unnerve me also, madam," John said. He didn't tell her about the five-inch *tete de mort* spider he'd killed the previous night under his desk.

"This may sound unkind to you," Emeille continued, "but the natives here are more of a trial than even the snakes and insects. Not only do they have no sense of Christian modesty—dare I say it, men and women bathing together in the bath houses—but these people stare at us constantly. We were loath to come even on this short excursion, weren't we, Josephine dearest?"

"I . . . I was pleased to accompany you, Mum." The young lady, in her early twenties, pinned a strand of thin blonde hair back into its chignon net. "I hoped to see a few sights outside the foreign sector." She smiled shyly at John.

"Then I'm sure you'll find today's outing a good opportunity." John didn't return the smile. The international settlement already treated him like bait for famished fish.

"Such a brave girl." Emeille patted her daughter's hand. "And do you know, Consul, one of the warlords has had the nerve to put a likeness of the poor British consul's wife on his rice whiskey bottles? A very unflattering likeness too, I'm told."

"That would be the Hizen warlord." John could imagine the fireworks if the lady knew comic caricatures of herself also existed and were for sale at local street stalls.

Mr. Morrow tapped his fingers on his walking stick. "Consul, I'd like to discuss a more pressing subject. I understand there is to be a trial of a certain American on smuggling charges."

"Mr. George Jennings, sir."

"As you may be aware, many of us in the settlement are concerned a guilty verdict would encourage the Japanese government to charge other foreigners with similar minor offenses."

Richard shook his head. "Excuse my interruption. The consul may not be free to share that Mr. Jennings has been implicated in such a scheme on a previous occasion."

"A scheme which he forsook, according to my good sources."

"Which has obviously come into question." Richard glanced at John. "Furthermore, smuggling can hardly be called a minor offense."

"My good man, the term 'smuggling' depends on one's viewpoint." Mr. Morrow produced a thin smile. "I've heard that in your country, Americans who *smuggle* runaway slaves through the so-called Underground Railroad are referred to as thieves by some and heroes by others. Along similar lines, you consider mission work to be a good thing, but the Japanese consider it to be criminal. Am I not right?"

Richard adjusted his spectacles, then looked over them. "To a degree, yes, but a question of semantics shouldn't be put on equal footing with clear issues of moral rectitude."

"Oh, I quite agree, but one can see the problem in judging these matters." Mr. Morrow flicked a fingernail and turned toward John. "We must also remember that opium trade is encouraged by most nations with commercial interests in China, and copper is freely traded in America. Of course, I'm not saying George Jennings handled either substance. But you follow my reasoning, don't you?"

"Yes. It's clear." John waited for the twist of the screw.

"Why then, I can be confident you will take into account the subjective nature of the charge against Mr. Jennings and the damage a guilty verdict would perpetrate. Isn't that so?"

John groaned inwardly. No wonder he lacked chances to be still and appreciate beauty. There were too many men like Robert Morrow and too few people like the Pendletons and Miss Taguchi. "As I see it, I'll simply have to judge whether Mr. Jennings broke any laws my country pledged to uphold. The treaties' extraterritorial rights don't let us ignore laws, recognized by civilized countries, prohibiting not only smuggling but the vile opium trade . . . if the defendant is so accused."

Angry lines creased the Englishman's brow. "And so you imply Britain is uncivilized because of the Opium War, a war of complex causes." His neck's veins puffed out. "Your duty is to protect your countrymen, not further a Japanese or Chinese peculiarity."

"I am bound, sir, to observe the evidence."

"Evidence? The only evidence against Mr. Jennings will be Japanese fabrication."

Mr. Morrow swept his top hat onto his head. "I warn you, if there's a miscarriage of justice, your State Department will hear about it." He nodded sharply at his wife, who was already raising her blue parasol. "Good day."

John and Richard rose to help the ladies. Neither took their proffered hands, choosing instead Mr. Morrow's aid one at a time.

Margaret Pendleton's gaze followed the departing Morrows. "What a shame." She smoothed the quilt's lines back to its original shape and looked at John. "I hoped we might have a friendly relationship with that family, especially for Josephine's sake."

John grimaced. "I shouldn't have been so blunt."

"Blunt?" Richard laughed. "You spoke what had to be said and in a more Christian manner than I'd have put it. When George Jennings overspent his line of credit at the hotel last month, Morrow covered his debt with a sizeable loan. At least that's the rumor circulating. I hate to repeat gossip, but it sheds light on his interest in the matter."

"Well then, we see once more how money affects values." John picked out one of the hard-boiled eggs. "Only he's not the first to tell me Jennings must be found innocent. Most members of the Nagasaki Club feel their white-skinned reputation lies under a cloud." He ran his finger over the egg's slick, white layer.

The remainder of the outing would have been uneventful except for John's chance meeting with the interpreter's family, who were also on their way home from cherry-blossom viewing. The Taguchi family, in turn, had met two additional acquaintances a few minutes earlier. These men were introduced to John as the eldest Kurohashi and his grandson, Keiji, neither of whom offered so much as a nod.

Mr. Taguchi spoke in English about the day's activities, while John managed the pleasantries in Japanese. Miss Taguchi remained a little apart, her face flushed.

The two Kurohashi men, eyes hooded, watched the interchange without comment, then abruptly turned aside and spoke to Sumi's grandfather, mother, and cousin.

Miss Taguchi glanced at the backs of the men and her father, who also spoke with the others. Then smiled at John as he joined her. "You are making excellent progress, Cardiff-*sama*. You carried on a real conversation." Despite her smile, her eyes appeared troubled.

"You're the one deserving that compliment." He reached for a cherry blossom and handed it to her, hoping to remove whatever thought worried her. "In recognition of your fine achievement. You sound more and more like someone whose mother tongue is English."

Brown eyes now sparkling, she bowed and tucked the blossom into her hair.

Remembering his manners, John stifled the urge to hand her another blossom and stepped into the group to face the Kurohashi men, noting their matching patterned *hakama* trousers and burnt-sienna tunics. When they finally gave him their attention, he told them in Japanese how much pleased he was to be living in their beautiful country with such gracious people.

The eldest glowered, and the younger's eyes sparked with anger. Neither spoke before they whipped back toward the grandfather, their sheathed swords close to swiping John. He had the distinct impression they would have liked to wield unsheathed swords against him.

"Good heavens," John said, approaching Miss Taguchi again. "I didn't mean to insult your friends." He went over the words in his mind.

"Your words did not insult them." Her soft voice shook. "The Kurohashi family is old, traditional, I think you say, and they were involved in a . . . difficulty with my family."

"In other words, they side with this country's anti-foreign element." Was the angry, sour-looking fellow the one the family had tried to foist on her? He clenched his jaw. He had to remember it was none of his business.

"I am sorry." She pushed the blossom farther into her hair.

"Don't be. I hate to think these men might be troubling you or your family, but a couple more cold shoulders don't bother me."

"Cold shoulders?"

"Not literally. Rejection—refusing friendship."

"I wish I could be strong like you. *Cold shoulders* trouble me." She began to fan herself. Her eyes appeared more haunted than ever.

The poor girl. How could her family allow these men to bring her such discomfort? If this were his country, he'd make sure the Kurohashi men didn't throw their weight around. But this wasn't his country.

The upcoming May Day Ball came to mind. Miss Taguchi would most certainly enjoy it. Women the world over liked parties. Of course, he wished more than ever that Catherine could be with him, but surely there would be no harm in having his tutor accompany him. They could both pick up more vocabulary, almost like a lesson if he watched his p's and q's.

"Miss Taguchi, perhaps you would like to see one of the

traditions we have in the West. If your family
be pleased to have you come with me to the
the Commercial Hotel. It'll be on the first day o
where it gets its name."

"May I ask the meaning of *ball*? It is not part ...ie, is it?"

He resisted a chuckle. "No. It's a formal party where people dance, talk, have refreshments. May Day parties celebrate the coming of warmer weather." As he hoped, a gleam of interest had replaced her troubled look.

"It sounds pleasant, but I don't know how to dance."

"That's all right. I don't intend to dance. I just think the ball would give us a good place to polish our language skills and also be of interest to you."

"Oh yes. I would like to see it if my elders give their permission." Her face turned a soft pink, similar to the cherry blossoms. She patted the flower in her hair and bowed.

Her family turned back toward John to say farewell following the Kurohashi men's unannounced departure. John promised to give Miss Taguchi and her father more information about the ball at a later date, bowed to the family, and resumed his stroll back to the compound. He whistled a tune until it attracted too much attention from passersby.

Having Miss Taguchi accompany him to the ball would be a welcome change from attending parties alone even though it would scandalize the prejudiced in the Caucasian international community, the Morrows in particular. Odd how many expatriates turned a blind eye to the "discreet" visits of men to a Peach Blossom or a Little Plum Tree in the nearby brothels, but looked down their noses at a British merchant's modest Japanese wife. That brave man had bucked the gossip and rancor for an honorable love. A downright admirable thing to

At any rate, it didn't matter what the social cliques thought about Miss Taguchi. It wouldn't be as though he were courting the young lady.

"Look at this." John slammed his fist onto the desk. He had been contentedly perusing the afternoon edition of Nagasaki's English-speaking newspaper, basking in the afterglow of the previous day's outing . . . until he came to the editorial page.

Henry Mann stopped his weekly check of the consulate's financial ledger and jumped up. He read the letter to the editor alongside John.

> *We are writing with regard to the coming trial of the respected American, Mr. George L. Jennings. We understand he is held in solitary confinement without the simplest amenities. Furthermore, reliable sources have reported that while Mr. Jennings engaged in lawful trade, the Japanese government, ever eager to thrust up hindrances to a foreign presence, commissioned its ubiquitous spies to manufacture "evidence" to "prove" his guilt.*
>
> *Finally, it has been noted that the honorary American consul could hardly be expected to function as an impartial judge, having become closely tied to more than one Japanese party.*

The letter was signed, "Concerned Citizens."

"*Respected American*, bloody nonsense," Henry huffed. "A pack of lies, all of it."

"Right, including that last line, no doubt talking about the Taguchi family. My impartiality isn't affected one iota by that relationship. And a relationship is quite natural. The Taguchis aren't machines, after all."

"Certainly not," Henry agreed.

"This letter makes it sound like friendship with the Japanese people is disgraceful. I admit I thought it prudent not to become closely associated initially, but I've broadened my outlook. Miss Taguchi will even be with me at the ball . . . as my tutor." He crumpled up the page and threw it in the trash.

Henry blinked, seemingly taken aback at John's last piece of information, but he recovered quickly. "I'm sorry you have to deal with these small-minded hypocrites. There are enough problems without being unfairly judged."

"That's just it. If I find a fellow American guilty and hand out a sentence matching the crime, Jennings' supporters will shout to the highest heaven about injustice. On the other hand, if I seem a tiny bit biased in favor of Jennings, our relationship with the Japanese officials will go to . . . er, be impaired. Chief Inspector Sato, no doubt, is already convinced of Jennings' guilt."

Henry slowly nodded, worry lines creasing his forehead. "These grumblers blithely go about their narrow lives, unaware of their own ignorance." He crossed over to the desk and closed the ledger book with a sigh. "Everything's in order here. If you don't mind, I'll head to Jake's General Store, see if they've gotten in some ink for us, and pick up a couple of items for Beth. While I'm out and about, I'll do my best to counteract the letter's falsehoods."

"May not be possible, but I appreciate your support, nevertheless."

John walked out of the consulate with Henry, and then went his separate way toward the Commercial Hotel. For a block or two, he didn't meet anyone, then noticed that people were crossing to the other side of the street for no apparent reason. When he entered the noisy Nagasaki Clubroom at the hotel, all the conversations stopped. He tried to join a card game while waiting for his appointment, only to have the players end their game as he drew up a chair.

"You shouldn't believe everything you read," John said to the two men who hadn't stalked out. "I work hard to be fair, to represent all our countrymen to the best of my ability."

"From what we hear," a merchant named Sam Thompkins said, curling his lip, "you need to try a good deal harder. Guess you can demonstrate all that fairness at Jennings' trial."

"Count on it, gentlemen."

The men pulled out cigars and walked out together without another word.

John recalled his brave words to Miss Taguchi. Yes, he could endure cold shoulders, but they were anything but pleasant.

The week of the trial, John's mind kept straying from his work to the lines of argument the two sides might offer. *Just be fair,* he firmly counseled himself the night before the trial. *Man proposes and God disposes.* Although he'd repeated the same thing dozens of times already, this time he said it with true conviction.

He awoke the next morning feeling composed until he entered the "courtroom" in his downstairs audience room. The spectators, every single one of them at first glance, glared at him—fifty or more pairs of angry, defiant eyes.

CHAPTER 21

Fuming at the ultimate insult, Nobumitsu pushed his way onto a back bench in the temporary *kotorumu*. He'd see this travesty for himself. The consul's undeniable honesty in dispensing wages and paying shopkeepers in no way qualified him to dispense justice. A barbarian ruling on a crime involving the Chōshū clan—repulsive!

Makeshift benches and folding chairs borrowed from the foreign hotel filled the room. It looked like all the pale devils fouling Nagasaki were in attendance.

From the first minute, the trial proved to be the sham Nobumitsu expected. How dare Jennings sit in a chair? He should be kneeling before his judge, begging for mercy.

Further, Jennings' lawyer was making a mockery of right procedure by arguing *against* the government. The consul should lay out the incriminating evidence and hand down the sentence, precisely as a competent Edo official would for a serious offense. And the penalty should be death. Death for the red-haired smuggler! Death for the invader!

As though throwing dung on the whole performance, Interpreter Taguchi stood in the center of the room, posing as important, promoting the farce.

John found it hard to endure the defense lawyer's none-too-subtle appeal to the spectators. *Good thing no whiskey's allowed. He'd incite a regular barroom brawl.*

Wilton Davis strode toward the observers. "As the Japanese government claims, my client bought a small amount of copper, a metal unworthy of protectionism. In fact, it is reported"—he swooped a paper into the air—"that the warlords hoard the copper to produce more guns. Guns that could be used against our women and little ones."

"Shame! Shame!" a voice shouted.

"God forbid!" two others chimed in.

John rapped his gavel. "The Japanese government's use for copper is not on trial, Counselor."

Davis raised an eyebrow. "Right, your Honor. But let us lay the blame for breaking this *peculiar* law where it belongs. What we have here is entrapment—entrapment of my client who had no premeditated plan to break the law."

Murmurs of agreement rippled throughout the room.

John rapped his gavel again. He looked over the crowd during the translation. Surprisingly, his groom Nobu sat at the back on the right, his face unreadable as usual. Too bad the Pendletons were under the weather and the Manns were on a trip to Yokohama. It would be nice to have one or two sympathetic spectators.

Then he spotted Miss Taguchi on the left, leaning forward, obviously attentive. Her friend from the English class sat next to her. He focused on Miss Taguchi for a second more. How good of her to come.

Their eyes met, and she offered a slight smile until looking down.

He dragged his gaze from her and turned back to the proceedings—the full burden of responsibility replacing the momentary uplift of spirit.

"I wish to enter into evidence the bill of lading for my client's imported goods and these three receipts documenting how Mr. Jennings obtained the silver coins in legitimate transactions." With a look of triumph, Davis slid the receipts toward John.

"Since these receipts have just come to light," John responded, "I would like this gentleman to verify his signature. Is he present?"

The spectators grumbled their disapproval.

After Davis conferred with Jennings, he reported, "Unfortunately the Englishman sailed for London last week. However, Mr. Robert Morrow can verify the signature." Davis swept the receipts back up and took them over to Morrow, who nodded assent without so much as a glance at the papers.

"Counselor Davis, this evidence lacks proper verification and will be noted as such," John said.

Mr. Morrow muttered indistinguishable words. His closest associates glared. Other spectators turned their thumbs down with muffled complaints.

John rapped for order. "The defendant will be accorded every opportunity for a fair trial, but this court will not be bullied into unlawful concessions."

Louder protests filled the crowded room. John pounded his gavel and motioned to the two American guards to move to the front. Chief Inspector Sato also walked forward and bowed. The courtroom became quiet, the anger palpable.

John dabbed the sweat pooling under his collar. A smoky haze from the cigar smokers next to the back window joined the high humidity swathing the crowded room. His eyes sought out Miss Taguchi.

Her jaw was set, much like her look when the arsonist died. At least, she stood with him. Or was he imagining her support? Maybe she was simply curious.

At that minute, she looked at him, paused, then swept her hand across both shoulders as though dusting them. She ducked her head while continuing to peer up at him.

Ah, cold shoulders shouldn't bother me. He nodded his agreement, thankful for her perception and even the slightest encouragement.

Davis wrapped up the defense, stating the silver coins should no longer be an issue due to the reliable evidence concerning their source.

While drinking the lukewarm tea his manservant Goda served, John considered the proceedings to that point. Was it possible the police had framed Jennings, as the Westerners firmly believed? Had Jennings' brashness and previous run-in with Chief Inspector Sato made him a convenient target? When John had half-heartedly studied law at Hamilton College, he never dreamed he would someday be a judge. *Lord, grant me signposts out of this quagmire.*

The Japanese government's representative, a slight, unpretentious lawyer, resumed the prosecution. The lawyer called three witnesses, who shuffled in, chained together.

"These three innkeepers owned neighboring inns on the route to the Chōshū domain," the lawyer stated. "Their conscientious neighbors noticed they had become unaccountably well-to-do. Upon examination, the police found this wealth came not from gambling, but from selling opium. The three independently asserted that a red-haired American was the intermediary between themselves and the Chinese suppliers."

Paper rustling and a few skeptical guffaws came from the spectators, who obviously thought the chained men, broken by torture, would only parrot what they'd been ordered to say.

The lawyer continued. "The High Council has found these men guilty of robbery, opium trade, and murder of a Chōshū courier. They are sentenced to be crucified at sunrise tomorrow. Their testimony today will *not* change their sentences."

No guffaws broke the dead silence.

One by one the lawyer asked each innkeeper whether Jennings had been the intermediary.

"Yes, his face is implanted in my mind."

"I have no doubt."

The last shamefaced innkeeper pointed a shaking finger at Jennings. "I paid the stolen silver to this devil. He supplied me with opium not just that one time, but four times before the robbery. I speak the truth! Now I beg the gods not to despise me when I enter their realm in the distant sea. I implore my victim's spirit not take revenge on my son and daughter."

Jennings shook his head in disgust.

The prosecutor pointed out that not only did one of the bundles of coins bear the Chōshū clan's seal, but also Jennings' current explanation of how he gained the coins contradicted the first one he gave the police. Mr. Taguchi was asked to read Jennings' original handwritten account.

Good move, John thought. *Impossible for the Japanese officials to fake this American's language.*

The prosecutor rested his case, and Davis changed his approach. In his closing statements, he echoed Morrow's argument that the law was based on subjective issues. His speech oozed less and less confidence. At length he sat down, avoiding his client's outraged stare.

John straightened his back. Maybe the crowd hadn't heard the ring of truth and reached the same conclusion, but he was the judge. He signaled to the accused to stand.

"George Leonard Jennings, I find you guilty as charged."

Jennings grasped the edge of the table next to him and turned toward Mr. Morrow.

Morrow jumped up and shouted, "You have no qualification to be a judge! This is an outrage!"

John motioned to a guard to escort the Englishman from the courtroom, but Morrow strode out of his own accord.

After a buzz of comments, a hush fell again. Sato kept his hand on his sword's scabbard and glared at Jennings, who kept his mouth shut.

"George Leonard Jennings,"—John spoke in a deliberate tone, conveying finality—"you have smuggled copper and dealt in opium trafficking, thereby supporting a destructive and illegal addiction in this host country. Moreover, you have contributed to a murder and to the downfall of these three witnesses. Your criminal activity has sullied the honor of the United States of America. By the power vested in me, I sentence you to permanent exile from Japan and to nine years of hard labor in a United States penitentiary."

A hum of agreement swelled from the transformed spectators.

Jennings shook his fist. "You'll hear from me again, Cardiff! You'll not bury me alive!" He yanked up his chair and smashed it onto the floor.

The American guards leapt forward before Sato reached the man. The guards handcuffed Jennings and gripped both his arms to return him to his cell.

Jennings' curses faded into the general noise of the spectators, many of whom told John they had doubted Jennings' innocence from the beginning. They just hadn't felt free to say so.

When the crowd dispersed, John stepped outside. He breathed in the fresh air and thanked the Almighty that the evidence had been clear after all. The tension of the last weeks melted away. Observing Miss Taguchi, her friend, and his interpreter preparing to get into three *kago,* he headed toward them. Miss Taguchi's presence had been like having a songbird inside a room of cawing crows and circling vultures. He should thank her for her thoughtfulness.

Before John reached the group, Sato walked up and began speaking with the three.

So, John wondered, could Miss Taguchi have come to the trial to see the chief inspector? He shrugged away the question, a question he had no business pursuing. Rather than interrupting, he'd thank her at the ball next week.

However, it was his business to make sure Jennings was held securely. He'd ask the captain of the naval frigate anchored in the bay to take immediate charge of the prisoner and to double the usual guard. If Jennings escaped, his revenge would far exceed a smashed chair.

CHAPTER 22

May (Month of the Horse)

Arriving at the Commercial Hotel for the May Day Ball, Sumi strolled respectfully three steps behind her father, who was to interpret for several Japanese dignitaries attending a small reception hosted by a visiting Australian. She gazed in rapt wonder at the sights. First one lady, then another, in billowing satin gowns and glittering jewels, stepped down from horse-drawn buggies. An attentive gentleman hurried around the buggy each time. The lady slipped her hand over the crook in the man's arm as if she were nobility.

Although the twilight still lingered, glowing copper lanterns intertwined with purple wisteria lit the walkway leading to the hotel. Near its entrance, a canopy of bright streamers stretched out from a center pole.

Her father slowed his pace so they could walk in together. "Acting as an interpreter will be a good experience for you," he said, "but do not become enamored with the different customs. Remember how privileged you are to have your feet touch the land of the gods, to be a daughter of samurai."

"Yes, I will never forget." How could she since she was always reminded? However, for the moment, she was in a world far removed from tea ceremonies and flower arrangements.

She paused at the door to the ballroom, stunned by its huge size. Hundreds of candles in the immense chandeliers shone down on foreigners filling the room. Trying to spot Cardiff, she peered around several couples, who turned to stare at her. Just then, he strode toward them. He wore a long black coat with something like two tails on the back, a white ruffled shirt, a scarf rolled at his neck, tight black trousers that stopped below the knee, and white stockings. A strange outfit, yet it enhanced his strong stature.

Why did he seem more handsome each time she saw him? More admirable? He no longer appeared foreign. He seemed to belong in her country. And in her life.

Her father's words reverberated: *Don't become enamored*. . . Yes. She wouldn't forget. The land of the gods had not succored him. But she wouldn't worry about that tonight.

After showing her father the direction to go to the reception, Cardiff-*sama* held out his arm for her to clasp. He gave her a sideways smile and raised an eyebrow. "As always, you look charming, Miss Taguchi. I hope you enjoy yourself tonight."

Warmth ran through her and wrapped her in its glow. "Thank you. I am sure I will." She lowered her eyes, careful not to show too much of her feeling.

As he escorted her toward the ball's hosts and hostesses, her confidence wavered despite his courtesy. Her kimono didn't dazzle like the shimmering gowns surrounding her even though she'd chosen her most elegant summer one, a dark green silk with pink azalea blossoms sprinkled on it. Her hairdresser had arranged her hair with her prettiest tortoise combs and silver beads, but she'd just passed a lady who wore something sparkling like a crown of spun glass.

And more troubling was her short stature, especially when compared to Cardiff's towering height and all the other foreigners who dwarfed her.

She peeked at Cardiff. His face wore a contented smile. He didn't look the least bit embarrassed to have her next to him. And he had complimented her. Enthusiastically. So she should stop worrying.

The hosts and hostesses focused their attention on them as they approached. The couples looked stiff and cool, perhaps due to the formal occasion. At least, she hoped that was the reason. Two of the men shook Cardiff's hand, and all of them listened intently as he introduced her as his tutor.

While her heart beat louder than a drum at one of the gods' festivals, she said "How do you do" and bowed.

The ladies looked at each other, and one lady coughed to cover what sounded like a snicker.

Maybe she should have just nodded, like some type of goddess.

The men engaged Cardiff in conversation, and she stood by, politely dropping her gaze. A strong, flowery odor from the closest plump woman assaulted her senses, but she feared offending the ladies by moving away. The hum of the other chatting guests didn't drown out the voices of the three hostesses, who had turned their backs and talked among themselves.

"We all know," said the one introduced as Emeille Morrow, "a few of the men make a practice of visiting the Willow World, but none of those geishas or common prostitutes have been introduced into our company. Now this American has the gall to bring a native into the ballroom—as his guest!"

Sumi drew in a breath. Was *gall* good or bad? Mrs. Morrow was referring to Cardiff-*sama*, so it should be good. But it sounded bad in combination with *native* and *prostitute.*

"He said she's his tutor," another lady said, "but a ball isn't really the place for a language lesson, is it?" She laughed.

"Even if she is his interpreter's daughter," Emeille Morrow sputtered, "she's a native, for heaven's sake!"

Gall definitely was not complimentary. Sumi suddenly realized where she had seen Mrs. Morrow's husband. He had been the loathsome man in the trial. No wonder his wife exhibited the same characteristics. The couple had better watch their loud pronouncements, or like the cicada in Bashō's haiku, they would cry themselves out and become empty shells stuck on tree bark— puffy shells that looked impressive, but held nothing.

Despite her determination to ignore the cold shoulders of the hostesses, she gave a sigh of relief when Cardiff guided her away.

No sooner had Cardiff seated her at a small, round table than several merchants descended on him. She could follow most of what she heard concerning Japan, but the heated words about the United States stymied her.

One red-faced man doubled his fists. "Those soft-bellied Southerners only know how to crack a whip. They demand to be waited on hand and foot. By Jove, slaveowners care more for their mules than their slaves."

Sumi hoped Cardiff wasn't a Southerner.

Cardiff nodded. "Far too many plantation owners can't see their own great wickedness. That's the truth. I'm as dead set against slavery as you, as all God-fearing men must be. Yet, I think of how Wilberforce and his cohorts achieved the peaceful abolition of slavery for Britain. I hate to see our Union facing dissolution or another war—brother against brother."

"Let 'em secede. Georgia, Alabama, Carolina, all the bloody rebels," the red-faced man growled. "Good riddance!"

After saying something that seemed to bring a sort of conclusion, Cardiff engaged in another conversation farther away from the table.

Sumi didn't mind. There was more than enough to observe. The small orchestra on a platform at one side of the ballroom began to play, and for the first time, the pianoforte was a tangible object, instead of a book's illustration. She tapped her fan in time to the music and studied how the ladies' dance steps fit with the men's.

After an hour had passed, a grinning Russian gentleman approached. "Miss, you speak English? Russian? French?"

"I speak a little English." She looked toward Cardiff for help, but he was facing the other direction.

"May I add my name to your dance card? Sit out every dance not good for you."

"Thank you, but I do not know how to dance. I am happy to watch."

Barely disguising a frown, he made a half bow and walked away.

She appreciated having had an excuse. But perhaps she might find a way to learn the skill, so if Cardiff-*sama* himself asked her to waltz at a future affair, she could accept. With a flutter of anticipation, she pictured herself curtsying, taking his hand, moving flawlessly with him around the ballroom floor. Thus far, however, just as he'd said when he'd invited her, he had not danced one step.

The music stopped, and the dancers returned to their tables. Waiters brought food around on large platters. Sumi sampled the chilled chicken, lobster, early strawberries, and too-sweet pastries. The little strawberries were sour, but they didn't present a problem. She hid the other unfinished items under her napkin.

During the toasts, a few of which were drunk to Cardiff's health, he rejoined her. "Are you enjoying yourself? I'm afraid I've been neglecting you." A waiter held a tray of food next to him, and he picked the lobster and strawberries.

"I'm having a splendid time. I wish I could always learn this much with pleasure." Did she dare tell him about her desire to learn the waltz?

"Westerners' lives aren't often this glamorous. We have to get back to the business of life, but that helps us appreciate these good times all the more, I suppose."

"I feel I'm becoming modern, learning about up-to-date fashions . . . the dance steps."

"And so you are. It's good to keep up with the changing times." Cardiff laid down the little knife he'd used to dissect the pitiful lobster. "Of course, a hundred years from now, our modern life will look old-fashioned. I try to remember not to waste too much time on insignificant things."

"You mean like fashions and dance steps?" A little uncomfortable, Sumi took a sip of water.

"The quiet simplicity of the rest house we visited and its lovely scenes may have more value."

"You sound almost Japanese."

"Thank you." He raised his glass to her.

"My country's simple ways fill my days," she continued,

surprised at her boldness. "When I get the chance, like tonight, I want to learn all I can. My cousin says it's dangerous to be like a turtle with its neck stuck out. But I want a bigger view than a shell's inside."

The consul smiled. "I hope a dear friend of mine will have the same brave attitude as you and will stick her neck out far enough to visit this country."

"Is your friend in a place called New York?"

"Yes, I haven't invited her here. I'm almost afraid to."

"You are afraid she feels uncomfortable in this country?"

"I guess that's part of it. At any rate, a thirst for knowledge, Miss Taguchi, is admirable, a fine trait."

She felt the warm glow envelop her again, dampened only by the idea of a good New York friend who was a woman.

"Actually," Cardiff continued, "for a diplomat, there's no nicer compliment than saying I sound Japanese. But I've got a long way to go in understanding your culture."

"I will help if I can."

"You may not realize how much you helped me recently—in a different way during George Jennings' trial. Yours was the only friendly face, and I caught your message about cold shoulders."

"The people acted like noisy cicadas, soon to become empty shells." He didn't need to know the ones in the room were still making a racket.

His mouth twitched with a hint of a smile. "What did you think of the trial itself, aside from the spectators' bawdy behavior?"

"Criminals don't have lawyers and can't argue against the officials here. But if arrested, I would like this method."

He laughed, but then became serious. "You'd like it

especially if you were wrongly accused. We'd rather let a guilty man escape occasionally than have an innocent man 'confess' because of torture. Does that make sense?"

"Yes . . . perhaps. But I think the trial turned out well because you were a good judge."

He laid his hand on hers. "You're a fine friend, Miss Taguchi. Is there any other subject I can help you investigate?"

His touch thrilled her. Dared she ask? "I would like to learn the waltz."

"Now?" He jerked his hand away.

"Oh no! Later." She felt her cheeks redden and raised her fan.

"Then I'm sure someone can be found to teach you."

At that moment, they were interrupted by a call for the young ladies to wrap the Maypole, which had been moved into the center of the ballroom.

"This is your chance, Miss Taguchi. Don't be shy."

One of the hostesses she'd met with Emeille Morrow was distributing the streamers. Sumi took several steps toward her, but the lady raised her chin and swished her skirt and herself toward another person.

Sumi retraced her steps.

Cardiff paused in his conversation with a man next to him. "Did you change your mind?"

"I decided to watch this time." She pushed away the disappointment. Directing her eyes away from the masquerading cicadas, she concentrated on the dancers weaving the ribbons back and forth until a rainbow of colors covered the bamboo pole.

Emeille Morrow clapped her hands to gain attention. She proceeded to announce that the foreign sector's village council had chosen a young French merchant to act as King of May. Several cheers erupted from the crowd. Mrs. Morrow clapped her hands again and swept the room with a commanding gaze until everyone quieted. "And now you will want to know which young lady is to be the Queen of May. The council unanimously chose"—she paused and beamed with delight—"our daughter Josephine for the honor."

Sumi hesitated, but then joined the subdued applause. After all, the daughter might not share the parents' barbarism.

During the remaining time, Josephine no longer sat the dances out. All the single men took turns dancing with her. When Cardiff danced with her in a four-couple quadrille, Sumi imagined herself in Josephine's place—Cardiff-*sama* promenading *her* in a circle. How stately he looked even when performing dance steps. How graceful the ladies in their sweeping curtsies.

She sighed. She'd better not dream too much. And she'd better keep her feet on the land of the gods. A foreigner would never be worthy of the devotion of a samurai's daughter, even such a splendid one as Cardiff-*sama*.

All too soon, the party ended. Her father waited for her by two *kago* in front of the hotel. Cardiff bid a cheery farewell, following the governor's orders for foreigners not to travel outside their sector at night without an armed escort.

She watched him walk up the hotel's sidewalk to wait until his horse was brought from the stable. She would never forget clasping his arm, seeing his look of contentment, sharing in his thoughts. Her feet still touched the sacred ground, but she couldn't help that her memories soared.

Her father said her name, and she blinked. He opened his mouth and she knew what he'd say: *Remember that you belong to the land of the gods. You are the daughter of samurai.*

CHAPTER 23

Sumi gathered her notes, sorry the tutoring session was drawing to a close. She had introduced many words from the previous week's ball. Cardiff-*sama*'s progress was amazing.

He smiled at her. "I haven't forgotten your desire to learn the waltz. I know just the right person to teach you."

"It was a foolish idea. Forgive me." He had definitely looked disconcerted when she'd made the request. Whatever the reason—Western customs and ideas were often unfathomable—she wouldn't misuse his kindness in having invited her to the ball. She began fanning herself.

"This is your chance to learn more of the modern ways."

"Please forget my silly request."

"You needn't be afraid of the teacher. Phillip Gray is an old acquaintance of mine who arrived from New York a few days ago. In fact, he's the brother of the lady I mentioned to you at the ball. He's staying in the hotel and could get here in no time."

"Please, I don't want to trouble your friend."

"Oh, pshaw! Then I'll teach you myself. It will take only twenty or thirty minutes, so we can fit it in before your father returns for you. And you'll be twice as skilled as Miss Josephine Morrow. There's enough space in this room if I scoot back a couple of chairs and that lamp table." He moved his own blue brocade armchair back a foot and took hold of the teakwood table.

Her heart sped up. He was mistaken. It would take much longer to become as skilled as any Westerner who had been doing the steps for years. Rather than graceful, he'd find her clumsy. Besides, in the same way a samurai's daughter could not become too intimate with Westerners, he might have similar constraints, especially as a high-status American.

She shook her head. "It is too much trouble for you. I—"

"Stand up. Please. And lay your slippers aside."

Taken aback, she obeyed.

He moved her chair back too. "Now count," he instructed. "1, 2, 3 . . . 1, 2, 3."

She counted. Her voice sounded far away, unattached to her body.

"A little louder, please."

She tried to oblige.

"That's it. Let me see you curtsy."

She sucked in her breath while managing to bend her knees and balance on her wobbly front leg. Her narrow kimono prevented her curtsy from being anything like the sweeping ones she'd seen at the ball.

"Fine." He bowed in return. "The orchestra is warming up. Just for us."

He placed her left hand on his shoulder and took her right hand in his. With his hand on her back, he guided her. "Back, side, together. Back, side, together."

She tried to concentrate on moving her feet rather than on

his touch. She had once thought she might faint when meeting a foreigner face-to-face. Now she was in the arms of one. So far, however, the waltz wasn't as difficult as she'd expected. Maybe she wouldn't make an utter fool of herself. *Back, side, together.*

He pulled against her in the other direction. She stepped tentatively toward him. He stepped back at the same time, but not before she had stepped on his foot. Her face burned with shame. Why had she ever asked to learn?

She dared a glance up at his face. His eyes held not only the familiar twinkle, but something else. Admiration? Her heart skipped a beat.

"You're getting it, Miss Taguchi. You needn't worry about injuring me. Even if you stomped on me, it would do no more harm than a kitten's paw."

She couldn't help smiling at the image.

"Let's try that last move again." He pulled her toward him a second time. "Forward, side, together. Forward, side, together. And repeat."

He stopped and nodded. "Now that you know the basic steps, we'll do the real thing with the orchestra. You're learning quickly." He started to hum a melody.

His touch in the middle of her back was firm as she stepped forward. After a few more minutes, she didn't have to concentrate as hard on the movements, and he increased the tempo. Uneasiness melted away. In fact, she'd never felt such exhilaration. She wanted to grasp the joy, to never lose the thrill of his low voice near her ear and his breath mingling with hers. *If "heaven" could be like this, I would want to live forever.*

Glancing to her right as they circled the parlor the third time, her attention was caught by a figure by the open door, half-hidden in the hallway's shadow. The person watched their actions for a moment and then was gone.

Sumi's breaths came faster. The observer seemed out of place, different from a servant, almost arrogant. But then, she reminded herself, anyone would be shocked to see a samurai's daughter in the consul's arms.

With a final flourish, Cardiff twirled her around and ended in a bow. She took hold of a chair to steady herself and curtsied. She suppressed a giggle that had bubbled from deep within.

"That wasn't so bad, was it now?" he asked. "You may need to wear a gown more fit for dancing next time."

She held onto his words, *next time*. How she hoped there would be a next time.

Rain splashed off the eaves the next morning. Sumi pulled her cherished moss-green shawl higher on her neck. The Pendletons had given her the cozy, western-style wrap the day after the cherry-blossom viewing, explaining that an American church had sent three expressly for the couple's Japanese friends. The shawl was a good reminder that not all foreigners were like the ball's hostesses.

Surrounded by the sheets of paper placed in small piles, she dipped her brush in ink and continued writing words from the dance lesson and the ball: "wisteria – *fuji-no-hana*." Then, "partnor," or was it "partner"? These would be added to the list of English words and phrases and their Japanese equivalents she'd begun after the climb to the rest house. Using the phonetic alphabet a foreigner invented for Japanese sounds, she had already written down several hundred words.

"Look at these papers! They're everywhere!" Her cousin's

loud complaint startled Sumi from her thoughts. "It is impossible to walk to my closet."

Sumi frowned. "You can walk *around* them, can't you?" She ought to be patient with her cousin's bad moods, increasingly foul since the fire destroyed Kiyo's dowry, interrupting negotiations for her marriage. But such forbearance at the moment seemed impossible. "Our family is indebted to the American consul, you remember. These pages will make a good gift for the American Independence Day. They'll help him learn our language faster."

"How thoughtful of you. Especially since the barbarian was more the cause than the cure of our loss." She kicked a pile of the papers on the way to her cupboard.

"Stop it! You're getting them out of order."

"Then clean them up. Now!" Kiyo roughly shoved another pile out of her way.

"I hope you can marry soon—a happy outcome for both of us." Sumi began to pick up the sheets that were helter-skelter.

Kiyo rummaged noisily in her cupboard and found what she wanted. "I'll tell you what *I* think." She headed for the door. "That consul does not belong in Nagasaki. He *will* leave sooner or later. And not only are those papers a waste of time, they are insulting to the gods. You are a simpleton to care about a barbarian!"

"You'd be amazed at all I've learned from him. Simpletons are people with closed minds."

Her cousin glowered at her and left the room.

"Like Kiyo," Sumi muttered to her cat, which stared at her from its cushion. But the prediction of Cardiff leaving Japan struck ice to her soul.

The rain drummed against the roof. The house grew darker,

as though the storm clouds moved inside. Soon their clothes and other objects would mildew as they did every rainy season.

She checked for smears and straightened the papers.

Never mind Kiyo. She would be able to give Cardiff-*sama* the dictionary and receive *his* approval . . . and gratefulness. A smile pulled at her lips.

His interest in her country caused him to try to communicate with any number of people. Sometimes she'd seen him speak even to street sweepers. One sweeper near the American consulate had bowed and returned his greeting although the others pretended not to see him.

Despite his limited vocabulary, he'd also gotten to know a group of children living close to the international sector. He called them by name and carried hard candies for them in his pocket. One time, much to her amazement, he accepted a boy's offer to let him fly his kite. Cardiff-*sama* had sprinted down the street, dodged the gaping gawkers, and returned breathing hard and grinning.

Kiyo was wrong. If he planned to leave, he would hardly be so interested in her country. He would find her dictionary very useful, and his pleasure would be worth every minute required for the undertaking.

The melody he had hummed close to her ear while they waltzed echoed in her mind. Even now she could feel his arm around her. Holding her papers out as her partner, she began to waltz. They were dancing, dancing, whirling around the room. Nothing could take away that wonderful memory, and there would be many more in the days to come.

John sat at his desk in his upstairs suite, working on a contract for purchasing teapots, but making little progress. He couldn't get the dance lesson off his mind. Waltzing with Miss Taguchi—holding her small hand in his, feeling her light touch on his shoulder—had been delightful. There was no other way to describe it.

Who wouldn't admire her delicate figure and fine oval face—brown eyes looking up at him, alternating between shyness and a shimmering joy, silken hair that made one want to run a hand through it, lips that produced demure smiles and kind words?

Catherine's framed likeness, resting above the desk's center compartment, caught his eye. His face heated. He'd always despised shallow men who couldn't stand by their commitments. How could he have allowed a young, unsophisticated native to entice him?

To be honest, it hadn't been her fault although he sensed a degree of mutual attraction. He'd better guard the wellsprings of his heart like the *Holy Bible* admonished.

"Don't worry, dearest," he told the image. "Miss Sumi Taguchi is charming, but you are my love. You always will be."

He picked up his quill pen and checked its tip. The time had come to write Catherine about visiting Japan. Although there had been recent threats to the safety of the foreigners living near Edo, no threats had come to light in Nagasaki since the arson. If she left the fourth week of July on a ship scheduled to meet up with his company's ship in Hawaii, she would arrive at the beginning of October, an ideal time to enjoy Japan's natural beauty.

He cut short his sudden vivid memory of Miss Taguchi at the grotto by the rest house and brought to mind the last time he'd escorted Catherine to a ball. While she had glided around the ballroom with him, the other men had fairly gawked with envy. He dipped his pen in the inkwell and addressed his letter to the "loveliest lady in both hemispheres." He had to keep his head on straight and his heart in the right place. That shouldn't be too difficult for a man of his experience.

CHAPTER 24

Five days after the dance lesson, John stepped outside for a stroll through the compound's front garden. The sunshine promised a pleasant day after the three rainy days. High above him, a breeze stirred the Stars and Stripes, which the guard had hauled up the consulate's flagpole a few minutes earlier. He stopped to smell the last of the purple irises next to the veranda. Miss Taguchi said irises spoke of homesickness because of an ancient tale about travelers. Thankfully, he hadn't felt homesick since his language study enabled him to communicate more freely, other than missing Catherine, of course.

The entrance bell interrupted his reminiscences. Interpreter Taguchi, looking apologetic, greeted him at the gate along with four government officials. Uneasy about such an early morning visit, John welcomed them and sent Goda to bring Henry Mann on the double. He chose to seat the men in the Western-style audience room as a reminder they were on American property.

After the requisite refreshments, the chief spokesman rose from his unsteady perch on the edge of the wingchair and withdrew a two-foot-long paper from a red lacquered box. "His Honor, Governor Nakamura, orders you to . . . to relinquish the

Edo map in your possession immediately," Mr. Taguchi translated, his eyes wide with shock.

"An Edo map?" John stood also, his wariness mounting. "I don't have an Edo map or any Japanese map, not even one of Nagasaki." He spread out his empty hands. "Your government bans the sale of maps to foreigners and severely prosecutes offenders."

The official frowned and addressed the interpreter with a harsher tone.

"Begging your pardon, a search is to be made for the map," Taguchi's voice quivered.

John's stomach knotted. "A search? Here? By whom?" These men had some gall giving such an order. Yet refusing would feed their suspicions.

"By Retainer Yamamoto and yourselves, honorable sir. Only the downstairs." Taguchi's voice had a pleading undertone.

"I'll help with the search, John," Henry volunteered. He had just arrived, short of breath.

In less than ten minutes, while the three remaining guests still puffed on their pipes with John, Henry returned with an Edo map in his hand. Retainer Yamamoto sported a grim, as-I-expected expression.

"You found one?" John unrolled the map part way. "Where on earth did you find it?"

"*I* didn't find it," Henry replied tersely and folded his arms. "The samurai here caught the slightest glimpse of it between two lower cabinets. Pulled it right out."

John gave a hard look at the retainer, who didn't blink, let alone flinch.

Standing by his interpreter at the side table, John dictated a letter to the governor, emphatically denying prior knowledge of the map and alleging foul play. After sealing the envelope himself, he handed it to the haughty Yamamoto, who picked up the map and strode out.

Mr. Taguchi, his face uncharacteristically flushed, bowed and followed the officials.

Turning back from the entrance, Henry balled his fist. "This reeks of a skunk."

John nodded and sank into the nearest chair. "If it's not one dilemma, it's another. I'd never have allowed a search on United States property if I'd thought the map could possibly be anywhere on the grounds."

"It would be nice if that logic occurs to Governor Nakamura—if he's *not* the one behind this."

"Yes, it certainly would." John motioned to Henry to take a seat on one of the velvet settees. "From what I know of Nakamura, I don't think this originated with him. And he knows me fairly well. Surely he wouldn't suspect I'd want to spy out the capital—of conspiring in an attack."

"We've suspected the governor of wrong motives in the past. Couldn't he suppose the same of us, with all the colonizing in this part of the world?"

"I guess it's possible. My threat last summer of a military reprisal for an attack on foreigners probably doesn't help." John pinched the bridge of his nose to fend off a developing headache. "Whether or not Nakamura suspects me, someone is slandering me with that retainer's help. And since no one could have gotten into our office except our staff, which trusted scoundrel took a bribe?"

"How about letting the whole bunch go, except Goda, naturally. The cook, groundskeeper, housekeeper, maid, groom—one of them's a rotten apple."

"I'll talk to Mr. Taguchi first. Maybe he can shed some light. Firing the whole staff at this stage wouldn't uncover the plot's originator. The damage's been done."

Henry sighed. "Beth's been fretting more about the *rōnin* and warlords ever since the Taguchis' home burned down, and now there's this. I just hope nothing blows up in our faces before July's departure. I'm not sure Beth could weather it."

"Looks like I'm the target. I doubt you're in danger." John forced a wry smirk. "After all, you can always claim you helped in the search."

Henry frowned. "And be like a turn-coat witness to the crime?"

After his secretary left, John poured himself a cup of the remaining tea to help his headache, now full-blown. After drinking a little, he paced, trying to make sense of the attack—a blast across the bow out of nowhere.

If the perpetrator's purpose was to accuse him of a plot against the government, much depended on who had the governor's ear. Mr. Taguchi's referral to the official as *retainer* portended trouble. A lot of trouble. Such a high-level samurai would, of course, serve an even more important master. A high-ranking official could ruin everything, just when his trading company was becoming more and more profitable and he was adjusting to the culture and . . . well . . . building friendships.

It was one thing to choose to leave a place, or even to be banished for upholding one's convictions, but another to be booted out by a false accusation. His mother would feel vindicated in her mistrust of his ventures. His fiancée would be horrified at his apparent ineptitude. If he lost his Japanese investment and the company disintegrated, working in her father's carpet factory loomed whether or not their engagement survived.

Still, he hadn't done anything wrong. He stopped pacing and picked up his cup again. The governor *should* believe his reply. Stewing over the situation wouldn't help.

Nobumitsu waited near the gate after the noon meal to see if his *master* needed a horse for the afternoon. To his relief, Cardiff set out on foot to inspect the materials delivered to his warehouse.

After returning the horse to the stable, he spotted Retainer Yamamoto striding through the consulate grounds, this time heading toward the rear kitchen area. No doubt the governor's second son was behind his retainer's visits. Kohei was wise to keep his plans a secret from everyone including Nobumitsu himself, but that wouldn't prevent his seeking answers.

He gave Yamamoto time to enter the kitchen, then edged toward its open window and knelt in the prickly shrubbery. Oddly, the retainer was speaking with the consulate's groundskeeper.

"We will not tolerate a slip-up. Now tell me how you know the map was of Edo."

"Knew it wasn't Nagasaki by its shape."

"No! Say you overheard Interpreter Taguchi tell the consul it was the Shōgun's city."

"I'll say anything you like."

"You had better. And the consul's response?"

"Said it'd help the Americans. Is that all right?"

"No," Yamamoto growled. "Say the consul bragged about

how the American military would analyze the map. Use your mind. The foreign devils already surveyed the coast. Knowledge of Edo would precede an attack."

"Yes, Sire. I can say that's why I'm reporting this . . . crime. The danger and all."

"Add that even a peasant like yourself can see the barbarians are thieves, using silver to cheat our country out of gold."

"Speaking of coins, Sire . . ."

Nobumitsu crept away. Back in the stable, he shot his hands up to the gods. Not just any map, an Edo map! This meant not only the consul's expulsion, but also Interpreter Taguchi's imprisonment or even better, his execution. The High Council would accuse Taguchi of supporting an invasion. Yes, Cardiff and his interpreter would not escape this ingenious trap.

CHAPTER 25

June (Month of the Sheep)

Kenshin hurried toward Governor Nakamura's residence. Clouds gathered overhead as they did all through the rainy season. Some people would no doubt grumble about the rain falling day after day, but he liked the calm *shito-shito* sound of a steady, cool drizzle splattering leaves and puddles. After this first tumultuous year of dealing with foreigners and the arson of his home, he appreciated anything soothing.

He relinquished his swords in the governor's antechamber as usual. Halfway to the audience room, a movement flashed in an adjoining passageway. Two guards burst out. They crossed their pikes, blocking his way.

Kenshin rocked back on his heels. "What is the meaning of this? Do you not know who I am—an interpreter in His Honor's service?"

The governor's second son's retainer, Yamamoto, stepped from the shadows. "We know who you are. Follow me."

One murky hallway led to another and then to yet another. The two guards walked close behind Kenshin. When he slowed his step, they clashed their pikes.

His anger simmered. Did the retainer really think he would try to escape? Why the show of force? The humiliation?

His only dealings with Retainer Yamamoto had been when the Edo map had been found in the consul's office. That had been weeks ago. A shiver ran up his spine. If this threatening behavior was connected to the map, he was at the mercy of the gods.

The guards ushered him into a room where the governor's son Kohei sat cross-legged on a dais. Retainer Yamamoto knelt down next to his master and held his unsheathed sword.

Kenshin bowed to the ground. When he raised his head, Kohei's eyes held an ominous glint.

"Why did you give the American consul the Edo map?"

Kenshin struggled to find his voice. "Begging your pardon, Sire. The map was discovered in my presence, but did not come from me." He touched his head to the mat. His body quivered.

"A lie!" Kohei sprang up. "A witness saw *you* give the map to the consul."

"I beg your pardon. I . . . I have been confused with someone else." He fought against the grayness overwhelming him.

Kohei crossed his arms and glowered. "Admit it! You want the foreigners to attack. If the foreign nations carved up this country, your position in the American portion would be important, would it not?"

"Sire, I am a loyal—"

"The witness knows what he saw. You face execution for this treason."

Kenshin's mind reeled. *A trap! By the governor's son? Could the man be that malicious?* "I did not touch—"

"My father will conduct the investigation. Your treachery is far worse than astronomer Takahashi's, imprisoned for trading maps for books with the German rascal, Siebold. You should have known treason is always discovered, always punished."

A wave of Kohei's hand dismissed him along with an order to leave the grounds.

Kenshin shuffled out of the building and toward the gate used by samurai, feeling as if the leaden sky above had crashed down on him. More terrible than torture, imprisonment, or death, would be the shame if found guilty. And with the governor's son accusing him, how could he not?

His father's honor would lie in the dust—first, the loss of the house and now a charge of treason against his heir. Haru would have to go to her brother's household, or if refused there, into a Buddhist nunnery. And Sumi? If she avoided life as a nun, she would be forced to marry far below their family's status.

And, of course, the consul would be expelled—the least troublesome consequence.

An official message box arrived the next morning. Fingers trembling, Kenshin took out the scroll and broke the governor's seal.

> *Taguchi Kenshin, Interpreter of the Second Rank, is under investigation for treason. He shall neither leave Nagasaki nor speak about this investigation. Failure to obey the injunctions is punishable by death.*

Kenshin leaned his hand on the wall so he wouldn't fall. If only this were a nightmare and he would wake to find the sun shining, birds singing, and everything fine. But no, a sword hovered over him and his family.

He composed an answer that he would be careful to abide by the requirements and that he fully expected the investigation to confirm his innocence. Then he ordered the maid to bring him a flask of *sake*.

After he had drunk three shots of the hot rice liquor, his daughter's voice came to him through a haze. "Father, may I help you?"

"The world has not ended. Leave me."

"I am sorry." She eyed the rolled-up scroll, bowed, and crept out.

CHAPTER 26

Clothed in her old brown riding outfit, Sumi mounted the small horse. She took the bow and a quiver of stone-tipped arrows from the attendant. She had suggested the riding course for the tutoring lesson when a clear morning interrupted the rainy season's downpours. Now her goal was to not make a fool of herself in front of Cardiff-*sama*.

It had been years since her grandfather had taught her to ride and shoot the bow and arrow. He'd taken her to the track weekly until the day she'd let slip her desire to ride into the countryside and even visit the main island and climb Fuji-*san*, disguised as a boy.

She'd never had another lesson.

She rode at a trot around the track. While passing the straw target, she stood in the stirrups and shot off two arrows, but missed. She grasped the bow more firmly. Surely she could remember something from her long-ago lessons. On the second go-round, one of the arrows did hit the target's extreme edge, vibrating in its precarious position.

"Forgive my poor showing." She shook her head and motioned for Cardiff to take his turn. "I am out of practice.

Grandfather would be disgusted."

He pointed to her arrow. "You hit the target. No one should disparage that. And this isn't an exhibition, I hope. My skills are rusty too."

After mounting his horse, he raised the much longer bow the attendant handed him. "I'm not used to a bow with so much of it above the hand grip, but I'll give it a try."

"I'm sure you'll do very well." Archery being the highest samurai skill, his arrows would zing right into the target's center point.

He galloped toward the target. The first arrow slipped out of his hands when he drew it back on the bow string. He got the second arrow off, but it wobbled and went far afield.

She could hardly bear to keep watching.

His third and fourth tries weren't any better.

Her heart squeezed, hating he had lost face. What type of warrior was he anyway? Or was his vision the problem? As he dismounted, she queried, "Cardiff-*sama,* are your eyes all right?"

He laughed. "I haven't shot arrows for a long time, but when I did, I shot on foot with a smaller bow."

"On foot? Why on foot? Not as a common foot soldier? Of course not." She mustn't insult him on top of his fiasco.

"Archery nowadays isn't primarily used for warfare in my country. It's a sport, at least in the Northeast, where I lived ... er, live." He brushed his hair back from his forehead. "At any rate, I shot at live targets. Deer, turkeys, and wild hogs. I preferred to blend in with the forest and let the animals come close to me, like our Indians did."

"You hunted *animals? Deer?*" An uncouth sport, suited only to barbarians.

"Not often with a bow and arrow. Usually with a gun."

"A *gun?* Why did you do that?" Gunnery was the lowest samurai skill. Maybe not even a skill. She'd heard untrained farmers could shoot guns and cause mass slaughter if they had a chance.

"It's a good sport, and we eat the meat. In your country, fishermen catch fish, and people eat them. Eating meat from deer isn't so different, is it? I've even heard it referred to in restaurants here as meat from the *land whale.* And hunting animals is better than shooting men in wars, don't you think?"

"I don't know. I haven't ever thought about it." She cleared her throat. "But I know you have some excellent martial skills—your training to be an important government official."

Cardiff wiped his brow, wet with sweat even in the cool air. "Let's find a place we can talk more easily, like over there." He motioned to the attendant and his groom to take their horses and turned his steps toward the small park bordering her home.

The groom's scornful look, visible for only a second, chilled Sumi. Two other grooms, who prepared to exercise their masters' horses, stared at Cardiff. She was glad to leave the site of his humiliation and her own disgrace.

Cardiff chose a spot halfway up the arch of a small bridge for their lesson. Sumi knelt opposite him and then sat flat on the wooden slats, slanting her legs to one side as she'd seen foreigners do.

He glanced at the stream, then focused on her. "I'm afraid my archery skills need a lot of work, much more than yours."

"It is easy to get out of practice." But she doubted he'd ever been good at archery. How had he possibly achieved his high position? In his confrontation with the Hizen samurai, he'd bluffed his way through, but surely that kind of bravado—

extraordinary as it was—wouldn't be enough to make him the consul.

"My training has had more to do with books, like your father's, I think."

"Oh, but I'm sure you have samurai skills besides hunting with guns and horseback riding." He *had* to. They just hadn't surfaced yet. "You do ride well," she added lamely.

"Tell me other ones your countrymen practice. Perhaps I have one or two of them."

"Swordsmanship?"

"No, never appealed to me."

"Military strategy?"

"Not much."

"*Jujutsu?*"

"What's that?"

"Turning your opponent's strength against him. Fighting with your hands, your body, your feet, but not usually with a weapon."

"Yes, I can wrestle—fairly well."

She was only a little relieved with the last affirmative, but then noticed his increased discomfort. "Maybe we should think about these times, right? Samurai don't fight much anymore."

"We can be thankful for that."

"My father especially likes the peace. And he says it is useless to train to fight shadows." She pushed away the painful thought of her father. Her duty right then lay with the consul. She forced a smile. "So, samurai skills are not as useful now."

The familiar twinkle's return to his eyes encouraged her to continue. "One of the great military strategists who lived hundreds of years ago talked like you. He said we can know happenings of thousands of years through books. If books are better for modern times, Soko—his name—was wise, wasn't he?"

"Clearly ahead of his time. Where did you hear about this strategist? From your father?"

"No, in school. The teacher admired him."

"Girls attend school here? Amazing. I'm glad to hear it."

"Mostly girls in samurai families, like mine, and rich merchants' daughters. I attended classes at a temple for three years and then had a tutor." She tingled with happiness at his approval, so different from Keiji-*sama*'s disgust at the idea of educated females.

"And what did you study?" He strummed his beard. "Military strategy?"

"First, I learned to write." She checked his face, not sure if he was teasing. "I memorized over three thousand *kanji*, our Chinese-style characters."

"Three thousand? I'd better be thankful for our twenty-six letters."

"My father taught me to write the English alphabet just two years ago. We called it crab-writing because of writing from side-to-side."

"Yes, and you begin from the back and we begin from the front, or is it the other way around?" He chuckled. "And then did you read about military strategies?"

"My tutor assigned *Higher Learning for Women* to teach me a woman's place. I preferred reading *Heike Monagatari, The Tale of the Heike,* about our country's history."

"I see." The consul stretched his long legs and leaned back against the railing, clasping his hands behind his head.

He looked relaxed, open to the world and to her—vulnerable, yet strong. Even with his low samurai skills, what woman wouldn't want to feel his embrace?

She tightened her jaw. *Not this samurai's daughter. Even if I didn't care he was a foreigner, my family would. My ancestors would. My countrymen would be aghast.*

She averted her eyes from his body and concentrated fully on the conversation. "*Bushido,* the way of the warrior, is more what excites me."

He raised his eyebrows. "You are full of surprises, Miss Taguchi."

"You remember the Gempei War, I'm sure."

"No, unfortunately our history books contain very little about Japan."

"Oh, I didn't know." She paused for a second, but there was no time to think about the implication. "People can read about the Gempei War in *Heike Monogatari.* It is full of schemes and the warriors' bravery. Tomoe, a female warrior, fought as skillfully as the men."

"Female warriors? Another surprise. I mean, the ladies here are demure. Quiet and a little shy. Very lovely. Not the least warlike."

Lovely—was he including her? His gray eyes were looking at her, appraising her. Her pulse throbbed. She hoped he couldn't tell.

"Women do what duty tells them to do. Samurai women are taught to use a weapon. My tutor taught me how to wield the *naginata,* a pole with a long-curved blade."

"I have trouble imagining you in a fight."

"The only fight I've actually had is with a snake. And I fatally injured one of the sparrows I was trying to protect. However, I'm fairly good at slicing pears from a tree." She raised her fan to hide her grin. It felt good to make light of her former depressing failures.

He laughed and shifted to an upright position. "Not to change the subject, but since you like to be up-to-date, let me mention an important skill government officials need these days. The ability to negotiate."

"I've only heard the word used for nee-go-shi-ating betrothals."

"Negotiations between opposing countries can take place, too, when they work to settle their differences by talking instead of fighting. For example, Commodore Perry began the negotiations for trade. Much better than war."

"I think I understand the word." A deceptive word. Perry's black warships, more than talk, persuaded the Shōgun to open the country, so nee-go-shi-ating was talk backed by power. "I will tell my father about this use of the skill."

"I admire your father, Miss Taguchi—his intelligence, his hard work. And I'd wager he used a form of negotiation to become a Dutch Scholar."

"He did get my grandfather's permission. Not easy to achieve."

He nodded. "Negotiation, like military strategy, requires unusual foresight and often the hand of providence, meaning God's help. You see, both a successful battle and negotiation can have unforeseen consequences, like in America when the Mexican army won the Alamo but lost the war." He sighed. "I don't mean to pry, Miss Taguchi, but I hope your father's success in becoming a Dutch Scholar hasn't come back to haunt him."

"Haunt him like ghosts?" Her father was troubled, but probably not by a revengeful spirit.

"No, I mean—I don't know how to phrase this—I hope

some difficulty hasn't developed in addition to the terrible loss of your home."

Sumi bit her lip. Her father's sudden despondency seemed too burdensome and personal to reveal. "I hope not too."

His eyes softened, encouraging her to say more.

"But something is wrong." The rolled-up scroll with the governor's broken seal flashed into her mind. "He might have displeased Governor Nakamura, but I don't know how." She covered her mouth, fighting for composure.

"I'm sorry. I shouldn't have brought up an unpleasant subject." He leaned forward almost as though he would embrace her, but then jerked back. "But if I can help, I will."

"I appreciate your words." What would she have done if he *had* embraced her? She didn't know, but she'd have wanted to melt into his arms. She blushed at the wayward thought. "You are always kind to our family."

He studied her for moment. "Have you possibly heard anything about an item being found in my possession? An item prohibited to foreigners?"

She shook her head. A new shaft of worry pierced her heart.

"Such an item was found weeks ago in the consulate. My groundskeeper took off the next week. No warning. Makes him look like a scoundrel trying to put me in a bad light. I can't imagine how that would impact your father unless . . ." He stroked his beard.

Swallowing a gasp, she tried to imagine the rest of his sentence.

"Well, I do have one idea that might help matters. I need to consider all the ramifications, however, before carrying out such an action . . . or divulging it. I don't want to stir up more trouble."

She struggled to keep a tremble from her voice. "You are wise, Cardiff-*sama*." *While stoking fear for my father and now for you as well.*

An hour later, Cardiff gathered up his lesson's notes. "It seems like only minutes since we started. Unfortunately, I've other obligations." He donned his wide-brimmed hat. "I won't forget about your father. We are in this together, Miss Taguchi."

He bid her goodbye at the track. She watched him ride away, his strangely haughty groom jogging beside him. She bowed both times Cardiff glanced back.

It was too bad, and really inexplicable, that he had mastered only a samurai's low skills. Still, despite his failings, he had *ki,* remarkable energy. His surroundings weren't shaping him. He was shaping them, not by force, by caring. Genuine, deep concern had shone in his gray eyes when he'd spoken of her father. Maybe kindness was more important than either samurai skills or nee-go-shi-ating.

At her home's front step, she slipped out of her sandals. She heard a groan and then noticed her father at the end of the veranda. He was kneeling, looking at their plum tree. She started to join him, to see if he could be composing a poem or observing the wren's nest she had seen earlier. Then she stopped. Her father, trance-like, wasn't looking at anything.

"Father, I am back from tutoring." She took another tentative step toward him and bowed.

He turned with a vacant air before he collected himself. "So I see, and did the lesson go well?"

"Oh, very well. Cardiff-*sama* learns quickly, doesn't he? But he asked a question, and it startled me."

"What question?" He swiveled to face her.

"He asked if I had heard anything about a prohibited item

being found in the consulate."

Her father leapt up and gripped her by the shoulders. "You must *never* speak of this again!"

"I won't." She choked back tears. "But I am worried—for you."

"I am samurai." He let go of her.

"Cardiff-*sama* said he might be able to help, that—"

"He is the *last* person who could help. Speak no more of this. Not to me, nor to your mother. Not to anyone. Do you understand?"

She bowed to hide a tear that escaped. "Yes, I understand."

"You go on with your life. Enjoy it for now. And I will go on with mine." He turned back to the tree, to stare at nothing.

Kenshin entered the room and bowed, dreading the confrontation.

His father slid his door shut, nodded for him to sit, and extended a cup of tea. "Our house is under a dark shadow. Tell me what has occurred."

Kenshin accepted the cup and stared into it before taking a sip. "I am under investigation. The governor forbids its discussion." His voice cracked. "I should not speak of it even now."

"Then you must obey the prohibition."

"I should not have studied the Western languages. You warned me of the danger. I apologize for bringing trouble, great trouble, on this noble house."

"No need to apologize. Wars are not always fought on the battlefield. Your service to Governor Nakamura, your liege now, demands strong bones and a steady hand . . . until the investigation demonstrates your innocence."

"I am afraid our family's name is endangered more than you can imagine."

His father paused and then waved his hand toward the back garden. "I liked the previous garden—its old moss and shrubbery, its *shibui* feel. This new garden is too fresh, too colorful."

"I am sorry." One more thing to regret.

"No. You and the groundskeeper have designed it with care. So the garden is not bad. I liked the old ways of our country too. But times have changed. I am pleased with your loyalty to your liege in these complicated days, even if other people disparage your good service."

Kenshin bowed low and slowly raised his head. The horror of the accusation lessened a little, yet the dishonor of the family name loomed as terrible as ever.

"Now, steps must be pursued once more for Sumi's betrothal."

"Kato-*dono* will be unable to help us with a match if the plot against me succeeds."

His father stiffened. "I no longer count on his representation. His contacts have no interest in our family. Some insects prefer bitter herbs. I am considering Chief Inspector Sato."

"A good match, but the false charge would also eliminate him."

"Then we will wait for this trouble's resolution." He leaned forward. "Listen to me. Our arrows are bound together like this." He clasped his hands.

"Thank you, Father." *But being bound together will not prevent our family's downfall. It means we fall together.*

CHAPTER 27

Sumi carried the dictionary's alphabetized pages from her cupboard and laid them on her dresser. They were ready to be bound, but the pile looked too small. She sorted through the pages twice and then again.

The H – M section wasn't there. Blood pounded in her ears. All that work—missing!

She pulled everything out of her storage cupboards. One by one, she unfolded and refolded every blanket and kimono. Then she checked her small chest. The missing papers had vanished.

Anger checked her tears. Kiyo! Hadn't she kicked the papers aside, called Sumi foolish, grumbled bitterly about the consul? She plopped down by her dresser and waited one agonizing hour after another for Kiyo's return.

Her cousin finally strolled into their room.

Sumi adopted her nicest voice, "Have you seen my missing dictionary pages?"

"Dictionary?"

"Yes." The niceness disappeared. "You know very well. The one I'm compiling for the consul."

"Oh that." Kiyo didn't meet Sumi's eyes. "For once, there

were no papers around when I straightened up my things this morning."

Obviously, her cousin wasn't going to confess. "Let's see what the kitchen's firebox shows me." Sumi padded down the stairs, nearly tripping on the bottom step.

The cook stopped chopping vegetables and bowed when Sumi entered. "May I do something for you, mistress?"

"No, go on with your work." Sumi used tongs to poke at the ashes in the large firebox, but found no remnants of paper. She knew better than to check the ashes under the separate rice pot, for Kiyo wouldn't think of insulting the kitchen god by burning paper there instead of straw.

Kiyo entered, hands on hips. "Look at you—pawing through ashes and dirtying your delicate hands. Do you plan to lend a hand while the assistant cook is gone?"

"Let's talk in private."

"You're the one who pranced in here."

Sumi looked at the cook, who instantly went back to chopping.

"You know I have no such plan." She lowered her voice to almost a growl. "But if I did help and forgot to put something in its place, I'm sure our cook would have enough restraint not to destroy it."

Kiyo got inches from her face. "I don't know what you're going on about, but I know what it is to have everything—my dowry and even my parents' mementos—destroyed because of the foreigner!"

"The arsonist wasn't a foreigner." Sumi fought the urge to yell. "I'm sorry for your losses, very sorry, but stop blaming the wrong people."

"I do not want your fake sympathy." Kiyo spoke through

clenched teeth.

"Then have the kitchen to yourself!" Sumi stormed out. *I hate her! She took those papers. She must have.*

Back in her room, Sumi stood in the growing dusk, thinking. Suppose Kiyo had hidden the papers instead of burning them?

She carefully opened her cousin's new chest and started a search of its neat little piles. She had never touched Kiyo's belongings before. A scroll of calligraphy extolling loyalty lay on one side, bearing the stamp of Kurohashi Keiji. What had possessed him to give Kiyo a gift? Had the despicable man transferred his attention to her equally despicable cousin? He *had* spoken to Kiyo during the cherry-blossom outing. How amazing if he had truly become interested in Kiyo.

The only other paper she found was a small yellowed scroll, tucked in a silk scarf near the bottom of the chest. Addressed to Sumi's father and mother, it told of Kiyo's parents' delight in the birth of their first child, a daughter named Kiyo. It had probably been in Sumi's parents' papers since Kiyo's had all burned up in the heavy wooden chest she hadn't rescued.

Sumi fingered the scroll, perhaps the only item left of her cousin's parents. How would Kiyo feel if it were destroyed?

She stood still, summoning the courage to tear the paper to shreds. She would do it. Yes! Even as her fingers moved, she heard Kiyo's furious voice behind her.

"What are you doing in my belongings?'

Sumi slipped the scroll into her kimono sleeve. Trembling with both fear and anger, she whirled to face her. "I was searching for the missing papers you found so irritating."

"You think *I* took them?"

"Someone did."

"Well, I did not. And don't you touch my things again!"

Sumi tossed her head and headed toward the door, still shaking inside. For a minute she'd thought Kiyo was going to slap her.

"Wait a minute, Sumi-*san*! Did you take anything of mine?"

"Of course not. *I'm* not a thief." Cheeks burning, she told herself that returning blow for blow wasn't stealing. She hurried down the stairs.

After making sure no one was in the guest room, she pulled out the letter and read it again. The little tear at the top tempted her to go ahead and rip the whole scroll. But no, she'd just keep it in her cupboard well-hidden and decide what to do with Kiyo's treasure when she could think clearly.

Two days later, Sumi relaxed in one of the puffy green armchairs in the Pendletons' familiar parlor, basking in the couple's reception. The rain poured outside, but the couple's cheery chatter warmed her heart. She told about the fine time at the May Day Ball, being careful not to mention the hostesses' rudeness. People resembling empty shells shouldn't bother her anyway. She also could not talk about her father's trouble. A much too private subject. But after a few minutes, she found herself telling her kind listeners about Kiyo's treachery.

"My cousin gets irritated over nothing." Sumi steadied her voice. "Small piles of pages I laid out on our bedroom floor inconvenienced her a while back. So now she has stolen the section I worked on for countless hours. Just for spite."

Mrs. Pendleton nodded, compassion in her eyes. "Oh, I understand. It must be very taxing to have to reconstruct so much work."

"I'll never forgive her."

The couple looked at each other. Some type of communication passed between them.

Mrs. Pendleton picked up her Bible. "Sumi dear, Jesus told a story about forgiveness in the Bible. Let me read it to you."

Sumi was in no mood to hear about forgiveness, but certainly couldn't say so.

Mrs. Pendleton read a parable about a king who forgave the huge debt of his servant, only to have the servant refuse to forgive the miniscule debt of a fellow servant. The king was angry at the hardness of heart of one who had been pardoned much. "So you see, the God of heaven and earth is commanding us to forgive each other," she concluded.

Sumi couldn't grasp Mrs. Pendleton's point at all. Why was she talking about debts?

"Miss Taguchi," Mr. Pendleton joined in, "the king symbolizes the one true God you learned about in the English class. God forgives our sins when we come to Him because Jesus died to be our Savior. Our sins are like the immense debt of the first servant. Because we are offered this forgiveness, we should forgive the smaller sins others do against us."

Mr. Pendleton looked at her expectantly over his square spectacles.

"It is difficult, but a good lesson." In reality, Sumi reasoned, forgiveness could upset the rules of nature. If a person jumped off a cliff, he shouldn't expect the ground to pardon him, should he? Facing revenge was a natural result of doing wrong. Every valiant samurai avenged his master. Forgiveness was unnatural. Weak. Disloyal.

"In time, it may mean more to you," Mrs. Pendleton said. "Excuse me for a minute. I have something I want you to taste." She turned to her husband. "Could you help me, please?"

Mr. Pendleton rose and held the kitchen door for his wife with his left hand and balanced his other hand on his cane's parrot head. Cardiff had often held the door for Sumi too. The strange custom always unnerved her, just as the story in the Bible unnerved her. Actually, the story exasperated her.

This "one true god" wasn't her god, and Jesus wasn't her savior, whatever that meant. She had no intention of deserting her country's gods. Not in a thousand lifetimes. Then too, the story seemed to imply Kiyo's debt was nothing compared to her own. That was nonsense. Kiyo's was larger than any wrong she'd committed, except possibly her deception of her grandfather. Even then, she hadn't intentionally hurt him or anyone else, unlike Kiyo.

She thought about the letter scroll she had taken from Kiyo's chest. The Pendletons would argue against its destruction. But that revenge would be justified. Anyway, she hadn't destroyed it yet.

Mrs. Pendleton came back from the kitchen, carrying a tray. She proudly set a round pan of food on their coffee table. "This is a pie I took out of the oven an hour ago. The apple-pears here add a more delicate flavor than American apples. Won't you try a piece?"

The *pie* gave off a strange odor of the spice called *shinnamon* and cooked fruit. Mrs. Pendleton cut a large slice and slid it onto a small, round plate decorated with pink roses.

Sumi couldn't refuse to eat the piece.

She used the unwieldy fork to cut off a bite, then

swallowed, forcing the sweet goo and soggy lumps of *nashi* down her throat. "It's delicious," she said, hoping the smiling couple wouldn't glimpse deceit in her eyes.

In spite of her rebelling stomach, she managed to eat almost the entire piece. However, she took only two sips from the cup of tea infused with cow milk. She wasn't superstitious about growing horns. Not at all. But cow milk on top of gooey pie couldn't possibly sit well.

"Thank you for your helpful advice and the tasty pie," she said at the end of her visit. At the gate, she cheerfully waved good-bye and then turned sadly toward home, the rain beating down on her umbrella. Had she misread the sign of the dragonfly? Had it merely taunted her with the hope of entering a bright new world?

CHAPTER 28

July (Month of the Monkey)

Oppressive heat bore down on the city after the rainy season. Uncomfortably warm in her summer silk kimono, Sumi envied the commoners' little children, who nonchalantly played by the road, devoid of all clothing. Her father wiped his brow, no doubt uncomfortable too, although he stayed wrapped up in his morose silence, not even inquiring about the package she carried. Wishing she could cheer him up, she searched for something to say, but gave up when they crossed the bridge to the foreign sector. As they approached the consulate, her expectation of Cardiff-*sama*'s joyous reaction to her gift replaced all other thoughts.

She hadn't finished the dictionary in time for the American Independence Day. It had taken two extra days, and even then she couldn't recall all the original words in the missing section. Still, neatly bound together were close to five hundred English words with their Japanese equivalents. Four small crepe prints by the artist Hokusai added depictions of daily life. She originally planned to affix her grandfather's watercolor to the cover, but it had turned up missing too. In its place, she'd drawn the American and Japanese flags and had decided they were more appropriate anyway.

When they arrived at the consulate, her father left her with a promise to return after two hours. Cardiff's manservant bowed and led her toward the parlor, informing her that the consul had an American visitor.

"Ah, Miss Taguchi, come in," Cardiff said, rising. "May I introduce my friend, Phillip Gray? He's making an exploratory visit to see if he'd like to become a partner in my trading company. He's just back from an extended jaunt to Yokohama. Naturally, I think there should be no question as to the suitability of Cardiff & Associates." He flashed his friend a smile. "And Phillip, this is my interpreter's daughter—the excellent tutor, Miss Sumi Taguchi."

The blond-haired Mr. Gray, who had also risen, bowed and arched an eyebrow.

The stranger's bow and direct gaze unsettled Sumi, but she managed to say "How do you do," which he echoed.

"Please sit down." Cardiff waved her toward an armchair. "We can get started. Phillip says he'd like to listen in."

Sumi took a seat, feeling uneasy. Cardiff-*sama* seemed different somehow, perhaps too eager to sound nonchalant. Pushing aside her concern, she turned her attention to his friend. "Would you like me to translate, so you can follow the lesson, Mr. Gray?" She made her face a mask to conceal her irritation with his unwavering stare.

"Not necessary." He grinned. "No doubt I'll find John's efforts most entertaining and your teaching inspiring to the utmost degree."

"I fear I will fail such high expectation."

Cardiff rolled his eyes at her. "You may need to ignore my guest. I'm sure I shall."

She took a deep breath. "Before we begin, Cardiff-*sama,* I brought something for you." She handed him her meticulously wrapped gift.

"Phillip, let me explain in case you haven't observed this custom." Cardiff seemed more on edge. "Japanese people bring gifts when visiting. Of course, I don't normally expect one from my tutor."

Mr. Gray tilted his head and smiled. "You never can tell about tutors."

Having no idea what the man meant, Sumi addressed Cardiff. "My poor effort won't begin to repay your kindness. I hope you find this useful."

A small frown knitted Cardiff's brow while he removed the red and white ribbon and little piece of seaweed.

"What's the seaweed for?" Mr. Gray asked. His blue eyes met hers before she could avoid them.

"A wish for the blessing of a strong shadow." Seeing his puzzled look, she explained, "A strong shadow means a long life."

She was almost afraid to move. Would Cardiff-*sama* like it? Recognize her hard work and her care . . . for his progress?

Cardiff lifted out the bound pages. "Why, it's a dictionary." His eyes showed the twinkle she adored for only a second before they became troubled. "What a mammoth task!" He thumbed through a few pages and handed it to Mr. Gray.

"It's not much," she said. "I meant to present it to you for the American Independence Day, but I couldn't finish it in time." *He hardly looked at it. What's wrong? What have I done?*

"For the American Independence Day? We don't usually give gifts for that holiday."

Acid wormed its way through her stomach.

"But thank you for your thoughtfulness," he added as though realizing her dismay. "This is really invaluable, and it may be the very first English/Japanese dictionary that exists anywhere. I'll keep it right here while we study." His lips formed a half smile.

Sumi fumbled with her notes. Why had Cardiff-*sama* been reserved? Ill at ease? Recently they seemed to understand each other remarkably well despite their different customs. He had emphasized being open and honest, so his friend's presence shouldn't make a difference. Was he disturbed over his lack of martial arts befitting a samurai? She thought she had smoothed over that calamity.

She tried to keep her mind on the translation of English to Japanese, and not on the disappointment stinging like scorpions.

Two hours later, John bowed to the solemn Sumi and her father at the consulate's gate and turned back to face Phillip's questions in the parlor.

"So that's your pretty little tutor," Phillip said, his voice half teasing, half serious. "And she must have been the *native* who was with you at the May Day Ball. Heard it mentioned at the club."

"I guess there's a lot of talk about it. Upset an uppity section of society. Believe me, if she could ever be more to me than just the daughter of my interpreter, I'd never have invited her."

"I know that, I think."

"She's a charming native, but a native nevertheless. And the daughter of a samurai would hardly have any romantic leanings toward an American like me."

"Well, leanings or not, I may ask her on an outing myself . . . to tutor *me*."

John scrutinized Phillip's face. Just what kind of *outing* did he plan?

"What the devil are you looking at? Do I have gravy on my beard or something? I wouldn't take advantage of the young lady if that's worrying you."

"Of course not." Having the thought cross his mind could hardly be termed *worrying*. "It's just that Miss Taguchi's a fragile thing and taken with Western ways. Her family, especially her samurai grandfather, would guard against any appearance of her being courted by a Westerner, no matter how upstanding."

Phillip shrugged. "So even the most innocuous outing could be a problem, I gather."

"Afraid so," John said, while thinking of a bigger drawback. Miss Taguchi could easily catch any man's fancy without intending to. After all, he'd found it hard to resist her charm at the grotto. And at the ball. And in his arms during the dance lesson. And even after the fiasco with the bow and arrow. But he had resisted, and was continuing to do so, like during the lesson that just finished. He forced his mind to bring up Catherine's image, replacing Miss Taguchi's beguiling one.

Wrinkling his nose, Phillip picked up the dictionary. "I can see why people planning to live here the rest of their lives tackle the language, but you puzzle me. Just how long *do* you plan to stay in Japan?"

"Five years, or seven at most. Long enough for the company to have a solid footing."

Phillip stared at him. "Are you serious? How could you endure these bizarre customs for years—eating with sticks, squatting on straw mats, the stares and snickers, swaggering samurai, and most irritating, the bows, bows, and more bows?"

"The customs don't seem all that bizarre now. It'll take time to train qualified managers. The company's got stiff competition. In fact, I communicate partly in code with my Chinese comprador and the clerks back in the States. The British firm Barton is nipping at our heels. If they knew my payment for the best silk, they could raise their offer and snatch the order."

"But what about Catherine? Do you honestly expect my sister to accept that long of a separation?"

"I'm encouraging Catherine to visit and see how it is." He leaned back in his chair, imagining her arrival. "Wouldn't she like the parks with their manicured gardens? Those farm cottages I told you about? Some of the thatched roofs even had irises sprouting out of them."

Phillip's brow creased. "She might if she ever saw the hinterlands. She'd much rather wait at the hotel and hear about any excursion of yours while drinking hot tea with lemon."

"Well, that'd be fine too. But I believe she'd at least enjoy the cultural aspects. If she comes, we could take her to a hillside rest house and a *kabuki* play right off. Miss Taguchi could help show her around."

"If you're going to count on Miss Taguchi's help, you should work on how you show your appreciation. Think about this dictionary she'd wrapped in such nice ribbons and, er, seaweed. When she arrived, she reminded me of a cat that caught a mouse, and she left looking as though the mouse trounced her."

"A belated gift for our Independence Day is stretching it, seems to me. And to be honest, I didn't want to give you any impression I'd wavered in my loyalty to Catherine."

"John, my infallible friend, you've always kept your commitments. I suppose the Indians out West could bury you in an ant bed up to your chin, and you'd refuse to break a promise."

John puffed out a self-deprecating huff. Little did his friend know that a bed of ants could be less of a problem than Miss Taguchi.

"But if the dictionary seems too risqué," Phillip continued, "you could just pass it on to that Pendleton couple. They could handle it, no doubt."

"All right. I'll try to be less of a cad, more appreciative next time I see her." He rubbed his forehead. "And a duplicate for the Pendletons is a fine idea. I'll get Henry to copy it as his last assignment."

Phillip was right, John thought. Miss Taguchi had deserved better. Much better. Sometimes knowing how to act with his charming tutor—with or without his fiancée's brother in the same room—was downright impossible.

CHAPTER 29

Chief Inspector Sato struggled to get his bearings. How could the accusations against Interpreter Taguchi and the American consul still be active? Weeks had gone by, at least five, since the map had been discovered by Kohei's retainer under suspicious circumstances. Sato had assumed the governor grasped the flimsiness of the charges.

Governor Nakamura, his round face a thundercloud, crumpled a report from Retainer Fujino, his most trusted official. Fujino, already kneeling, touched his brow to the mat.

"I have no more patience," the governor railed as Sato knelt beside the retainer. "A man cannot disappear on an island no larger than Shikoku. In a month you should have found him."

Fujino raised his head. "I regret my dismal failure. The conspiracy of the groundkeeper's village to hide him offers no excuse."

A short, nearly bald man in his forties, Fujino was known for his relentless persistence in tracking criminals. Sato suspected the Shikoku clan's warlord, who often flaunted his semi-independence, had facilitated the disappearance of the United States consulate's groundskeeper.

The governor turned to Sato. "Why did you fail to assure that the only witness to the crime stayed in Nagasaki?"

"I regret this lapse. The groundskeeper had disappeared by the time I was privy to the accusation." He touched his brow to the mat too. His mind objected to the path he was taking. Pointing out the flaws in the accusation risked his position. Did he want that? Was a possible betrothal to Taguchi Sumi truly a big enough reason?

"The accusation was made without your knowledge, *Chief Inspector Sato?*" The governor tapped his foot.

"Kohei-*sama* took sole charge of the map's discovery." The icy hardness that gripped Sato overwhelmed his hesitancy. Kohei had waved the Edo map in his face and rebuked him for not detecting the alleged conspiracy. Sato could still taste the dust in his mouth from bowing his head to the ground. He owed the second son no favors.

Only an eye's tic revealed the governor's surprise. "Why do you think my second son worked outside your purview?"

"I apologize." Sato bowed deeply. "I can voice no opinion on his honorable reasons." *Especially since I doubt any honorable one exists.* A bead of sweat trickled down the side of his face.

The governor's eyes narrowed. "A strange answer."

"Since the only witness is missing," Fujino interjected, "I respectfully recommend that Interpreter Taguchi be imprisoned and interrogated. If he is guilty of supplying the map to the consul, he will confess. If not guilty, his brave persistence under duress will eliminate him as a suspect."

Sato groaned inwardly. If the interpreter was innocent, but found guilty, his daughter would be ineligible for marriage to a samurai like himself. "May I offer my humble opinion?" he heard himself say.

The governor scanned Sato's face and nodded.

"May I suggest someone could have paid the groundskeeper for *false* testimony?" Sato sucked in his breath. Had he pushed too far? Why was he doing this when he detested the foreigners, and Taguchi Sumi's father spent all his time with them?

The governor trained his eyes on Sato again. "You took no part in the investigation, you say, but voice strong opinions, stronger than warranted."

Fujino hissed out a breath. "If a conspiracy to attack the capital exists, examining Interpreter Taguchi could produce a conclusive answer."

"Sire, I—"

The governor held up his hand. His eyes glinted. "The government provided land and workers for Interpreter Taguchi's new house at the consul's request, which may have prompted Taguchi to give him the map. I don't fancy a repayment of treason for my provisions."

The governor grasped his fan and pointed it at Sato. "Arrange for Interpreter Taguchi's arrest today." His iron look allowed no objection. "Have him interrogated at the central prison. If he fails the test, the High Council will want his confession before his execution and Consul Cardiff's expulsion."

Sato bowed and left to carry out his liege's order.

Insistent shouts from the front entrance demanded Interpreter Taguchi's appearance. His heart hammering, Kenshin rushed to the vestibule. Two policemen seized him by both arms and pulled him down the step.

"I have done nothing!" To his shame, he couldn't stop his voice's tremor.

"No!" Haru cried out from the veranda. "Stop!"

Sumi burst from the house. "Let him go! Let my father go!"

His wife and daughter, holding each other, collapsed together onto the front step. Their maid Kin, moaning, stumbled after him.

At the gate, he managed to turn back toward the women. "Calm yourselves. It is a misunderstanding." Then seeing his father standing motionless in the entrance's shadow, he choked up.

The policemen shoved the maid back. Rough hands pushed Kenshin out the gate. They forced him into the waiting bamboo cage. The two porters lifted its attached beam onto their shoulders and started off toward the city prison. Kenshin kept his head bowed, hating the disgrace far more than the discomfort.

Citizens yelled at him when they saw the cage.

"Thief!"

"Murderer!"

"No escape now!"

At the prison, guards thrust him into a cell with wooden bars on the front side, as if he were a wild animal. Light already faded in the late afternoon. He knelt in the corner on the stained mat, nauseated by the stench of human waste.

Thoughts of the impending torture seized his mind. Unless he confessed guilt, his interrogators would wring the supposed *truth* out. He tightened his muscles to keep from flinching, anticipating a rod pummeling his bare back and shoulders—

fifty blows, not one less. Then the crushing of the bones in his legs and arms by piling on stone after stone. Drawn-out, excruciating agony.

He forced himself to concentrate on his early training as a samurai. His emotions must not paralyze him. He pictured a maple tree and focused on a single leaf. He was one with the leaf, bearing the wind and rain, the summer sun, the winter cold.

The withered leaf fluttered into the snow. Dead.

Unexpectedly, he saw his childhood memory of the unknown god vividly as though experiencing it for the first time. During his family's pilgrimage to Ise's shrine, they had spent the night at a nearby inn. He'd awakened the next morning to brilliance—sunshine glinting off the surrounding snow-covered fields.

"How powerful the Sun Goddess is," he had said to his older brother.

A voice inside his head had replied. "No! *I* made the sun, moon, and stars, and everything that exists. Only I command the morning. Only I have entered into the treasure of the snow."

He had been thunderstruck and after that, thoroughly frightened. Something existed outside what he'd been taught.

From time to time he'd repeated the words to himself, wary but not wanting to forget the mysterious message. Then two months ago, he had found the same words in the writings of an English missionary who had taught Christianity in China. In order to increase his English fluency, Kenshin had been comparing the original English publication with the companion Dutch translation he'd found in a dismantled Dejima storehouse. The missionary quoted from a book called *Job*. Trying to convince himself that his memory had played a terrible trick on him, he hadn't dared tell anyone in the family, especially not Sumi.

Yet now he faced the threat of death as the missionary and his companions had. Although not samurai, they had stood strong, unafraid to die.

He repeated the words from *Job* out loud. Then straightened, sensing a new mystery. The words no longer troubled him. Instead, they comforted him. His interrogators were not all-powerful, not like the source of the amazing words. They had not made the heavens and the earth; they did not cause the sun to rise every day; they had not set any constellations in place; and best of all, they had not entered into the treasures of the snow where his leaf lay.

Sumi sipped the scalding tea. The pain on the roof of her mouth indicated she still functioned. She had been unable to eat one bite of the evening meal.

Her grandfather set down his bowl and rapped his low stand with his fan. "A samurai's family must be strong, as unyielding as the samurai himself, giving in to no one." His eyes blazed as he faced her mother and her. "This is the time you show what you are made of."

Sumi bowed her outward acquiescence while thoughts roiled beneath. Was that it? Just have mental hardness? Be self-sufficient while her father suffered in prison? Their family's enemies were powerful this time, not a lone *rōnin*. Since her father would never admit guilt to something he didn't commit, his interrogation would go on and on, increasingly horrible.

She shuddered. What if all this trouble were her fault? Like pepper pods and dragonflies, everything in life was connected.

Their home might have burned, and her father might die from torture because of her deceitful actions last fall.

A tear hit her hand, and she swiped at her wet cheek. She had to *do* something, not weep. Swallowing the last of her tea, she asked to be excused.

Her mother gave a slight nod. Her grandfather, sitting stiff and immobile, didn't acknowledge her departure.

Pacing in her room, she thought of Cardiff-*sama*'s desire to help. He'd even hinted of a possible way to do so. His inexplicable coolness about the dictionary wouldn't have destroyed his willingness to help her father. But what about her father's claim that Cardiff was the last person who could help? And, she'd certainly been forbidden to speak of the prohibited item ever again—in spite of not even knowing what it was.

But didn't the arrest change things? Didn't loyalty mean taking blame if necessary? Unless Cardiff acted immediately, it would be too late. It might already be too late. If there was still a chance for his idea to work, he had to hear about the arrest.

A courier couldn't be trusted to take such a sensitive message past the international sector's guards, if they even allowed a messenger in at night. That left only her. But going to the consulate by herself in the dark would be scandalous. She had to meet Cardiff-*sama* at the Pendletons' home. Secretly.

Checking that no one was nearby, she unbarred the shutters to the guest room's outside panel in case the back entrance was locked later. She drew her cloak around her and made sure the dirk she wore for the first time was secure in her sash. Then she slipped out their gate and crept beyond the park to the main street.

The dark shadows helped hide her while she waited for a *kago*. Distant stars twinkled, yet the night's suffocating darkness stole her breath.

Would a *kago* ever pass by? Time was her enemy.

Finally porters stopped to let out a passenger a little distance down the street. One of the men leered at her when she approached. "Too late for a samurai princess to be out, don'cha think?" he remarked to his partner.

Fear squeezing her heart, she allowed a glimpse of her dirk as she drew out coins.

"I reckon it's the lady's affair," the other responded.

She set her jaw and climbed in. She couldn't fail in her mission. A prison held her father like an injured water buffalo waiting to be slaughtered.

A guard at the first gate between the city's sections demanded to know her business.

She hid her trembling hands and spoke in a forceful voice. "A relative requires the Western medicine."

He narrowed his eyes. A minute ticked by that seemed like a lifetime. Finally, he muttered for them to proceed.

When the *kago* had passed beyond the light from the gate's lanterns, she fell back against the cushion. She'd made it through the first barrier.

At each succeeding checkpoint, the lead porter spoke for her, his gravelly voice exuding more and more confidence. As Sumi expected, however, the unbending guards at the international sector stopped the porters and motioned for the *kago* to withdraw.

She alighted, raised her chin, and walked up to the gate. "Mrs. Pendleton waits for my translation work," she said in both English and Japanese. Her voice's tremor threatened to expose the falsehood. She bowed, then pointed in the direction of the Pendletons' home. Suddenly remembering the excuse given at the previous checkpoints, she quickly added, "My relative is in dire need of the Western medicine the lady promised as payment."

One guard shook his head, and another said, "An improbable story. More likely a rendezvous."

Black despair threatened her. Her father's life could be lost because of these two unfeeling men.

Then a British redcoat, posted inside the gate, waved for her to enter. One of the guards shrugged and opened the gate. After promising the staring porters two extra coins to hold the *kago* for her return, she walked into the international sector with all the dignity she could muster.

Mr. Pendleton opened the door after her first knock. He looked beyond her as though expecting an escort, then welcomed her into the parlor, not betraying any astonishment. At her tense request, he agreed to fetch Cardiff.

She struggled to breathe when she heard Cardiff-*sama*'s voice in the vestibule. Was she hoping for the impossible? No matter how exceptional, how much could a foreigner do?

Mrs. Pendleton asked her husband's assistance in the kitchen, providing privacy.

"Miss Taguchi, how can I help you?" Concern shone in Cardiff's eyes. "Richard indicated an emergency, and certainly it must be a serious one for you to be out at night . . . alone."

"My father was arrested today." Her voice cracked. "He's innocent!"

He slapped his hand down on the back of a chair. "Of course he is innocent! What was the charge? Did you hear?"

"No. They just dragged him off." Her voice shook despite her efforts.

Cardiff's fist clenched. "His arrest must be connected to the illegal item found at the consulate. At the time, its discovery seemed a grim threat, but only to me, not to anyone else."

Sumi swallowed. What item? Could she ask?

"It's better not to know the exact details," Cardiff continued, as though reading her mind, "in case an official questions you."

"You're an extraordinary foreigner," she blurted out. "Is there anything you can do? A kind of *negotiation*?"

"I'm an ordinary man, Miss Taguchi. But I do have an extraordinary source to turn to—the Almighty's good hands. I'll pay Governor Nakamura a visit first thing in the morning. If what I suspect is the cause, I *might* have a solution."

A thin thread of hope glimmered. Cardiff-*sama*'s god probably had no more interest in helping than hers, but the man himself could sway people. She'd seen the effects of his *ki*, his calm determination while facing the samurai's sword, also during the trial, and at the ball, in fact, every time she'd been with him.

She stood. "Thank you. You are always kind beyond what we deserve."

He rose quickly. "No. As I said before, you and I are in this together. Now, we'd best get you home." His brow wrinkled. "How did you pass through all the sectors' gates? I would think a samurai's daughter moving through the city by herself at night would raise suspicions."

"I said Western medicine was needed for a relative. It's somewhat true. Rescue for my father would be the best medicine."

"Indeed." He rubbed his forehead. "I'll ask Mrs. Pendleton to give you a packet of herbs to satisfy any overly officious guard. Richard and I can accompany you home if that wouldn't draw too much attention."

"I won't need an escort, but thank you. A *kago* is waiting at the gate."

"Then we'll escort you to the gate." He took her hand and squeezed it for a second. "Let's trust that the truth will set your father free."

His tender touch brought her close to tears again.

When two guards asked to see the medicine on the return trip, Sumi held up the packet, thankful for Cardiff's foresight. After reaching home, she crept around the outside of the house. The back entrance was shuttered, so she slipped in through the guest room.

"Where have you been?" Kiyo accosted her in the hall, her eyes glinting in the lantern's light.

Sumi jerked back. "I've been . . . in the garden. Where else?"

"I think not. I looked behind *every* tree, bush, and rock."

"Then you need spectacles. I sat there, meditating."

Kiyo put a hand on her hip. "My eyesight is fine. What is not fine is your honesty. Meditate about that."

Sumi looked Kiyo right in the eye, pushing away the paralyzing thought of being reported to her grandfather. "And you had better meditate on caring about your aunt's husband. While you were senselessly hunting for me, you could have done something worthwhile. You could have . . . burned incense."

Kiyo harrumphed. "You don't fool me. Not for one instant." She wagged her finger. "To sneak out after what happened today is disgusting beyond words."

Sumi gasped. What was Kiyo implying? Whatever, it wasn't good. She clasped her hands to keep from slapping her.

Hatred mingled with grief for her father. Her chest heaved with silent sobs as she shoved past her loathsome cousin.

Muffled chants led her to her mother and grandfather, bowing before the god shelf. She joined in although beseeching the gods and spirits never seemed effective. At least, her show of outward piety would make any tattle by Kiyo less believable. Besides, she couldn't bear to be near her cousin, or even worse—alone.

CHAPTER 30

John entered the audience room and bowed to Governor Nakamura, noticing the British consulate's interpreter had been called to translate in Taguchi's place.

The governor frowned and motioned for John to sit. "My time is short. State your pressing business." He offered no refreshments or pipes, a definite insult.

John folded his arms and nodded. As if enticing a fierce dog with red meat, he would dangle a hint of his proposal. "My trading company has reached a new understanding. It concerns munitions."

The governor arched an eyebrow, indicating interest or suspicion.

"I assume the Japanese government still has a need to purchase guns," John added.

The governor's eyes narrowed. "Yes, of course."

"Because of our new stance, Cardiff & Associates is willing to import and sell a limited number to the shogunate through your office."

"What has caused this *new* inclination?" The governor's voice carried unmistakable sarcasm.

John inhaled. Instead of an adversarial attitude, the governor should be delighted. So, most likely he really suspected John of spying.

"Trade is dependent on a country's law and order." He maintained a tone of deliberate patience. "I have invested a goodly amount of my resources here, as have the other American traders I represent. All our assets and profits hinge on stability."

He handed the governor the contract with only a slight bow. "My company wants to contribute to your government's strength."

The governor had the interpreter translate the contract's words twice, then stopped the flustered translator from finishing the third attempt. "It appears you are offering to sell ten *cases* of Spencer repeating rifles." He stared at John.

"Precisely." John met the governor's eyes and saw bewilderment there, far greater than when he'd finagled the governor's gift of land for the Taguchis' home. John waited, giving Nakamura time to gather his wits and reach the only possible conclusion: no one guilty of aiding a United States invasion would build up the Shōgun's armaments.

Nakamura, brow furrowed, stamped the contract and had his retainer show it briefly to the Shōgun's agent, who was earnestly recording the transaction, his glass of sherry all but forgotten.

John affixed his signature next to the governor's stamp. "I will place the order immediately." He cleared his throat. "I would like to bring up an unrelated matter. Although I am grateful for this translator, I am concerned about Interpreter Taguchi's absence."

The governor pursed his lips. "He is indisposed."

"I am sorry to hear that. The United States values his excellent work."

Nakamura inclined his head, but made no reply. He spoke to the retainer holding his sword. John had learned enough Japanese to understand the words "halt" and "questioning" among a few others surrounding Taguchi's name. The next moment, the governor bowed curtly to John, announced the end of the interview, and walked straight into the garden adjoining the audience room.

John rose and looked around until a vice governor hurried forward, bowed, and offered to accompany John out of the residency. John walked next to the official, silently bemoaning his vulnerability. It was one thing to negotiate with foresight. It was entirely different while blindfolded.

Yet the Almighty's eyes were not closed nor his hand shortened.

Shortly after noon, footsteps stopped outside Kenshin's cell.

He sprang up. *The ultimate test!* He recalled the missionaries' words.

Another prisoner's shrieks kept time with the cracks of a bamboo rod. Kenshin steeled himself to bear the pain in silence.

The door grated open. The guard, steely eyed, motioned for Kenshin to come to the opening. He thrust out a scroll bearing the governor's seal.

Kenshin broke the seal and unrolled the parchment. The words blurred too much to read.

The guard huffed impatiently, but bowed abruptly after apparently glimpsing the message.

Blinking, Kenshin forced his eyes to move from one word to the next.

An investigation has been duly carried out.

Interpreter Taguchi Kenshin is no longer suspected in any crime.

No longer suspected! His vision cleared.

His release is thereby ordered.

He is not to speak of this matter.

Failure to keep this prohibition carries the penalty of banishment.

He touched the scroll to his forehead in thanksgiving, then squatted down to steady himself.

After giving him a minute to regain his senses, the guard led him out the building. Breathing in the fresh air, Kenshin exclaimed, "I'm free!" Unable to hold in his relief and astonishment, he started laughing.

A passing guard pointed at him. "The man's gone berserk."

Because of the prohibition, Kenshin didn't answer. But he thought, *Berserk? No! I've regained my mind. My life. My family's honor!*

Sumi heard a voice that sounded like her father's. Was she imagining it? She jumped up to investigate. Halfway down the stairs, she heard her father's voice again. "Is there no one to greet me? To rejoice at my freedom?"

She bounded down the rest of the stairs and flung herself down on the vestibule in front of him. "You're home! You're home!" Tears flowed in torrents. She couldn't stop them.

Her mother came sobbing and hiccupping behind her.

"Tears of happiness, I hope," he teased. He didn't reprove either of them for showing feelings so openly.

Sumi rose and dabbed at her wet cheeks. Her father looked uninjured. Healthy. Joyful.

"Seeing the light return to your eyes is what I have waited for," her mother sobbed out.

"I'd like to explain." Her father gazed at both of them. "But I am forbidden to speak about the trouble. I can just say that at noon today I ceased being a suspect. I endured no torture to prove my innocence. My release came like a bolt of lightning. Sudden. Unexpected."

Her mother ran a hand across his chest. "To be dragged off to prison while doing your best to serve the governor—horrible, unbelievable!" She mustered a shaky smile. "But you have returned."

Sumi's grandfather stepped onto the veranda. "You conquered." His solemn tone and stiff back didn't mask the underlying elation.

Warmth flowed through Sumi as if the sun itself shone inside her. Yes, her father conquered. He had withstood the evil threat. But the lightning bolt most likely came from Cardiff-*sama*. Her family had been vulnerable, even having four arrows united—one more than the three the Mori *daimyō* had prescribed. But a fifth arrow from a foreigner, certainly not from her cousin, made the difference.

She followed her parents inside, then stood stock still. Was she forgetting another arrow? Could the *good hands* of the foreign god have helped after all? How much power did this so-called *Almighty* one really possess?

Nobumitsu sauntered through a grove of towering fir trees toward the Shinto shrine's posterior building. He had been given a space to sleep there for the times he wanted to avoid the consulate's servant quarters. This night he wanted to avoid everyone—the barbarians and fellow countrymen alike.

He looked through the evergreen branches at the dark sky. The gods were like the glittering stars, aloof and indifferent. They had watched the removal of the charges against Interpreter Taguchi and the consul without interfering. Even worse, they allowed the loss of the second son's small force in the future joint strike. Retainer Yamamoto no longer walked the earth. Kohei had sworn to spread seeds of rebellion during his forced pilgrimage, but that didn't compare to providing warriors and their swords.

Nobumitsu stopped walking at an explosive sound from the dark wood. A shadowy shape flew straight toward him. He swung his arm up to protect his head. The ghost of his clansman, clearer than ever! Still shielding his head, he dropped to his knees, ready to plead for mercy, for who could stand against a spirit?

Then the heron settled on its nest.

He groaned. Could he never be free from this haunting? Eight years had passed since he'd stealthily struck down his sweetheart's father for betrothing his daughter to another. Nobumitsu's initial satisfaction in exacting revenge had dissolved into self-loathing for his murder of a loyal clansman.

His mission had to succeed even without Kohei's help. Perhaps then the gods would overlook his long-ago betrayal.

CHAPTER 31

August (Month of the Rooster)

"Dog days." Sumi wrote the newest phrase for Cardiff's dictionary with the quill pen she'd finally mastered. She cocked her head. "You said we're experiencing them now, but next month is the month of the dog, and the day of the dog won't be for another nine days. Although this is the year of the monkey, I don't believe translating them as "monkey days" would be any better."

The corner of Cardiff's lips hinted at a smile. "Dog days aren't connected to the zodiac. They're hot and humid summer days, muggy days. The name's related to a group of stars called Canis Major. The constellation reminds people of the outline of a dog."

"Then I suggest *mushi atsui* to describe this month's weather. Maybe the idea of dogs would be hard to explain."

While writing the Japanese, she imagined sitting next to Cardiff under a starry sky, instead of across the table from him in his library. Perhaps they would be on a grassy hillside. He would scan the sky, point at what resembled an aerial dog, then watch her upturned gaze.

She quickly blotted the drop of ink that fell on the page and gave Cardiff-*sama* a wobbly smile, very glad he wasn't a mind reader.

He patted the sweat from his brow with a handkerchief and glanced across the table at her work. "This dictionary is invaluable and so is your tutoring. I can't tell you how thankful I am for these lessons, both your father's and yours. You are especially quick to catch meanings and see implications."

Impossible implications. The daughter of a samurai would *not* be gazing at stars with any man outside her family, let alone with a foreigner, no matter how extraordinary.

She added the finished page to the dictionary's pile. "Tutoring will never repay you for the help you gave my father. Your negotiation with the governor was powerful."

"I don't know how effective it was, but it came about because of your bravery. Almost like a Japanese Paul Revere." He smiled and took a sip of tea.

"Paro?"

"Paul Revere. He made a daring trip at night to warn the Americans about the enemy's action."

She treasured his look of approval. "I've kept that trip a secret."

"I thought as much. I'll guard my words."

"I've been curious about the negotiation." She fanned herself, suddenly more aware of the dog day's heat. "Is it still a secret?"

"No, I can talk about it now. I believe the charge against your father stemmed from a map Retainer Yamamoto found in the consulate's office."

"A Japanese map?"

"One of the capital, Edo."

Sumi felt faint. How easily her father could have been killed, her family ruined, Cardiff-*sama* expelled. "It was worse than my greatest fears. How did you persuade the governor that you and my father were innocent?"

"You may not approve." He straightened the papers and notebooks in front of him and then looked at her. "I agreed for my company to sell guns to the shogunate. However, I'm not sure how much difference that made."

Her heart lurched. "Guns! For hunting?"

"They aren't for shooting animals." He took a deep breath. "Maybe an additional militia trained in their use can help deter any revolt. Save lives."

"Aah, I see." *Not so barbaric.* "Only an ally would provide weapons. Governor Nakamura must have realized that."

"Right. But I still wonder who took the blame for concocting the false charge. Surely the governor didn't believe the groundskeeper —my suspect for placing the map—did it alone. And the government couldn't just bury the case."

"I'll tell what I overheard my father tell my mother, but it is in *confidence*, as you say. One day last week, Chief Inspector Sato visited with my grandfather in a teahouse. I think he wanted our family to know that justice had been carried out. He mentioned that Retainer Yamamoto committed ceremonial suicide to atone for failure in serving his master."

"So it sounds like he was what we'd call a sacrificial lamb, taking the blame."

"There was more. The chief inspector also said Governor Nakamura ordered his second son to set out on a religious pilgrimage—for two years."

"A two-year pilgrimage?" Cardiff leaned forward. "Is that common here?"

"Unheard of for someone like Kohei-*sama*, and this pilgrimage, on foot, will be hard. He must visit every Buddhist temple on this island and the eighty-eight Shingon Buddhist temples on the island of Shikoku."

"Well, with that kind of discipline meted out, I'd say the governor suspected his son of going astray. Of masterminding the plot. Wouldn't you agree?"

"Yes, even though the chief inspector didn't explain. He told my grandfather he couldn't discuss the matter further."

"So blame fell on both the retainer and the son. Yet their guilt had to be established somehow."

"In the United States of America, there may not be so many observers. Here, almost everything that happens is witnessed by both friend and enemy—government *metsuke,* priests, headmen, neighbors, workmen, and servants. Especially servants. I heard Chief Inspector Sato interviewed many people, including your housekeeper."

He shook his head in apparent wonderment. "Thank God the truth came out no matter the source."

Just then a boom in the harbor announced an incoming ship. Cardiff jumped up and rushed to the door, then stopped and turned slowly around, shaking his head. "Only the local steamer from Edo. Forgot this is the second Tuesday. I'm waiting for important news from back home." He sank back into his chair. "Anyway, our study session is a splendid change from refereeing disagreements, dealing with suppliers, and writing reports. Endless reports."

"Maybe I can offer you another good change." She started to pick up her fan, but resisted. "My family asked me to invite you for dinner on Thursday. We are planning appetizing dishes."

"I can think of nothing I'd like better. Much better than shooting billiards with Phillip Gray on Thursday by a long shot, who by the way sends his regards. He's given up studying Japanese."

"Please give him my regards too." Although she wouldn't miss him at all.

Cardiff's eyes held a teasing twinkle. "Appetizing dishes? I wonder if sea slugs are in the offering."

"We could add them." She paused. The twinkle had disappeared. "No, now I remember the sea slugs at the rest house. Your face turned a strange color—almost green. So, you don't really want any."

His grin confirmed her assumption.

"We've planned tempura, spinach and sesame salad, summer oranges—all your favorites, I think—and a surprise for what you call dessert."

"More than enough without the slugs."

She wondered if he'd actually winked.

Sumi checked with the cook on the final touches to the stewed apple-pears she had ordered in an imitation of Mrs. Pendleton's pie filling. Her father's restored wellbeing, her grandfather's approval of the foreigner, Kiyo's visit to a friend's house—everything was perfect for the consul's visit.

Cardiff, dressed in a fawn-colored suit and white waistcoat, arrived exactly on time. He presented the family with a large basket of fruit, including an imported pineapple and bananas, which Sumi's mother set as a display in their main room's *tokonoma*.

Sumi knelt on a cushion an acceptable distance from

Cardiff and listened proudly as her pupil praised the meal's dishes and made small talk with her father and grandfather in Japanese. At her mother's cough, she startled, aware she'd been staring. She darted her eyes to the men's trays to check for dishes that needed replenishing and reminded herself to keep tight control over her feelings. She was Cardiff-*sama's* tutor first and then his friend. A good friend. Nothing more.

The conversation turned to the furnishings in the new home. Cardiff reverted to English, so translations became necessary.

"The paintings on those screens are beautiful. Did a professional artist create them?" Cardiff looked at Sumi for the answer, and the family's gaze followed his.

She silently thanked him for his effort to include her. "Grandfather painted those scenes. He's bringing us more of our previous home's beauty little by little."

Her grandfather motioned for Sumi to continue translating. "We elders cherish the ancient and subtle," he said with the hint of a challenge. "But the younger generation likes the new and vivid. What do you think, Cardiff-*dono?*"

"Hmm." Cardiff held up his hand in the pose of an art admirer. "I like the traditional subject of nature. It pulls the garden with its delicate shades into the house." He smiled at Sumi's grandfather. "And I like the fresh colors that celebrate this family's power to prosper." He smiled at her and her father.

"Some are artists with paint. You are an artist with diplomacy," her grandfather responded.

Sumi nodded with her parents. The consul's answer couldn't have been better. Even if he still had one or two of the barbarians' customs, his visit to their home made her feel—how did the Pendletons describe it—as happy as a clam at high tide.

"I must say," Cardiff added, "the beauty everywhere in this

country is impressive. I'm looking forward to showing my fiancée—the lady I intend to marry—some of the charming places in this city and the nearby countryside. I hope Miss Gray will visit Japan this fall. Mr. Taguchi, you and Miss Taguchi know her brother, Phillip Gray."

Sumi caught her breath, going over the words with the sharp, cutting edges, scarcely believing she'd heard correctly. She struggled to look cheerful despite her churning stomach.

"Ah yes, a fine gentleman," her father said. "My family and I will be happy to help during your betrothed's visit any way we can."

Sumi rose and began refilling each person's cup of tea. Bowing and murmuring the required responses, she moved from person to person. She couldn't trust herself to say anything else.

The consul's marital status had never been mentioned. She'd assumed he had no ties other than the female friend he'd mentioned in faraway New York. So, his betrothal was why he had been more reserved than other foreigners in the presence of women. More than that, it explained why he had initially shown no enthusiasm for the dictionary. She must have seemed very foolish standing before him and his *fiancée's brother,* expecting his praise.

Her heart ached as much as when she had faced the betrothal to the Kurohashi grandson. Yet she never dreamed of marrying a Westerner. Certainly not! How could she? The foreign lady's presence need not affect her relationship with Cardiff-*sama*. All could continue unchanged. Should she be upset? Of course not.

Despite assuring herself all was still well, each minute dragged by until Cardiff exited their gate and she escaped to her room.

CHAPTER 32

October (Month of the Pig)

John's heart sang when he saw Catherine wave from the steamer. Springing up the ladder from his company's cutter to his ship's deck, he felt as though he were living out a dream. But this time he wouldn't wake up to disappointment.

"Darling, you're here at last!" He couldn't restrain himself from kissing her cheek.

"Now, John. Let's not make ourselves a spectacle." She glanced at the captain standing nearby.

John stepped back. He should have been more thoughtful. Naturally she would be on edge in these strange surroundings. He turned to greet Captain Whitson.

Whitson grinned at them. "Madam, one of my duties is to report to the American consul whenever one is stationed at my port of call. I also have to report to the ship's owner. Since the consul and owner are one and the same, I appreciate the remarkable service here."

"Well then, all is forgiven." Catherine adjusted her hat with its ostrich feather and tilted her head. "I might have been out of my mind to take this trip, but now that I've survived, it's wonderful to see you too, John. I'm relieved you're in such good health, and also you, Phillip." She offered her hand to Phillip, who had followed John up the ladder. He gave her gloved hand a quick peck.

"I've been counting the days and hours." John gazed at her face, mesmerized by her blue eyes and rosy lips.

"As have I. You can't imagine how eager I am to be rid of this ship even if it is your company's. Let me just say my goodbyes."

While Catherine bid others on board farewell, John set a later time to hear the captain's full report, then instructed his staring stevedore to see to unloading the imports of patterned cotton material, sugar, farming implements, and blacksmith tools. It was too soon for his munitions' order to arrive.

He helped Catherine into the wooden gamming chair that lowered her from the steamer to the cutter's deck. Her poise and the way she kept her blue gown modestly arranged struck him as admirable, yet he couldn't help but wonder at the long-lived fashion of frilly, ballooning skirts with a bustle on the back. He must have become too accustomed to the kimono's simple lines. He pushed away an image of Miss Taguchi gracefully serving him tea.

After guiding Catherine through the customs house formalities, he helped her into his rented buggy for the ride to the Commercial Hotel. She seemed more intent on recounting the voyage to him and Phillip than seeing the sights, but he didn't mind. She'd had a long, taxing trip.

"We saw only the ocean's surface day after day," she complained, "and when we did reach ports of call on the South American coast, Cousin Elizabeth didn't want to venture onto land and advised me to stay on board too. We didn't even spend the night in a hotel in Honolulu, but transferred directly onto the *Retriever*."

"You're fortunate both ships avoided any major storms," John inserted when she paused for breath. "I hope Miss Elizabeth enjoys visiting her uncle. How did she feel about her stopover in Yokohama?"

"She expressed relief at seeing people who looked like Americans on the pier. Although I imagine she crocheted in the hotel room while waiting to board for Shanghai."

Catherine suddenly pointed out the carriage window. "Oh, those men with the split-skirt trousers and tunics must be the samurai. Look how their swords stick up like a rooster's tail when they bow." She stifled a laugh. "Are you sure they're friendly?"

"They serve the governor, and if a problem arose, they would quickly come to our aid." How lucky she'd glimpsed those particular samurai first, John thought. Perhaps she wouldn't ask about others—ones who might not be as friendly.

While the buggy was passing along the settlement's second block of stores, a small group of children followed along and shouted with hands held out. Catherine clutched her reticule. "You didn't mention beggars in your letters, John."

"They aren't beggars. The populace has enough to eat these days, at least in this area. Those rascals are just asking for the candies I usually have in my pocket."

"So you're at it again with the little ones. What a soft touch you are."

"You disapprove?"

"No, no. I'm glad you haven't changed, at least in that respect."

Had he changed? New York and home seemed like a fictional place. Even his beloved Catherine appeared almost a stranger. But she was finally next to him again, and he had the coming days to rejuvenate their relationship.

John noted Catherine's pleased look as she looked around the hotel's European-style lobby. She'd see Japan offered comforting touches of the West along with the country's fascinating uniqueness. He led her and Phillip toward the reception desk. Just as he rang the little bell to call the clerk, the grandfather clock John faced began swaying back and forth. The next second the whole room was moving and rattling. And then the tremor stopped. Those around them resumed business as though nothing had happened.

Catherine's face paled. "Good heavens! Is it safe? Was that an earthquake?"

John put his hands on her shoulders, shaking his head at the timing. "Just a tremor. They won't worry you as much after you've been here a while, will they, Phillip?"

When her brother rolled his eyes, John went on. "Really, you won't even notice them. None of the hotel staff got excited, did they? Of course, if the shaking should grow in intensity, then you'd need to get out of the building."

"But if I'm in my room on the second floor, I won't be able to escape before the building collapses."

"It won't collapse, Sis," Phillip said, finally doing his part. "There are lots of tremors, but virtually no killer quakes. I've been told there's only one or two in a century in the whole country."

"Right," John said. "An old wives' tale here claims the catfish under the islands cause the quakes, and that only happens when the gods aren't carefully watching them. The gods were probably distracted when they saw a beautiful lady disembark a short time ago."

Catherine took a deep breath. "At any rate, I'm glad I have two brave men here with me."

"It'll take a while to get used to all the new sights and sounds. But you'll come to love this country as I do." John paused to sign a paper and initial a chit for the clerk. "I'll enjoy showing you my favorite spots. We'll have a great time—guaranteed."

He slid the papers across the counter and gazed into her eyes. "You're not planning on returning to New York any time soon, are you? Your letter didn't say."

Catherine looked down and smoothed her shawl. "I haven't decided yet. Let's just see how things go. I hope you're right. I hope very much I will love this country."

"Just don't tell her the tale about the forty-seven *rōnin*," Phillip said dryly.

"Yes, I'll wait on that one." John winked at Catherine, pretending lightness. Before talking about any menace—unlikely as danger might be—he'd introduce his fiancée to the grand sights and fine people. She'd catch the spirit of adventure, and *her* loveliness would recapture his thoughts—as well they should.

To John's relief, Catherine announced the next day that she looked forward to sightseeing. Having studied the vicinity of the hotel from her balcony, she'd been impressed by the clean streets. When John assured her that his *kago* would lead the way, she even agreed to ride in one to a nearby temple's park.

Interpreter Taguchi joined them on the park's stone path, which led to a ceremonial teahouse. John greeted him cheerfully although disappointed that Miss Taguchi hadn't come instead. It would have been nice for Catherine to not only meet Miss Taguchi but also hear her livelier explanations.

They approached the teahouse and met a diminutive, yellow-robed monk.

"Come with me," Taguchi translated for the Buddhist monk. "I will explain the truth underlying what you see."

The monk paused outside the teahouse and pointed to the roof. "These beams protect us from the changeable weather. The Buddha tells us change is the only certainty."

"What a strange thought," Catherine said after the translation, "but I suppose it may be true."

John could think of other certainties. Perhaps he'd return another time and engage the monk in a deeper discussion.

Everyone slipped off their shoes and bent down to enter the building's interior through the low door, constructed to induce humility. Catherine's olive-green gown dragged the floor and nearly tripped her. John steadied her while bending over double.

The small matted room they entered was bare except for the tea ceremony's instruments and a hibachi for heating the water. With John's help, Catherine managed to kneel and rest back on her heels in the midst of her ruffled skirt. John knelt next to her, forming a semi-circle with Mr. Taguchi.

Once they were situated, she pursed her lips. "I must say this room is a letdown. There's nothing to see."

"I believe the sparseness is on purpose." John kept his voice low. "It's meant to refresh us. Allow our overtaxed senses to focus."

The sight of Miss Taguchi at the grotto glided into his

mind—the musical note of the bamboo, the butterflies, her closeness. The quietness. Her long lashes had curved up from her eyes, intent on watching the miniature waterfall.

The monk's soft cough tore him loose from the picture that should not have captivated him. He promised himself to do better as he listened to Mr. Taguchi's translation.

"The chirp of a bird or cricket makes us notice the room's silence. The simple adornment makes us aware of empty space, not cluttered by things and desires. We can imagine the peace of uniting with the universal force."

"Is what he's describing like heaven?" Catherine asked.

John resisted his impulse to ask her to speak more softly. Was he indeed being affected too much by this culture? In a loud whisper, he explained, "Not like heaven. All of a person's desire is replaced by the soul's absorption into that universal force." He would have broached the disturbing concept of the self's loss of identity, but Catherine straightened, and the monk appeared displeased with the distraction.

Once the tea had been whisked, they each swallowed their cup's bitter, foaming liquid, using just three-and-a-half gulps as instructed. Catherine had grimaced after the first gulp, but stoically completed the task. In fact, as they exited the teahouse a few minutes later, she joined John in thanking Mr. Taguchi and the monk for the memorable experience.

The positive outing encouraged John to schedule the climb to the place he was keenest to show Catherine. They would visit the grotto near the rest house and feel at one with nature and with each other.

The day started off well with a cool breeze blowing from the ocean. The housekeeper had adamantly refused to go this time, and Phillip had begged off with other plans. But John didn't worry about having a third person. After all, Catherine and he were engaged adults, and the hike would be on a well-traveled path.

As they climbed, Catherine remarked several times on the good view of the city stretching out beneath them toward the silver sheen of the bay. However, two-thirds of the way, she stopped and crossed her arms. "This is as far as I go."

John took a step back and stared at her. "Catherine, dear, the rest house is in a gorgeous spot. There's a miniature waterfall, a beautiful little pool. Aren't you eager to see it, so we can cherish the memory? You might even make sketches for a later painting."

"Let me repeat, John. This is as far as I go."

"How about resting, then taking a slower pace? The interpreter's daughter and my middle-aged housekeeper managed it in kimonos last spring."

"The interpreter's daughter wasn't recovering from an extremely hard journey, was she?" Her eyes squinted in irritation. "I also doubt a kimono poses more of a problem than a day dress. A lady's modest apparel isn't designed for climbing steep slopes."

"All right. I see the difficulty." He didn't remember her being so sensitive.

"Yes, and you should have considered the difficulty *before* we started on this exhausting trek." She shook her striped teal skirt to remove the dust and checked the heels on her Balmoral boots.

"Your being here is all that matters, whether we're on a hilltop or on level ground." He forbore mentioning she might have chosen shoes more suitable for a hike.

A Japanese family of four, clambering along the path, paused to give them the once over. Catherine looked away. John said *konichi-wa* to the giggling children and handed each a brass button, then bowed to their wide-eyed parents. The family bowed in return, thanked him profusely, and continued on their way, the middle-aged mother seeming to handle the hike well.

"I suppose you think I should pull myself together, do as well as those natives."

"I'm sure you would surpass them . . . under different conditions." Phillip was right, John reflected. Catherine preferred drinking tea with lemon to exploring.

"I'm not a native," she snapped. "And I have no intention of living like one!" She whipped around and began the descent.

Swallowing his disappointment and a retort that natives were structurally no different, he took her arm. "Here. Let me help you. A hike is not worth arguing over."

At the bottom of the hill, he paused, surveying the tree he had climbed on the previous jaunt. When Chief Inspector Sato had greeted Miss Taguchi, something had passed between the two—an understanding because of their culture. He'd felt cheated, a little like his present feeling. But then, he had no right or reason to feel that way with Miss Taguchi or Catherine.

He glanced at his sweetheart, who waited with a perplexed expression. "I chased a monkey up that tree once to rescue my keys," he admitted a bit sheepishly. "But no sign of it."

She glanced up at the tree. "It might be interesting to see a monkey outside a zoo, but I've no desire to watch for it now."

"Nor do I." He held out his arm for her to take.

Here was the one he had adored for years. Each venture simply brought its own rewards and challenges. Hefty challenges.

CHAPTER 33

Listening to their maid Kin's description of the current *kabuki* dramas, Sumi bemoaned her dilemma. Making arrangements for Catherine and Phillip Gray to attend the theater was more demanding than she'd expected.

Cardiff had asked her to escort the two in his stead since the commoners' plays were considered beneath the dignity of samurai and officials like the consul. The stories might cause a display of forbidden emotions, especially laughter or tears that signified childishness or weakness.

After making his request, Cardiff-*sama* had stood at the consulate gate, a beseeching look in his eyes. "I'm depending on your good judgment to select an appropriate play, Miss Taguchi," he'd instructed. "No violent revenge in the plot, please. No drama like that of the forty-seven *rōnin*. Perhaps you can understand how much I want Miss Gray to be favorably impressed."

She'd promised to do her best, for how could she possibly refuse anything he asked? But she couldn't magically make a suitable play appear. The current ones not containing revenge did contain prostitution, and she'd learned Christians disapproved, at least in theory, of extramarital sex.

A temptation crossed her mind while she held the handbill of one of the seamiest plays. Since the selection was so difficult anyway, perhaps if she chose this one, Catherine Gray would return more quickly to America, where she couldn't monopolize so much of Cardiff's time.

But no, after all Cardiff had done for her family, she could never be so disloyal.

She spent another hour of consultation with Kin, who attended the plays at every opportunity, and finally settled upon *The Fatal-Love of Kamiya-Jihei*. She supposed the foreigners would approve of the wife's devotion. At any rate, it appeared the best one available.

Enthusiastic theater-goers made a practice of arriving as early as 9:00 a.m. and staying as late as 9:00 p.m. for a series of plays. When Sumi arrived at 9:30 with her two charges, a large audience was already there. According to Catherine Gray, the building resembled a Western-style theater in that it had a stage, albeit a revolving one, a pit for the musicians, and balconies. The biggest difference, she remarked, was that everyone squatted on the floor, each family or party within its own enclosure.

Railings separating the various enclosures were used as aisles. Sumi bravely led the two foreigners down the narrow passageways, amid scores of exclamations about the *gaijin*. Miss Gray used her hands to press her hooped, peach-colored skirt so that much of its fluffy volume ballooned to the front or behind her. She tilted precariously several times.

249

Sumi breathed a sigh of relief when they arrived at their reserved area without mishap and just in time for the opening act.

After they were settled, Miss Gray studied the people around them, then frowned. "Why aren't the people listening to the play? Aren't they interested?" she asked Sumi.

Although the questions didn't make sense, Sumi replied the best she could. "The people *are* interested. This is a famous production with several of our country's best actors. In fact, you can see their crests on five of those lanterns hanging above us." She pointed toward the rafters.

"What I mean is"—Miss Gray sniffed and pointed at the group sitting next to them—"that the audience behaves as though they're at a church social."

"A church social?"

"What we're curious about," her brother said, "is why people are chatting and partaking of refreshments rather than paying attention to the story."

"That's because everyone here, except you and Miss Gray, knows all the details of the story. They care about the quality of acting and especially the poses."

"Poses? I don't follow you." Miss Gray sounded irritated, or at least impatient. The lady's genteel exterior might camouflage a short temper.

Careful not to respond in kind, Sumi pointed to the two motionless actors, one having a fist raised against the other. "You see what is happening now. This is an important time in the story. The pose—not moving at all—draws attention to this moment's event."

Miss Gray pursed her lips. "A very unusual custom. Those wailing noises and masks are peculiar too." She turned to her brother. "Unsettling, wouldn't you say?"

Her brother shrugged. "Not for me, but it's going to be a long day."

Sumi congratulated herself that neither of the Grays had voiced any objection to the story itself despite their other criticisms. Cardiff-*sama* would be pleased with her selection . . . and with her polite explanations if he knew.

Then halfway through the play, Miss Gray began to fidget. "It's a sordid theme," she pronounced.

Her brother had an amused look.

Sumi tensed and redoubled her efforts at translation, trying to phrase her words just right. If only the Grays would give the play a chance, they wouldn't find so much to censure. "Don't you think the male actors show admirable skill in the female roles?" Surely they'd agree to one good point.

"They're men?" the two exclaimed in unison.

"Why don't women play those roles?" Miss Gray asked.

"Years ago, women of the street—I think you call them *prostitutes*—did act in them. The Shōgun of that time wanted to protect the people from bad influence, so he banned actresses from *kabuki*."

"Evidently he didn't succeed in his puritanical efforts," Miss Gray muttered.

The lady complained several more times, primarily disapproving of the wife's role. She announced the minute the play ended that one drama was sufficient. She wished to return to her hotel immediately.

Sumi was more than happy to oblige.

Once outside, Sumi procured two *kago* right away, but they had to wait on the theater's front pavilion for a porter to bring the last one. During a lull in the street noises, Sumi ventured to ask if the Grays' father was a samurai in New York.

"I suppose you mean a soldier," Miss Gray replied. "No, he isn't. Is yours?"

"Oh yes, my family line has been samurai for hundreds of years."

Miss Gray lifted her chin proudly. "Our father is the owner of a carpet manufacturing company."

"Then your family is in the artisan class, I believe." Sumi tried to think how to be most tactful. "I'm sure we agree that's much better than being merchants. Your family must have wonderful—"

"Why is that? I'm not sure we do agree."

"I'm sorry. I didn't mean to bring up an unpleasant subject." Perhaps Catherine Gray wasn't proud of her family's status after all. Her strange blue eyes certainly looked disturbed.

"No, I'd like to know why you're saying the artisan class is better than merchants."

"Because the merchant class doesn't produce anything." Absurd question or not, she had to show patience for Cardiff's sake. "Merchants are unavoidable in these modern times, but they live off other people's work. Although artisans are not as important as the farmers, who produce our food, they contribute many appreciated items. I'm sure your family is talented, Miss Gray."

Sumi waved away a vendor carrying two water buckets. She wished the sellers of amulets, bamboo whisks, and countless other items would stop jostling them and pursue the many other people entering and exiting the theater.

Miss Gray shot an angry look at a seller of wash basins, who banged them noisily as he walked by, then tilted her head toward Sumi. "I see. So which do you deem to be a higher class, soldiers or artisans?"

Sumi almost laughed. "Samurai, the 'soldiers.' They protect us. Of course, we have to fulfill the duties where we find ourselves, don't we? We have a saying that if one is a pepper, he should the best pepper, not try to be a squash or an eggplant. Perhaps you have the same saying in America."

She paused, expecting a word of agreement. When the Grays remained silent and stared at her, she opted for a compliment. "Your artisan family did amazingly well in your betrothal to one of samurai status. Such a match would be very difficult to achieve here."

The lady still seemed to be at a loss for words, and her brother snickered. Sumi decided to change the subject. "I hope you liked the play and my translation was not too poor."

"Your translation was satisfactory, I'm sure, but the subject matter was deplorable."

"Now be careful what you say," her brother said. He frowned at another water vendor, who circled them warily. "Miss Taguchi accompanied us as a favor. Don't make a mountain out of a molehill."

"Well, she did choose the play, you know."

Sumi's heart beat faster. "I thought you might approve of the wife's loyalty even though the husband made many mistakes. The family sacrificed the children's clothes, but at least they didn't sell their daughter to a pleasure house . . . like some poor peasant families."

At that moment the third *kago* arrived, and they got into their individual conveyances. At the hotel, Miss Gray offered the most perfunctory of thanks.

Sumi watched her walk slowly toward the hotel, the gown's bustle exaggerating the lady's posterior. How inscrutable the foreigner was. What did Cardiff-*sama* find delightful about Miss Gray? His status was much higher than her family's. The *equality* Sumi had heard about must make that less of a problem in America, at least for those not owned as slaves.

John joined Catherine in the hotel for dinner. After they were seated, he smiled at her over the candle floating in a bowl topped with rose petals. "Well, how did you like the play? As good as expected?"

She didn't return his smile. "The costumes were gorgeous. The unique style of acting was interesting, especially how males played the female roles. But the play itself, I'm sorry to say, was utterly disgusting."

"Disgusting?" He was ready to order his favorite dish of prawns, but pushed aside thoughts of food, hoping Miss Taguchi hadn't made too bad a selection.

"Yes, the hero, for lack of a better term, was a good-for-nothing who deserted his family for a woman of ill-repute. Finally, due to the husband's stupidity, he and his paramour perished, and none too soon."

"Not the best of themes. Of course, Shakespeare also talked of women of ill-repute at times. I suppose the heroine came out looking better in contrast to the rotten husband."

"No, I'm afraid not. The wife actually encouraged her husband to redeem the immoral tramp." Catherine met his eyes with a determined squint. "Unbelievably, the inane wife offered to take a position in her *own* household no better than a maid. A maid, John! As if that were not insanity enough, she offered to let the husband pawn all her clothes and the children's clothes.

And, I might add, the fawning audience heartily approved. I tell you, I'll never get over my repulsion!"

"And Miss Taguchi, did she also seem repulsed? Or apologetic?"

"Why no. She seemed to think pawning clothes wasn't so bad because at least the daughter hadn't been sold to a 'pleasure house.' Can you imagine?"

"Pawning the family's clothes is a new low, I agree." *What has Miss Taguchi done?* "And Phillip? What did he think?"

"Why, he concurred with my assessment. Surely you wouldn't value his opinion over mine if he hadn't."

"Of course not. I'm just having a hard time understanding how Miss Taguchi could make such a poor selection, or not mention a problem if nothing better was available."

"John, I must tell you, she also explained why my family's status ranks below soldiers and peasants. Father's manufacturing business places him in the *artisan* class, putting my status far below hers in the *highest* class."

"She knows very little about the outside world."

"That's not all. She congratulated me on my good fortune of being promised to one of *your* status."

In an entirely different situation, John would have laughed.

Catherine frowned. "It sounds rather funny now, but at the time, it seemed quite rude."

"I can't imagine why Miss Taguchi would be anything less than courteous. I've never seen her be rude. Like I said, she hasn't been exposed to much besides her own culture."

Catherine gazed at him and cleared her throat. "There's also the possibility she doesn't like her friendship with you being interrupted—by me. Maybe she wanted to show me this country's seamier side. If so, she succeeded royally."

John rubbed the back of his neck, wishing there was a way to undo the harm. Whether or not tainted by a predisposition to find fault, Catherine's opinion was what mattered. "I'm sorry you and Phillip had such an unpleasant time."

Catherine slipped a handkerchief from her reticule and patted her forehead. "We survived, but it *has* brought on a headache, so if you don't mind, I'll skip dinner and retire early. I'm sure I'll be in better spirits tomorrow." She moved her menu to one side.

"I guess I was plain wrong to depend on my tutor's judgment."

"Or perhaps the difficulty lies more with her character. It's good to become aware of someone's true nature, isn't it? People can fool us when we see them in only one type of setting."

"In that case, I should thank you for pointing out her flaws." But he felt no gratitude whatsoever.

After escorting Catherine to the hotel's second-floor landing, he returned to his table, but the formerly enticing odors now irritated him. He left a tip for the waiter and walked out. Taking a seat in the lobby, he prepared his pipe and marshaled his thoughts.

In all his interaction with Miss Taguchi, he'd sensed a deeply rooted integrity and sensitivity. But she had clearly chosen an inappropriate play. She couldn't really be that ignorant of some of his culture's most cherished values, could she?

And what was this business about telling Catherine her family was in a low class? Yes, he knew the pecking order of the four classes in Japan—samurai, then farmer, then artisan, and last merchant—but that wouldn't give her the right to be impolite.

He lit his pipe and took several puffs. Then snuffed it out. Unable to stay seated, he rose and headed for the door, still digesting the situation.

Miss Taguchi must have spent hundreds of hours on the dictionary to please him. Recently—in fact, since the evening he'd mentioned his fiancée—she hadn't been her buoyant self. So Catherine's accusation of jealousy could indeed be a possibility.

He kicked a stone off the road and let out a breath. The last thing he needed was for Miss Taguchi to try to contend with the lady he was committed to marry.

CHAPTER 34

Arriving at the hotel the next morning, Sumi found Cardiff and the Grays seated in the lobby. The men rose and returned her bow, but Catherine Gray merely tipped her head. *Like an imperial princess might acknowledge a commoner*, Sumi thought.

"We've been discussing our plans for today." Cardiff drew a chair into the circle for her. "I'm encouraging the Grays to ride on an excursion with us into the countryside. Phillip is leaning toward visiting the Russian bazaar instead. What is your opinion?"

Sumi carefully arranged her green-and-gold kimono as she sat and then took a second to weigh the options, determined to give good advice. "The horseback ride would provide beautiful scenes—bamboo and evergreen groves, and maybe a nice riverbank for a picnic, but a lady rider might draw a lot of attention and also be tiring to anyone used to carriages." Sumi glanced at Miss Gray. "The bazaar is a good place to find the items foreigners prefer."

"Ah, Catherine, you see," Cardiff said, a smile replacing his worry lines, "Miss Taguchi is looking out for you despite my preference."

No smile brightened the lady's face. "Perhaps she doesn't realize American women can and do ride horseback."

Sumi blinked. How had her advice turned into an insult?

Phillip Gray snorted. "Maybe you've given that mistaken impression, Sis. But I have a different reason for recommending the bazaar. I took a little jaunt of my own while you two were roaming around town. I've seen just as pretty scenes in the Adirondacks, and none quite as disturbing as the five skinned monkeys that hung for sale in one of the village stalls. They looked for all the world like children."

Catherine gasped in horror.

Sumi sniffed. The lady shouldn't be shocked. After all, Americans hunted deer and ate soft, wooly sheep.

"Don't judge too—" Cardiff clamped his mouth shut.

The floor was shaking. Several chairs slid toward the window, and a vase wobbled on the table in front of them, then flew off the table and shattered on the floor. A row of books clattered off a shelf.

"An earthquake!" Miss Gray shrieked. She jumped up and headed for the door.

Cardiff caught up with her. "It's over, dear. Just a tremor."

His fiancée's feather-covered hat had moved to one side of her head.

A giggle escaped Sumi's lips before she could stop it.

Miss Gray glared at her. "I don't see anything funny about fearing for one's life."

Sumi lowered her hand from her mouth. "I am sorry. I did not mean . . . er, it is not funny."

"It's your hat." Cardiff pulled his lips into a solemn line. "And the fact we weren't really in danger."

Miss Gray adjusted her hat and tilted her chin toward Sumi. "I suppose *she* thinks the catfish under Japan are a trifle upset."

John frowned. "I doubt it, but you two can converse directly. You both speak English."

"Well, then, Miss Taguchi, are the catfish upset? Did they cause the tremor?"

Sumi managed to hold back another snicker. "Why no. I'm sure Cardiff-*sama* can tell you about the shifts in the earth better than I."

"Oh, for heaven's sake! Of course, I know the real cause." Miss Gray sat again and turned toward Cardiff. "While we're on the subject of earthquakes, it seems strange I've felt a *tremor* in this place twice and no place else. Is the building's foundation on solid ground?" She narrowed her gaze at Sumi. "By chance, John, did you receive bad advice in choosing this hotel for me . . . and Phillip?"

Sumi was too puzzled by the lady's line of reasoning to be tempted to laugh.

Cardiff took his seat and grimaced. "No one gave me advice. I could have reserved a room in one of the Japanese inns outside this area, but I assumed you'd prefer the European style to the Japanese one with *communal* bathing. Was I wrong?"

Miss Gray's mouth fell open. "Uh, no."

"Just a day ago," Cardiff continued, "I felt a tremor while we were getting out of the *kago* by the silk shop. You probably attributed it to the hammock's movements. I assure you, this hotel does *not* hold a monopoly on tremors."

"I see. Well, at any rate, I'm not putting up with any more of your tutor's discourtesy," Miss Gray muttered, patting her hat. "We three can go to the bazaar. If your Japanese isn't good enough, John, ask her father to come with us. He's doubtless more experienced in negotiations. And manners."

Cardiff leaned forward. "Try to see things from a Japanese person's perspective, will you? You're not being reasonable."

Sumi couldn't agree more.

"Reasonable!" Miss Gray's eyes flashed. "This native chose a repulsive play, insulted my family, and now laughs at me. She may pull the wool over your eyes, but not over mine."

Sumi recoiled. *She's talking about me!*

"Let's not drag this out," Mr. Gray interjected. "Your Japanese is good enough, John. We'll venture to the bazaar without an interpreter. I, for one, would enjoy the pretty tutor's company again, but I'm not the star of the show."

Miss Gray harrumphed.

Sumi clutched her chest in disbelief. How could this be happening? She had tried every way possible to please the impossible lady.

Cardiff's jaw tightened. "Well, the differences appear irreconcilable for now." He turned toward Sumi. "Let me help you get a *kago*. I regret you made the trip here in vain, and I'm even sorrier for the misunderstanding."

At the hotel's entrance, he paused. His gray eyes looked into hers as though he searched her mind. "I'm afraid we won't need your kind services during the rest of my fiancée's visit." He took a deep breath. "It's too bad. I had hoped you might become friends."

Flustered, she lowered her eyes. "I don't understand how I offended her."

"Well, Catherine *is* still adjusting to the cultural differences here. And because we belong to such different worlds, perhaps you didn't know how to choose a worthwhile play, one that would be agreeable to her."

"Did she dislike the play that much?" She glanced back at the lady, who turned her head away.

"She said it depicted the very worst about the Japanese society. So it gave her a terrible impression of your fine country."

"I tried to choose one she would approve of. I even asked our maid for advice since she's seen so many." Sumi shook her head. "And Miss Gray said . . . she said I insulted her family. Cardiff-*sama,* I would never do that."

"You need to know it's impolite in our culture to tell people they are in a lower class. People aren't born into classes in the United States as people are here. And as for Miss Gray's father, being the owner of a manufacturing company is considered much more important than being a warrior."

"More important? I don't understand." She tried hard to calm herself.

"Manufacturers and merchants are useful to everyone, making it easier to obtain what we need." His voice resembled a teacher's while instructing a dull student. "I'm not just a government official. I'm also a merchant. So you see, I am part of your country's highest class and also belong to its lowest class, except for Untouchables."

Cardiff had never lectured her before. Apparently she had committed a huge error. She swallowed a lump in her throat. "Then is it my fault Miss Gray may not stay here?"

His gaze softened. "Well, as I said, we live in two different worlds. Perhaps her displeasure was unavoidable unless . . ." He studied her face.

"Unless what? Please say it right out, as you like to do."

"Unless you chose an unsuitable play on purpose. And intentionally pointed out your idea of her family's lower status."

"Why would you think that?" She could feel her face burning.

"Because you don't approve of Catherine . . . of Miss Gray for me."

She stepped back as though he'd struck her. Yes, in selecting the play, she had been tempted for a second to do just that, but instead had tried her best to fulfill his trust. Didn't he know that? She wanted to ask how she could have done better, but she couldn't get the words out. She fought against tears.

"Miss Taguchi, please accept the fact I *will* honor my commitment to marry my fiancée, no matter what she thinks of Japan."

"I, I do . . ." Sumi struggled to claw her way out of the deep well engulfing her, but instead kept falling deeper.

After helping her into the *kago*, Cardiff reentered the hotel without his customary second bow or even a look back.

During the ride home, Sumi repeated his words over and over to herself. Why had she been blamed for the Floating Pleasure World's unsuitable plays? That wasn't her fault. Or for describing society's classes? And how could his fiancée have spoken against her in the face of her supreme efforts to please? The lady had been very unkind.

Cardiff didn't want her with him during his fiancée's visit. Perhaps he wouldn't want her company any longer even after Miss Gray departed. Grief tore at her heart. What could she do to change things?

Nothing. Absolutely nothing!

Busy with Catherine's entertainment, his business allocations, and the duties of his office, which mushroomed with the return of more pleasant weather, John refused to dwell on the rift with Miss Taguchi. Whenever he let down his guard and her troubled face floated before his eyes, he reminded himself that his fiancée's feelings were paramount. Besides, he'd too often indulged in affectionate thoughts about Miss Taguchi, and such fickleness had to be curtailed.

Together with Phillip and Catherine, he planned a trip to Shanghai for a three-day stay. Catherine had urged the trip to introduce him to her cousin Elizabeth and to hear a troupe of opera "stars" on world tour. She insisted she appreciated the *geisha's* "shrill voice" accompanied by the tom-tom, lute, and *samisen*, which she called a Japanese banjo. But wouldn't it be more of a treat, she'd suggested, to hear the music of their own culture?

John didn't object to the fifteen-day round trip. He could enjoy a more relaxed time with Catherine on the ship as well as survey a tract of land north of Shanghai's American sector. He could also check on two of his company's suppliers since his brother Edward had extended his visit at their family home. And truth be told, it wouldn't hurt to be away from his interpreter's family. For the time being, he'd just as soon not meet Miss Taguchi.

While the two stood on the deck during the return voyage, watching a fishing boat maneuver off a small island, Catherine gave John one of her most enchanting smiles. "I . . . uh, hope you'll understand what I'm about to say."

Apprehension coiled around his chest.

"Phillip has booked staterooms on a merchantman for himself and me, departing the middle of next week."

John lurched against the railing. "What! Why so soon? And

without even consulting me?"

"I knew you'd try to talk us out of it, and there was no time to delay. Phillip was only able to get the reservations because a couple he met wanted to cancel theirs."

"Why, there's so much more to see, Catherine! You haven't even tried your hand at painting the scenes." He forced a smile. "You can't imagine how beautiful the countryside is—like a fairyland once you get beyond the village Phillip saw. I wouldn't have wasted our time on this blasted trip if you'd just confided in me."

He'd been thinking minutes earlier how attractive she looked as a breeze blew wisps of her auburn hair, but a good part of the charm had disappeared as if a sudden gust blew it out to sea.

"I did so enjoy the opera and shopping," she said, running her finger down his forehead and nose. "And you don't fool me. You found this trip worthwhile because you could explore. You go right ahead and explore, just so you return to me."

"How can I return to you if you leave in a week?"

"John, I refuse to join you in this uncivilized land. I could never feel at home. The culture of this country has nothing in common with ours."

"You haven't given it enough time. I felt that way at first, too, but the people here—"

"No! Even before I left New York, I suspected a large cultural chasm. And the chasm is actually a bottomless canyon. Everything in this country—its music, ideas of heaven and marriage, the stern 'samurai' in the *highest* class, the outrageous drama—everything is utterly different from what I know to be right and true." Catherine's lips formed a thin, pink line.

"But think about *our* culture." He struggled to keep his

voice even. "It's not perfect either."

"It's based on equality. The idea that soldiers, peasants, and artisans are all better than merchants and that one must remain where one is born is rotten, rotten to the core."

"Don't snobs in our country look down their noses at the poor who are mired in the tenements? Don't many Southerners keep and mistreat slaves?"

"Yes, but you know my meaning. You do, don't you?"

"No culture is all good or bad. I see a lot to value here, and we could make a contribution to it too. A Christian one."

"You've changed, John."

"Well, you can't live in another culture and come close to meeting your Maker at the hands of pirates and a raging storm on the East China Sea without gaining a new perspective."

"Yes, I'm sure it's unavoidable."

"Unavoidable and with desirable outcomes. But my experiences haven't changed my basic beliefs." He sought her eyes.

"I'm glad of that. Very." She turned abruptly and looked steadily out at the sea.

A couple walked by, laughing merrily. A mother farther down the railing helped her cooing child throw crumbs into the air to attract a sea bird. How ironic. The world under his feet had turned upside down, and the rest of its inhabitants went on blissfully.

John set his jaw. "So you would only be content to marry me if we lived in New York?" *With me working in the wretched carpet factory.*

"Not New York necessarily, but a *civilized* place. Even a city like Cape Town if you yearn for overseas adventure. People speak highly of the colony." She motioned toward the toddler.

"Don't we have to think about the best place to raise children?"

"Cape Town is just a stuffy European settlement."

Her mouth drooped. Tears gathered in her eyes.

He took both her hands. "Leaving Japan would be a hard blow, but losing you? A much worse one." He wrapped his arms around her and hugged her to himself, noticing her feminine curves. Yes, they did need to think about future children. Yet the thought of returning home to her each night had lost part of its luster.

Miss Taguchi came to mind, unbidden as usual. He couldn't seem to shake the pesky attraction he felt to the young lady. Not only did his mind connect most of the Japanese language to her, remembering her patient explanations of the meanings, but he also found himself constantly trying to reconcile Catherine's low opinion of her with his high one. He'd never once seen his tutor be inconsiderate. Was he really such a poor judge of character?

He steadied his thoughts. Catherine's insight deserved his trust. He had pledged himself to her, and he would not waver now.

At the end of the three and a half weeks, the fourth week of October, Catherine, accompanied by Phillip, boarded the merchantman with John's promise that he would seek ways to expedite his return to the United States. He agreed to explore a means to recoup his investment by selling the Japanese portion of Cardiff & Associates, while leaving the three-mast ship and the company's West Coast and Chinese offices in the hands of his brother Edward. Catherine emphasized more than once that a position in the carpet factory could be his, but only if he wanted it.

The steamship moved away from its anchorage, and Catherine's figure became smaller in the distance. After other well-wishers left the dock, John told the Pendletons, who had also come to see off the Grays, more about what had happened during the visit. He ended by explaining Miss Taguchi's unexpected part in the *kabuki* debacle.

"I keep thinking about a certain proverb," John said, sensing a heaviness he couldn't blame altogether on his fiancée's departure. *Confidence in an unfaithful man*—or woman—*in time of trouble is like a broken tooth.* For me, the results have been much worse. As for Miss Taguchi . . . I expected her to have better judgment. Catherine felt she purposefully chose a repulsive play because of jealousy. I have trouble believing that about Miss Taguchi, but a woman's wiles may be beyond me."

John adjusted his Munich spyglass and looked for the ship. Seeing only its dark shape with a thin filament of smoke, he turned back toward the Pendletons.

Richard's brow wrinkled. "Ah yes," he said after a moment. "I seem to recall another proverb from that same chapter: *Go not forth hastily to strive,* it says, *lest thou know not what to do in the end when thy neighbour puts thee to shame.*"

"So you're saying I've drawn a wrong conclusion?" John hid his surprise that his friend could so easily pull up Scripture references.

"You're not the sworn enemy of Miss Taguchi's family, are you?"

"And your point?" He'd be offended at the simplistic question if he didn't have so much respect for the older man.

"Sumi Taguchi's Confucian training would require loyalty to you as her friend and as her father's superior no matter how she felt about Miss Gray. Moreover, she faced a major problem in trying to select a decent drama. Last August, we wanted to take the Browns to one of the plays while they were here. We imagined we could find at least one that suited. We couldn't."

Margaret nodded her agreement.

John rebuffed the strange rise in his spirits. "Isn't depicting a wife's sacrifice of her position and even her children's clothing for a husband's immorality going too far, even for here?"

"This country's idea of the ultimate female is a wife who lives only for her husband's desires." Richard cupped his hand to shade his eyes against a ray of sunlight. "And there's more. A Dutch translator we met explained that the play's main character often pursues a forbidden passion. The audience enjoys an emotional release with him, while approving those who preserve society's harmony."

"Like the poor wife, I suppose. Nothing's quite what it seems, is it? Always another layer to look at."

"Although a *Noh* drama might have been less objectionable, a Japanese young lady wouldn't feel at liberty to suggest an alternative as though she were smarter. Sumi Taguchi's invariably polite, I've noticed, even when our ways don't appeal to her."

John winced. What was it about his tutor that made him react irrationally? "It seems I did misjudge her. At the least, I should have given her the benefit of the doubt. I was trying to keep Catherine's trip from turning out the way it did. But that was no excuse for shifting blame onto Miss Taguchi."

He'd visit Miss Taguchi and make things right. Although

she wasn't his love like Catherine, he could relax with her and discuss all kinds of topics. If he guarded himself against any wayward affection, they could resume their good relationship until . . . until he left Japan.

His renewed sense of well-being vanished. The dock workers' shouts, the milling crowd, the incessant clangs and whistles grated. He and Catherine had supposedly settled his future, but nothing about it seemed right. He glanced at the Pendletons.

"It would take a very unusual American lady to adjust to such a different life," Margaret put in as her husband pocketed their spyglass. "Some Westerners here avoid all contact with the Japanese citizenry. Others struggle to fit into their new surroundings, but never fully succeed."

"I tried to shield Catherine from this country's most disturbing aspects, especially from the reactionaries' opposition to Westerners—that we're 'barbarians.' I wanted her to see the culture's fascinating parts first." He took one last look at the ship's dot of smoke as it slipped behind an incoming one, then pushed back from the railing. "I expected her to be enchanted with Japan, never imagining she'd detest it. I guess a monk came close to the truth when he said 'nothing is certain in life—except change.'"

Margaret gently tilted her head. "And the Almighty."

CHAPTER 35

So that's how it is. I'm a speck on a tiny planet in a universe of thousands of stars. An insignificant speck! Sumi closed the astronomy book Phillip Gray sent as a parting gift. *The gods didn't specially create this country. That's why nothing's recorded about it in Chinese books. That's why foreigners don't know anything about the Sun Goddess. My country seems important, but it's not. The earth appears still, but it's spinning. Nothing is as it seems.* She glanced around. *The foreigners' bright light isn't a light at all. It's a shifting mirage. I've been a fool, like Kiyo said, grasping at clouds!*

She blinked to rid her mind of Cardiff's accusing eyes. His fiancée had finally left the day before, but that wouldn't change anything. Rebuffing tears, she inspected the other books on the shelves over her father's low desk. There had to be a more appealing one.

Thumbing through an old collection of poetry, she came across a *tanka* poem by Tsurayuki.

>*The cherry blossom*
>*Said to be most transient*
>*Yet I disagree*

More fleeting still—a man's heart
Even with no breath of wind

She copied the poem and walked over to her grandfather, who was smoking his pipe while he watched the misting rain drip from the eaves and trickle down the rain chain. Her father was a scholar, and that was excellent, but her grandfather was a warrior with his sword's steel in his bones. What had once repulsed her as unbearable stubbornness now appeared admirable strength.

Feeling her face heat, she bowed and gave him the copy. "I like this poem. It is true to life." She bowed again.

He didn't question her, but grunted and took the paper to his room. That afternoon he handed her a copy of a poem by the same poet.

A heart is hidden
From people's understanding
But in the old site
Blossoms from ancient eras
Give out their fragrance

"Are you planning to visit Hagi?" she asked, incredulous.

"I am considering it. If I go, you may accompany me."

Her pulse quickened. She could get away from Nagasaki. Perhaps find relief from her depressing thoughts. On top of that, she'd wanted to visit their ancestral village in the Chōshū domain all her life. But was it safe? What about their warlord's anger Kiyo ranted about? Or an unknown radical clansman, like the crazed Chōshū samurai who died at the toy store? Yet her grandfather wasn't a foreigner's interpreter. He was their clan's hero.

"I would like that."

"The weather should improve by tomorrow. If we go, you

must be ready in two days."

"I will be ready."

He nodded and left the room.

After selecting paper to write her friend Taki a note about the trip, she headed for the stairs. On the bottom step, she heard her father and grandfather talking on the front veranda. When she caught the word Hagi, she crept closer.

"I need to see the place once more before I am too old to travel," her grandfather said. "Good for Sumi to go. Might stiffen her spine."

"So you're definitely going. How long will you stay?"

"Three weeks. My sister would object to a shorter visit."

"Any risk, as you see it?" Her father's attempt at a nonchalant tone betrayed his worry.

"The warlord cannot ignore my brother-in-law's years of faithful service."

"Nor your well-known valor." He paused. "I have been concerned about Sumi too. I understand your wisdom, enabling her to see she comes from a root of a thousand years."

Sumi tiptoed away. She disliked the notion her grandfather might take an unnecessary risk for her. She'd rather think he was simply acting on what he already wished to do.

The toll of passing years struck Yoshikatsu from the minute his sister and brother-in-law greeted them at the port near Hagi. Gray hair, deep wrinkles, and slow gaits replaced the vigorous images he had from their last reunion. Still, the couple's natures seemed unchanged. His sister chattered about how Sumi had become a lovely lady and asked question after question. Her husband added a word or two and sighed.

While Yoshikatsu was pointing out their packages to the porters, a messenger strode up and made a cursory bow. "Lord Ōta summons you. Do not delay." The young man smirked and handed him a scroll.

"So you have read this?" Yoshikatsu took hold of his sword's hilt. "A messenger has lost his head for less."

"I beg your pardon. I did not dare read it. Lord Ōta issued the command in my presence." The youth backed away, bowing several times.

"Then you had better remember whose command it is. Not yours."

"Yes, Sire." He bowed twice more and scurried away.

Yoshikatsu fought against sudden weariness. The upstart young man and the terse message did not bode well. But he was samurai. He would handle whatever lay ahead.

Leaving Sumi in their relatives' care, he headed for the castle.

After navigating the maze of alleys, he crossed the moat and passed through the heavy gate. The high-ranking style of his stiff-shoulder tunic and *hakama* stopped any guard from detaining him. Archers, stationed behind high-up windows, no doubt watched his progress along the spiraling pathway to the main courtyard, yet no warning came. He'd been proud of his ease of access through the years. But experience told him that access didn't always come because of honor. A hunted animal was welcomed too—through the open door of a cage.

He threw off the cloud of misgiving. His own years of service, despite his son's position as interpreter, should insulate him from charges of disloyalty—unless the clan's inner circle plotted outright rebellion against the Shōgun. He strode into the massive castle's dark, inner recesses.

The awe he'd felt as a youth gripped him. The gold leaf in the six-fold screen behind the warlord's dais still glittered in the glow of an oily candle, giving life to the screen's two fierce Chinese lions. A faint smell of musk incense seeped in from an adjoining room. Nothing in the immense chamber had changed except what was the most significant of all—the current warlord.

Yoshikatsu approached the dais, taking several steps between each bow. Lord Ōta, remaining seated, offered no greeting and beckoned him forward each time with a flip of his wrist.

After prolonging his deepest bow, Yoshikatsu presented a scroll expressing loyalty, written with his precisely executed calligraphy, and knelt before the warlord.

Lord Ōta stroked his chin and narrowed his sharp eyes. "These *kanji*—the ideographs—may not be the same as the *kanji*—the sentiment—of your house at Nagasaki. Is that not so?"

"In the same way I have always served your honorable house, I remain true to my vows."

"Your vows were to *both* the Shōgun and the Chōshū house of Ōta. Is that not a predicament?"

"Should I change my vows?" *You speak the treason.*

"No one doubts your devotion to the Shōgun. Your loyalty to *me* is what lacks proof. You must be aware I receive missives from all sections of the country, including Nagasaki."

Yoshikatsu met the warlord's eyes without flinching before lowering his gaze. "I am ready to obey your every word." He bowed his forehead to the mat.

Lord Ōta said nothing. A samurai approached and asked

permission to flog two disruptive servants in the courtyard. The warlord consented, then ordered a servant to fill his tea *chawan*.

Yoshikatsu sat back on his heels, pondering the most likely test of his allegiance.

A requirement to reside in Hagi? Doubtful.

Disembowelment?

Like a coiled serpent, repulsion flared. All his life, he'd considered *seppuku* the pinnacle of service, but he had no desire to discard his life for a warlord's whim. Furthermore, his granddaughter had turned to him for help, something she had not done in a long time. He wanted to live long enough to see her exuberance renewed.

He carefully kept his face a mask. No muscle's flicker could signal dismay.

The warlord's gaze lit on him again, as if measuring him. Despising him.

Yoshikatsu walled out thoughts of family. He focused his mind on a tiny point deep within—virtual emptiness. The room around him and the warlord—illusions. They receded into whiteness. The point was the only reality. It too would disappear with his blade's deep stab into his intestines. Pain would ensue, but then—hopefully—rest.

"Leave me, and take this with you." Lord Ōta flung the open scroll, jerking Yoshikatsu out of his meditation. The scroll crumpled into a pile next to him. "I have more important matters than dealing with one more worrisome vassal, a decrepit one."

Yoshikatsu drew his mind to the present and the fact he was to live. The unmerited insult registered, but oddly invoked no anger. With all the dignity he could muster, he bowed his head to the mat and picked up the ruined gift.

The rows of samurai he passed in the castle's shadowy antechamber shimmered like phantoms. In the courtyard, the shrieks of the servants being flogged reverberated in a world different from his. Only a hair's breadth had existed between life and death, and against expectation, he held on to the edge of life.

Following the narrow lane to his relatives' home, he came to a field where bloody battles had been fought hundreds of years earlier. He had honed his own samurai skills there in his youth. Memory after memory rushed in as though eager to be embraced one last time. The pungent smell from a nearby clump of pines reminded him of a departure for battle when he had been nineteen.

He and the other samurai had led their horses up a path swathed in mist. The dew on the evergreen needles clung to their bodies as they brushed past. After two hours of climbing, they burst out on a high meadow. Sunlight danced off the metallic chain threaded into their thick leather armor. His gray speckled horse pawed and whinnied. Flags fluttered in the brisk air, and his heart had raced with the thrill of adventure and danger.

What he wouldn't give to go back and relive the next few days. The shunned noble's uprising had been a lost cause, yet the noble only pretended surrender. Yoshikatsu's alertness and quick parry saved his warlord's life. When his liege publicly expressed gratitude upon their return, Yoshikatsu's father beamed and his brother-in-law had stood by proudly.

The blood no longer surged through his veins. His father's pride, his mother's love, his lord's appreciation were only memories. The current warlord had been right about one thing: Yoshikatsu was old. The buildings he'd seen as a youth looked almost the same, but the faces inside were different. How ironic that the man-made structures survived, and the people who built them did not.

But his granddaughter still had her life ahead of her, and he would be part of it, at least for a time. For that, he could be grateful.

CHAPTER 36

The fog on the third day of the Hagi visit smothered everything, even the tangerine tree next to the eaves. Sumi kept close to the outside wall of the house and picked a short camellia branch with a white blossom and shiny leaves to add to the flower arrangement her great-aunt requested. The impenetrable fog chilled her. The flower drooped a little, just as *The Tale of the Heike* proclaimed. *Flourishing flowers* all decayed.

Reentering the house, she sighed—too loudly, she realized when her grandfather looked up from his scroll.

"Your effort is appreciated." His posture was stiff, but his tone conveyed unusual warmth. "You continue to make progress." He rose and moved the sputtering candle, still needed in the muted daylight, closer to where she knelt in front of the partially finished arrangement.

"I hope my stumbling effort pleases you." She blotted the water droplets off the flower's petals and trimmed the stem to the right length.

"You labored diligently, too, on those long lists of foreign words. A task very few could do."

She caught her breath. "I didn't know you saw those pages—the dictionary."

He frowned. "I came across them when your mother and I retrieved a painting from your cupboard. I wished to check the shading in the hydrangea."

"May I ask when that was?"

"Near the end of the rainy season. I borrowed one section. It helped take my mind off your father's trouble." He crossed his arms. "I thought you would realize I had the papers when you missed the painting. The words have proved impossible to remember. Good exercise for an old mind, however." He scanned her face. "Is something wrong? I have kept the list safe, in readiness to return it when you need it."

"No, I do not need it, but I thought Kiyo . . ." She searched for words. "I am happy you think the lists worthwhile." Managing a wavering smile, she poked the flower into the vase.

After a polite interval, she gathered up her traveling bag and retired to a small room attached to her great-uncle's storage closet. His daggers, an extra sword, and long-disused armor cluttered the space. A musty smell emanated from the darker corners. She didn't mind. She needed to be alone.

Her eyes gradually adjusted to the faint light coming through the adjoining paper panels. Leaning back against a wall, she tried to think. Her grandfather—tackling the English language? How could that be? But that wasn't the sole puzzle. Everything was bewildering.

She should have believed her cousin's innocence. But Kiyo hadn't sympathized about the missing papers. Not one bit. No, her grandfather's disclosure didn't change anything with Kiyo. She despised her cousin and always would.

And how about Cardiff-*sama*? Digging out her mirror from

the traveling bag, she inspected her reflection. He'd said she was pretty once. Before his fiancée came, he seemed to relish their time together. She'd marveled at how frequently his thinking fit with hers. She didn't know his zodiac sign, but surely it matched hers well.

"Why does he prefer Miss Gray?" She lurched forward, startled she'd spoken out loud. Glancing around, she let out a breath. No one could have heard her muttering.

Catherine Gray's face sprang up in her mind. Round bluish eyes. A mouth spouting perfect English. Hair arranged in a customary style for foreigners with a curl dangling in front of each ear. Pale skin. She was an American, not a *native*. So, Cardiff desired Miss Gray's company.

Not hers.

She shivered at how aghast her family would be at her feelings for Cardiff, a barbarian. She never thought of him as an outsider now. He was a friend. More than a friend, but that could never, never be. Her chest ached, making it hard to breathe.

One of her great-uncle's daggers lay close by. Picking it up, she found it heavier and colder than she'd expected. She rummaged in her bag for the English Bible, carefully wrapped in a scarf. The Pendletons had called the book a *balm* for the soul. Balancing the book and dagger in each hand, she closed her eyes. Could either of the yin-yang objects bring relief?

The dagger would have the swiftest answer. Why should people live and face suffering when they were only insignificant specks? But would dying be an end?

She might be reborn as an Untouchable or even as an animal, bird, or insect. Possibly she deserved such karma. She certainly hadn't come close to following the eight-fold path to enlightenment.

Or she might roam the earth after dying, the way Bashō intimated.

> *Struck ill journeying,*
> *My dreams are wandering still*
> *Through the dried-up fields*

Anger and rejection could still haunt her wanderings. And it would be too late to change anything.

She flipped through a section of the Bible and leaned over a page to read its lines, all filled with difficult English words. It would require months, even years, to comprehend the book's lessons. Take the parable on forgiveness. The idea of forgiving Kiyo's *debt* still repulsed her. Not only that, but Cardiff-*sama* and Mrs. Pendleton had talked about *blessing* one's enemy. Admittedly, the story she'd heard in the English class about the good *Sa-ma-ri-tan*'s kindness to his country's sworn enemy was noble in a strange way, but unattainable. Blessing Kiyo? Or Miss Gray? Impossible!

She gripped the two objects. Although unlikely, how magnificent if the dagger brought peace. Yet how terrible if it brought dried up fields or life as an ant.

She rubbed her hand over the Bible's leather cover. Odd that this ancient, baffling book had been banned for hundreds of years—feared and despised in her country, yet cherished elsewhere. She should at least try to discover why Cardiff-*sama* believed living forever could be joyful.

The wind during the night blew away the fog, and the late fall day dawned clear and brisk. After Sumi finished breakfast, her great-aunt handed her a lunch she'd packed.

"A young lady like you needs a little time out of the house, away from her elders. There is a grove of maples, dressed in their fall colors, halfway to the castle. You can enjoy the beauty of that place."

"Oh, I do not—" Her grandfather's firm nod of approval and the pleading in her great-aunt's eyes stopped her. "Thank you. A walk is a good idea on a fine day." She should please her elders. It didn't matter where she spent her time.

On her way to the grove, she came to a field of autumn grasses, broken in places by large boulders, clumps of brush, and a few pine trees. The field must be the one her grandfather mentioned. A prickling raised hairs on her neck. What had the battling warriors been like? Fathers, brothers, sons—all struck down for some warlord's cause.

Another of Bashō's poems flitted through her mind:

Summer field of grass
Of warriors' glorious dreams
Only it remains

The Buddha said life was laced with suffering. Science reduced people to specks. The dead heroes became a field of grass. Why couldn't life be truly precious? Why did *futility* have to be the answer to the poet Issa's ponderings about what lay between the first washbasin and the final washbasin?

A puff of wind rippled through the field. Her heart skipped a beat. Could any spirits of slain warriors still hover close by? She picked up her pace until she reached the grove.

The maple trees' scarlet leaves gleamed against the blue sky. Her aunt was right about the beauty. She should treasure the splendor now because those brilliant leaves would fall to the ground whether or not they were gifts from Cardiff-*sama*'s eternal *giver*.

Sitting carefully so as not to damage her kimono, she braced herself against the trunk of a large oak tree in the middle of the grove. Only the distant chirp of a solitary cricket broke the silence.

Drawing out her aunt's provisions, she obediently ate a rice ball. Although moist, the second ball became more difficult to swallow. She tossed the third one into the yellowish-brown underbrush.

The closest bush quivered. Sumi put both hands on the ground, poised to move.

A long, gray snake slithered out.

She yelped and leapt up, then backed away.

The snake lifted its head, darting its tongue in and out of its mouth.

She backed up farther and stumbled over a knobby root. Her hands latched onto the tree trunk and stopped her fall. She edged to the backside of the tree, and peered around it.

The snake raised its head higher and faced her directly.

A sensation of ill will washed over her. She hardly dared breathe. Had a dead samurai's spirit sent the snake? Did the spirit resent her intrusion?

Lowering its head, the snake turned and zigzagged back into the brush.

Sumi walked in the opposite direction, her heart beating erratically. At the edge of the grove, she sat near a maple tree in an open, clear space, bordered only by low grass and a few straggling wildflowers.

Was she foolish to be frightened by either the snake or lurking spirits? She imagined Cardiff-*sama* would insist the snake had simply come out to protect its territory from a bombardment of more rice balls. Or he might joke that it was thanking her for the unexpected meal. She couldn't help smiling at the thought, so like him.

In fact, they'd both laugh and agree their cultures looked at the same event in different ways, but that didn't prevent them from understanding each other. Round eyes, slant eyes, frank talk, or unspoken words—all insignificant distinctions. Affection shining in his gray eyes, he would put his hand on hers . . . *Stop it! Don't be a greater fool.*

She would not think of the consul. What good would it do? She'd find something else to occupy her mind.

A dragonfly darted past her and circled the nearest clump of wildflowers before zipping away. She checked over the plants for any insect the dragonfly might have been hunting, then picked one of the delicate yellow daisies and spun it in her hand. Its petals were precisely geometrical. Its loveliness— amazing.

If a person was a speck in the universe, the flower was the tiniest fraction of a speck. Yet it had an exquisite design. She put the flower in her hair, thought of how she had done the same with Cardiff-*sama*'s cherry blossom, and snatched it out.

She sniffed the flower's mild fragrance and studied it again—a small treasure soothing her deep ache. And the masterpiece had grown from a miniscule seed. But how was that possible? How had the directions for such beauty gotten into its seed, just a little larger than a grain of sand, an even smaller fraction of a speck?

She'd never seen a shrine to a wildflower. None of the gods would care about such an insignificant object. But if a power, even a deity like Cardiff's Giver, had put so much effort into the flower's beauty, could that power care about people . . . a little?

She paused and then said aloud, "Flower maker, if you are listening, show me please."

Other than a slight breeze rustling the maple leaves high above, all was quiet. She grimaced at her presumption. How could a speck like her demand a sign? The sense of emptiness brought a lump to her throat.

As the fiery ball of the sun began its descent, Sumi laid the little flower aside and set off at a brisk pace in order to arrive back at her great-uncle's home before the evening meal. When she approached the ancient battle site, a shadow rose up and then dropped back behind a boulder. An apparition? She walked faster.

"Traitor's daughter," a voice shouted. "Go away!"

Her stomach knotting, she wheeled around to see who, or what, had spoken.

A gangly boy dashed through the tall grass to another rock. "Traitor's daughter, you are not wanted here!" A shower of pebbles peppered her.

She brushed off her kimono and called out, "Stop it! You know nothing!"

Running was impossible in her kimono and thick-soled sandals, but she tripped along as fast as she could. The boy made another dash, and she turned quickly, but the sun's rays impeded her vision. The boy didn't stop taunting her until he ran out of rocks to hide behind at the edge of the field.

She continued on her way, aware she still valued her health and life. Such ridicule, she lectured herself, was not a great catastrophe—not like being targeted with a dagger. Or having their home burned to the ground or her father imprisoned. Or losing her most cherished foreign friend.

She told her grandfather about the boy, passing it off as a trifle. He narrowed his eyes and, to her surprise, reported the incident to her great-uncle.

"Earlier today a fox crossed my path," her great-uncle said. "It didn't hide in the brush. It came right out in the open. It stopped and stared straight at me, defiant."

Sumi shivered at the similarity to the snake, but then shrugged off the resemblance. It had to be coincidental. Cardiff-*sama* would think so.

"A harbinger of calamity!" Her great-aunt's eyes radiated fear. "An evil spirit in disguise, ready to use its power against us!"

The couple looked at Sumi's grandfather.

"If the gods do not help us," he said, laying aside his pipe, "that spirit will work our destruction. I am sorry we came and hastened the evil day."

"No, do not say such words." Her great-uncle rapped his knuckles on the low stand next to him. "You and our niece are welcome. This trouble has been building ever since Lord Ōta took his father's place."

Sumi's palms dampened. The incidents upsetting her elders weren't dire enough to predict the family's destruction unless they were on shakier ground than she'd suspected. Had the clan forgotten her grandfather's famous heroism? Her great-uncle's unflagging service?

After the tense meal, her elders offered incense at the family *Butsudan* and implored the spirits at the separate god shelf for help. Sumi joined them with a show of piety but inward reservations. She'd much rather leave all the spirits in the Hagi area alone.

If only she and her grandfather had stayed in Nagasaki.

CHAPTER 37

Sumi's great-uncle slowly unrolled the scroll delivered by Lord Ōta's messengers early the next day. His face paled, and his wife's crinkled into a mosaic of despair. Her grandfather, frowning, read it next. Then Sumi was allowed to take a look.

She shuddered at the cold, hard characters, so irreversibly brushed onto the paper. Her great-aunt and uncle, together with Sumi and her grandfather, were banished from Hagi—never to return. The next sentences proclaimed the transfer of the house, which the couple had occupied for fifty-two years, to another retainer's family. Any belongings left in the residence after three days would be confiscated.

Sumi groaned. Lord Ōta had ice for a soul.

The old couple uttered no complaints. Her great-aunt's deep sigh when her husband shuttered their home for the last time was the only show of emotion.

The warlord had put three samurai in charge of their journey to Nagasaki. Sumi detested the men from the minute they swaggered onto the Chōshū coastal ship. One named Maeda, with no concern for damage, ordered the porters to sling her great-aunt and uncle's seven lacquered boxes, holding their most treasured possessions, into an inner walkway.

Another one of the three, leering at her great-aunt, halved her allotment of rice for the noon meal. "That's enough for an old woman." Sniggering, he pushed a bowl of persimmons toward her. "Eat these instead, as many as you want." The persimmons were overly ripe.

Sumi wanted to spit in the tormenter's face, but her grandfather shot her a look that forbade any reaction.

On the way to the family's cabin after the meal, she overheard Maeda defending himself against his companions' charge that he always claimed the young women for himself. Shaken, she crept away and vowed to stay close by her elders.

In the late afternoon of the second day, clouds lowered over the open seas. When the sails' adjustment distracted the ship's crew and the three samurai, Sumi's grandfather beckoned her and her great-aunt and uncle to join him at the end of the deck. "There is no time to lose," he warned. "We must let the small boat down as soon as we get a chance. We were lucky to wake up this morning. Our escorts' mood grows blacker by the moment."

"The rough waters will overwhelm us," Sumi's great-uncle replied. "The strength is gone from my arms."

"At least we'd have a chance out there." Her grandfather glanced down at his sash where his swords had hung before they were confiscated. "Lord Ōta has ordered a dishonorable death for us. The fox that crossed your path sensed our spirits' desolation."

Her great-uncle shook his head. "We will perish in the sea."

"If we do, the gods will it, not our assassins."

Over her grandfather's left shoulder, Sumi saw Maeda

approaching on the gangway. To delay him, she pretended seasickness and reeled toward the ship's railing.

Maeda roughly grabbed her arm. "Not feeling good, are you?" He pulled her away from the railing. "You'll feel better in my cabin."

"Stop!" her grandfather ordered. "Leave her alone!"

"Release her!" Her great-uncle started toward her.

Maeda drew his sword. Sumi's grandfather yanked her great-uncle back. The samurai, wild eyed, cursed them both. Then he grabbed Sumi again and propelled her to his interior cabin.

Maeda thrust her down on his stained mat. "You lie here and rest, little lady."

Fury repulsed fear, and she started to rise. "How dare you! You will be punished!"

He shoved her back down. "Who will punish me? Huh? Not those tottering, swordless fools out there!" The air he drew in through a missing front tooth made a whistling sound. "I'll check your condition later." He slowly ran his eyes over her sprawled body.

Her skin became clammy. Yearning to crawl under the mat, she drew the folds of her kimono closer around her neck.

"Do as I say, and *you* won't lose your life. Can't promise that for the others."

He strode out of the room and slid the door shut. A heavy object was shoved against it.

Coldness encased her. Her eyes roved the room for a weapon. Spotting a metal pipe sticking out of the floor in the corner, she stood up, fighting against dizziness. She struggled to wrench the pipe loose, but it wouldn't budge. A cabinet next to it held only a blanket and smelly clothes.

Could she kick her way through the door? Possibly, but with the sailors, the four of them would be far outnumbered even if they could reach their stored weapons. And she was no female warrior like the heroine of the Gempei War.

She sat back down and drew her trembling knees up to her chin. One thing for sure—the next time Maeda touched her, she would force him to kill her if she couldn't somehow kill him first.

A half hour later, a noise outside the door alerted her. The heavy object was being moved. She grasped one of her sharp cylindrical pins from her hair, ready to ram it into Maeda's throat. The door slid open. She sprang up— coming face-to-face with her great-uncle.

"Hurry!" he whispered. "Head for the small boat. Your grandfather is preparing to launch it."

She stepped forward and heard a movement behind her. Maeda—with his sword raised! She screamed.

The sword whipped through the air, slashing her great-uncle from his shoulder to his groin. Blood gushed from his body.

"No! No! You monster!" Sobs wracked her body.

Maeda's eyes gleamed. She backed away.

He stepped over her great-uncle's corpse. "Stop right there, you wench."

She turned and raced toward the side of the ship.

"You'll be sorry when I catch you!" He lunged for her.

She flung herself over the side.

The ocean's surface dealt her a powerful, stinging blow. The blast of dark water swallowed her up. She plummeted down deeper and deeper. Kicking frantically, she struggled to stop the descent, to climb upwards. She ripped off her kimono and pushed its clinging folds away. Her lungs burned. Light rippled too far above. She strained with all her might to hold her remaining breath and swim upwards.

Bursting onto the surface, she coughed and sputtered, then gulped the air. A series of enormous ocean swells bore her away from the ship. She shot a glance toward the distant shore, a hazy, gray line in the twilight. She could never swim that far, but turned in that direction anyway.

Her great-uncle's bloody, sliced body filled her mind. When the next wave washed over her, she welcomed the cold, clean water. More waves rolled over her. The shouts of Maeda and the other samurai faded.

Strength ebbing, she slackened her strokes. If she ceased swimming altogether, she would know within moments whether her afterlife consisted of peace, or withered fields, or a rebirth. Yet beyond all reason, she couldn't give up.

Something sharp jabbed her side. An oar! Terror surged through her again. She shoved the oar away.

"Stop! Grab hold!" It was her grandfather's voice.

He pulled her up over the edge of the boat and wrapped her in his outer cloak. She dropped down, crying and gasping for breath.

"Your great-uncle? Is he dead?"

She tried to speak, but made a wheezing sound.

"Tell me!" His voice shook. "We have to know for certain!"

"Dead. He's dead!" she wailed. She heard her great-aunt moan.

Her grandfather bent over in silent grief. Her great-aunt continued to moan. The last light of dusk vanished into the night. The storm edged closer, and a rough wave spun the boat around.

Still gasping out sobs, Sumi pulled herself up and peered into the enveloping blackness. The large craft belonging to the Chōshū warlord had disappeared. The overcast obscured the moon and the stars. The rocky promontories and sandy beaches were invisible. In all but one unknown direction, a dark ocean stretched interminably.

Desperation silenced her sobs. The boat would soon flounder amid the rising waves. Her grandfather and great-aunt had held onto life, somehow escaping the warlord's trap. They couldn't perish now.

The wind whistled. Sea foam splashed into the boat. Sumi looked in every direction.

Her grandfather twisted around, also searching for a sign of the distant shore.

A pang of sadness swept through her. She'd never see Cardiff-*sama* again . . . or her parents, or her friend Taki, or the Pendletons. Where were their ancestors' spirits her elders beseeched for hours in Hagi? Why weren't they helping? She slumped down and put her face in her hands.

An image of the tiny wildflower arrested her. What about the wildflower's maker . . . or Cardiff-*sama*'s god? Could the power that wove such beauty save them? Or would such a deity turn away, disgusted by the evil?

She raised her head, then blinked. A faint ray glimmered through the waves in front of her. She grabbed her grandfather's arm and pointed. But when he looked, nothing was there.

She saw it again. "It *is* a light! Look! There it is!"

He shook off her hand a second time. She continued to point at the almost imperceptible twinkle glancing across the swells. Possibly a lantern's glow from a faraway fisherman's quarters or—horror of horrors—from the Chōshū ship. At any rate, the glimmer was their only hope.

At last he saw it. He picked up a pair of oars. "You row too," he ordered. "Watch and do what I do."

Sumi grabbed the oars and tried to copy his movements. The buffeting wind and waves made the oars rebel, but she forced them to duplicate his moves as often as she could.

Her great-aunt's moans had become inaudible in the growing storm. Sumi glanced back at her. She was gripping one side of the boat and staring into the blackness behind them. Did she have a vain idea her husband might follow them? Sumi couldn't bear to look at her more than a second.

When Sumi turned back around, the glimmer had disappeared. Panic froze her arms. Her grandfather shouted for her to row, but she couldn't make herself move until the twinkle reappeared.

The little light continued to disappear behind the larger swells. Fear gripped her each time it vanished, and relief washed over her every time it returned slightly to the right or left. Her mind might welcome the release of death, but her body clearly wanted to live.

The spray from the wind and waves deposited a thick layer of salt on her face and hands and drenched the cloak. She shivered despite the fiery pain gripping her shoulders. It seemed like they had been rowing long enough to reach the southern tip of Kyushu.

At long last, the twinkle developed into a distinct light. A surprised fisherman welcomed them into his rough shack as the full blast of the storm hit. Twenty minutes later, Sumi lay on the empty rice sacks their host had spread for the three of them on the dirt floor. A rough straw blanket covered her. The fearsome struggle against the ocean melted into a memory. All that filled her mind was her great-uncle's death.

He had been motioning to her one moment and the next moment lay dead at her feet. If only she hadn't pretended to be seasick. If only they hadn't gone to Hagi. Why had she needed cheering up? Because of the foreigners. Why had she become so well acquainted with the foreigners? Because of the English classes. She'd deceived her grandfather and set terrible things in motion.

Regret skinned her layer upon layer. The anguish was unbearable, knowing nothing could be changed. She lay awake the rest of the night, tears streaming down her face.

By the next morning, the last of the storm clouds had moved over the distant high hills, leaving only a white wisp in their wake. The kind fisherman rowed the three of them to a nearby village. From there, they returned to Nagasaki by a larger fishing boat.

The three samurai also went on to Nagasaki. To hide their identity, they donned the basket-type headgear of penitent pilgrims. The Chōshū warlord's ship remained in the harbor only long enough to unload its cargo before it headed north for the more welcoming waters of the clan's domain.

The three sought out the American consul's groom and reported on their mission.

Nobumitsu glared at them. "You *helped* lower the boat into the sea? What possessed you?"

"Didn't want more assassinations to turn the sailors. Some of the weaker ones felt sorry for the girl. Impossible for those two old people, almost in their graves, to rescue her and make it to land. With that storm and darkness, even the strongest of us couldn't do it. You'll never see them again."

"You think not? I saw the girl last evening. You should have taken care of the traitors when they were in your hands."

Maeda's jaw tightened. "What kind of people are these? I tell you, no one I know could've got that boat to shore." He gritted his teeth. "We won't fail again. I'll do whatever—"

"Are you sure you weren't followed?" Nobumitsu knew the noises of the stable. A different creak had sounded from a corner of the roof.

"Yes," Maeda answered, "we checked."

"So you say."

Nobumitsu strode outside. For more than a year, he had kept his identity hidden at great cost. By the gods, he would not allow a slip up now. The three men had better not be as inept in staying undercover and in fighting as they'd been as assassins.

He checked the environs thoroughly, even scaling half-way up a tree to get a full view. But whatever had caused the irregular sound was nowhere to be found.

When he reentered the stable, Maeda's eyes flashed with anger before he bowed and repeated, "We checked."

Nobumitsu scowled at him, then shrugged. "It seems you did one thing right." At least this one had passion.

An English couple walking toward George Jennings glanced at him, then took a second look as they passed by. Jennings resisted ducking his head. He had to get off the dock and out of sight.

Dodging sailors and longshoremen, he headed for the steps

leading up the embankment that ran along the harbor. Where was his contact? His disguise as an English sailor wasn't good enough here in Nagasaki although his masquerade had worked well during the passage from Hong Kong. Dying his red hair a dark brown and shaving his beard and sideburns had done the trick.

    His incarceration in the Hong Kong prison until a ship could transport him to the United States had played right into his hands. If he'd been allowed to choose any city's prison in the world, he'd have chosen Hong Kong's. The chief Chinese prison cook, a relative of Cardiff's former cook accused of collaborating with pirates, had helped him escape.

    Jennings reached the top step, and to his relief saw the one person expecting him. He doffed his sailor hat, and the Englishman waved his arm for him to follow.

CHAPTER 38

November (Month of the Rat)

Not again! The housekeeper's new spaniel had already waked John up two previous nights, barking at what turned out to be a stray cat teasing the dog from the top of the wall. He lit the oil lantern with a Lucifer match and found his night robe. Maybe he could scare the cat so thoroughly it would never come back.

A thump sounded from downstairs. Most likely Goda heard the dog too and was investigating. In the off chance of an intruder, John grabbed his loaded revolver from the dresser drawer.

His manservant's muffled voice came from downstairs. "*Abunai! Abunai!*"

John took the stairs two at a time and pounded down the hallway toward the flickering light coming from the audience room. He slid to a stop before entering. Goda hadn't yelled again. Leaves rustled from outside the room's open window, a window that shouldn't have been open.

Keeping his finger on the revolver's trigger, he stepped

sideways into the doorway.

His gaze swept from a swaying window curtain to a large, prone body in an expanding pool of blood—headless. The head lay a foot away. John sucked in his breath. George Jennings! Then he spied his servant by the room's back wall—motionless.

"No! Don't let it be!" He skirted the blood spurting from Jennings' torso and bent over Goda's body. A ghost of a pulse beat in his servant's throat. "Oh, Lord, help!" Ripping off a section of his robe, he pressed it against Goda's jagged head wound. Blood instantly soaked the cloth. A doctor's stitches were crucial.

He closed and locked the window to stop any further attack. Surely his elderly servant couldn't have killed Jennings with just the broken knife lying next to the dead man. But if a third person had been in the fight, who was he? Where was he? Racing away or lurking close by?

Heading for the door, he glanced away from Jennings, sickened by the death's grotesqueness. He dashed toward the servants' quarters, yelling for his housekeeper and groom.

Kuma and her husband both came running. There was no sign of Nobu.

"Goda is hurt." Urgency made it harder to recall the Japanese words. "Bad American dead. Put new cloth on wound of Goda. I get doctor."

He tore off on foot, thankful the recently arrived English doctor had settled in the neighborhood.

Fifteen minutes later, Doctor Hughes briefly scrutinized the corpse. "An American?"

"Afraid so. An unsavory one. His victim's why you're needed."

The doctor strode across the room. "Your manservant, I presume. He's bloody well gone."

John's eyes watered. "Do whatever you can. Please. I've never met a better man."

His housekeeper stood a foot away, wringing her hands, while her husband muttered. John ordered them to heat up water, mainly to keep them occupied.

After wiping the blood from the wound, the doctor cradled the back of Goda's head with one hand while he examined the gash. His face hardened, and he gestured for his bag.

John handed it to him and squatted. "Does he have a chance?"

"The wound's wide and the man's in shock. I doubt he'll survive the night."

John rocked on his heels. "No! He's got to make it!"

"There's an outside chance, a small one. You don't know why he was attacked?"

"That devil was coming after me, no doubt. I'd sentenced him to prison."

"I see." He swabbed alcohol onto the slash and his needle, then began stitching it up.

John felt each prick's pain.

"So he figured murder would prove the injustice of his sentence." Bitterness tinged Doctor Hughes' words. "Plenty of scoundrels at ports. Drawn like filthy flies to honey." He tied off the last stitch.

John mumbled his agreement and then checked the servant's nearby room. A futon was already laid out, and the two moved Goda onto it.

"He's lost a lot of blood. You'll need to keep him covered and also sedated if he regains consciousness. I'll leave laudanum for him." The doctor checked a bottle's label and gave it to John. "Most important—swab the wounds with this alcohol every three hours throughout the night, and be careful not to get it into his eyes." He placed the bottle of alcohol by the futon.

"I'd do anything to save him, anything at all."

"Don't get your hopes up. Even if he survives the first critical hours, infection could set in. I'll come back in the morning." He picked up his medical bag. "Too bad! Such senseless violence."

Doctor Hughes pocketed his small fee and left, shaking his head.

John took the pot of hot water from Kuma's quivering hands and instructed the couple to get some rest. He seated himself beside Goda.

"Steady, my friend! You're going to pull through. You've got to."

Goda moaned.

John started to administer the painkiller, but the man was out cold. He placed his hands on Goda's chest and bowed his head. "Lord, you promised that even a cup of water given in your name would earn a reward. This man's given his blood for me, not in your name, but I am one of yours. Have mercy. Mercy! Please!"

Leaning his head against the wall, he thought back to the risk Goda had taken for him during the Hizen warlord's procession, just days after being hired. Even life-long friends would rarely be so selfless. "Almighty God, don't let him die!"

John woke with a start, a shaft of sunlight in his eyes. He lay on the floor next to Goda. He must have dozed off right before dawn. Holding his breath, he put his ear to his servant's chest.

Thank the Lord! He lived although still unconscious.

Kuma came to relieve John and was prepared to apply a *moxa*. She used gestures to show how she would place a paper cone holding ground-up bark and pith on powered charcoal and then ignite it on top of the skin.

John cringed. "*Moxa* may be good," he said in Japanese. "But *moxa* and foreign medicine not good together." Picking up the ingredients, he carried them to her bag. "We use doctor's medicine this time."

She frowned, but followed his example of pouring the alcohol on a piece of gauze and carefully patting it on the wound.

John checked on Goda throughout the morning and slipped a drop of the laudanum between his lips twice. Doctor Hughes still expressed little hope during his examination toward noon.

When two American sailors from a ship in the harbor came to remove Jennings' body, they tried to postulate how the servant, one hundred pounds lighter than Jennings, could have decapitated him.

"Dangest thing! Looks like he swung down from a crossbeam, don't it now?" one man remarked. "Some of that jujutsu voodoo?"

"If . . . not if, *when* he can speak, I'm going to find out what happened," John said. "Not even martial arts could account for this. But if there was a third person, he vanished like a phantom."

"Yeah, well, seems to be an off-with-the-American's-head phantom. Glad you're stationed here, not me, sir."

"We'll sort this out, find the hero or villain, when my manservant's back on his feet." *Make it so, Lord! Make it so!*

That afternoon Goda's sister came to care for him. The doctor agreed with John that a family member would make the best nurse.

Barely able to breathe, Sumi listened to her father's account of the gory attack. The poor servant! George Jennings had already shown his villainy during the trial. Now doubly so in trying to hunt down Cardiff and attacking a good, brave man like Goda.

"Mr. Robert Morrow," her father said, "is rumored to have been the criminal's accomplice." He paused and glanced at Sumi.

She realized her mouth hung open and closed it. Even though Mr. Morrow and his wife were like locust shells, his aid for a murderer seemed beyond possibility.

"People say the American hid in the Morrows' home before the attack," her father added as though to offer Sumi evidence. "I guess the rumor's true, seeing as the family returned to England two days ago."

When her parents began discussing the servant's chances for survival, Sumi asked to be excused and fled upstairs. She paced the room, trying to calm herself. Thank the gods, Cardiff-*sama* hadn't died! Every night when she strove to fall asleep, she saw her great-uncle's corpse. She couldn't have borne another loss. Although the consul and she would never be in a close relationship again, at least he was alive and not far away.

She looked toward her dresser, resisting the urge to reread the note that lay there. She'd first read it on the day of their return from Hagi. Actually she didn't need to see the note. She knew the words from memory.

> *Dear Miss Taguchi,*
>
> *I apologize for misjudging your fine effort in selecting a play for my fiancée to view. I realize now you did the best you could, considering the available plays. Please forgive my thoughtless manner in speaking with you at the hotel. I value our long friendship and your dedicated tutoring.*
>
> *Yours sincerely,*
> *John Cardiff*

Bittersweet words. He no longer blamed her, yet he'd cast aside their *long friendship*, at least until Miss Gray left Japan. When the consul had called on the family the day after their return to express his sympathy at her great-uncle's murder, she'd stayed in her room, sending word she was indisposed, as she truly was. She still couldn't face him in the following days and had beseeched her father to take over all of the lessons. He'd readily agreed.

Rising, she straightened her kimono and counseled herself to stay the course. Thankfully Cardiff-*sama* hadn't been killed, but his horrible fiancée possessed his heart and mind.

Kiyo's imperious voice called from downstairs. Sumi took a deep breath. Her cousin's insufferable attitude now reached the highest heavens. While Sumi had been in Hagi, the Kurohashi family had put forth a proposal for Keiji to marry

Kiyo despite her small dowry. Kiyo assumed a new role as a result, posing as a vastly superior elder relative—someone to be *obeyed*. Sumi nearly gagged at the thought.

Frowning as usual, her cousin met her at the bottom step. "There you are. You need to answer me when I call. Fetch today's food to offer before your great-uncle's tablet while I prepare the incense sticks."

Sumi headed for the kitchen, relieved to get away from Kiyo for even a minute. The cook, compassion in her eyes, had the steamed red snapper ready, a dish her great-uncle had especially liked. Sumi reverently carried the dish. Her great-uncle's spirit, if it was hovering near the eaves, would see her desire to honor him. The fifty days a spirit remained close to its bereaved family would pass all too soon, especially for his widow.

"After we finish, you must check on your great-aunt," Kiyo said when Sumi laid the dish at the front of the *Butsudan*. "She has so little left."

"I checked on her early this morning. She doesn't want me to move in with her." Her great-aunt had been given their guest room.

"See that you fully carry out your duty. She must deeply regret your ill-fated visit."

"We're doing all we can, and you've reminded me of her plight a hundred times." Sumi furtively wiped a tear. The worst part about Kiyo's taunting was its element of truth.

"And I'll continue to remind you." Kiyo poured fresh rapeseed oil into the little lantern in front of the great-uncle's stone tablet. "I warned you that a turtle sticking out its neck could get it cut off. But the neck wasn't yours this time, was it? I guess you're thankful for that. Nevertheless . . ."

Sumi stopped listening. What could she say? Kiyo was sure she'd foreseen the tragedy. Her tongue was sharper than the sharpest sword. Everyone would despise Kiyo if they had to live with her day in and day out. The *Holy Bible*'s parable about forgiveness was an impossible fantasy. In fact, destroying Kiyo's only memento of her parents would serve her right.

Kiyo stopped speaking, apparently expecting an answer to a question. Sumi ignored her glare and bowed to the altar. She would take care of that letter right then.

She started up the stairs at a fast pace, but then slowed her steps and stopped at the top. Now that she knew the truth about the dictionary pages, destroying the letter might make her uncomfortable the next time she talked with the Pendletons or even the consul—if she ever talked with *him* again.

She squared her shoulders. Let the *Kirishitan*s follow their own outlandish teaching. Kiyo deserved some anguish. She'd been harassing Sumi every chance she got, not caring a bit about her despair.

After making sure Kiyo hadn't followed her, she slid open the cupboard.

The letter wasn't where she thought she'd placed it. She took everything out of her side of the cupboard, shook out each kimono, sash, and undergarment, and put them back one by one. The letter wasn't there.

Maybe her cousin had found it while she'd been in Hagi. She checked Kiyo's side of the cupboard.

Not there.

Trembling, she opened Kiyo's chest.

Not there either.

Of course not, she told herself. If Kiyo had found it, she'd have let the whole world know about the *treachery*.

Steps creaked on the staircase. Breathlessly, Sumi finished putting everything back in the chest and whirled around. Kin entered with clean laundry and laid it on the chest with a puzzled look.

After the maid left the room, Sumi gave up searching. She must have thrown the letter away, mixed in perhaps with other papers—an unbelievably careless action. Was losing the letter the same as destroying it? Kiyo's dismay would be the same when she discovered the loss. Sumi's jaw tightened. Let her cousin suffer. If possible, let Kiyo feel as much debilitating agony as Sumi felt when her great-uncle died.

She gasped. She was *worse* than her cousin. What kind of goblin lived in her to make her want to inflict so much pain? Moaning, she dropped to her knees and bent over, her forehead hitting the mat. Any little variance from the righteous eight-fold path brought disaster. Look what happened after she deceived her grandfather. Now taking the letter and losing it would bring more troubles. Was there no escape from misery?

CHAPTER 39

Water cascaded from the eave outside Sumi's room. The storm bent and twisted their garden's younger trees. But in a neighbor's garden, the muted-green tip of an ancient pine tree held firm despite the blowing rain. Sumi couldn't tear her eyes away from the splendid tree, strong and resolute with deep roots.

She sighed, thinking back to the visit to Hagi. In all the turmoil, the perfect little wildflower had slipped her mind. Had the flower's maker helped in the storm, or had the twinkling light been a coincidence? She drummed her fingers on the open panel's post. Would it hurt to ask Cardiff-*sama* about this incident? Could she bear to see him, perhaps tutor him for one or two lessons, and then let go of him?

The room's shutters slammed shut in front of her. She jumped back.

"There you go staring into space again," Kiyo grumbled, hands on hips. "You need to prepare for dinner. You've been spending an inordinate amount of time staring at nothing—like a mindless fool without a sensible thought."

"That's not true," Sumi sputtered. "What's more, telling

you my thoughts would be like *neko ni koban,* putting gold coins before a cat."

"Kiyo clucked her tongue. "And I'm the cat, am I?"

"Since you say I'm a mindless fool."

"Looking at raindrops and moping all day *is* stupid. You had better learn how to handle my tasks. After I join the fine Kurohashi family"—Kiyo tilted her head up—"overseeing the cook and her assistant will fall to your oh-so-delicate hands."

"If I'm given your responsibilities, my oh-so-able hands will have no trouble."

As usual, Kiyo left the room in a huff.

Sumi repressed an urge to shove the shutters open. Admittedly, her unbearable cousin had a point. Other than spinning a little thread and checking on a few of Kin's household duties, she had contributed almost nothing to the family. Just to get up in the mornings was a struggle. But she couldn't stay in a stupor the rest of her life.

She would look at raindrops whenever she wanted. But tonight she'd offer—in front of Kiyo at dinner—to take her father's place at the next tutoring session. And the consul's indifference wouldn't defeat her either. She needed answers—a root.

Crossing the bridge into the foreign sector by herself three days later, Sumi wove her way through the crush of carriages and people dressed in Persian *pyjamas,* Chinese *qipao,* English waistcoats and trousers, military uniforms, and other strange apparel from unidentifiable places. Like a living organism, the area had mushroomed. Many more houses of foreign design, as well as boarding houses, eating establishments, and saloons, lined the crisscrossing roads. Trading companies crowded one another near the river leading to the bay. The new additions blocked her view of Cardiff & Associates' warehouse and offices, but she pictured their prominent positions facing the harbor. She'd like to explore the area's expansion, but without her father, she had to go directly to the consulate.

At the consulate's gate, she pulled the knob on the end of a wire running to an inside bell. Her rapid pulse refused to slow.

Cardiff himself let her into the grounds. After a surprised step back, a big smile had lit up his face. "I was hoping you'd come soon. It's been far too long. I suppose your father has other business today?"

"He does, but he will meet me at the new teahouse at the end of our session. I—I've had a lot to attend to recently myself." She gripped her green shawl as a gust of wind took hold of it.

"This north wind is getting stronger. Let me help you inside."

"I can manage, but thank you." She hoped she sounded independent. Maybe he hadn't noticed her voice's tremble.

He looked at her and nodded while positioning his body to shield her. His small kindnesses always pleased her. She warmed to his nearness despite her resolve to resist his charms.

After hanging her shawl in its usual place by the door, he motioned for her to enter the parlor. "I've missed our lessons. It's strange how isolated we can feel even when surrounded by people. But you and I have gotten well acquainted, I'm glad to say."

She nodded and accepted his gesture to sit in a velvet wing chair. "I'm afraid my chatter might use the whole time if I'm not careful." *And we will never be acquainted well enough.*

"If time's a problem, let's do away with the lesson. I always learn a lot just talking with you."

"But—"

"No, I insist. Give me a minute to order us tea and slices of the cake the cook has mastered after much trial and error." He headed for the hallway, and a bell jingled a minute later.

While she waited for his return, the memory of the dance lesson came back—Cardiff's touch, the wisp of his warm breath, the thrill of being in step with him. That would be the only day they would ever dance together. She fought against the lump in her throat. She was finished with tears, even the threat of tears.

Her gaze rested on the door to the hallway. The strange shadowy person watching them waltz had seemed out of place, sinister. Where had she seen that figure?

Cardiff strode back across the room. "You did receive my note?" He sat down in the matching wing chair.

"Yes, the day we returned."

"I am sorry I was a beast about the *kabuki* play. I'm the one who didn't understand a thing."

"You should not apologize. I should have used more wisdom." His face registered unbelief. "I'm sorry. My country's ways don't let you take blame."

He reached out and squeezed her hand. "I think highly of your ways."

She felt herself blushing.

He removed his hand and straightened his cuffs. "Also, I've wanted to offer you my deepest sympathy concerning your great-uncle. Such a terrible blow to you and your family."

Her chest tightened. If only his eyes weren't so tender.

"Yes. We'll never get over it."

"I believe I mentioned once that my father died in an accident at his mill during my college years. Not under such terrible circumstances as your relative, but I understand the loss, the feeling of finality."

"I wish I'd wake up and find it a nightmare." She fought for control. If she broke down sobbing, she'd never be able to face him again.

"I trust the police will bring the criminals to justice. Every one of you could have easily perished because of those evil men. Thank God the rest of you escaped!"

She blinked. "Should I thank a god, perhaps your god? That was . . . a question I had."

"What a splendid question, Miss Taguchi! I can't imagine answering anything but yes." He leaned forward and faced her more fully. "But may I ask why you have this question?"

"It would take a while to explain."

"I'd like to hear, no matter how long it takes." He gestured toward the cups of tea and white slices of cake Kuma set on the nearby table. "And please have some refreshments."

"Thank you." She picked up a small plate with a slice of cake and a tiny fork, then took a big breath. "To begin, I have to tell you what I found out from a Western astronomy book—that we are only specks in a universe of ten-thousands of stars. I guess you know that."

He nodded.

"Then, while in Hagi, I looked at a simple wildflower in a new way, maybe because of the Western science . . . or maybe because of Mrs. Pendleton's classes. I'm not sure."

"English classes and science." He leaned forward. "I'm eager to hear."

She sat straighter. "At first, I just noticed that a yellow daisy was a tinier speck than me. But the petals had such a beautiful pattern"—she steadied her voice—"I asked whatever power made the flower to let me know if it also cared for people. At the same time, I was afraid."

"Afraid of what?"

"That this flower's maker might be the Christian god you and the Pendletons talk about because I didn't know any gods in my country connected to wildflowers."

Cardiff stared at her for a minute. "You've been on a long journey since September," he said at last. "Not the trip to Hagi. I think Almighty God led you to this insight. It's extraordinary."

His enthusiasm brought her a flush of pleasure, but also greater anxiety. What if the flower's maker really was *Almighty God*?

"There's more to tell." She tried to smile. "The flower's maker may have helped us on the rough sea. Right after I questioned if that deity could help, we saw a glimmer from a fisherman's lantern, and we made it to the shore in spite of the wind and waves."

"Yes, you should thank God. I'm sure he helped you, because of your prayer to learn about him."

"But why didn't the maker—your god, you think—help my great-uncle too? Why let me live, when my deception about the English classes led to his death? And why let the one who killed him also live?"

"Those are difficult questions, the most distressing kind." He rubbed the back of his neck. "Many factors must have led to your great-uncle's death. We understand only a tiny part. I do believe God helps us because we turn to him, not because we deserve it. But some questions can't be answered in this life.

Goda, too, was an innocent victim of an evil plot."

She sighed. So many puzzles. So much unknown.

"I'm afraid I can't be much help with those enigmas. But as you're convinced your deception was wrong, I can tell you the Maker holds out an offer of forgiveness."

"Don't you think my deception was wrong? It led to much trouble."

"When you mentioned it after the class last fall, it seemed almost inconsequential, a small sin. To me, as a Westerner, your grandfather was unreasonable in forbidding you to study English."

"But deception is wrong in both our countries, isn't it?"

"True enough. Only I don't see why attending the English classes would lead to your great-uncle's assassination. That's a big leap."

She paused, fearing Cardiff-*sama* would guess his role. But she had to say something. "One thing led to another, and finally to Hagi."

"Like a tiny pebble that begins a rockslide, then. But one has to be careful not to misapply the principle of cause and effect. That principle doesn't make you responsible for the evil someone else carried out."

"Pepper pods and dragonfly wings—they're like my deception and my great-uncle's death. It's all one, don't you see? Perhaps my deception was like that Alamo battle you mentioned. I didn't see the unwanted results of what looked good in the beginning."

"Oh, my dear Miss Taguchi, your deception was nothing like the Alamo. And that famous *haiku* might not have all the answers either. If my company sold silk to someone and later an evil person killed my customer to get that silk, I wouldn't be responsible for the murder, would I?"

"I guess not. I'm not sure." Why couldn't she gather her thoughts? Was her confusion due to Cardiff-*sama*'s nearness and his slight scent of spice and tobacco? Or was it because the ideas floated like unreachable clouds high above her?

"Clearly, I would not be liable. Otherwise, no one would dare do anything at all because of the possible consequences." Cardiff's gray eyes shone with concern.

She turned his words over in her mind. If only his explanation were right, how reassuring that would be. Yet somehow her situation seemed different.

The mention of forgiveness reminded her of Kiyo. Although she hated to reveal the bitterness between the two of them, her words spilled out. However, she carefully omitted the attempt to take revenge by almost destroying—and then losing—the irreplaceable letter.

"To be honest," the consul said at the end of her account, "I've recently had feelings much stronger than yours. I hated someone so much I would have rejoiced at that person's death."

"I cannot imagine you hating anyone."

"Well, I don't know even now if the Englishman Morrow aided Jennings when he came back to do me in. But for those first two weeks, whenever I thought of Goda lying there, struggling for his life, white-hot fury possessed me. Even during the Sunday services, hatred for Robert Morrow sprang up. I wanted to smash in his face."

"But your hatred for Mr. Morrow seems right," Sumi ventured.

"The initial anger, yes. My hatred, no. My problem was assuming God's position as judge. Once I called to mind that I also needed God's mercy—not a little mercy, a great deal of mercy—it changed me."

"Just like that, your hate disappeared? Completely?"

"No, even now that Goda's getting better, it still returns. Sometimes as strong as ever. I have to remind myself each time that the Almighty is the ultimate judge. I'm not."

Sumi took a deep breath. His words echoed the parable's lesson about forgiving debts, and they were just as hard to accept, even coming from him.

Cardiff's brow furrowed. "I'm afraid I haven't had much experience in counseling people in spiritual matters. Perhaps you could talk with the Pendletons. In fact, Richard told me the other day he'd discovered biblical truth in the Japanese ideograph for *gi*, for 'righteousness.' I think Mr. and Mrs. Pendleton would explain these truths better."

"The Pendletons are very kind . . . and wise." She pictured the ideograph for *gi*. How could the symbols for a *lamb over oneself* have anything to do with the Christians' belief about righteousness? One more puzzle to tease her mind, like a lantern that didn't illuminate the pathway sufficiently, yet attracted attention.

"Thank you for the suggestion. I will visit the couple." She took a bite of the cake, then noticed his furrowed brow. "But you are a great help. I hope my words haven't tired you."

"Certainly not. Your candor makes you an even more valued friend. I can't tell you how much I'll miss you and your gracious family."

"Why do you say *miss*?" Dread entwined her. She nearly choked on the cake.

"Why, I promised Catherine I'd return to the United States more quickly than originally planned. Perhaps even by the end of next summer. You didn't know? I think I told your father."

"Next summer!" Her hand flew to her throat, where a big

lump blocked her breath. "But you will return here? Together with her?"

"We plan to stay in New York indefinitely." A wounded look escaped before he looked away.

"And not ever return?" She swallowed hard. The woman should follow the man, not vice versa. Cardiff-*sama* was intelligent, brave, kind . . . with high status. How could his fiancée exert such power over him?

"It appears unavoidable. Miss Gray feels New York would be the best place for us to raise a family."

A wild, unheard of thought captured Sumi. "Couldn't I go to the United States too? To teach Japanese for a year or so? Isn't there a need for Japanese language teachers in your city?"

"I'm afraid not. And life in the U.S. is very, very different, very strange compared to here. It wouldn't do to pull up a charming flower like you by the roots. You might not thrive in different soil."

"Roots? Cardiff-*sama*, I think my roots can grow in a new place. Like a tall pine—"

He shook his head. "No, it's impossible. I'm sorry. Sorrier than you can possibly know." His tone carried a sad finality. With a thin smile, he raised his teacup. "A toast to your brave spirit."

While Cardiff walked her to the consulate gate, Sumi lectured herself. She had to accept the inevitable. Not only would she not have a special relationship with Cardiff-*sama*, she would have none at all. No chance to hear about him from her father. No chance to pass him on the road. No chance to see the twinkle in his eyes.

A temple bell sounded in the distance, mimicking *The Tale of Heike*'s beginning words: *In the sound of the Gion Temple's bell, the impermanence of all things reverberates.* Each reverberation differed, a perfect example of change. So, it was true—nothing lasted in the world, including friendships.

She pulled her shawl closer. The cold wind chilled her neck despite Cardiff's attempt to shield her from the blast.

John bowed to Miss Taguchi as he opened the gate. "Until next time. And please, don't wait so long. You are my favorite female tutor."

"Your *only* female tutor." Her downcast face became more cheerful as she smiled and looked up at him through her long lashes.

He made the obligatory second bow to mask the unexpected rush of longing that flooded him.

She walked toward the nearby teahouse, and he waited, ignoring the biting wind, knowing she would turn and bow a final time. He couldn't help noticing her graceful figure, enhanced by the kimono's lines and her mincing steps.

For a moment, when she'd described her heartache and her search to understand the traumatic events during her trip, he'd yearned to put his arm around her and comfort her. The thought of Catherine hadn't held him back as much as the desire not to let passing feelings—and they definitely had to be passing—interfere with discussing such important truths. What a wonderful discovery she'd made—a shift from the Shinto and Buddhist ideas of spirits and gods and impersonal enlightenment to a caring creator.

She turned and they exchanged the final bows. He batted away a desire to escort her farther. He had to guard against getting carried away. After all, she simply happened to be the only Japanese lady he could talk to without a language barrier.

He grunted at that last bit of foolishness. In reality, Miss Taguchi happened to be the only lady in the *world*, besides Catherine, whose every word and insight he treasured.

What set Miss Taguchi apart? Not just her pretty face or figure. Her thoughtfulness? Her curiosity? She definitely had many qualities he sought in his closest friendships. She would make some Japanese man of adventuresome spirit and intelligence an extraordinarily fine wife. In fact, in some respects, she outshone Catherine.

Whoa! What was he thinking? Miss Taguchi was only beginning to learn about the world—about literature and science and the Almighty. She couldn't hold a candle to Catherine, really. Could she?

CHAPTER 40

Sumi swallowed the last of the too-sweet cookie and patted her mouth with the small white napkin. "Thank you for the treat and for taking time to talk with me. Today I have many questions." If the Pendletons couldn't clarify her jumbled thoughts, she'd just have to give up trying to figure out the flower maker.

"You are always welcome here." Mrs. Pendleton, facing her across their parlor's coffee table, offered an encouraging smile.

Her husband, sitting in a nearby puffy armchair, nodded his agreement. "We're never too busy to talk with you. Ask to your heart's content."

Despite resolving to be brave, Sumi's voice trembled when she began to tell about the Hagi wildflower. Her nervousness increased when the couple turned to each other, not concealing their astonishment.

Mr. Pendleton adjusted his square spectacles, picked up the *Holy Bible*, and read sentences aloud about the world's creation. "You see," he said, looking over his glasses' rims, "rather than dripping water from a jeweled sword to create these islands,

God spoke successive commands and the entire universe came into being. Yes, he is the wildflower's maker."

Sumi offered a faint "I see," already fairly certain the *Holy Bible*'s record of creation matched reality better than her country's traditional account.

He turned to another place in the book. "The Creator proved his love for all of us"—he ran his finger over the page's words and then looked up—"by giving his Son, Jesus, to take the low status of man. Jesus suffered a criminal's death so *our* sins, every one of them, could be forgiven."

"I'm sorry. I cannot understand that part." She clenched her hands. She would have to risk asking rude questions if the Pendletons were to help with the taunting riddles. "When we do wrong, there must be suffering, a penalty. How can this 'forgiveness' be right?"

"I have a question," Mrs. Pendleton said. "When a warlord does wrong, can one of his samurai suffer in his place? Would that satisfy justice, or offset what some people here call karma?" She spoke more slowly, more carefully than usual.

Sumi pondered the strange question. "It sometimes happens," she answered, remembering Retainer Yamamoto's suicide. But I still don't understand. Please excuse my slowness."

"Let's turn it around. Suppose a warlord had a samurai whom he greatly loved. If that samurai did wrong, could the *warlord or the warlord's son* suffer in the *warrior's* place?"

"It's unheard of." Such an outrageous question was obviously irrelevant.

"But could the warlord or his son suffer in the warrior's place if he really wanted to?" Mrs. Pendleton persisted.

"Yes. Yes, he could. But it would never happen. A warlord

is too highly esteemed. The samurai must serve him and his family—*always*." Instantly regretting her forcefulness, she softened her tone. "Would it happen in America?"

"Perhaps, if we had warlords. But the point I want to make is that Almighty God, who created the wildflowers and the whole universe, chose to give his Son to suffer a cruel death in *our* place."

"Please pardon me, but why would this god do something like that if he is truly almighty, the lord of everything?" Sumi sighed. The idea made even less sense than the parable about forgiveness. Grasping the Christians' ideas was like trying to grab hold of carp swimming in a fast stream.

"Because he *loves* each of us more than we can ever fathom, and only his Son was good enough to sacrifice himself for us." Mrs. Pendleton touched Sumi's hand. "His Son Jesus paid our penalty. Justice is satisfied, don't you see?"

Sumi clasped her chest. Could this maker care that much about people, who were just specks? No, it was too good to be true. Yet . . . the consul had cared enough about her standoffish grandfather to risk his life in their burning house. The Pendletons always welcomed her, taught her, showed concern for her even though she couldn't repay them. If the believers cared that much, then why not the one they believed in?

When she'd heard about Jesus in the English class, she'd thought the execution of such a respected teacher deplorable. She hadn't understood the magnificent purpose. How could her countrymen have thought the religion was evil, forcing every person to stomp on Jesus' image? She had done so herself. Yet despite this, the maker had evidently helped them on the ocean—because of *love*. Years earlier, she'd secretly read and puzzled over one sentence from the *Holy Bible*: *God is love*.

Now the words made more sense.

A shiver of delight wound its way around her heart.

"Sumi, would you like to thank Jesus for what he's done for you?" Mrs. Pendleton looked into her eyes. "Would you like to accept him as your Lord? We know that's a . . . a very momentous decision for you."

As if she plummeted from a cloud to the hard earth, pain struck her mid section. Her heart beat wildly. "I don't know. I don't know what to say."

"We don't want to rush you. Consider carefully," Mr. Pendleton advised.

Sumi sat still, saying nothing, trying to calm herself. The couple also were quiet.

The offer of forgiveness squeezed her heart. She already knew her deception deserved judgment. And since the almighty god required Cardiff-*sama* to forsake his hatred of Mr. Morrow, her own smoldering hatred of Kiyo had to be wrong too . . . and her strong dislike of Miss Catherine Gray. She had strayed a great distance from the right meditation required in the Eightfold Path to enlightenment.

But what about her parents and especially her grandfather? Could she bear to cause them grief yet again? How could she turn away from her family? She wanted this master—one who didn't want to kill her, who loved her instead. But were the obstacles too great? The aftermath too dire?

The Pendletons began speaking to each other in soft voices. Sumi kept her head down, struggling to make up her mind. A decision seemed impossible. Maybe she should *wait* until she learned more. Mr. and Mrs. Pendleton wouldn't object. They'd help her.

But if she waited, what would happen to her little root?

And, oh those ancestor spirits! They would fight against this.

She sensed a spiteful spirit rebuking her. How would she bow at the god shelf, it asked, or honor her forebears at the *obon* observance, or protect her future children through their dedications at Suwa Shrine? But children, the spirit cackled, wouldn't be in her future anyway. The dedications wouldn't pose a problem, for she'd never marry!

She shivered, then steadied herself. When she'd been on the verge of marrying Keiji-*sama*, she'd been willing to sacrifice her desires in order to be loyal to her family. How could she not offer her loyalty to the one who made the universe?

She clenched her hands. She was not a female warrior, but she could take the step, no matter how hard.

"I think I should take your god to be my lord. But I don't know how."

The couple looked at each other again, their faces radiant.

"That's the most wonderful decision you could ever make," Mr. Pendleton said. "I can explain how . . . if you are sure."

"I am."

He paused, then nodded. "Very good." His voice carried a quiver. "Now, to take God as your Lord, you talk to him in much the same way as you did on your trip. Use your own words. Tell him you accept his Son Jesus' sacrifice for your sin. Then welcome him into your life as your liege."

Sumi bowed her head and closed her eyes as she'd seen the Christians do. "Please help me overcome my weakness," she whispered in Japanese. "Before today, I never understood about your son. Thank you for having him die for me." She choked back tears. "I am honored to have you as my liege. I pledge my loyalty."

She opened her eyes and sighed, relief washing over her. She'd taken an incredible step. Maybe the Maker had helped her do it. Anyway, it was done.

Mrs. Pendleton hugged her. Mr. Pendleton enthusiastically shook her hand. For a few minutes, he pointed out additional information in the *Holy Bible*, but Sumi couldn't absorb any more. The Pendletons encouraged her to read a chapter every day in the English Bible, especially in the New Testament. They promised to get her a Japanese one as soon as it became available.

While walking home, she told herself over and over she'd made the right decision. But her stomach churned as she envisioned the storm when she told her family. She'd have to tell them sometime, but not yet.

She paused when she came to the chipped wall, remembering the feel of the dagger catching several of her hairs as it missed its mark. Had the Maker intervened? Perhaps. The samurai hadn't hurled a second dagger.

In her home, she found her flower arrangement in the *tokonoma* had withered. She hurriedly disposed of it, hoping Kiyo hadn't noticed she'd neglected to add water.

The wilted laurel leaves and branch of purplish bush clover reminded her of the battlefield at Hagi and Bashō's words: only a *summer field of grass* remained of *the glorious warriors' dreams*. What difference might this new liege make after her own death? Would the Maker of everything rescue her from wandering in the poet's *withered fields*?

She dug the *Holy Bible* out of its hiding place in her cupboard and curled up in the corner of her room, welcoming her yellow cat beside her. Opening it in the middle, she read a few lines down from the top of the page. Then reread: *As for man, his days are as grass: as a flower of the field, so he flourisheth. For the wind passeth over it, and it is gone; and the place thereof shall know it no more.*

Amazing! Exactly like the poem! She read on. *But the mercy of the Lord is from everlasting to everlasting upon them that fear him.*

She clasped the book to her forehead, tingling with excitement. The Maker had just spoken to her! He had perceived her unspoken question and answered it. Precisely. He was talking to her through these pages! Despite the old English, she'd grasped the meaning—*everlasting* mercy was given to her. Tears ran down her cheeks. It was the first time she'd ever cried from joy.

John issued a proclamation for the American community to observe a Thanksgiving Day. The foreigners had been blessed during the year with unusually good weather, acceptance by the local Japanese citizens, and financial opportunities. More importantly, John's heart filled with gratitude for Goda's improved condition. His servant could not only walk short distances, but had also begun practicing a few moves in the martial arts.

Goda made it clear, however, that *jujutsu* hadn't saved him. A mysterious samurai, whose sword came from nowhere, deserved the honor. Furthermore, the sword's scabbard carried the Chōshū clan's symbol. Such a shadowy warrior arriving in the nick of time, no matter how baffling, was an added cause for thanks.

During the celebration at the Commercial Hotel, the

Pendletons pulled John aside. Their countenances radiated excitement.

John could hardly keep himself from interrupting, waiting breathlessly to hear the end of their detailed account. Was it possible the dear girl had entered the kingdom of God? At their confirmation, he exclaimed, "Thank God!" A couple next to him turned their heads, and he lowered his voice. "Why, that's the best news ever! I prayed our Lord would help her find the answers to her questions. I never dreamed it would be this soon."

"She'll be tested in greater ways than she's ever been," Richard said, "and she's been through more difficulty in the last year and a half than many people experience in their lifetime."

"Right you are. But she's a determined young lady." John glanced at Margaret. "And the Almighty will continue what only he could have begun."

She smiled. "You read my mind."

The hotel's head chef, standing next to the buffet, beckoned to John. He reluctantly excused himself to check on the refreshments.

"Just replenish all the dishes." John swept his hand toward the end of the table. He couldn't concentrate on something as ordinary as food when he'd just heard about a miracle. Even while greeting several guests who were helping themselves to the array of desserts, his mind dwelled on Miss Taguchi. Yes, God would sustain her, but he hated to think of the trouble she'd face. Would her family require her to worship their gods? If she refused, would they threaten to disown her, or actually do so? If only he could stay in Japan a year or two longer, but that would never do. Catherine would point out—reasonably enough—that the Pendletons could lend Miss Taguchi support.

He grimaced. He didn't actually want to stay just a few more years. His irrational yearning was to make Nagasaki his second home. Yes, to visit New York from time to time, see his mother and brothers, but settle down right where he was.

He could buck Catherine. He could break their engagement. It had crossed his mind they weren't suited for each other. But he'd loved her for years. And besides that, what kind of man would propose marriage and persuade his sweetheart to visit him halfway around the world only to break her heart? He wasn't that kind of person.

He threw back his shoulders. This was a day for rejoicing. He wouldn't yield to his dismay about leaving this country . . . and its people.

CHAPTER 41

First of December (Month of the Ox)

In contrast to the snowy New York winters, gold and russet chrysanthemums still bloomed by the consulate's wall even though Christmas was around the corner. The number of social events on John's calendar confirmed the holiday season's arrival. One small consolation of leaving Japan, he told himself, would be the end of *making merry* while being true to a faraway sweetheart.

Because of the intervening ocean, he'd received just one letter from Catherine since her departure. She'd posted it from Yokohama before heading across the Pacific. Although interested as always in everything she'd discussed, even her description of another passenger's dowdy attire, he clung to a hope she would reconsider living in Japan—at least offer to try it for a time after their marriage.

When her next letter finally arrived, he tore it open. Had she reconsidered?

He read her greetings and description of Hawaii with a smile, and then stunned, raced through the remainder. Although he'd stopped drinking, he dug out a bottle of whiskey from the back of the cabinet and poured himself a capful. Sinking into a chair before his desk, he scanned the shattering words.

> *. . . I was dismayed to learn in a back edition of the* San Francisco Bulletin *that special armed detachments guard the foreign legations in Edo against attack. The June 28 article stated, "The white men here are in a state of constant alarm."*
>
> *Honestly, John, I cannot understand how you can remain in such a dangerous place and could have encouraged my visit. You gave me no hint of the peril. I question now whether I could ever feel secure with you, always worrying about not only our safety but also our little ones' welfare.*
>
> *However, I hesitate to break our long-standing engagement. But to continue our understanding, I ask you to return to the United States no later than June and to give me your solemn promise you will settle down in New York permanently. I ask this for your safety and my peace of mind.*
>
> *If you cannot find it in your heart to affirm these two requests, I will release you from your marriage proposal.*

He grabbed his pen to respond, to argue that neither of them had been in danger. Other than the criminal Jennings, no American had been injured or slain.

He dipped the pen in ink but stopped with it halfway to the

paper. Danger did threaten whenever one met a warlord's procession or ventured beyond the settlement at night. And he couldn't contradict the newspaper article she'd found so disturbing. Americans and Europeans were alarmed—although more so in Yokohama and Edo than in Nagasaki.

And besides, that wasn't the real problem. Her feelings for him were where the trouble lay.

I won't phrase things right if I write now. Better wait till tomorrow.

The next day he took up his pen again. But after writing his first sentence, he remembered Miss Taguchi's willingness to follow him to New York, not as his sweetheart but as a friend and adventurer. On the other hand, Catherine demanded he follow her dictates.

He felt nauseous. For him, their relationship had trumped everything except the Almighty. So much so, he'd agreed to sell out and leave Japan—just not as soon nor as shackled as she demanded. He thumped down his pen. He'd answer her the following day with a calmer spirit.

That evening, he walked along the seashore, little noticing the chilly wind. Lights winked from the ships out in the harbor as though beckoning him on board. The faint outline of a steamer anchored far out promised a fast journey. He could easily meet Catherine's deadline, or even beat it, if he sold the trading company's Japanese holdings for whatever he could get—to the delight of his competitors—and gave up his post. Mr. Pendleton could step in as vice-consul temporarily.

He picked up a handful of shells and tossed them out into the waves one by one, picturing her gay laugh, her tendrils of hair swept back by the breeze. So what would it be?

A white gull cried and whirled away, abandoning the shore's lean pickings, vanishing into the dark sky. A surge of anger ripped through John. It wasn't a case of Catherine rejecting Japan and danger. She had abandoned *him*—not finding juicy enough pickings to continue with him unless he changed! He swallowed a curse word.

Ripples of water lapped at his boots, and he stepped back onto higher ground. A straggling fishing boat, prow high, headed toward the city docks. Fragments of banter and guffaws traveled across the water. The fishermen no doubt looked forward to going home to wives and children, not to being set adrift from all their future plans.

Silvery light from the moon, high above, reflected on the foamy waves between the boat and the shore. He watched the water for a minute. Since he and his company's ship had survived the edge of a typhoon, he'd been drawn to the Scripture: *The Lord on high is mightier than the noise of many waters.* But knowing the Creator was in charge was one thing, and feeling it was another.

He climbed back up the embankment and avoided looking at the shadowy man and wife he passed, returning their greeting in a barely audible voice. He nodded to three sentries patrolling the street and waited to extinguish the two lamps at the consulate's gate until the men passed by. Hopefully anyone wishing to visit would take the hint. He sure wasn't up to entertaining.

His trousers brushed a chrysanthemum plant when he turned toward the house. Its flowers brought back Miss Taguchi's discovery of the Flower Maker, who cared for her even though she was a speck. Last week her eyes had shone when she'd told him about her new allegiance. He walked into the house, reliving the moment. What a breakthrough she'd had. His own life was in disarray, but at least hers was starting to bloom.

Drawing a chair to his desk, he composed his response to Catherine—that he understood her fears, but could not meet her demands. He accepted the consequence with regret and wished her much future happiness.

Picking up her framed likeness, he started to slide it into the desk drawer, but paused and studied her face. He'd never imagined their engagement's dissolution. Yet she had changed, and he had too.

With an ache, he tucked the image away.

CHAPTER 42

John stepped back and admired the small pine tree he'd decorated for the consulate. Now that the first shock about Catherine had subsided, the hustle and bustle before the Christmas holiday helped lift his spirits. In fact, he prided himself on his resilience, even having the sense a fresh adventure lay ahead.

A problem stared him in the face, however.

The Christmas ball.

He could no longer use his fiancée as an excuse for not showing interest in the young ladies in the foreign community. At the news he wouldn't be leaving Japan after all, his acquaintances deduced the reason. Twice he'd barely avoided being roped into escorting someone's relative to the affair.

There was a solution he'd like to take. And why not? Why not once again invite the one young lady he couldn't get off his mind? Then too, the ball would give him more time to encourage her new faith. Two trade contracts needed translations. He'd take care of the task by looking up Mr. Taguchi that very afternoon.

At his interpreter's home, John focused his attention on the translation work with Mr. Taguchi until Miss Taguchi poured his tea and served him his favorite sponge cake, introduced by the Portuguese hundreds of years earlier. While he observed her graceful movements, his powers of concentration evaporated.

He adjusted his jacket and warned himself against sounding too eager. "Next week on Friday, there's a Christmas ball at the Commercial Hotel. A festive occasion, really grand, with all kinds of beautiful decorations befitting the season. Would you care to attend another ball as my guest, Miss Taguchi? I can ride here and bring an extra horse for your father so we can escort you to the hotel in style."

"Next week, Cardiff-*sama*? I, uh, don't know if that is possible." She blushed.

"It seems you have other plans." His heart sank despite telling himself her refusal wasn't the end of the world.

"No, I don't have plans, but . . ." She bit her bottom lip.

John hesitated to force the issue, but unless her answer was an unspoken one, it didn't seem to be a firm refusal. "I thought you might want to practice those waltz steps you learned."

"You are kind to invite me, but I . . ." Her voice trailed off, and she resorted to fanning herself.

John huffed out a breath. How stupid he was to leave her in the dark about Catherine. "Not to change the subject, but I don't believe I've told you my latest news. I won't be returning to New York to marry." He mustered a smile. "So I'm looking forward to learning more about this country and spending time with my good friends."

"You're not returning to America? You'll live in Nagasaki? With Miss Gray?" Her cheeks grew rosier.

Mr. Taguchi stirred at his desk, no doubt reminding his daughter to behave with decorum.

"In our last correspondence, we released each other from our engagement."

A light flickered in Miss Taguchi's eyes before she blinked and ran her hand over her forehead. "I am sorry. Then my mistakes while trying to entertain Miss Gray turned out to be terrible. They ruined everything."

"Actually, that had nothing to do with it. I've come to see that Catherine and I belong to two different worlds. She grasped that before I did." Just a couple of months earlier, he'd described *Miss Taguchi* as belonging to a different world. Life could turn a corner without warning.

"This must be hard for you. The Western style of love is powerful, isn't it? The stronger the feeling, the worse the heartbreak."

"Any loss is painful, but I'm optimistic about the future."

She nodded and poured more tea for him.

John blew on the nearly boiling liquid while mulling over her strange words about Western love, then noticed the lull in the conversation. "So concerning the ball? May I have the pleasure of your company? We both enjoyed ourselves at the one last May, did we not?"

"Yes, last May's ball was splendid." She glanced at her father, who kept on working. "Father, Cardiff-*sama* requests our presence at the ball next week."

After studying her for a minute, her father rose and bowed. "We would be honored to observe the holiday celebration."

Relief flooded John. Then he looked from the one to the other. Had unspoken communication taken place this time?

Her brow wrinkled. "Cardiff-*sama*, I wonder if a kimono can be suitable for dancing."

"More than suitable. Any of your beautiful kimonos would

be perfect." No doubt she would be striking in a ball gown, but at the expense of her own style of beauty.

Her eyes smiled at him. "I'm looking forward to the evening."

"I'll come for you both at seven o'clock. We'll have a grand time."

John grinned at his next thought. *Those old biddies will be beside themselves when the lovely Miss Taguchi and I do turns around the ballroom floor. They'll be downright aghast.*

The next day, John felt he'd landed in another universe as he absorbed the news Mr. Taguchi brought about his groom.

"Incredible! Could your aunt possibly be mistaken about Nobu's identity?"

"She saw his profile clearly when you mounted your horse yesterday."

"Whew!" John shook his head. "I knew something was odd about him, but a nobleman? Unbelievable!" He paused to hand his interpreter one of the cups of tea Kuma brought in. "Why would the warlord's cousin disguise himself? Some trouble with his clan?"

"Not that we know of. My aunt said he suddenly left the Chōshū domain, but was not banished." Mr. Taguchi took a slurp of the steaming tea. "His parents still live in Hagi."

"With a background like that, he couldn't be desperate for employment, certainly not one as lowly as a groom. Makes a sinister reason for his masquerade likely, I'm afraid. Sort of reminds me of the tale about the forty-seven *rōnin*." John searched his interpreter's face. "What do you think? You remember, I'm sure, that your former neighbor, the bronzeware merchant, recommended the man."

"And the brother of the merchant's servant was the arsonist."

John nodded. "An improbable coincidence." He pictured the squat proprietor patting his chest when the police approached after the fire. "Mr. Omura appears either to be part of a conspiracy or to have terrible judgment. Both strange possibilities for a well-off merchant."

"There is another part to the riddle, sir. Your groom, Ōta Nobumitsu, was probably the Chōshū samurai who saved your manservant's life."

"Yes, had to be. Nobu's action may have saved my life too. Remarkable! Of course, he did strike down an American, but who could fault his killing such a reprehensible criminal and saving Goda? It's been the only violence in the man's long service." John got up and stirred the coals in the fireplace, then turned back toward Mr. Taguchi. "Maybe his constant contact with foreigners is having a beneficial effect. If there was a conspiracy, it may be defunct." He took his seat again.

"I doubt . . . I don't know, sir. It is hard for me to trust him. I think you said you had a loaded gun when you found your injured servant. Maybe your groom heard you coming, knew you would have a weapon."

"True. That might have caused him not to take me on." John rubbed his brow. "But the man, in spite of his mood swings, has had an impressive dedication to duty as my groom. What will happen when he's reported to the governor?"

"An interrogation. Then probably banishment to the northernmost island's wilderness. A Chōshū nobleman disguised as a foreigner's groom? The governor will suspect a bad purpose. A *very* bad purpose. Also, the High Council could call him to Edo for more questioning."

John winced. "I've survived having him with me for almost a year and a half. Let's hold off reporting the situation for a week or so. I'd like to try one course of action first."

A worry line wrinkled Taguchi's forehead. "As you wish, but may I make a suggestion?"

"Certainly."

"Chief Inspector Sato is an acquaintance of mine and a friend to my father. May I notify him of the deception? He would not want to anger the Chōshū clan without good reason. Informing the inspector would let him investigate quietly before making an accusation."

"Go ahead, then, but please be sure to relay my request to delay any interrogation."

Mr. Taguchi bowed his assent, but paused at the gate. "May I say, sir, I am worried about your safety."

"I'll keep my revolver at hand, just in case. But I appreciate your concern."

"A disgruntled *rōnin* could be more deadly than poisonous puffer fish." He started to enter the *kago,* but turned toward John again. "Samurai have years of training in surprise attacks."

With that, Taguchi departed.

CHAPTER 43

Nobumitsu tensed as the cutter carrying him and the consul drew broadside to the American steamship. He'd like to sink the disgusting vessel, used to carry a Japanese delegation to America earlier that year. He had ignored Cardiff's own ship with its three masts and smoking black funnel when it came into port a few months earlier, consoling himself that the attack on the foreign settlement would stop the intrusions of these ocean-going monstrosities. But now, his own countrymen were using the ships, sailing them, and even starting to build them.

Despite the massive iron hulk that dwarfed him and the mountains of coal reportedly under the deck, the enormous vessel rode well in the bay waters. But no matter how advanced the engineering, he would not be moved from his goal. No doubt the old woman from Hagi had identified him, and now, instead of turning him in, Cardiff hoped to bring him over to the barbarians' side. How preposterous!

Once on board, an American officer showed them the ship's inner workings. Nobumitsu ran his eyes over the three-story-high engines—huffing giants flexing their muscles. He had never seen the like. But he would not be dissuaded.

The ship's captain invited the consul to his private quarters after the tour. Retainer Aomura, a clan elder who had been part of the delegation, requested that Nobumitsu follow him. His deferential choice of words revealed he had guessed Nobumitsu's identity.

They sat on a bench in the deserted billiards room. The retainer opened a box of daguerreotypes from the trip. Parades and people shaking hands with the delegation filled photograph after photograph. Nobumitsu itched to toss the thick set into the bay.

Then Retainer Aomura turned to sketches showing factories with puffing smokestacks, iron warships at a naval base, and steamers filling a gigantic seaport rimmed with buildings three-or-four-stories tall.

How dare the man try to intimidate him and his countrymen. Nobumitsu leapt to his feet. "These pictures are misleading. Reprehensible! They make the barbarians appear powerful."

Aomura set the box aside and rose also. "They *are* powerful. In our own country's present condition, the United States would be a formidable foe."

"Traitor's words!"

Aomura bowed. "Before the trip, I would have agreed. But I witnessed the Americans' factories and military might. The American naval fleet has 86 ships, heavily armed, like *The Roanoke*'s forty large guns I saw with my own eyes."

"Our warriors' strength of character is more than a match for barbarians, no matter what weapons they brandish!" Nobumitsu thought of Cardiff's use of the bow and arrow. "Their military training is pathetic. They are worms to be crushed."

"Then how can we explain the tiny British Isles' defeat of mammoth China's forces? The second time happened earlier *this* year." The retainer reached over for two billiard balls and sent them rolling into the table's pockets. "Britain put China in its sleeve *twice*."

Nobumitsu took a step back. "Are the British Isles small for a fact?" He had always discounted foreign maps.

"Without question. Yet the British rule half the world because of their gunships and weaponry. A few foreign ships could easily bombard and take Nagasaki or even our fortified port of Shimonoseki. If weapons are strong enough, anyone who wields them can win. Think of the utter disgrace of a defeat by the Americans or the British. But if we fought a war against either of them now, we would suffer a massacre."

Nobumitsu resisted retching. "We can't stand by and let the barbarians overrun our sacred soil! It's unthinkable!"

"Not stand by. Our country must adopt our enemy's scientific knowledge and build up an invincible military. Then we can launch an all-out war for the Divine Emperor. With patience and this strategy, we *can* crush our enemies!"

When Nobumitsu left the steamship, Aomori's words reverberated in his soul. Patience! Patience—a necessity. Martial arts had taught him to turn an opponent's strength into a weapon to use against him. But to do that, his country had to access the source of the enemy's strength. He saw that now.

Still, the coming attack could not be called off. A samurai did not commit to an assault—did not pull out his sword—without drawing blood. Restraining the Hagi samurai who had let the three traitors escape their ship would be impossible. Maeda in particular thirsted for a slaughter.

The company boat cut through the waves on the return

toward land. Nobumitsu frowned, watching Cardiff lean forward in the prow, eager to reach shore. Unexpectedly the consul's fate nettled him. This barbarian had risked his life for the eldest Taguchi. He had an odd mannerism of treating even the lowest individuals with respect. Strange but somewhat likeable, especially when on the receiving end as a groom. And now the consul had apparently not reported his disguise.

Of course, that kind of soft heartedness was one more sign of barbarian weakness. He hadn't asked for, never wanted, the consul's forbearance. What's more, the good actions of one foreigner could not erase the damage from the other barbarians.

The consul should have stayed in America, out of trouble. Nobumitsu was sacrificing his own life. Why should he spare Cardiff's?

CHAPTER 44

Sumi imagined the wondrous evening as she readied her blue kimono, embossed with swirls of silver stars. While they waltzed, the consul would hold her in his arms and sweep her around the ballroom. And at one of the small, round tables, they would discuss all manner of things. Such joy had seemed unattainable a few weeks ago, and now her heart overflowed with happiness.

Kiyo puttered with items on her dressing stand, making more noise than usual.

Sumi turned to see what she was doing and noticed her cousin's mouth droop. Unaccustomed pity pricked her. What a horribly dull life awaited her cousin as the wife of Keiji-*sama*. Sumi's own happiness mysteriously dimmed.

Kiyo shot her a quizzical look. "Are you having a deep thought?" She smirked.

"Not deep, but unusual." Sumi ignored the blare of her inner warning. "The Christmas decorations tonight will be beautiful, I expect. Even though you don't care at all for foreigners, wouldn't you like to see the sights? You could come with us."

Kiyo's mouth curled. "I have no desire whatsoever to see men and women shamelessly swaying in each other's arms."

What had she been thinking? Of course, her cousin would despise the idea. Then she caught a hint of a smile cross Kiyo's lips. "What is it?"

"Nothing, nothing at all."

Sumi shrugged and sat down to finish her preparations. Right away, she had trouble managing her hair. She was too excited, she supposed. She was about to summon Kin to apply more camellia oil and tame the loose strands when Kiyo rose and came over behind her.

"All that fumbling is getting on my nerves. Here, I'll help." Her tone had become milder.

Over a year had passed since either had assisted the other in doing anything. Swallowing her surprise, Sumi handed Kiyo her combs and beads. "I can't get those straggling hairs to stay in place." She hoped her effort to smile wasn't a grimace.

"You can't control your hair unless you control yourself. That's your problem."

Sumi held her tongue and picked up her mirror to watch the progress. Examining her own face for a few seconds, she noted the slant of her eyes and their intent expression. Would the consul think she was pretty compared to the round-eyed foreigners in their flouncy gowns, jewels, and curled tendrils? Was it significant he had invited her and not one of the sophisticated ladies who had eyed him even when he'd been betrothed? Goose bumps shivered up her arms.

Kiyo swept Sumi's loose tresses up and slipped them into her hairs' main loop, already wrapped around hidden dark blue paper pasted in place. Then Kiyo leaned over and caught Sumi's eyes in the mirror. "I've been meaning to tell you something for a long time . . . about your dictionary." She straightened. "I saw your grandfather take those missing pages along with his painting."

Sumi let go of the mirror. "You did? Why didn't you tell me? It took me days to replace those words. I never could entirely."

"I'll tell you why. The Eldest acts like I don't exist even though I must respect him above all others. In spite of painting an untold number of pictures for other people, he's never painted one for me. I decided if he wanted you to know, he could inform you himself. But after you were so upset, I came back to tell you. Only, you were looking through my things. So I didn't."

Sumi flinched. "I *was* upset, too upset. I shouldn't have touched your belongings."

"So you acknowledge your wrongdoing. You are full of surprises today, aren't you?" Wrapping the final string of silver beads around Sumi's chignon, Kiyo pulled hard on several hairs, causing Sumi to make a face.

"I have something to tell you too." Sumi took a deep breath. Her cheeks burned. "I took your father's letter announcing your birth. I put it in my closet, but now it's missing." Tears came to her eyes unexpectedly.

"You took it? I should have known when it was out of place, but I never thought even you would steal something so precious."

"Out of place?"

"If you wanted to make me miserable, you failed. While you were in Hagi, my aunt found the letter when she and Kin took our clothing out to be aired. She told me she would keep it for me so it wouldn't get damaged. I assumed I had mistakenly put it in the cupboard with my other scarves."

Sumi breathed a sigh of relief.

Kiyo shoved the remaining comb into Sumi's hair and stamped her foot. "Don't for a minute think you are excused. Your action reeked of evil even if I didn't know about it. And I believe you damaged the letter. The top has a tear."

"I am sorry."

Her cousin glared.

"The loss of so much hard work kept me from thinking clearly." Sumi blinked back the tears.

"That's no excuse, and you know it." Kiyo, scowling, flopped down in front of her own dresser.

Sumi bit back a retort. She'd admitted her fault. Why couldn't Kiyo accept her apology? But then her cousin's words registered, dampening her ire. "I didn't know the Eldest never painted anything for you, or that it bothered you."

"That is what I *just* said."

"I guess you'd have felt a bigger part of our family if—"

"I have never belonged here. At least Keiji-*sama* has truly welcomed me into *his* family." Kiyo slipped a tortoise-shell comb into her own hair, which, as usual, was impeccably neat. "How you raged against the prospect of having him as your betrothed." She snickered. "Short-sightedness like that causes grave mistakes."

"At any rate, it worked out well for you." Sumi congratulated herself for rising above Kiyo's spitefulness.

A faint smile didn't reach Kiyo's eyes. "On second thought, I believe I would like to see the strange decorations tonight."

"Truly? You'll come with us?"

"Must I repeat everything?"

"Then I'll tell Father. You can't imagine the magnificent sights you'll see."

"No doubt there will be surprising ones."

One hour before time for his son, granddaughter, and niece to leave for the ball, Yoshikatsu received a scroll bearing the seal of their former neighbor, Merchant Omura. He broke the seal cautiously, as if he might find a viper poised to strike, and read the message, obviously written in haste:

> *Secret papers have come into my possession. They give vital information about a Chōshū clan member and his plan for this evening. I ask that you and your son visit my home without a second's delay.*

Yoshikatsu acquiesced. A viper could not be ignored.

As soon as he and Kenshin arrived, Omura insisted on serving refreshments. After nearly twenty minutes, the tea and bean cakes were finished, and the papers still had not materialized. The merchant, a nervous twitch in his hand, rummaged through his desk as though he'd misplaced them.

At the sound of horses trotting past, Kenshin jumped up and bowed. *"*Excuse me. Sorry to leave, but I have previous plans—related to those horses, I believe.*"* He bowed again and dashed out the door.

"Stop!" Omura shouted from the entrance. He spun toward Yoshikatsu. "Stop him, I beg you! He must *not* leave! His life depends on it!"

The truth struck Yoshikatsu like a crack of lightning. "Neighbor, you have been found out!"

The merchant paled. "How? What? What are you talking about?"

"The nobleman's disguise. The Honorable Governor knows."

"I don't understand."

Yoshikatsu lied with greater assurance. "He knows *your* traitorous connection with the disguised groom."

Omura crumpled. His fist beat the mat.

"Quick! Tell me all!" Yoshikatsu held back from rising and kicking the merchant.

Omura stilled, then straightened. "I was assigned to poison Kenshin-*sama*," he jerked out, "at this very time."

"Poison! What have you—"

"I couldn't do it. Naturally, I couldn't! So I planned to delay him until after the other assassinations. When Ōta Nobumitsu-*sama* and the rest were killed or forced to flee, no one would investigate my failure." He wrung his hands. "Don't you see? I wanted to *protect* your son."

Yoshikatsu gripped the low stand in front of him. "What assassinations? Speak up! If people die, so will you!"

"You need not threaten me, neighbor. I will tell you the little I know." He puffed out a breath. "Nobumistu-*sama* will kill the British consul on his way to the ball. Other samurai will attack the French and Russian consuls. But I tell you"—he jammed his fist into his palm—"the Chōshū nobleman planned it! He trapped me, threatened to kill my family! At the beginning, I just had to report the goings on in the neighborhood. I—"

"Tell *everything* about *tonight*! Or I will oversee the

crushing of your bones myself."

"A fire!"

"Where?"

"I don't know. I tell you, I didn't make the plans."

"What else? What about the American consul?"

Omura scrunched his face as if expecting a blow. "The scholar, Kurohashi Keiji-*sama,* and a Chōshū samurai named Maeda will kill the American consul and . . . and anyone accompanying him."

Yoshikatsu sprang up, knocking over the stand and splaying its contents onto the floor. Maeda—no doubt the Chōshū samurai who had slain his brother-in-law! But Keiji? Unbelievable! And their prey was Consul Cardiff, along with *anyone accompanying him*—his son, granddaughter, and Kiyo!

He grabbed up his swords from Omura's vestibule and clattered down the street toward the riding course's stable.

A track attendant was unsaddling one of the racehorses. Yoshikatsu pushed the boy aside, threw himself onto the animal, and rode away at breakneck speed.

Flouting the law against galloping through city streets, he raced by blurring faces. At each ward gate, he shouted his name and ordered the guards to let him pass. All cooperated except the guards at the next to last post.

Every muscle straining, Yoshikatsu gave the horse a sharp kick and shot past the gesturing men.

Near the Oura River Bridge, *kago* and loitering people clogged the street. "You there," he shouted at a man strolling directly in front of him. "Make way! The gods curse me if I won't run you down!" He drew his sword, and all the people scattered.

The governor's guards at the foreign sector's gate stood

aside, bowing to his retainer status. The foreigners' guards were preoccupied with a string of *kago* and waved him on. But a cluster of arriving carriages and foreigners near the hotel caused the horse to shy. Dismounting, he ran the last stretch the best he could, his heart hammering its protest.

Maeda waited in the darkening shadows on one side of the hotel. Cardiff and Interpreter Taguchi rode up behind two arriving *kago*. The consul helped Taguchi's daughter and another female step from their conveyances.

Maeda slipped a dagger into his hand. The American would be the first to die.

All at once, a terrific pain rippled up his arm. A knife stuck through his wrist! The next second, a coil of rope encircled his body and forced his arms against his sides. He began cursing his captor, Chief Inspector Sato.

Sato yanked the rope tighter. "Three of your intended victims on the Chōshū ship escaped death. You will not."

Maeda cursed his own stupidity. Nobumitsu-*sama*'s suspicions had been right. They had been followed from their ship.

Sumi kept her hand tucked around the consul's arm as they walked through the huge ballroom, where dozens of couples already chatted. The ladies' satiny gowns, necklaces, and bracelets shone in the light from the chandeliers' candles. Men, dressed like Cardiff in black coats with tails, elaborate scarves, trousers, and long white stockings, stood next to their wives or female companions, nodding and smiling. Flowery perfumes tickled her nose.

The members of the orchestra filed onto the little stage to take their seats. The music would begin momentarily, and she'd be waltzing with Cardiff-*sama* once again. She tingled with anticipation.

Her father gazed at the orchestra, then turned to Cardiff. "I see an acquaintance." He pointed toward the one Japanese member in the orchestra. "Kiyo and I will give him our regards. Excuse us please."

Suddenly startled exclamations swept through the room. Sumi peered around a tall couple to see what had happened.

She gasped. *Her grandfather*—swords still on—stood at the edge of a group of the guests, who were rapidly backing away from him. He began to turn slowly, eyeing each person.

Why? What on earth? He couldn't have lost his mind! He'd always had his wits about him. Breathing heavily, she began fanning herself,

Her father started toward him, but her grandfather waved him back.

Except for a few whisperers, everyone became silent, their attention riveted on her grandfather. Then someone bellowed, "Get the loony fellow out of here!"

More guests joined in. Sumi's face burned with shame.

Cardiff-*sama* glanced at her, patted her arm, then hurried into the center of the room. "Quiet!" he yelled. "I know this man. He's not crazy. Let him speak."

Her grandfather swept his eyes over the guests again. What could he possibly be looking for?

Suddenly he pointed toward a yellow-haired lady in a billowing purple gown. The lady put her hand to her heart, looking like she would faint.

Shock ricocheted through Sumi. Her grandfather was pointing at the man behind the lady. Keiji-*sama*! The Kurohashi grandson had come to the ball!

"Danger!" her grandfather shouted in Japanese. "That man intends murder!"

Her father, rocking back on his heels, translated the warning.

Instantly the place was in an uproar.

Sumi could not believe her ears. Keiji-*sama* was a scholar, not a murderer!

The scholar squatted and put a dagger up to his abdomen.

Sumi's scream joined those of the other ladies. Several foreign men headed toward Keiji.

Her grandfather drew his sword and waved it, ordering them back. He commanded her father to translate again. "Leave him alone! This is not your country. In our custom, a man commits *seppuku* to save his family's honor."

The crowd obeyed, though many objected, shouting about "rule of law" and other incomprehensible phrases.

Keiji plunged his dagger into his left side.

Sumi flinched and forced herself to keep watching.

He slid his dagger to the right and twisted it upward, then leaned forward with an agonized look, but uttered no sound. Motioning to her grandfather, he stretched out his neck.

Her grandfather raised his sword high.

Sumi moaned.

He swung the sword down. A sickening thud and a ringing noise filled her ears. The next thing she knew, the consul had helped her to a chair.

Several ladies had fainted dead away. Others were weeping. Sumi felt detached, as though dreaming, and shook her head to clear the images from her mind.

Her grandfather leaned over the body and appeared to slip something into his sleeve. Then he called for the gawking hotel staff to remove the corpse and swab up the expanding pool of blood. He beckoned to her father, and they came to where Cardiff stood next to her, trying to comfort her.

"Assassinations are not the only plot," her grandfather told them in a low voice, translated simultaneously by her father in case Cardiff needed it. "The villain Omura spoke of a fire too, at an unknown location."

Sumi grasped the edge of the chair as though the floor were tilting. Their neighbor? A greedy, slippery man, yes, she knew that. But a villain? First Keiji-sama, next the merchant?

Cardiff's face contorted into a look of horror. "Tonight's *location* is likely this hotel!" He wheeled and waved for them to follow. "The building's rear! The rear's the most vulnerable!"

Sumi started to rise, but he turned back.

"No, Miss Taguchi! Please stay here. I'd never forgive myself if any harm came to you."

She stopped and nodded. Silently, her heart cried out. *But what if harm comes to you?*

CHAPTER 45

Nobumitsu scooted along a high wall to a place across from the entrance to the hotel's grounds. He watched two foreign couples talk and gesture. Four gas lamps along the front of the hotel in addition to the moon provided a good deal of light. He recognized the British consul, whom he had waited in vain to accost on the town's main street. The Englishman and his wife must have taken a roundabout way, but now the man, clothed in more ludicrous garb than usual, was within range.

He hesitated, fingering his dagger. In addition to Maeda, the police had captured the other two Chōshū samurai, assigned to assassinate the French and Russian consuls. Six officers on high alert waited near the couples to escort them to the hotel's entrance. Nobumitsu would hit his target, but he would not survive the aftermath.

Suddenly, Maeda shouted, "We are not to end our lives! It is our *daimyō*'s command."

His liege's command! Even though the words were intended for the captured samurai, the message had to be from the gods. The fire demons could take care of the consuls still alive as well as the other depraved barbarians reveling in their ill-gotten wealth.

He slipped down behind the wall and circled toward the back of the hotel. In the hotel's garden, he picked up one of the strange red and green lanterns casting an eerie light.

Nothing would stop him. Just a spark from the glowing oil lantern would ignite the straw matting he'd put in place that afternoon—matting supposedly to replace worn tatami in four of the hotel's *Japan* rooms. The inferno would consume the bulky wooden hotel, the arrogant officials, the hotel's guests, then the entire foreign sector in an hour or two. Warehouses would explode into flames. Barbarians trying to escape at the edge of the bay would disappear into watery graves. The gods would smile on him again.

Rounding the hotel's corner, he heard voices—Cardiff, issuing commands, and Interpreter Taguchi shouting for help! His enemies were pulling the matting and oily rags under the straw away from the building.

Nobumitsu hissed curses.

Hotel guards and policemen came running from the other end with sloshing water buckets.

How many of the devils could he slay before he was slain himself?

More men sprang out the hotel's rear door.

He couldn't slay enough.

Retainer Aomura's words came back—patience, a necessity. He had to leave the fight for a later day or face certain defeat.

Defeat was not an option.

He would ride up the coast, where the governor's second son waited with a Satsuma coastal ship to pick up any survivors. His message for his warlord would not be one of failure, but enlightenment. He would advise true patriots to infiltrate the enemy. Learn the language. Master the skills. But still strike the enemy with the sword when the gods gave the chance.

After toppling the traitorous Shōgun in the coming years, the imperial forces would be able to assemble a fleet of warships, heavily armed, not just with forty guns, but with fifty or sixty guns. If the barbarians continued to hang onto their settlements, those guns would pound their businesses, homes, stores, and hotels into mounds of rubbish.

He retraced his steps to the front of the hotel. To his amazement, a loose horse snorted on the other side of a carriage. He whistled and coaxed its approach. Clicking his tongue, he prepared to mount.

Just then, the interpreter's daughter peered out the hotel entrance.

Ah! He would take the clan's wretched member to Lord Ōta. The warlord would make her wish she had never betrayed her country.

Assuming his former pose as a groom, he led the horse up the walkway, bowed, and then beckoned to the girl.

She took one step toward him and paused, glancing around.

He bowed low and gestured toward the horse.

Wrinkling her brow, she shook her head, but took another step.

That was all he needed. He mounted the horse and grasped her arms, dragging her onto the horse in front of the saddle.

She jerked and screamed. Onlookers yelled. Three policemen and Chief Inspector Sato rushed toward him.

Tightening his hold on the girl, he spurred the horse into a gallop. Sato would have to get his horse from the hotel stables. He wouldn't catch up.

Nobumitsu kept the girl's right arm bent behind her and leaned over her body, pinning it down. She continued to scream and squirm. He yanked on her until her legs were under his right leg and pushed down hard on her neck, forcing her head into the horse's side. Wrapping the end of one of the corded reins into a noose around her neck, he pulled it until just short of choking her.

He shouted in her ear, "If you move, I'll pull this tighter. You *will* die!"

She stiffened, and her left hand reached to grip the saddle's edge.

Ears laid back, the horse raced at top speed. Nobumitsu leaned into the wind, inviting its onslaught. They would soon reach the countryside on the coastal road leading northward. He congratulated himself. Each minute put more distance between him and his pursuers.

Sumi gasped for breath while her body jounced on the galloping horse. Her head was just above the horse's powerful left front leg. It was racing faster than any she had ever ridden. No one would catch up with them. Where was he taking her?

"No!" Her shout vanished into the wind. Hagi! It had to be Hagi with the abhorred warlord. She could never escape from there! Lord Ōta could sell her to a Pleasure House, where she would disappear, in every way a prisoner—never to surface. Or he would have her *married* to a widowed peasant to keep him warm in bed in his old age. No one, not her father or grandfather or anyone else, would be able to undo the union. And she would never see Cardiff-*sama* again. She had never stopped loving him. She never would!

In spite of the rein's noose, she had to do something even if she died as a result. She must not enter Hagi! With a sudden vengeance, she bit into the horse's side. The hide's thick, coarse hair filled her mouth, but she held on to the sliver of skin and ground it between her teeth. Maybe it wouldn't make a difference, maybe it was little more than a horsefly's irritation, but she had to try.

With no warning, the horse sped at an angle into the woods lining a side of the road. Sumi heard a branch smack the samurai and a thump. The horse came to a standstill farther into the trees. She struggled to loosen the rein wrapped around her neck.

Her fingers trembled. She couldn't get a good grip on the rein's knot behind her head. Was the noose getting tighter? If the samurai hadn't been knocked out, he'd reach her any moment.

The horse neighed. Could she make it take off? She prodded it with her feet.

It didn't budge.

She prodded it harder, but it still didn't move. Instead, it shook its body. She grabbed the mane and held on. Her hands were sweating now in the cold air.

When the horse finally stopped shaking, she tugged at the knot again.

It gave!

Yanking the noose open, she slid off the horse. The thick undergrowth would hinder her running, but not her hiding. She dove under the nearest bushes, ignoring the pain throbbing in her arm.

Lying as still as a stone, she heard her kidnapper approach. He trampled the undergrowth and probed it, calling down the gods' vengeance.

"You think you can hide from me?" He stopped moving as though listening for her movement, her breath. "I will find you, and this time my weapon *will* hit its mark." For a few seconds he moved away from where she lay and then turned back in her direction. Just a few feet from her, he paused next to the horse.

"Oh, Maker," she begged silently, "I can't die like one of your flowers in a field. No one in my family knows about you. Please, please let me live! Let me see Cardiff-*sama* again!"

She bit her lip hard, preparing to endure the searing pain from his dagger's stab.

In the rear of the hotel, the flammable material had been carted away.

"A lady's been kidnapped!" someone yelled out the door.

John stopped his survey of the grounds. He dashed inside. Seeing Kiyo, he tried to question her, but she turned her back. In all the confusion, no one seemed to know where Miss Taguchi was and whether she was the one who had been taken.

Then the British consul's wife came rushing up, exclaiming, "The poor dear! What will your horrible groom do to your friend?"

John ran for his horse in the stable and rode off in the direction a witness said the chief inspector and groom had taken. "If you harm her," John muttered, "I'll hunt you down if it takes the rest of my life!"

He spurred the horse on. "Dear God, let me reach her in time. Help me!"

Yoshikatsu, still outside, saw the consul ride off, apparently chasing after the arsonists. Although a brave act, particularly alone, Cardiff could be riding into a trap. It was too late to stop him, however. Perhaps the man's gods or spirits would protect him. He hoped so. The consul was a valiant man.

He entered the ballroom to find his daughter-in-law's niece. When he approached Kiyo, she stood rigid. Drawing her roughly aside, he asked, "Did you know anything of this scheme?"

"Yes, I knew." Her voice filled with defiance.

He glowered at her. "You knew the Kurohashi grandson intended to kill anyone with the consul? You knew Merchant Omura meant to assassinate your aunt's husband—your benefactor—yet you said nothing? Nothing to warn your own family!" His gruffness mirrored the emotions churning within him.

An incredulous expression spread over her face. "Oh! I didn't know! I swear I didn't know!"

Kiyo knelt and took hold of his tunic's sleeve. "I knew only that Consul Cardiff would be attacked." She began to cry. "I ask for your mercy. I despise the barbarian. But I would never do anything against my benefactor . . . or cousin."

"So you beg for mercy you were not willing to give." He wanted to shake her. "There's no time to talk. Leave now before the police ask questions."

Yoshikatsu watched the weeping girl stumble out of the room. Then he started looking for his granddaughter. Kenshin, who had finished his inspection of the hotel's exterior, soon joined his anxious search.

His son questioned one of the milling foreigners, then dashed toward Yoshikatsu. "If this person is not mistaken"—his fist struck his forehead—"Sumi has been kidnapped!"

CHAPTER 46

In the woods, Nobumitsu's eyes swept the undergrowth. Something gray protruded from under the rhododendron bushes. He stepped toward it, then recognized what it was. The edge of the girl's white *tabi* sock contrasted enough with the surroundings to be visible.

He stared at the bushes. His former sweetheart, the girl he'd lost, had picked blossoms from a bush like the ones before him. The old ache gripped his chest. The consul genuinely cared for the traitorous girl hiding beneath the leaves. He'd seen it numerous times, even when the consul's absurd betrothed claimed the man's attention.

Bushido's code dictated he owed the consul a debt for not reporting his disguise. It had been a favor, small and unsought, but given. He would like to sever a foreigner's head to present to his cousin, but this female's head—not even a foreign female's—would be a laughable trophy.

He bent over the bush. The softness for the girl disappeared. She was his country's betrayer!

He raised his dagger to strike.

But what about the consul?

He stabbed his dagger into the ground next to her neck, and heard her moan. "You are an accursed traitor. I should have aimed the second dagger at you when the first one missed. You deserve to die—doubly so now." He yanked his dagger out of the ground. "But I owe the devilish consul a debt."

A horse galloped past and on down the road. He listened to make sure the rider, no doubt Sato, didn't turn around. Continuing to the ship with the female would be difficult, especially with his pursuer ahead of him. Yet a hostage might be convenient if he didn't reach the fork in the road before Sato backtracked.

"My cousin will handle you!" He pulled her up and twisted her arm behind her. The girl cried out. He wrenched it harder, taking pleasure in her shriek, and reached for the horse.

A bullet whistled over his head, barely missing him. Shocked, he jerked aside.

A second pursuer, a stealthy one at that! And did his adversary have the eyes of an owl? No, of course not. The smart attacker saw the broken bushes, then heard the noises. He'd shot high to hit him but not the girl. The gun meant the man was a foreigner. Good! He'd get a foreigner's head for his cousin after all.

He drew out his dagger, relishing the opportunity.

He moved slightly out of the direct range of fire and leaned forward to get a clearer view. He instantly recognized the dark shape. His *master* had dismounted and crept to the edge of the woods. A revolver glinted in the shadows while the consul waited for a movement or sound.

The girl's life had been spared for the debt, but the bullet changed everything. Nobumitsu shoved Sumi down and heard her fall sideways into the bushes. Another bullet whistled by just above his head.

He drew back his arm. *He* wouldn't miss. His weapon would go right under the low branch and into his target's chest. His hand quivered for the first time since he'd killed his sweetheart's father. But the man before him was not a revered clan elder. The consul was a barbarian, not worth a minute's consideration. He held his breath, taking careful aim.

As his arm moved to let the dagger fly, he lurched forward and sprawled on the ground. The dagger flopped into the bushes.

The wretch had grabbed his ankles and was lying on top of his legs.

He tried to kick her off, but she held on. The she-devil! Why had he spared her?

Through her shrieks, he heard the consul ordering him in Japanese to stand up with his arms raised. Sweat ran down his back. He could never endure the shame of being captured by a barbarian—with a female's help.

He pretended to obey, rising to his knees and stretching up his arms. The girl let go. The horse was right behind him.

In the blink of an eye, Nobumitsu slid under the belly of the horse, released it, and slung himself up and onto the far side. He had just one leg on the animal's back, and his arms encircled its neck. He spoke in the horse's ear, hoping desperately it recognized his authority.

It turned and took off.

Once on the road, Nobumitsu leaned over on the horse's back. The consul would have his gun trained on him any second now.

No bullet came. Were the gods repaying him for his mercy on the girl? He grunted. No! They could never overlook her disloyalty. But good or bad, the consul would be happy.

Nobumitsu laughed out loud—at himself, for thinking about a barbarian's feelings.

CHAPTER 47

Miss Taguchi collapsed in John's arms. His pulse accelerating with each step, he carried her limp body to the roadside and knelt down, cradling her buckled form. He checked her breath, his face inches from hers. She still breathed!

He gently laid her down, folding his coat under her head. Kneeling next to her, he moved some fallen strands of hair to one side of her forehead and stroked her cheek, her skin soft under his fingers. Warmth ran through him. How could he have gone on if she hadn't escaped from that madman?

Sato came tearing around a curve, urging his horse forward. "Is she alive?" he shouted in Japanese. He jumped down and ran toward them.

"*Hai, hai,* she is!"

She stirred and opened her eyes, then lifted her hand toward John. "Thank you, Cardiff-*sama*," she murmured.

"Thank God, you're alive!" John took her hand and held it.

The chief inspector cleared his throat.

John looked up. The official appeared both relieved and angry. "Chief Inspector Sato, thank you. You also chased that villain." The Japanese words came out effortlessly.

"My duty," Sato replied drily.

"You were ahead of him. Did he pass you?"

"The road divided." Sato showed how it forked with his hands. "A rider kicked up dust. Moving fast. I did not follow. The gunshots came from here."

"So, no chance he's returning to fight us?"

"None."

One piece of good news, John thought. The woods no longer cast threatening shadows impersonating the samurai.

Miss Taguchi started to lift her head, but hunched her shoulders in pain instead.

"Lie still," John said, feeling a sympathetic pain in his own head. He looked up at Sato again. "Please ride back for a doctor, the one from England. She needs a doctor before we move her."

Sato nodded. "As you wish." His face was a mask.

John watched him remount. The man on whose *good hands* the foreigners relied was performing well tonight, very well. But there would never be a connection between them.

Miss Taguchi started to praise John for what he'd done, but he said, "Just rest. You're safe now. Our enemy's fled, and more help is on the way."

He reluctantly released her hand in order to check his gun, and then sat down next to her. Tucking his coat's sleeve better into the makeshift pillow, he stared at the red welts encircling her neck. *The monster! Look how he repaid my kindness—attempting to incinerate hundreds of people. Then tormenting this dearest one of all!*

He listened for any sound on the road that might indicate his vile groom was backtracking in spite of Sato's expectations. Surprise attacks, like Mr. Taguchi had warned, never agreed with assumptions. Except for the rustle of a breeze and the staccato of night insects, all was quiet. But he kept his gun next to him, ready.

He gazed at Miss Taguchi's face. How sweet and vulnerable she appeared as she lay, eyes closed. He wished he had more than his coat to make her comfortable. He longed to wrap his arms around her again, protect her, care for her. When he'd fired into the woods, his life had meant nothing—hers everything! Nationality, race—those things hadn't mattered. She was his dear friend.

But she was more than that. An indescribable feeling, alive and untamed, possessed him—not just tonight—frequently when he saw her these days. He exhaled. Was he in love? Had he somehow, without noticing, fallen in love with his tutor?

If the feelings welling up inside him were any indication, he was indeed in love. Inexorably in love.

While Sato rode back to the city, he contemplated the look that had passed between Sumi-*san* and the consul. Surely a samurai's daughter could not feel more than a passing interest in the American. Although not totally barbaric, the foreigners were uncultured oafs. They always wanted to be in charge, just as Cardiff had taken charge minutes earlier without a thought for Sato's own authority. The ignorant consul had asked for the British doctor, who practiced only Western medicine. Nagasaki doctors had been trained in Japanese, Chinese, and Western medical knowledge.

Foreigners were lacking in modesty and humility and especially in commitment. Already degenerate merchants had discarded their Japanese wives, like worn-out toys, when they returned to their home countries. Worst of all, Cardiff and his closest associates held to the Evil Religion, a curse for those ignorant enough to believe the lunacy. Praise to the gods, the belief was still illegal for his countrymen, and few foreigners outside Cardiff's circle seemed to care for it.

Without further delay, he would ask an intermediary to propose marriage to the young lady on his behalf. A samurai's daughter deserved a far better life than any foreigner could hope to provide, let alone one who professed loyalty to a false god.

Sumi managed a smile when her father, the British doctor, and Chief Inspector Sato hurried to where she lay. Her father leaned over her, and she thought for a minute he might cry. Then Doctor Hughes began to probe her ribs and check her limbs. She squeezed her eyes shut and barely kept from crying herself.

Her arm was beginning to swell, the doctor said, due to a broken or sprained wrist. She couldn't help but whimper when he put her wrist in a makeshift splint. He also reported signs of a concussion, but predicted her full recovery after a few days' rest.

Her father decided to take her with him on his horse, and the men gathered their coats to cushion her ride. While the preparations were made, she listened, forgetting her throbbing wrist and head.

"This is the second violent scene you've called me to, you know," the doctor said.

"Yes," Cardiff replied, "and it's been good of you to come at a moment's notice."

"That comes with my job, but I wonder if the forced opening of Japan was a mistake. Commodore Perry's desire to bring it into the 'family of civilized nations' may have wakened a hibernating beast."

Doctor Hughes and Cardiff stopped talking in order to help her. Together they lifted her onto the horse. She leaned back into her father's waiting arms.

Cardiff mounted his horse and resumed the conversation. "My hope is the beast represents a small minority and will be subdued. What do you think, Mr. Taguchi?"

"Trouble has been brewing for years," her father answered. "A future uprising may be unavoidable. However, tonight's attack has yielded one bright spot. I believe Nagasaki's chief conspirator has been uncloaked and has fled."

"Couldn't he return?" Cardiff asked.

The men turned toward the chief inspector, and Sumi's father translated.

"We will put out an order for his arrest," Sato answered gruffly. "He won't dare come back here. The roads and checkpoints will be guarded. He will have to lie low wherever he goes."

Cardiff looked over at her. "In that case, we've yanked one victory from what could have been the worst night of all our lives."

The horse began to move, and Sumi positioned her wrist to receive the least jarring. She shivered in spite of the strong men around her. The groom Nobu—*not* the crazed samurai killed by the toy store—had thrown the dagger at her from the noodle shop's wall. He had probably watched her learn to waltz from the doorway's shadows. He had sneered at Cardiff's poor showing with the bow and arrows. The fiend had been nearby since the foreigners' arrival.

Yet the groom hadn't overcome them. Death had loomed just a finger-width away, but she was alive. Delivered.

She closed her eyes, picturing how she had wakened to see Cardiff-*sama* bending over her, touching her cheek. Perhaps it was just her groggy imagination, but wonder of wonders, she had felt his gaze caressing her—as though he felt the same desire for her that she felt for him. Nothing could come of it. She knew that. But now she had that memory. She would never let herself forget the feel of his gentle touch and that look—imagined or not.

Despite her strong headache, she tilted her head back to see the sky. Her new liege, who had made all those stars, had answered her prayer from under the rhododendron bush. Could a person—a woman—be like a retainer to the Maker of the universe?

CHAPTER 48

John escorted the Taguchi family to their home, determined to see them safely inside its walls. His eyes lingered on Miss Taguchi before her father helped her through their gate. He longed to stay and help ensure her protection, but duty compelled him to check on the Americans in the foreign sector.

For several more hours, the foreigners traded rumors of skulking *rōnin* waiting to assassinate passersby. They swore they'd seen arsonists by the warehouses, up on the bluff, and in the dark alleyways between their tinderbox homes. While attempting to reassure his countrymen, John was stopped several times by Japanese policemen and British sentries advising him to return to his residence. Finally following their instruction in the early morning hours, he tried to get a few hours of sleep.

Every time the building creaked, he jerked and felt for his revolver. Goda had not fully resumed his duties, so he was alone in the consulate. What if Sato were wrong, and the groom returned to Nagasaki? But most likely, Sato didn't make mistakes.

John fidgeted, unable to slow down his thoughts. He should

have immediately reported Nobu's disguise. He had endangered many lives by his misjudgment. The groom's web had even extended to the Confucian scholar.

But he had rescued Miss Taguchi. Thank heavens for that! He imagined her lovely form in his arms again. Why hadn't he seen the priceless jewel beside him week after week? How had he missed what was right in front of his eyes? Had his fiancée blinded him?

In contrast to the way his heart soared at the thought of Miss Taguchi, his attachment to Catherine had amounted more to admiration of an exquisite prize—one not nearly so fine as he'd first thought. When tested, his so-called love had dissolved more quickly than sugar in hot tea. What a fool he'd been!

But he had to admit an additional reason for his blindness. When Miss Taguchi talked about how the trappings of culture weren't all that important, he hadn't thought to apply her insights to himself. In fact, he hadn't even recognized his biases.

Giving up all hope of sleeping, he got out of bed and began to pace. If he married a native, what would the family back home say? The neighbors? His good friends? How many would understand?

None!

Marriage between races? In their eyes, unacceptable.

How attached was he to his homeland? His heart skipped a beat. To the woods? The villages? The church spires? His home itself? There was no denying his love for his family and America. Although he could still make brief trips to New York, and family members could visit Nagasaki, he would be irrevocably fastened to Japan for the rest of his life.

He sat on the edge of the bed and watched the flickering

shadows caused by his lamp. He would never find another like Miss Taguchi. Wasn't she more important than land masses?

As if to answer, her beauty at the grotto swept over him. He had admired her raven black hair and light olive skin, while struggling not to be attracted. And during the tutoring classes, he'd always watched for the endearing way her brow furrowed when she tried to think of just the right word. And her figure wasn't lacking either. He couldn't deny having taken glances at her gentle curves—the little he could glimpse.

But good looks were only the beginning. Her personality was everything he'd ever yearned for in a sweetheart: thoughtful, perceptive, adventurous . . . while still thoroughly feminine.

One more question remained, however. He couldn't get this answer wrong. Other people's opinions didn't matter so much, but would the Almighty approve? He searched his memory of the Scriptures.

Ah, such good words: *For man looketh on the outward appearance, but the Lord looketh on the heart.* The heart mattered, and Miss Taguchi had taken the Lord to be her liege. Yes, she was a babe in the faith, but he was too in many respects.

He pictured Miss Taguchi in his arms again and grinned. He wanted to shout his terrific conclusion to the world.

He sobered the next minute. In the area of courtship, he had fallen dismally short. Their future together was possible *only if* she loved him, *only if* she thought him suitable for marriage. Perhaps marrying a barbarian would bring too much hardship. Would she be happier with a samurai, someone like the chief inspector? Pain clutched his stomach, as strong as when a stray horseshoe had slammed into him. He hoped to heaven she wouldn't prefer a samurai.

He lay back down. Sleep continued to elude him while he debated just how much Miss Sumi Taguchi might care for him or, on the other hand, thoroughly discount him.

Yoshikatsu, alone in his room, read the note he'd found by the Kurohashi grandson's side.

> *If this note comes to light, it will be because of my suicide. I must explain. Although the signs of the zodiac agreed for marriage, the one promised to me succumbed to the barbarians' spell.*
>
> *I agreed to help eliminate the contemptable consul, but was assigned to kill his companion, the one stolen from me. If I cannot strike the blow, my death must proclaim the invaders' many crimes.*
>
> *This is my death poem: Revere the Emperor! Expel the barbarian!*

Yoshikatsu wadded the note and watched his brazier's flame turn the paper to ashes. The Confucian scholar's naivety and blind passion let him fall prey to the groom's folly. The note said nothing about Kiyo. How much had she actually known ahead of time? A new home for her would have to be found before her bitterness poisoned all their family relations.

The night had again demonstrated the danger the foreign associations created. However, this time he had feared not only for his family but also for the consul. Cardiff once more risked his life on their behalf. And against all odds—triumphed. The old alliances had demanded loyalty. The new alliances demanded the same.

CHAPTER 49

The day following the kidnapping, Sumi recovered enough to join the family for the evening meal. After everyone finished eating, they began gathering around the *kotatsu* to ward off the night's chill.

Sumi's father lit his pipe over the brazier's glowing coals and was the first to speak. "Sumi was very lucky to escape Ōta Nobumitsu's clutches. I can't rid my mind of the horror."

"Nor can I," her mother said. "Powerful ancestors' spirits surely intervened."

Sumi's grandfather took his place of honor. They all bowed to him and then were quiet while her mother poured his tea. After drinking a little, he said, "Of course, it was the spirits. Nothing else could account for such good fortune." He gazed at Sumi, raising an eyebrow as though inviting her to speak.

"The strangest part," Sumi said, ignoring the reference to spirits, "happened when the groom found me under the bush. He said he was sparing my life because he owed Cardiff-*sama* a debt."

"A debt! Strange, indeed." Her father scratched his head. "What debt could cause that man to show even the smallest amount of mercy?"

Sumi's great-aunt grunted. "He is one of the Ōta nobility. Their younger generation has never shown mercy, especially not to our family."

All murmured their agreement except Kiyo, who sat back from the *kotatsu* with a morose expression.

Sumi's great-aunt rose and hobbled toward her room. Regret squeezed Sumi's heart. The widow had withdrawn into a world of her own, no longer the outgoing chatterer. Warlord Ōta and Maeda deserved the blame for her great-uncle's death— Sumi grasped that now—yet remorse about going to Hagi always lurked at the edge of her mind.

"The fiend, Ōta Nobumitsu, is a fanatic." her grandfather said. "Give up trying to understand him. Consul Cardiff and Chief Inspector Sato risked their lives last night. We can understand that."

"Yes, we owe both men an incalculable debt," her father joined in.

Sumi's spirit warmed, remembering the consul's gentle touch, his caring eyes. They owed Chief Inspector Sato a debt, no doubt, but Cardiff-*sama* was the one who rescued her, the one she would cherish as long as she lived.

Her grandfather lit his pipe and appeared lost in thought for a moment. Then he drew a rolled-up scroll from his kimono's sleeve and held it up. "In view of Chief Inspector Sato's excellent character, I have a good announcement." He looked at Sumi. "Today an intermediary approached me about a marriage proposal for you."

"Oh!" her mother exclaimed, eyes sparkling.

A flush seared Sumi, then numbing dread. Her elders would never understand her objections. Her grandfather would again envision her as a peacock shorn of its feathers as he had when she'd escaped the betrothal to Keiji-*sama*.

"Sato-*dono*'s family is of good lineage," her grandfather continued. "I planned to tell you when Sumi-*san* was stronger, but she is recovering well. According to the intermediary, after his wife died, Chief Inspector Sato could find no one suitable to take her place until he recognized my granddaughter's qualities."

Kiyo stood up quickly, made a small bow, and left the room.

Sumi couldn't speak. Her parents stared at her.

"Surely you are pleased," her father said. "He is brave, loyal—a woman's dream, it seems."

Her mother tapped the *kotatsu*. "He is exactly what you desire."

Sumi pictured the chief inspector and shuddered. He was strong and dedicated, but too dedicated. In the last year, he had been courteous to her. But she'd never forget how he rebuked her three years earlier because she questioned the arrest of her friend's neighbor, who as a secret Christian had committed the gravest of crimes in the inspector's opinion.

She took a deep breath. She couldn't delay the inevitable blow. "Do you think Chief Inspector Sato would marry a Christ follower?" She closed her eyes for a second, bracing for the onslaught.

"Why? What are you saying?" It was her mother who had jumped up.

"Do you think he would approve of a Christ follower? I—I am one now."

"No, you cannot do this!" Her mother, invariably composed, was shouting. "It is an evil religion! And illegal! An abomination to our ancestors and the gods! You will seal the fate of us all, and you will never be able to marry even if we are not arrested, tortured, and banished to the coalmines!"

Her mother twisted toward Sumi's silent father. "I beg you for our family's sake. Talk sense into our daughter before it is too late! Before she seals our doom!"

Her father bobbed his hand, motioning for her mother to be seated. "This is troublesome . . . and precarious," he said after a minute, "but the religion is not *evil* so far as I can tell. In my studies last spring, I read reports of the brave Christian missionaries in China."

"Why would you read such . . . such obnoxious materials?" Her mother had regained her cushion, but, eyes glinting, remained upright on her knees.

"The original reports were in English. I had the Dutch translations, allowing me to build my vocabulary. I also translated, with the Eldest's permission"—he glanced at Sumi's grandfather, who sat straight and grim—"several lessons for Mr. Pendleton. The first one, quoting the religion's book, said to live in harmony and obey those over you. No one can argue with that."

Her mother's jaw dropped.

"In fact, after my imprisonment, I considered, for the briefest time, studying the religion further myself. I recognized a god existed somewhere who was powerful, far more powerful than my accusers . . . or any gods I knew."

Sumi could hardly believe her ears. What a wonderful revelation!

"But your sanity prevailed." Her mother wrung her hands. "Our daughter will not be able to put her foot on the Christ image during any future inspection. She *will* be discovered!"

Sumi swayed, feeling as though she clung to a side of a cliff. No sooner did rescue seem imminent than rock crumbled beneath her.

"The inspections have been permanently discontinued," her father said. "The ban against the religion will be lifted eventually. The foreigners are pushing hard for that. News of Sumi's kidnapping will foster sympathy. If all of us are circumspect, the officials should leave us alone."

"But she is throwing away her great chance with Chief Inspector Sato, a fine man from a fine family! Now no one will have her even if we avoid banishment. How can you be so calm? The Eldest One too?" Forbidden tears watered in her eyes.

Sumi's chest ached. But she couldn't give in. If only her bones had more of her grandfather's strength.

Her grandfather, brow furrowed, put down his pipe and leaned forward. "We can see that Sumi was wise in her rejection of the reprobate, Keiji. None of us saw it at first. I, least of all. It seems for her that *no* marriage would be better than a *wrong* marriage."

For the first time in Sumi's memory, her mother shook her head in disagreement with her elder.

Sumi gathered her courage. "Isn't it possible that a fine man exists who will not care I am a Christian after the religion becomes legal? And if not, I will be content staying with you, Mother, with my family here."

Her mother jerked her head toward her. "You have not the faintest idea what you are talking about!"

Sumi clasped her hands, a sense of helplessness swamping her. Who was she to oppose her family? To not obey? The flower arrangement in the *tokonoma* caught her eye. The Maker had spoken beautiful words directly to her through the *Holy Bible*. Didn't she owe him her allegiance, not for a few days, but for all her life?

"Sumi has made a decision to be a Christ follower." Her grandfather motioned to her mother not to interrupt. "A commitment these days is rare, but a worthy liege rarer still. Think of my murdered brother-in-law's long, unfailing service to Lord Ōta—curse him!" His eyes narrowed with a look of steel. "I have always said my granddaughter was stubborn. Considering this, I do not believe any argument will change her resolve. She has fought through a fog, endured much. She must find her way, like the samurai's daughter she is."

Fighting back tears at the unexpected defense, Sumi murmured, "Thank you."

Her grandfather stood up. "Sumi has found a liege. This god may prove worthy of her loyalty, or perhaps not. We shall wait and see." He turned away, frowning. The discussion had ended.

Her mother retired to her room, the sound of muffled sobs penetrating the closed panels.

Weariness settled heavily on Sumi, but at the same time, relief that she no longer hid her new allegiance. The beginning of a root? She looked at her father.

He simply said, "You had better get some rest."

The next morning Kiyo, who was never late, entered the main room when the breakfast time was nearly over. Seeing the telltale redness in her cousin's eyes, a feeling close to sympathy stirred in Sumi. As bad as Keiji turned out to be, how devastating it must have been for Kiyo to endure her betrothed's suicide.

Kiyo bowed to Sumi's grandfather, who had already finished breakfast and was kneeling back on a cushion by the room's outside panel. He made no move to acknowledge her. Instead, he picked up a scroll to read.

Shoulders sagging, Kiyo turned away. The room's tension, already high from the previous evening, rose several notches.

Sumi studied her grandfather. Why his show of indifference?

Lifting her chin, Kiyo approached Sumi's parents next. "I appreciate your providing a place for me to stay these past three years."

They responded with nods.

The corners of her cousin's mouth tightened. "I will leave you . . . to become a nun."

Sumi nearly choked on her *miso* soup. Impossible!

"No!" Sumi's mother set her bowl down so hard the contents splattered. "A nun?"

"In the Buddhist nunnery north of the city. I . . . I decided last night."

Sumi's mother's eyes grew huge. "You cannot make a decision in one night that will revolutionize the rest of your life. Whatever are you thinking?"

"You have suffered a shocking loss," Sumi's father added. "Wait a little."

"Don't do it," Sumi said, finding her voice. "You will enter a dark, dark tunnel that has no exit." She could actually sense the suffocating gloom.

"I cannot be at peace in this house."

Sumi winced at Kiyo's frozen tone and rose on her knees.

"Don't snuff out your future. You will have another good marriage arrangement."

"How would *you* know?" Kiyo's voice grew louder. "One thing *I* know—the foreigner has once again robbed me of a husband. Even more this time."

"The Maker of the world is kind, good." Sumi desperately searched for the right words. "He can take care of you."

"Maker? Here's more of your stupid foreign talk. Dangerous talk. No, my mind is made up unless the Eldest forbids me."

Kiyo gazed at Sumi's grandfather—wistfully.

He fixed Kiyo with a stern stare. "Since this house does not suit you, you can seek another relative's roof. You are still young, ignorant of the world. You have time to form new, better opinions."

Sumi felt the verbal slap as though he'd struck her instead. But her cousin stood straight, seeming to find empowerment.

"I will take the vow today unless you forbid it."

Forbid it, Sumi begged in her heart.

"You know, all too well, the one reason I approve your decision."

Kiyo bowed.

Helplessness pinched Sumi's chest. Whatever her grandfather's cryptic reason, he didn't know how he and the rest of the family had helped foster Kiyo's sense of isolation.

"Don't leave. Please." Sumi's mother scrambled up and gripped Kiyo's shoulders. "You are all I have left of my sister. I don't know if I can stand another loss."

"I will not stay here." Kiyo jerked a few steps away. "But please join me in the nunnery if you also find the foreigner's presence detestable. An insult to the gods."

Sumi's mother shook her head. "I cannot leave my home. Certainly not, no matter how troublesome." She glanced at Sumi, accusation in her eyes. "So much sadness in two days! Nothing will be right again."

"How could you think my wife would leave, Kiyo-*san*?" Sumi's father's head quivered. "You are not thinking clearly. But this confusion is understandable after the horrors in the hotel."

"Thank you for your concern." She bowed in his direction. "I will try to regain my calm mind at the nunnery."

Sumi's mother sighed. "I did not think greater sorrow was possible, but I see it is. However"—she paused and her eyes sought Kiyo's—"if we cannot change your mind, I have a request. An indulgence to ask for *all* of us."

"Please name it."

"During your meditations, if you will burn incense on our behalf, perhaps the merciful Buddha will protect us if foreign gods threaten our home and our honor."

Her mother's next look at Sumi hardened into a scowl.

Sumi stood quickly and offered a small bow. "Mother—"

"The foreigners' god must not enter here." Kiyo waved her arm in an arc. "It is terrible enough to have the foreign man intrude. I will burn incense for you as long as I breathe."

"But that won't be necessary." Heat rose to Sumi's cheeks. "The Maker helped me in the woods and in the storm on the sea. He is not really foreign. He can aid our family without an offering of incense. Wouldn't it be wise to honor the almighty god who really cares for us?"

Kiyo snorted with disgust.

Her mother paled. "Quiet! Do not rile the spirits further!"

"Too much questioning, Sumi, causes unnecessary strife,"

her father said with a sigh.

Her grandfather slapped down his pipe. "Your mother has made a correct request. Your new beliefs will not force out our gods nor eliminate the honor due our ancestors."

"Don't worry, Sumi-*chan*." Kiyo put her hands on her hips. "I will not burn any incense for you."

Sumi bowed to her grandfather and parents. Averting her eyes from Kiyo's challenging ones, she picked up the teapot to refill her parents' *chawan* bowls. Her mother had already covered their shrine's god shelf with paper so the spirits wouldn't hear about her desertion. Clearly, this gulf dwarfed every previous one between her and her family. She swallowed back her embarrassment as she poured the tea.

Later that morning, Kiyo left for the nunnery without a backward glance. In order to embrace the Buddhist beliefs, she would take a vow to meditate in search of enlightenment, live with the barest necessities, and not seek marriage while in the order's confines.

When her cousin was lost from view, Sumi went up to her room. Kiyo's dresser was starkly bare. Her chest had been moved to the outside storage building. The room had a surprising sense of emptiness and loss, especially considering how Sumi had yearned month after month for her cousin's departure. What was most disturbing, however, was her memory of Kiyo's red-rimmed eyes.

She sat on the *tatami* and leaned her head back against the wall, resting her sprained wrist on a cushion. Kiyo was gone. Her mother was heartbroken, and everyone had rejected all she'd tried to say. Lying under the bushes, so close to death, she'd begged the Maker for another day, for an opportunity to tell her family about him. No question—she'd been granted another day. But if the breakfast conversation amounted to the begged-for opportunity, she'd made a muddled mess of it.

She mulled over what each person had said and her responses. Actually, it seemed she had explained quite a bit about the Maker after all. Maybe it wasn't as disastrous as she'd thought. One tiny step across the chasm between her beliefs and her family's was better than none. A flicker of hope sprang up.

Bowing her head, she imagined herself approaching the lord of the universe. After a moment, she whispered, "Thank you." She sat unmoving, not able to think of more to say, but sensing she'd said enough.

When her cat rubbed up against her, she stretched out her legs and welcomed it onto her lap. Maybe there wasn't anything more she could do right then for her family. But she could seek out Cardiff-*sama* as soon as she recovered enough to leave her home.

She rubbed the cat behind its ears. "I have to make sure Cardiff-*sama* is all right, don't I?" The cat stretched out its paws. "Naturally, I'll thank him again for risking his life. And"—she dropped her voice—"I'll look into his wonderful gray eyes."

Her cat purred its approval.

CHAPTER 50

After enduring a day of waiting for politeness' sake, John called at the Taguchi home. His interpreter greeted him at the door with many words of thanks. Then apologizing profusely, Mr. Taguchi asked if it would be too much trouble to delay any business until the next day. The household was recovering from unexpected developments.

John broke out in a sweat. "Is Miss Taguchi recuperating as we hoped? Should I fetch the doctor?"

"No, nothing like that. She has almost fully recovered except for a sprained wrist. Health-wise, she is fine." He lowered his voice. "I'll come to the consulate tomorrow if that would suit you and explain."

John's heart plunged. "I don't want to trouble you. Actually, the consulate will be closed for Christmas tomorrow, and Miss Taguchi is the one I wish to see." He felt close to bending his knee and pleading. "Would it be possible to meet with her here, perhaps in the morning—seeing as she is doing so much better?"

Her father rubbed the back of his neck and sighed. "Yes, our house should be more settled by then. I will tell her to expect you."

John returned to the consulate to suffer through another interminable afternoon and night.

The next morning, he retraced his steps as early as he dared. Finding from Mr. Taguchi that his daughter was in the back garden, John chose to follow the stone path on the side of the house rather than disturb the household.

While he walked along the flagstones, he silently rehearsed what he had already practiced saying hundreds of times. Would she find his words outrageous? Maybe she would think him fickle, turning so quickly from Catherine to her. And yet his appreciation for her had been planted the day they met. He'd tried to uproot the attraction—again and again—but that initial growth had kept on sending down deeper roots, impossible to extract. Thankfully.

He rounded the corner and stopped, entranced. Miss Taguchi was sitting on a granite boulder by the fishpond. Her light purple kimono suited her perfectly. A ray of sunlight glinted off a sparkling comb in her piled-up hair. Everything together formed a picture of loveliness.

She looked up from the pond, and her face brightened, lighting up his heart all the more.

"Are you all right?" he asked, trying to keep his composure. "I didn't expect you to be up and about so soon."

"I'm feeling much better, thank you. I'm cobbling . . . uh, coddling my wrist, to use the doctor's word. But he thinks it's just a sprain." She started to rise.

"Please don't get up. I hope I'm not interrupting you."

"No, I am happy you are here, How can I thank you enough for everything you did?" She motioned for him to join her.

"Thank me? I should thank you." He took a seat on a low rock, making his height even with hers. "I found out how effective a female samurai can be." At her smile, he said, "I'm serious. You saved the day."

"Perhaps military strategies are not too out of place for women."

"You've convinced me." After all that happened, she was still able to tease. "I never would have forgiven myself if that villain's plot had succeeded. To think, he hid in the consulate all those months, waiting to attack. I should have seen it."

"None of us considers any of this your fault, Cardiff-*sama*. How could we? He fooled everyone."

"I'm glad your family doesn't blame me." At least, he had that point in his favor.

"Thank the gods, you found us in the woods. Oh"—she put her hand to her mouth—"I should say to thank the Maker."

"I do credit him. I pled for his help more desperately than even the time you and I faced the Hizen samurai . . . or when I faced pirates and a typhoon before that." He looked into her eyes before she dropped her gaze and took out her fan.

He tried to swallow. His mouth had never felt so dry.

She began to fan herself.

He tore his gaze away from her and gestured toward the pond. "Remember the little pond near the hillside rest house? We stood watching the butterflies there." He turned back toward her. "Did you know I thought you were beautiful?"

"I had no idea." She blushed. "Truthfully, I thought you were . . . handsome." She raised her fan so that it almost hid the twinkle in her eyes.

He wanted to kiss her right then, but she would be shocked.

She lowered her fan. "The butterflies and the rocks and the evergreen aren't disturbed by what people do and say. They are simply doing what they're supposed to do." A yearning slipped into her eyes. "If only people could fill their role just as well."

"I think you fulfill your role admirably."

"I'm afraid I don't fit my country's ideal." She pointed toward the house. "My mother says I'll never marry now I'm a Christ follower. In fact, she fears I'm endangering the family although my father hopes otherwise and my grandfather is fearless."

So, she had already told her family about her new faith. Obviously, she hadn't been disowned. But questions on that topic had to wait.

He shifted his position to face her more directly and sat up taller. "I know someone right now who wants to marry you. He's been blind, utterly blind. But at last he's discovered what real love is."

Her forehead wrinkled. "You don't mean the chief inspector, do you? Because he wouldn't marry a Christ follower. . . even if he discovered *love*."

"Sato? No, I don't mean Chief Inspector Sato! I mean myself! I—I've waked up."

She drew in her breath. Her eyes widened.

"I know this is a big surprise, a shock. I haven't shown my deep affection—my love for you. I was so focused on Catherine, I couldn't see what was right before my eyes. But I can't imagine life without you. I'm asking: Would you be willing to spend the rest of your life with me?"

She stared at him. "As your wife?" Her voice was a whisper.

"Yes, as my wife." He swallowed hard and pressed on. "Now don't make a quick decision—well, unless your answer is a decided *no*. I am a Christ follower too, but also a foreigner, a barbarian as your countrymen often say. I would try my best to make you happy, but maybe marrying a foreigner is too much to ask." His question hung in the air.

"No, it's . . . I mean, yes! Oh, of course, I want to be with *you*, more than anything, Cardiff-*sama*!"

He moved to embrace her but felt her hand against his chest, holding him back.

"I'm sorry." Her voice quivered.

She looked up at him, and time stopped.

"First, we must have my grandfather's permission. I don't know if he will give it."

Fear pierced his joy. He desperately wanted to hold her to himself. "After finding out your feelings toward me . . . and if marrying a foreigner was even a possibility, I'd planned to ask for your family's approval." He took her hand. "Should I be the one to approach your grandfather?"

"A *nakōdo*, a matchmaker, is necessary." She looked into his eyes and quirked a sad smile.

"Is it hopeless?" How could such a dark shadow descend out of the cloudless sky? "Completely hopeless?"

"No. You rescued my grandfather . . . and me. He will never forget that. Yet taking a barb . . . a foreigner into the family line is a gigantic step."

John tried to calm his galloping heart. He leaned back to look at her fully. "Apart from receiving permission, what about all the difficulties you'd face being the wife of a foreigner? Are you sure you want to face them?"

"Nothing, except my grandfather's disapproval, could stop me from . . . from accepting this honor."

"You're shaking."

"I'm trying not to cry—because I'm scared and yet so happy."

This time he yielded to the impulse that had gripped him first at the rest house. He leaned over and kissed her—on her forehead. A more demonstrative kiss in this culture had to wait until the wedding night. *If* there was to be one.

She turned scarlet, but her smile proclaimed her heart. He gathered all his strength to refrain from another kiss.

CHAPTER 51

Four weeks later—two weeks before the beginning of the Year of the Rooster—Yoshikatsu called the obligatory family council to discuss the practically unheard-of proposition of joining a samurai's family line with a foreigner's. Governor Nakamura had already given his half-hearted permission in return for Cardiff's heroism and Yoshikatsu's role in unmasking the groom's plot. Although the next step was for him as eldest to make the ultimate decision, he sought unified opinions, necessary to hold the family together.

"In my association with the American consul," his son said after the preliminary pleasantries, "I have found he manages well in our culture. Still he is not our countryman."

"Yes," Haru chimed in.

But before his wife could speak further, Kenshin signaled her to be quiet. "He is not our countryman, but he risked his life for our family. Twice. A fine or not-so-fine exterior means little. Consul Cardiff is a brave and upright man." He shot his wife a determined look. "I favor the union."

"I respect your opinion of the consul's good nature." The tone of Haru's brother commanded attention. "But I foresee grave difficulties. Your beautiful home of forty-three years was destroyed, and your honorable aunt, sitting here, lost her husband because of the barbarians. A union of your noble house with the American would intensify the traditionalists' reprisals. I advise seeking a safer situation not only for Sumi-*san*, but for the entire family."

"Your advice is appreciated." Haru gave a quick bow to her brother and glanced away from her husband's frown. "For my humble part, I feel the foreigner's customs would be impossible to endure."

Yoshikatsu raised his hand for silence as he thought. Sumi had gained enough inner strength to accept a denial, perhaps even without outward complaint. Yet for too long, his family and his countrymen had been bound by constraints that were proving to be unreasonable. Why should he bow to those forces when Cardiff had proven his worth?

"Don't blame the barbarian for our troubles," his elder sister blurted out. "Blame Lord Ōta!" Everyone pivoted toward her in astonishment. "I was married to a man who was faithful and caring for more than fifty years. Now I am enduring both losses you describe." Her eyes watered. "I can tell you *great loss* proves *great worth*. I am thankful for my memories. Affection is a treasure. Let your daughter have that treasure, and every one of us can find pleasure in her happiness."

The group continued to stare at his sister in profound silence until Yoshikatsu nodded to her. "Well spoken." An inner shaft of sunshine warmed his bones. He turned toward Haru and her brother. "Then, I will give my consent for Sumi to marry Consul Cardiff unless larger objections remain."

Haru's brother shrugged. "Continuing opposition is futile if the rest of the family is willing to face the censure."

Haru dropped her head, acknowledging her brother's capitulation.

Through the intermediary, Yoshikatsu sent word the marriage could take place on two conditions: Cardiff would have to add the surname of Taguchi to any child so the family line would have an heir added through Sumi, and he would have to promise not to take Sumi away from Japan as long as Yoshikatsu lived.

The consul replied through the intermediary that he would be honored to add the Taguchi name and that he planned to live in Japan the rest of his life.

The wedding was scheduled for the first of May on the Western calendar. As Japanese custom required, John sent a courier seven times to the Taguchi house to welcome Sumi to her new home in the consulate. The eighth time, Sumi's palanquin, along with those of the family, met the courier halfway. Porters trailed them with her dowry in five lacquered boxes swaying from poles. The courier sent the lacquered boxes on to the consulate. The palanquins proceeded to the Pendletons' home, where the ceremony would take place following Western tradition.

Yoshikatsu took his seat at the front of the foreigners' parlor. The *armchair* he sat in was a strange contraption, good for old bones, but a temptation that could lead to softness. He breathed in the flowery scent permeating the room. The foreign lady had decorated her house with clusters of red lilies in honor of the consul's adoption into the Taguchi line, and large white bows in honor of the bride. His granddaughter had been thrilled with the ceremony's setting, a very familiar one to her, so he could put up with the frills.

He looked over the crowd. Many pale faces with round eyes and quite a few of his family's friends and neighbors filled the room and one beyond, all wishing Sumi and the consul well. Enemies might still lurk beyond the walls. But the foreign god had rewarded Sumi's loyalty, providing a husband she finally found acceptable—even loved—and one Yoshikatsu genuinely liked. Her decision to become a Christ follower posed the biggest threat for the couple's future, but it was time for his countrymen to stop being irrational about the religion.

Cardiff strode out and stood to Yoshikatsu's left. The audience rose. Yoshikatsu chose to remain seated. A lady ran her fingers over the music instrument borrowed from the hotel, causing it to issue a string of strange sounds. Keeping the music's rhythm, Sumi walked toward Cardiff, who seemed transfixed as though looking at beauty personified. Cardiff hadn't learned yet that high officials should not show emotion.

Yoshikatsu swallowed an unexpected lump in his throat. More passion in marriage, he reflected, might be a good aspect of the West for his countrymen to adopt.

Sumi was not wearing any white powder, and the pink in her cheeks reflected the red lining under her white and pink kimono. Drawing near to the consul, her eyes danced with delight and a smile dared twitch the corners of her mouth.

Yoshikatsu thought back to Hagi castle. This was what he'd wanted to live to see. Sumi's exuberance had not only returned. Her joy swept over all those around her—even him.

In addition to the Edo cousins, she would have a part in continuing the family line, and he would not be alone in his last days. He carefully maintained his solemn expression. Samurai should *not* show emotion. He hoped his eyes would not betray him.

Sumi took the final step to reach Cardiff-*sama*. His face shone with love, and her heart fluttered, like a bird about to fly, not away but homeward. He extended his arm and turned with her to face Mr. Pendleton.

She forced herself to concentrate in order to respond at the right times. The fact the consul had chosen her above all others still took her breath away.

His strong voice promised to love her, for better or for worse, in sickness and in health, until death. The words reverberated in her soul.

Awe streamed through her. Because of the Flower Maker, she no longer stood outside, yearning for a new world and for the man she loved. She was crossing the threshold into his arms—permanently.

"I do," she replied and met his eyes.

CHAPTER 52

July 4, 1861(Month of the Monkey)

Sumi heard John's footsteps on the stairs, taking two at a time. It still jolted her not to kneel and help him put on his slippers. He had made his feelings in the matter clear when he'd insisted on kneeling and helping with her slippers as well.

He entered their sitting room and gave her a gentle kiss—how she loved those Western-style kisses—and sat next to her on their couch.

"I've heard from Phillip Gray. You remember him? Catherine's brother? He just found out about our marriage plans before he wrote."

"I hope he doesn't disapprove."

"No, but he has his own unique style. Here. You can read it if you like."

She read the letter and handed it back. "One thing puzzles me—his question about how you managed the marriage without getting involved with the natives. An unusual question."

"It's a long story. Phillip's always been a bit sarcastic."

"I guess you became more involved than you first

intended." She raised her eyebrows, knowing they had shared a similar resolve.

"Well, one thing led to another. Like pepper pods and dragonflies—didn't you tell me, once or twice?" His eyes twinkled.

She laughed at the memory, but then a preoccupied look came over his face, checking her amusement. "Maybe it is harder than you expected to call this country your home. Do you have any second thoughts?"

He paused, and her eyes misted. "Are you thinking about America?"

"It *is* Independence Day, exactly two years since I set foot here. So much has happened, so many turns in the road. But I was thinking about a trivial thing just now—the parade and picnic in my hometown. This evening's celebration at the hotel won't be the same. So yes, I do miss parts of my former life from time to time. A little homesickness is only natural, I suppose. But no second thoughts, my dear native."

He put the letter in its envelope. "This is where I want to be, where I'm meant to be. And how about you? Living with a hairy barbarian?"

"A halfway civilized one makes a good husband." She smiled up at him. "I think you have given me wings."

She recognized his philosophical look and quickly added, "Actually the *Maker* of the wildflowers, dragonflies, and everything else gave me wings. I believe that. But you did help him do it."

He chuckled and rubbed his chin. "You're quick on the draw. That's an American saying from out West."

"Do you know why I am sure of the wings?"

"Not by looking in the mirror, I'd wager."

She smiled at the image. "It's here in the *Holy Bible*." She opened to the page she'd marked. "In Isaiah, chapter 40. *But they that wait upon the Lord shall renew their strength; they shall mount up with wings as eagles* . . . That proves it, don't you think?"

"Without question." He thumped the Bible and grinned. "Not only were you quick on the draw, you hit the bull's eye, the center of the target."

He reached for her, drawing her closer. "Now that I think about it, not one July Fourth activity can compete with what I have right here." He lifted her chin and kissed her again—a long, drawn-out kiss that made her soul seem to melt into his.

She nestled against him, loving everything about him. She never could have dreamed how it felt to walk with him on the beach or ride their two horses into the hills, which he called a storybook kingdom. Nor imagine the contentment of worshiping the Maker with him at the Pendletons' home and the joy of seeing happiness fill his clear, gray eyes simply because she walked into the room.

Naturally, not all was easy. She worried sometimes that an official would object to her participation in Christian activities despite her position as a consul's wife. She found it challenging to be outgoing with American guests, yet reticent with the Japanese ones. The occasional "cold shoulder" still bothered her, and she might never grow accustomed to eating meat. Strangely enough, at times she even missed the simplicity of her old routine.

But she had no second thoughts either. She put her hand in his large one, reveling in how he had invited her into the depths of his being.

They would continue to discover the wonder of those wings.

Together.

AFTERWORD

My great-great-uncle, John Greer Walsh, the first American consul to Nagasaki, served as honorary consul from 1859, the year the city opened for foreign residence, to 1865. At the age of thirty-four, he married Yamaguchi Rin. The couple lived the rest of their lives in Japan.

John Walsh with the help of his brothers, Thomas and Robert, began the first American trading firm in Japan, known as American House No. 1. My great grandparents, Richard and Eliza Walsh, joined the brothers later. Eliza died in Japan, and Richard returned to New York.

The story *Dragonfly Wings* is fiction. At the time of this writing, no facts are known to me about the courtship of the real consul and Yamaguchi Rin. Although used fictitiously, references in the story to the assassinations of the Shōgun's regent and the British legation's chief interpreter are based on those actual occurrences.

As I researched the setting, I tried to imagine the first foreigners' reactions as they encountered exotic sights, vastly different customs, novel ideas, and real-life dangers. Like the story's characters, many of them undoubtedly developed warm, lasting friendships with the Japanese people. The ancient land and its people, once shrouded in mystery, revealed a fascinating vista—one easy to love.

A NOTE FROM ELIZABETH ANN

Thank you for taking time to read *Dragonfly Wings*. If you enjoyed the story, please consider leaving a review on Amazon or Goodreads even if it's only a line or two.

Do you want to know what dangers threaten and how Sumi and John navigate the challenges of their two disparate cultures? Don't miss the release of Book Three of the *Dragonfly Trilogy*! A preview of *Two Autumns, One Spring* is at the back of this book.

Curious about John and Sumi's earlier adventures? The series' first book, *The Year of the Barbarian,* invites you to follow John in his risky venture to the far side of the world, and to experience life with Sumi as disaster looms.

To discover more about the unique culture underlying the story world and receive writing updates and giveaways, please subscribe to Elizabeth Ann's newsletter at:

https://elizabethannboyles.com/my-books/

I hope we can stay in touch. You are greatly appreciated!

THE NOVEL'S CHARACTERS

In the general order of the name's appearance

Taguchi Yoshikatsu* – An elderly retainer of the Chōshū clan
Taguchi Kenshin* – Yoshikatsu's son and a linguist, having a rank as a Dutch Scholar
Haru – Taguchi Kenshin's wife
Sumi – Kenshin and Haru's daughter
Kiyo – Haru's orphaned niece, Sumi's cousin
Kurohashi Keiji* – A Confucian scholar desiring to marry Sumi
John Cardiff – A trader who is the American consul in Nagasaki
Catherine Gray – John Cardiff's fiancée
The Pendletons – An American couple teaching English and doing missionary work
Goda – The American consul's manservant
Ōta Nobumitsu* – A reactionary Chōshū samurai who is the warlord's cousin
Omura – A bronze-ware merchant living close to the Taguchi family's home
Governor Nakamura – One of the two Nagasaki governors
Nakamura Kohei* – The anti-foreign second son of Governor Nakamura
Sato Rinzo* – Chief Inspector in Nagasaki
Kin – One of the Taguchi family's maids
Sir David Edman – The British consul in Nagasaki
The Manns – The secretary for the American consulate in Nagasaki and his wife Beth

Taki – Sumi's close friend in the English class
Yamamoto – Nakamura Kohei's retainer
Matsukichi – A Hizen samurai and the brother of Omura's servant
Kuma – John Cardiff's housekeeper
George Jennings – A trader accused of smuggling
Robert and Emeille Morrow – A British businessman and his wife
Josephine Morrow – Robert and Emeille's daughter
Wilton Davis – George Jennings' lawyer
Phillip Gray – Catherine's brother
Fujino – Governor Nakamura's highest retainer
Lord Ōta – The Chōshū warlord
Maeda – One of three Chōshū samurai who escorted the Taguchis from Hagi
Doctor Hughes – A British medical doctor
Aomori – A Chōshū clan elder who was a member of the delegation to the U.S.

* The surname is given first in the Japanese names.

JAPANESE TERMS

These definitions are specific for *Dragonfly Wings*, not comprehensive in scope.

Abunai – Danger.
Amaterasu Ōmikami – The Sun Goddess.
Anata-wa doko desuka? – Where are you?
Bashō – A famous 17th century poet, the greatest master of linked *haiku*.
Biwa – A four-or-five stringed musical instrument with a short neck, somewhat resembling a violin. The strings are plucked.
Bushido – Moral code of the samurai.
Butsudan – An altar or cabinet for a Buddhist icon.
Chan, Dono, Sama, San – Titles affixed to names, like Miss, Mr., Mrs. in English, but reflecting status.
Chawan – A large bowl for drinking tea.
Chōshū no Ōta Nobumitsu to mousu – I am called Ōta Nobumitsu of the Chōshū clan.
Daimyō – A feudal warlord.
Edo – The city which was the seat of power for the secular government from 1603-1868. Renamed Tokyo.
Fuji-san – Mount Fuji, Japan's highest mountain.
Gaijin – Foreigner.
Gi – Righteousness, written by the ideograph for lamb over the ideograph for oneself.
Go – A board game in which the player tries to surround more area than his opponent.

Hagi – A castle town formerly belonging to the Chōshū clan.

Haiku – A poem whose first line consists of five syllables, the second of seven, and the third of five. Its meaning relies on cultural understanding.

Hakama – Wide skirt/trousers worn by samurai.

Heike Monogatari – The Tale of the Heike gives an epic account of the Genpei war between the Minamoto clan and the Taira clan in the 12th century.

Ikebana – The art of flower arrangement.

Kabuki – A stylized play often based on popular legends, performed by an all-male cast.

Kago – A litter having a basket seat slung from a pole, carried on the shoulders of two porters.

Kanji – Chinese-style characters used in writing; also sentiment.

Ki – A person's life force in this story.

Kirishitan – Christian.

Kojiki – An ancient chronicle containing myth and a semi-history of Japan's origins and its rulers.

Konichiwa – Hello, used from midmorning until evening.

Kotatsu – The *kotatsu*'s wooden frame is placed over a recess in the floor. The frame is covered by a heavy blanket, and a charcoal heater is placed under a bottom grate.

Koto – A 13-stringed zither about six feet long.

Kurisumasu – Christmas.

Metsuke – An enforcement official whose duties can include recording the actions and words of other important officials and acting as censor.

Moxa – Medical treatment in which a cone of ground bark is placed on charcoal and ignited on the skin.

Naginata – A smooth, long spear ending in a curved steel blade, used for defense especially by women in very old samurai families.
Nakōdo – Matchmaker.
Nattō – Food made from soybean.
Neko no koban – A Japanese proverb indicating unworthiness, literally, a cat's gold piece.
Obi – A wide sash for a woman's kimono, tied in decorative knot at the back.
Ojii-sama – Grandfather.
Ojō-sama – Polite word to refer to a young lady.
Omochi – A soft rice ball made of pounded rice and additional ingredients.
Onmyōji – A diviner of luck, using cosmology based on Eastern philosophy, such as ying yang.
Renga – Collaborative poetry having more than one author and at least two stanzas.
Rōnin – A masterless samurai.
Sake – A rice liquor.
Samisen – A long-necked, three-stringed musical instrument, slightly resembling a banjo.
Samurai – A warrior in the service of a clan's warlord. Samurai is the singular and plural form.
Sandome no shojiki – The third calamity commonly prophesied for nineteen-year-old females.
Seppuku – The polite term for *harikiri*. It is ritual suicide by cutting into one's intestines, carried out with a short blade. The suicide is completed by an assistant using a sword.
Shibui – Subtle, simple, and often old and muted beauty.

Shinjinai – I don't believe.

Shōgun – The title of the supreme secular dictator.

Shogunate – The national government, led by the Shōgun and supported by the Council of Elders.

Shōji – A sliding panel used as a door, window, or room divider, made of translucent paper covering a lattice.

Sumimasen – A humble apology; excuse me.

Tanka – A poem having phrases of 5-7-5-7-7 syllables.

Tatami – Framed mats of rice straw that make up a traditional room's flooring. One mat is approximately three feet by six feet.

Tokonoma – The main room's decorative alcove, often displaying a scroll and flower arrangement.

Torii – The gate of a Shinto shrine.

Toso – A mildly sweet drink made with *sake* and herbs, drunk at New Years.

Tsurayuki – A Japanese poet who composed *waka* poems in the 9th century.

Urashima Tarō – A boy in a fairytale who was kind to a turtle, which took him to a sea palace.

Uta-garuta – A game based on 100 famous waka poems. The players try to be the quickest in matching the card having the last two lines of a poem with the card having the poem's full text.

DISCUSSION QUESTIONS

1. Was Sumi wise to disobey her grandfather? Was she justified in doing so? Should Kenshin have suggested not telling the grandfather? What does Chapter Two tell us about Kenshin's character?

2. The dragonfly symbolically represents Sumi's aspirations. Why is this an appropriate symbol?

3. Was John asking for trouble when he didn't kneel for the Hizen procession? Do you have any theory as to why the samurai didn't kill him? Did you catch the trouble portended by John's groom having been recommended by Merchant Omura?

4. John felt bad that he was a tiny point of light in the country's spiritual darkness. What truths in Scripture could have encouraged him?

5. What traits and factors do you think caused Sumi and John to be attracted to each other?

6. As the story progresses, we see more about Sumi's attitude toward her native religion. In what ways does she embrace it, and in what ways does she question it? Do you have trouble understanding how someone could consider differences in the nature of things an illusion?

7. Do you approve of John's company selling guns to the government? A larger question is whether or not the U.S should have sent warships to force Japan into a trade agreement. Do you have an opinion about that action?

8. Sumi sensed the Creator from a daisy's beauty. Her father was touched by words from the biblical Job. Have you had a similar experience that resulted in seeing life very differently?

9. Many analogies can be given to explain Jesus' substitutionary death for us. Do you think Mrs. Pendleton's analogy of the warlord and samurai is a good one? Do you think Sumi should have waited to become a Christian until she had learned more?

10. What later events provide evidence that Sumi's conversion was genuine?

11. Did John do the right thing in ending his engagement? What are John's best strengths? What are his weaknesses?

12. Did you find yourself liking the grandfather more as the story progressed? If so, why? Did you feel any sympathy for Kiyo? Did you feel any empathy for Nobumitsu, the fiercest antagonist?

13. Do you expect John and Sumi to have a happy marriage? What problems are likely to develop? (If you read Book Three, *Two Autumns, One Spring,* you can see if you foretold any that occur in the story.)

14. Did anything in the story disappoint you? What appealed to you most in the story?

ACKNOWLEDGMENTS

During the many years I worked on the *Dragonfly Trilogy*, numerous people kindly offered suggestions and encouragement. Here, I'll mention just those who contributed improvements specifically for *Dragonfly Wings* although I deeply appreciate all of the help.

Thank you to members of critique groups who read all or most of this book's manuscript and offered advice: Janice Olson, Lyndie Blevins, Lynne Gentry, Jan Johnson, Kellie Coates Gilbert, Michelle Stimpson, Dana Red, Patricia Carroll, Jackie Castle, Steve Miller, Daniel Miller, and Kay Learned.

Rebecca Brown kindly read three different drafts of the story. Many others read one of the various drafts over the years. You are treasured for being a friend willing to donate your time!

And last of all, a big thank you to my family, who put up with my book chatter and time-consuming writing day after day.

ABOUT THE AUTHOR

Elizabeth Ann's love for Japan developed when she lived there for several years while in her twenties. The Japanese people went out of their way to help her become acquainted with the food, language, flower arrangement, tea ceremony, and other unique and wonderful customs. She found the Far East to be like a second home. She also met her missionary husband in Japan, and they were married in a bilingual ceremony in Tokyo.

These days Elizabeth Ann teaches at a Christian university with a global outreach and is privileged to spend time with international students from Japan and many other fascinating countries as well.

She and her husband live in a suburb of Dallas, where they enjoy family times with their two grown children and grandchildren as often as possible.

Please visit Elizabeth Ann:
Facebook.com/elizabethannboyles
Twitter.com/AnnBoylesTX

**Read on for an excerpt from
Two Autumns, One Spring,
Book Three of the *Dragonfly Trilogy***

CHAPTER 1

August 1861, Year of the Rooster, Nagasaki, Japan

Hearing John rushing up the stairs from the first-floor consulate to their residence, Sumi Taguchi Cardiff headed toward the door. What could have caused her husband to abandon his usual decorum? Before she took more than a few steps, John burst into the room and planted a gentle kiss on her cheek.

"Come, have a seat." He crossed the soft Persian rug in his stocking feet and sat in one of their mahogany armchairs, stretching out his long legs. "I have important news. Very unexpected. A real revelation."

She sat in the chair's twin, scooting back the astral lamp on the round table between them so she could see him better. Was the shocking news good? Or terrible?

He pulled a letter from a pocket in his waistcoat. "Now, this may sound a little menacing, but you'll charm the dragon."

"Dragon?" Her stomach turned over. From what she'd heard of Western tales, dragons were fearful, never helpful like in some of her country's myths.

"Amazingly, my mother is on her way for a visit." John's tone was cheerful, but his eyes brimmed with concern.

"Your mother? My honorable mother-in-law? Coming here?" She realized her mouth hung open and closed it.

"Yes. The steamer's due this Thursday, believe it or not."

She drew in a breath. "I don't know what to say." Four days! Her mother-in-law—due in four days? What if the lady truly resembled a fire-breathing dragon and disliked her? Despised her?

"Her letter was sent from New York in May, five weeks prior to the ship's departure, but apparently was delayed. Probably routed overland because of the Union blockade along the southeast coast."

"Such a . . . surprise. She must be very brave."

"Determined, more than brave. She's staying only ten days, but long enough, I believe, for you to detect her softer side." His smile struck Sumi as close to a grimace.

"Can ten days be right? Might she have meant ten weeks?" But if American mothers-in-law were as demanding as Japanese ones, even ten days would be too long. And if she were a particularly fierce mother-in-law, her claws could cut out Sumi's throat in just one day.

"Sounds outrageous, doesn't it?" He unfolded the letter and glanced at it. "Her journey here and back will take far longer than her visit. I had to read the dates twice to believe it myself." He tapped a line in the letter. "She's traveling with a lady friend, who is disembarking in Hong Kong. Seems the woman's elderly relative passed away, and she's the only person eligible to sign for the sale of his residence. Mother will meet up with her friend's ship for the return voyage."

"To travel such a long way, your mother must be very eager to see you. I can understand why." She mustered a weak smile.

He exhaled. "I wonder if wanting to see me is all there is to her visit. The more I think about it, the stranger it seems." He ran his finger partway down the page. "She even mentions a newspaper article that quotes a visitor to Yokohama. This self-proclaimed expert says our islands are *overrun* by peril from outlaw samurai. I guess that helped her decide on a brief stay . . . as well as allowing for her companion's needs." He arched his eyebrows at Sumi. "I bet she'll have braved more danger from Confederate pirates than from anyone here. But considering the situation in both countries, not the best time for a journey." He folded up the letter.

"What will you tell her about the rumors she mentioned?" Maybe a nice visit with her on the ship would suffice, and the lady could go safely on to Hong Kong with her companion.

"Only that Nagasaki isn't at all like the area around Edo and Yokohama. That Edo's a magnet for hotheads, like many capital cities. No need to mention the samurai attack on the British consulate there if she hasn't already heard. It'd only increase her anxiety."

He rubbed the back of his neck. "Now I need to explain a problem. My mother appears to have started her journey before the arrival of my letter telling of our marriage plans."

"She doesn't know we married?" Sumi took hold of the chair's arms, feeling lightheaded.

"I think not."

"But you told her about me, mentioned me in previous

letters, right?" Acid began to eat at her stomach.

"As my wonderful, smart tutor for the Japanese language, yes."

"Oh John, what will happen when she finds out we *are* married?"

"Well, first I need to say that she's a Christian. However, she clings to a narrow outlook on certain aspects of life, like your grandfather once did. But like your grandfather, she can widen her thinking."

A chill slithered up Sumi's spine. "What are you preparing me to hear?"

"She'll be upset at first. In our culture, men in their thirties aren't obliged to ask permission, but she'll think that marrying a lady from a different background should have involved quite a bit of discussion. But then after getting to know all your charms"—he extended his palm toward her as though introducing nobility—"she'll forgive me."

Sumi tried to smile at his gesture, but couldn't. "I think I understand. I'll be a native in her eyes, an ordinary one. Even though my family all agreed you were an extraordinary Westerner, our marriage still troubled *my* mother." The room suddenly turned hot, oppressive in spite of a slight afternoon breeze coming in the open windows. She drew out her fan.

"You're anything but ordinary, my dear. She can't help but admire you, inside and out." He gestured toward her hair, a twinkle in his eyes. "Take the way your hairdo forms those intricate spools, held in place with those chopsticks." He chuckled.

"Cylinders. Glass cylinders." She felt the corner of her mouth curve up.

"Right. And your lovely complexion that turns rosy, right

before you fan yourself."

"She may not see me the way you do." She slid her fan back inside her kimono's broad sash. "Women judge each other differently."

"Well then, there's your ability to think and your endless curiosity. Those are traits she's got to appreciate. She kept urging me to acquire knowledge while I was growing up." His eyes became pensive. "But if she doesn't understand why I married you at first, let's trust the Almighty to open her eyes."

"I hope he does. Right away." She attempted to look assured, as though she trusted her new Liege. But in her country's history, the Almighty had permitted difficulties much worse than a draconian mother-in-law.

"Too bad I planned tomorrow's trip. However, the governor might drag his feet another month before issuing a new travel permit. Our company has to export better porcelain. And from what everyone says, I'm tracking down the world's best." He tucked away the letter and looked at her.

"If only you didn't have to go to the Hizen Domain to find it." Another reason to worry. In the midst of the new trouble, his overnight trip had completely left her mind.

"I honestly doubt there's a reactionary element left. Seems just a small fringe wanted to get rid of us Western barbarians. Besides, it's a quick foray in and out of the domain. Any remaining rabble-rouser won't have time to react."

Words formed on the tip of her tongue, but good wives didn't argue. She'd have a lot more peace of mind if her husband would delegate his trading business to his trainees, and become the American consul full time. But maybe the battles taking place in the United States delayed his country's offer of such a position.

As though he read her skepticism, he shook his head and smiled. "The four samurai escorting me—*courtesy* of the city's governor as usual—are more than enough to see that everyone behaves properly. And then there's your father. Thank goodness for him. His translation will transform my fumbles. The tradesmen there don't have to know my Japanese is . . . well, not great, but passable."

"Your Japanese amazes everyone." Her whole being wanted to enumerate reasons against the trip, a list that had grown every time he'd mentioned the Hizen Domain, but she forced herself to guard her tongue.

"Anyway, I should be back in plenty of time to help with any last-minute needs before Mother arrives."

She swallowed, steadying her voice. "The household staff will help. We'll be ready. Please just return safe and sound."

He stood and pulled her up in an embrace. "That's the exact plan."

When John laid down his fork after devouring his breakfast of poached eggs and tinned ham, Sumi put aside her *miso* soup. The wind chime outside the open window in their downstairs dining room tingled in a wisp of a breeze, but the bright sunshine flooding through the arched upper glass already foretold a scorching day.

"I'm afraid the time has come to head out." John gulped the rest of his coffee and reached for his tan frock coat.

Her poor husband. He hated the Western fashion requirements that made summers even more uncomfortable than crepe undergarments and a silk kimono did for her.

Resisting the urge to kneel and help John pull on his boots at the vestibule, she handed him his broad-brimmed hat.

"I'll be back by suppertime tomorrow, barring any trouble with the weather."

"Look at these geese bumps, John. Cardiff and Associates' investors should appreciate how you stick out your neck."

"Goosebumps, dearest. But aren't you the one who said people shouldn't be timid turtles, pulling their heads into their shells?"

"I guess I did."

"And hasn't all that boldness turned out well so far?"

"Much better than *well*." She grinned although tears scalded her eyes. "Still, I can't help worrying."

He ran his finger along her jawline, and she felt the familiar thrill at his touch.

"I'll be fine. I've got my six shooter right here." He pointed to his side and the hidden holster carrying his revolver. "It'll stop an attack if all else fails."

His groom met them at the gate, holding the reins of the large, chestnut-colored horse, for some reason named Shakespeare. John patted Shakespeare's forehead, then bent down and kissed Sumi.

Rubbing her chin after he'd relinquished his hold, she realized for the hundredth time that she'd not only become accustomed to his beard's tickle, she liked it.

He mounted, and she gazed up at him, tall in his Western saddle, a breeze ruffling his thick brown hair. The leader of a huge army couldn't look more assured. Although America didn't have warlords and samurai, he was samurai at heart. The most extraordinary one she'd ever known. *Almighty God, keep him safe. Bring him back to me.*

Her husband, horse, and groom disappeared around a curve in the road, heading toward the international sector's jetty, where the company cutter would ferry him to the Japanese coastal ship farther out in the harbor. She forced herself to stop staring at the spot she'd last seen him. He wasn't going to reappear.

She turned in the opposite direction and joined the foreign soldiers, merchants, servants, and unidentifiable drifters, as well as her own country's peddlers and laborers, crowding the cobblestone road that passed through the center of the settlement. Reaching the international sector's gate on the far side, she bowed to the sentries.

One of her country's guards glowered at her. She faced forward as though she hadn't noticed, while mulling the reason for his anger. Did he think she had betrayed *Nippon* by becoming intimate with a foreign man, or worse, did he actually know who she was? A shiver sliced through her. Her attendance at the Christian services in an American couple's home was illegal. Until this point, nothing had happened. Either the officials were unaware of her participation in what the government termed the Evil Religion, or the chief inspector overlooked it because of John's position. Sooner or later, however, the officials would take note. Had it already happened? Should she return to the safety of the consulate?

She nearly scolded herself out loud for her cowardice. The daughter of a samurai didn't hide behind glass windows. Besides, she shouldn't imagine the worst because of one moody guard. She raised her chin and crossed the Oura River Bridge into Nagasaki proper.

Although a piece of her heart had ridden away with John, at least his absence provided a chance to demonstrate her loyalty, both to him and to the soon-coming dragon. She passed the strong-smelling fish stalls and more sedate stores displaying rolls of colorful silk, shimmering in the sunlight. Entering the dental practitioner's shop, she sat back on her heels at one of the low tables. Once the specialist covered her teeth with his black-enamel potion, she'd look properly married.

For more information and to purchase
Two Autumns, One Spring, go to
www.elizabethannboyles.com/my-books

Made in the USA
Las Vegas, NV
30 August 2022